SAILING TO ALLUVIUM

ALSO BY JOHN PRITCHARD

Junior Ray (2005)

The Yazoo Blues (2008)

SAILING TO ALLUVIUM

A Novel

JOHN PRITCHARD

To my wonderful friend John Willcox. Love, John Pritchard S.W.A.K.! 10/31/13

NEWSOUTH BOOKS
Montgomery

NewSouth Books
105 S. Court Street
Montgomery, AL 36104

Copyright © 2013 by John Pritchard
All rights reserved under International and Pan-American Copyright
Conventions. Published in the United States by NewSouth Books, a
division of NewSouth, Inc., Montgomery, Alabama.

Library of Congress Cataloging-in-Publication Data

Pritchard, John, 1938–
Sailing to Alluvium : a novel / John Pritchard.
pages cm
Sequel to: Yazoo blues.

ISBN 978-1-58838-269-6 (hardcover)
ISBN 978-1-60306-124-7 (ebook)

1. Rednecks—Fiction. 2. Delta (Miss. : Region)—Fiction. 3.
Mississippi—Fiction.
4. Satire. I. Title.
PS3616.R5725S25 2013
813'.6—dc23
2013026124

Edited and designed by Randall Williams

Printed in the United States of America

This book is dedicated to my deeply beloved child,

my wonderful son, John Hayes Pritchard III.

He is excellent in all the most important ways

and is the man I wish I were.

Contents

A TIMELY(-ASS) REMINDER FROM McKINNEY LAKE

The Delta might appear plain to some, but it is dark and mysterious to those who know it. This low place of mostly legend and stage is not really a region at all; it is a psycho-topographic construct unlike anything else in the known world. And it is indeed a mystery—a mystery made of myth and of truth, so tightly interwoven that one is just as easily the other . . . and the people who "made" this enormous, deep Southern river-bottom complexity were in turn made by *it*.

The mystery is multi-dimensional. It can be *heard* in the genius of the incomparable Afro-Deltan single notes and chords of B. V. Roy's heart-piercing guitar, and it can be *felt* in the exquisite clear-eyed craftsmanship and point-blank, polished, high-octane prose of Steven Yarville, as well as in the eloquent beauty and brilliant accuracy of Teoc Longshot's essays.

The Delta can be *seen* rather perfectly in the magnetic, rich, un-reachable distances of Bill Dunsipp's graphic art and in the camera's captured magic of Jane Rayner Borden's golden metaphysical light. The photogeneity of the land is also locked in the eye's profound understanding of place-as-meaning by the photographic work of Becky Washington. And one can see the shape of time itself—shot clean—through the fourth-dimensional, indelible veracity of Madeline Romana Clay's black-and-white lens.

Even the Delta's roads do not obey the ordinary laws of physics. My father, a man who dealt in epiphanies and from whom I got, if not the absolute truth, always something extraordinary and far better, told me the engineers had to put curves every now and then in Highway 61 to keep it from leaving the earth, because without the curves it would be a *line-tangent* that would not follow the curvature of the planet's surface and would go straight out into space.

As I grew older I discovered that Highway 61 did leave the earth, curves and all. No road anywhere between Lake Cormorant and Eagle Bend is an ordinary road. They all rise above the surface of the expected.

An awful lot of the Delta is *inside* the Deltans, located, Dad believed, in special fiction glands. That kind of intimacy with a piece of the earth may be why much of the Delta's history is fiction, and truth becomes elastic.

— McKinney Lake

Publisher's Note to Readers

Junior Ray Loveblood has benefitted from the facilitational services of two people: In his first book, eponymously entitled *Junior Ray*, it was young Mr. Owen G. Brainsong II who "interviewed" the writer, or more accurately in Junior Ray's case, the "talker." In the second book, *The Yazoo Blues*, Junior Ray's guide and editorial assistant was McKinney Lake, who has just spoken to the reader of *Sailing to Alluvium* in the preceding "Preface."

As it turned out—and as will be explained by Junior Ray in the first chapter—McKinney Lake and young Mr. Brainsong II both agreed to help him with the editorial tasks of this, his third book. Thus, both have served Mr. Loveblood and reader alike, as literary and historical guides and as expositors on many matters, while simultaneously, in the main and for the most part, supporting Mr. Loveblood in their best capacity as that of just plain good friends and necessary "company"—for as Mr. Loveblood tells the reader, ". . . I just figured I'd go at it all alone. . . . But I couldn't do it. . . . So I went, hat in hand, to McKinney and also to Brainy and begged their ass to do what they did before, just one mo time, and they said, Yes, they would, and now I am back . . . on the fukkin track!"

In the pages that follow, both Lake ("—ml") and Brainsong ("—ogbii") have inserted footnotes where necessary to clarify Mr. Loveblood's narrative.

Pro Log[1]

Junior Ray Loveblood

Forty years ago I'da said foodledoodle[2] *to* all of that *gabuffalo* McKinney just told you about the Delta. But now I know— or at least have been able to see—that what McKinney has wrote is the gotdam truth. You may remember in my first book I said everything has changed down here except me, but the fact is that's not exactly so no more. It was then, of course. I don't know what happened. I didn get no smarter nor no dumber. I guess I just got older. Crap.

Anyway, I do not always understand everything McKinney is talkin about, but even if I don't, I am confi-DENT she's right just as a matter of principle. And I do have one or two muthafukkin principles even if you might not think so. The thing is if you're a *R-ther*, which is what I have become, and if you're older, which is also what I have become, you have to think a good bit more than you'd normally expect to have to.

Plus, I have come to see that a lot of the changes aint so bad.

---

1   After being informed of the proper spelling of "Prologue," the author declared he "didn want no *kew-yew-eeez* on the end of [his] word cause it looked like something a queer might do." No amount of explaining or urging, nor pointing out that there was no "q" in the word, was enough to change Mr. Junior Ray Loveblood's position, which has no more permanency than that of a sparrow. —ml

2   Junior Ray would most certainly not have said "foodledoodle." —ml

For instance, I don't really give a shit whether that Worthless
Nigga Ezell can now vote, mainly, *one*, cause he don't never do
it, and *two*, even if he did, him and me is mostly always for the
same gotdam candidate, even if the particular greedy, lyin, power-
lustin politickin fukhed of the moment is black hisself. I don't
care. It's white people that ruint the world. And, I suppose the
reason Ezell and me is in the same canebrake together is because
I have come to realize that me and him has more we agree on
than what we don't—in other words I now see it crystal-ass clear
that Ezell and me was in the same position all along when it
come to this place and them Planters (Big Shot Muthafukkas!).
And bygod still are.

You do need to know, though, that the title of this new book
is rilly only the title of half of it. In fact it's rilly just the title of
PART TWO, which is actually a semi-separate-ass book, itsef, a
larger version of which—like the en-tire stick 'a the whole baloney!—was supposed to be published somehow or another by young
Mr. Brainsong II, but so far he aint got around to it. So my PART
TWO is "selections" from his Notes of Leland Shaw. And, if you
remember, you saw some of that horsefluff in my first book.

So, here it is in a fukkin flea skin: You'll just find "selections"
here; whereas down the line some time soon, I reg'n, Brainy is goin
to publish just about all of Shaw's "Notes."

Anyway, to keep from bein confusin, if you just call the whole
fukkin book *Sailing to Alluvium*, you'll be in the right rabbit field.
Aint no sense in getn too technical.

You may remember that those so-called "Notes" was the googah
that Shaw wrote in all them *ledgers* I give to young Mr. Brainsong
II when he came here some years ago to be my *interviewer*, and
it was what I then told him that become my first book, which, as
you know, they named after my ass. As you also know, young Mr.
Brainsong II came to the Delta, and right here to St. Leo, wantn

to take a look at—and to get hold of!—all that fukkin goopydoo
of Shaw's that I happened to have kept, stored up in a closet at my
house. Why I had even kept that stuff I just couldn say. But I did.

Anyway, they—and by *they* I mean young Mr. Brainsong *the
Second*, McKinney, and the publisher!—decided to include in my
book this time a PART TWO. They only did it because some fat
old butt-wad four-eyed professor over at the university said he
"strongly believed" Shaw's crapola was "highly relevant." But I had
to ast mysef: "What the fuk does that mean?"

I coulda told you everything you wanted to know and showed
you a little piece or two of Shaw's crazy so-called "Notes" like I did
in the first book, and that, to me, woulda been way more'n enough
of Shaw to last my ass, and yours as well, for a hunnud years. But,
oh hell no!—every-fukkin-body had to chime in and put *PART
TWO* in MY gotdam book. Sumbiches. And gotdammit, McKinney went right along with it!

I s'pose you do realize this book, *number three*, more or less
makes a *Delta Trio*; only there's gonna be a fourth one, so I expect
we're lookin at a possible quartet. I like to think of my "talkin"
books sorta like they was singers without no musical instruments
or nothin, you know, kinda like them Church'a ChrEYEsters doin
it *Acapulco!*[3]

But back to what I was tellin you: *Natchaly*, young Mr. Brainsong
was all for it, too, because he has what he calls a "vested interest" in
seein his *editin-work* get spread around out there in the coksukkin
world, mostly amongst a buncha beard-sportn, tea-sippin college
muthafukkas setn around in skinny-ass chairs, holdin little flowery-
ass tweety-tweet tea cups with their pinky fingers stuck out. Young
Mr. Brainsong II says havin some of his new "publication" in my
book will give him a kind of *pre-ass*-publication toward his forthco-

---

3   Usage may be attributed to Ray Stevens and John Ragsdale. —ml

min actual *publication* publication, if you know what I mean, and which, I do have to tell you, is what coulda got his ass finally killed.

If I'da had my way the title of the new book—*MY* fukkin book—*PART ONE*—*this one here*—woulda been something on the order of:

How Voyd and Me—With the Help of Our Stethoscopes and Po-Lice Chief Secundus J. Shipp, Plus That Worthless Nigga Ezell, Along with Judge "Rusty" Justiss Jr., and a Favor from Multiple-Agent Eagle Swoop—Put an End to the Death Threats Young Mr. Brainsong Was Getn Through the U.S. Mail and Nailed Miss Attica Rummage for Killin Three Innocent Sumbiches on Purpose . . . by Mistake.

That run-down right there, woulda pretty much summed it up, and if you was interested you coulda read on to see how we done it. Plus, it woulda saved the Publisher some money because it would have filled up the whole cover of the book and there wouldn't been no need for no fancy artist.

I'D BE LYIN IF I said I didn like the sound of my own voice. But who the fuk don't? The fact is most people aint inter-rested in but one thing, and that's their own *sevs*. I am not no different.

I have come to love bein a *talkin* book-writer. On the other hand, it is possible the world needs another *write'n*-writer like the city of Meffis needs another *crack-ho* . . . or gotdam bobbakew joint. Anyway, the point here is you're about to get a two-for-one deal, and I expect *women*—who, you and I know, can't never resist a bargain—especially a bargain with a buncha new "recipes"!—which they will find in this new book, in PART ONE—and then also they'll get to read Shaw's dumb-ass poetry in PART TWO, which, as you know, is sure to have em all *oooin* and *aahhin*—will be dyin to buy the book. So I guess I can't totally keep bad-mouthin Shaw. Anyway, my experience as a fukkin R-ther has led my ass to see that *women* will go for just about any kind of a book that has recipes.

They'll fall in love with a fartn dog if the sumbich has recipes, or, ChrEYEst!—forget the dog and the book, women'll go for just for the recipes *a-gotdam-lone*!

Whereas most men . . . don't give a dynamite-shit about recipes, even if they're expert cooks, which a lot of em are. Plus, they would probably rather eat a cold paper plate of week-old boiled okra on a bed'a rock-hard grits than ever—and I mean *ever!*—read one single-ass page of poetry. But they'll love to hear about what happens in PART ONE when Voyd and me become diktectives.

There you have it.

I wouldna never thought for a minute nothin like what I'm about to pass on to you could ever have happened. On the other hand, I am not surprised by none of it. And when people ast me when all this I'mo tell you about went on . . . I just say it's all more like *up-around now* than it was; in other words I had already become a *R-ther*.

Also, McKinney called my ass a "shaggy" redneck, and I said, "Fuk that, McKinney. I aint *shaggy* one gotdam bit!" And she said, "Well, Junior Ray it's 'figurative,' and it's not all that bad a thing to be." That lost my ass, but, if McKinney says I am one then bygod I "figure" I'm lucky, even if, as I have said, I aint especially bushy. I do shave and get my hair cut on a regular basis over at the Beauty Bin, which is a ladies' beauty salon, and that's because the City Barber Shop and the other one, McCain's, has been closed for a long-ass time now. So, anyway, I go to the coksukkin beauty parlor for a haircut, and Claudette, who does the snippin, calls it a fukkin "style." ChrEYEst! It aint a style, it's a gotdam haircut! . . . . Day-um.

When I was a lot younger, I believed I was just fine the way I was, but that turned out not to be true, and I would like to say right now that I have gotdam fukkinwell improved. And that is probably the single most reason that I, *one*, become a historian and, *two*, near 'bout become a philosopher, and, *three*, got myself involved with *litter-tour*—although McKinney believes if you're a Mississippian that is not so unusual—and she pointed out that even though Mississippians may not read or think much, they sure as hell can write like a muthafukka and can start talkin the minute they're born and keep it up till the gotdam cows come home . . . from, I guess, wherever the fuk it is they've been to.

Anyhow, if all of what she says is true, I'm alive to tell the tale.

This whole story I am getn ready to th'ow on your ass has three killings; a possibly murderous old woman; a definitely murderous younger woman; Voyd and me; a buncha other, no-doubt lethal-ass, largely Delta women, some of which you won't never see, called *The Aunty Belles*; Secundus Shipp; Judge Russell "Rusty" Justiss Jr.; plus a few other muthafukkas you don't yet know about. It includes actual death threats wrote in handwrite'n which was wrote down, put in a en-velop, stamped, and sent to young Mr. Brainsong II—all because word got out he was aimin to publish some more of Leland Shaw's *Notebooks*, which Shaw wrote on all them gotdam commissary[4] ledgers. And you'll also get an explanation, which may have been provided by a gotdam *bird*, on how that submarine I told you about in the first book was able to come up the Mississippi River to the place where me and Voyd found it. And, bygod, you'll finally see some kind of a' reason, possibly even a double one, why Leland Shaw's footprints disappeared. Plus, you'll probably believe it.

You recall it was young Mr. Brainsong II who was my *interviewer* on the first book I ever *talked*. The crazy fukka had been livin in *Lost Angeleez* where he was teachin at some big-ass college. Before that I think he *DID live* in Cinci-fukkin-nati, wherever that is, but I believe, like most people, he moved from there out West.

---

4   Plantation office and store. —ml

Anyway, what you need to know is that, from where he was hangin out—way out there in *Cali-diklikkin-fornia*—he finally moved his ass right here to St. Leo!

It also turns out he, too—like, I guess, the whole fukkin rest of the gotdam world—is a queer, just like his uncle, and has got hissef a boyfriend, but Voyd and me don't give a crap about none of that because it has further come to be we truly love and admire young Mr. Brainsong the Second and so, now, as you already know, we call his ass "Brainy"—which, I am certain you bygod have come to realize, he dam-sure is. Plus, I'mo tellya, anybody that tries to fuk over him or don't treat him right is gon have to deal with me and Voyd—well, mainly with me . . . cause I don't know if Voyd's up for a scrap.

Queers is like bird dogs and coon hounds. Coksukkin is just bred into em. And they can't help bein queers no more'n a Blue Tick can stop chasin' coons or a pointer can keep hissef from pokin' his nose at a covey of quail. I finally just come to see all that *because* I couldn't think of no other excuse for bein a queer. So, I said, "That's got to be it. There ain't no other *sign'tific-ass* way they can be the way they are!"

I don't know. Sometimes it seems like a lotta sumbiches in this world who's got any sense or who does something unusual—and possibly great as well—is one way or another gon turn out to be some kind of a queer. But the way I see it, you got to pick your queers, namely the ones you like and who likes you, and, well, gotdammit, fuk the rest.

Anyhow, just as in the first "book I talked," I will let you look at a little bit of the other stuff Leland Shaw wrote down, and then in PART TWO of *this* book, you can see a lot more of it if you want to, especially if you're a woman, but even what's in the book ain't, by a longshot, all of what that crazy sumbich wrote. As I have told you, it is this and more of that pile of paper-ized bird farts that Brainy was goin to get published and *for which,* it turns out, he was apt to have got his ass killed.

But, now—without *"whichin"* mysef to death—most all of that goofy Leland Shaw crap-oleum, as you know, I personally think is horse-shit. But, other people feel like it's *litter-tour* and think it's gotdam *poetry*! Furthermore, they say Shaw, that sunnavabitch—who, truthfully, I really don't hate so much no more even though, as General Forrest mighta said, I do try *to keep up the scare*—anyway, back to "they-say," *there are those who claim* that googoohead Shaw is way-ass better at bein a poet than *that other marshmella fellow* down in Greenville—the one that's been dead quite a long time, you know, William-Ass *Peepeetweety,* or sumpm or other. I'm referrin to the sumbich who wrote a famous book called *Lanterns or Your Levis* or some such double-clutchin possum-slobber as that.

But, hole-ass on! I need to remind you again that at the end of each and every chapter in PART ONE, you are goin to see one of my famous recipes. I gave you a few of em in *The Yazoo Blues.* But, *Son!* You will *love* these other delicious-ass little *sukkumups.*

And you'll love this, too. An eighteen-wheeler turned over at the Coldwater River bridge on Highway Number 6 at Marks, and two hippopotamuses *ek*scaped out of the trailer and loped off into the Coldwater. Voyd called me on the cellphone and told me about it and said he heard that all the state troopers, po-licemans, constables, sheriff's deputies, volunteer firefighters, and every swingindik in the whole State of Miss'ssippi's *Gay Men's Fish Commission*[5] has done come out to try to catch them sumbiches. I'll find out what I can and get back to you. These days it just looks like if it aint one fukkin kinda *crisis,* it's a gotdam nuther. But that don't necessarily bother me none.

---

5   What Junior Ray's friend D. W. thought, as a child, the Game and Fish Commission was called. —ml

Sailing to Alluvium

PART ONE

Junior Ray's Narrative About What Happened and Why

*Southerners so often confuse violence with
entertainment and justify both as duty, which is
little more than a fanciful array of unexamined
obligation born neither of belief nor of truth but
merely from whiskey and habit.*

— SYLVIA ODCLUBB, author of
Katherine of Arrogance, *Knight
Sweats*, and *Gloria's Hallelujah*

CHAPTER ONE

Brainy (Young Mr. Brainsong II) Reappears—Death Threats—
The Threaters Want to Protect an Image—Junior Ray Begins
a New Masterpiece—A Sex Doll "Facilitator"—McKinney
Returns—Part Two Is Mentioned—"Life Aint Got No Plot"—
Recipe No. 1: Delta Catfish Delux!

I t was the gotdamdest thing. I hadn heard nothin from young
Mr. Brainsong Number Two—or even nothin *about* him—for
the longest time, when, one day, there he is. He knocks on my
door, right here in St. Leo, and says, "Mr. Loveblood, I very much
need to talk to you and get your advice."

Holy Life-Ruinin Cut Worm! That knocked me back. Not
many people ever wanted my *advice*, and I didn want none of theirs
neither. Anyway, I said, "Hell, yeah, *Young Mister Brainsong*, get
your ass on in here." The po' bastuhd looked like he hadn slep in a
year. So, I told him I could see something was botherin him pretty
bad, and I ast him what I could do to hep—and what the fuk was
it? Plus, I said, "Call me Junior Ray."

"Thank you," he said, "and you can call me Brainy."

Then, he come out with it: "I have received death threats . . .
Junior Ray, three, to be exact."

I said, "Jeezus ChrEYEst! What the fuk would a nice-ass sumbich
like you be getn death threats for?"

He said, "Apparently for letting it be known that I intend to
publish *The Notebooks of Leland Shaw*."

He handed me one of the letters. It was already took out of the envelope and was unfolded. This is what it said—

Hazardous Sodomite! And afterwards, we shall send you to the Maker your very existence insults.

Whoa! I have to say this was the first time I ever knowed young Mr. Brainsong II—I mean to say, Brainy!—had ever worked as a soda jerk. I could see, right then, there was some strange-ass doo-dywah already harnessed up and in the field. Then I kept on readin:

This is a travesty![1] *Our fair land has suffered enough! No more! There will be no more! This outrage you plan, which, I assure you, we have known about for some time, must be stopped. Yes! You cannot deny that you plan to publish the mentally disturbed scribblings of that embarrassing Leland Shaw whose public exposure in the book you helped to produce some years ago through your collaboration, if not in fact your "collusion," with Mr. Junior Ray Loveblood was an assault on all of us who love our Southern Culture and have sworn to protect it—to protect it indeed, along with the image of our Southern men, from pseudo-literary discoverers, Northern liberal literati, intellectual opportunists, nest-feathering academics, and pusillanimous Ganymedes, all of which, my dear Mr. Brainsong Number Two, describes yourself. Therefore:*
  Whereas: We have suffered the shame of Mr. Erskine Caldwell;
  Whereas: We have endured the horror of Mr. William Faulkner;
  Whereas: We have quietly borne the pathetic mischaracterizations of Mr. Walker Percy;

---

1   Some have declared that although the writer was apparently confusing the word "travesty" with "tragedy," the events that unfold are exactly in that specific category of satire, i,e., "travesty." I was of course terrified; yet, I tend to agree that "travesty" precisely names what took place. —ogbii

Whereas: All named above are traitors to our proud but defeated Southern Nation;

We here-in anonymously serve notice upon you once again—you abominable Antinoüs—that you shall not live to see your proposed work in print. For what it may be worth, we can stomach Mr. Loveblood because no decent human being can take him seriously, but there is a danger—a monstrous danger when it comes to poetry!—which is the core of Mr. Shaw's so-called "masterpiece"! And we who are ever vigilant realize that some who read it, though they be pure and entirely innocent, may be taken in unaware.

Why can't you find within the shallows of your being the nobleness of heart to edit and seek the publishing of something written by our beloved Stark Young? Albeit he was from the Hills. Still . . .

Oh, no. You intend to foist upon a credulous and largely non-Southern and of course non-Deltan readership the works of a misleading mental defective, one who not only hallucinates but who embodies the very shape of weakness and instability; yet, worse, exhibits a shameful lack of true manliness.

Why can't you promote something by Joyce Kilmer?

Oh, no. You are worse than that twisted Flannery O'Connor whose work has twisted the mere thought of the American South into one of disastrous grotesquerie. My Lord and Fathers! Where did she get those people!

Why can you not publish a delightful collection of Allen Tate?

Oh, no. You, sir, are beneath even the abysmal muck of that horrible Mr. Tennessee Williams! To think, he sat in our houses! He drank our Co'-Colas. He fanned himself with our fans! Surely he knew the Delta was not as it was made to seem in his plays and—it causes me to feel ill just to recall the shock of it all—in those motion pictures! Baby Doll did not live in Benoit. And her people were not like that! She would not have taken up with a foreigner. Or at least not that particular foreigner.

We were swindled by Mr. Williams, but we are on to you. You are worse than General Butler—I do mean "Beast" Butler—down in New Orleans. But you, young Mr. Brainsong II, are more harmful to our treasured image as the greatest example of civilization's finest hour than even the perverse calumniations of Mr. Robert Penn Warren.

Why? Why!? Do you not wish to announce the loveliness of our region, our fertile fields, our haunting swamps—especially those in our beloved Mississippi Delta—by showing the world once more the exquisite prose and poetry of William Alexander Percy? He did not feel it necessary, as did Mr. Shaw, to invent his own unintelligible language, nor did he believe he could converse in the tongues of marsh hawks!

Oh, No, Sir. You are convinced it is somehow your duty to attack us en derriere *by allowing the universe to view our men as babbling hallucinators who plop their psychotic drooling upon the pages of unused plantation commissary ledgers!*

Why can't you publish the works of Sir Walter Scott?

Oh, No! Sirrah, you shame us! We cannot permit it. And we intend to put an end to your ability to humiliate our countrymen. If General Nathan Bedford Forrest were alive today, he would thrash you and send you back whence you were spawned.

Alack a day! Time has taken the General, and he is no longer with us save in our hearts and history, thus it is we who will do his work for him and for the sake of who we are, what we stood for, and in the name of all we are taught to cherish about our illustrious heritage. We will do the General's work. But you, young Mr. Brainsong II, you shall not do yours.

Your most humble & obedient servant,

Anonymous

Holy nit spit. If this'd been on TV, this is where you'da heard the music go *DADA DA DUM!* Anyhow, I had to set there real still for a minute on that one before, natchaly, I ast him: "Why would any muthafukka on this gotdam earth want to kill your ass for that!?" See, I was thinkin if somebody was goin to kill Mr. Brainsong's nephew—remember, Voyd and me calls him *Brainy* now—over what Leland Shaw wrote in them weird-ass notebooks, then he probably shoulda been dead two or three times before now for helpin' put out that first book on me!

And I was right. Brainy, setn there that day in my livin room, claimed the threaters wuddn too happy about that neither. Then he told me that all three of the letters had said just about the same thing: namely, that the sender, or senders—whoever he, she, or they was—is de-fukkin-termined that no more *"works of so-called literature uncomplimentary to our way of life shall be published."*

He futher told me that the threater or threaters is hell-bent on sandbaggin' and generally preventn anything that *"does not portray Mississippi and Mississippians as the brave, intelligent, cultured, and decent* muthafukkas[2] *they are from ever again bein foisted on the American readin public."*

I said, "I didn know *there was* one." I really don't have much knowledge about the American readin public; mainly I meant that bein complimentary wuddn somethin I normally gave much thought to and that, personally I didn give a shit what people said about Mississippi because as far as I was concerned whatever anybody said about Mississippi and the whole bunch of know-nothin pekkawoods, Planters, politicians, bootleggers, beauty queens, bankers, and cornholers was *all* true—and if it wuddn, it probably ought to be or was gon be. Plus, I didn know what "foisted" was, but it sure as skeetshot did not sound like something I want to ever do. I figured it might be some kind of a word people in California come up with. Maybe they foisted

---

2   Junior Ray's word. —ml

a good bit. I don't know. Still, I didn want anything to get by me. Fukkum.

But here's the thing that caught my attention. Brainy said the letters wuddn postmarked in California. They was *mailed from Clarksdale*, Mississippi! And I thought, damn, I'll be a red-headed *step*-sheep! Even Voyd wouldna been that fukkin dumb . . . to mail something like that from *Clarksdale*.

Anyway, it was still hard for me to understand why somebody'd want to kill Mr. Brainsong's nephew just for little or nothin such as what he told me about. On the other hand, I remembered my own need to shoot the shit out of Leland Shaw. That hept me to see the picture somewhat clearer, and that's when I realized I was getn ready to become a diktective . . . a *private* diktective.

And the first suspect I thought about was nonefukkinother than Miss Attica Rummage!

Sumpm else, though, was that the threatERS—and I am indicatin that at the time we thought there mighta been more than one, because you need to bear in mind young Mr. Brainsong said whoever was write'n the letters always referred to themsevz as *"we"*—appeared to feel like the rest of the world would think all Mississippians was silly-headed, crazy-assed, and more or less totally outa their fukkin minds like Shaw was. But I told Brainy I figured the threaters was about a day late and seventy-five cents short and that *that* dog was already off the truck and chasin chickens.

Now, about this book: I may not can write worth a shit, but I sure-as-Shuqualak[3]—which is a town in Miss'ssippi but it AINT in the Delta—can talk. And as you know that is the way I write my books.

Anyway, when I began to go to work on this fukkin new mas-

---

3   Pronounced *shook-a-lock*. —ml

terpiece, I just didn feel I could ast McKinney to hep me with it, although, after a while, she did. Plus, since I am talkin a good deal about young Mr. Brainsong—Brainy!—and his *problem* with the threaters, I guaran-dam-tee you he wuddn in no shape to be carryin' on no interview nor no kind of facilitate'n with me, nor doin no kinda *extra* book work at all. I could see—and Voyd could, too—that them letters he had got was worryin the crap out of him and outright visibly-ass agin the sumbich.

Anyway, I just figured I'd go at it all alone, so I set in to try to do what I *been* doin: Namely, talkin into a gotdam *recordn* thing, and this time just that, plus, of course, getn Miss Minnie MacDonald to type it all up for me on a floppy. The publisher, NewSouth, said it was okay with them. So I went up to Meffis to the big *CheapCo store*—out there the other side of the city, half-ass way to Nashville—and bought me a fairly good little cassette recorder. I didn have one of my own and, durin the other two times, I had used Brainy's and McKinney's. Then I came on back home to St. Leo and went to work.

But, I couldn't do it. I couldn't get nothin done setn there in the house on my own. And I knew what it was. I had to have somebody *there*, like McKinney or Brainy—not just *anybody* but *somebody* nonethefukkinless—to look at and to talk my gotdam book to.

Thinkin I could fool mysef, I bought another one of them blow-up sex dolls like the one Mad and me stuck up in the sand out in front of his tent flap when he was down there on Horn Island in the GuffaFukkinMexico, with his pet one-legged parrot, Gene LaFoote. But me and the new blowup doll didn last two minutes. Frankly I don't know how ANY sumbich can stand to *look at* one nem things, much less poke his deeber up in one! That's way beyond my ass. ChrEYEst. Them things make a Holstein look like a mooo-vie star. That's a joke, muthafukka. Anyway, you sure as hell can't talk to one nem wide-eyed sex balloons! And you definitely wouldn want anybody to know you tried. Uh-oh. I guess I just let *that* cat out of the crokersack.

So I went, hat in hand, to McKinney and also to Brainy and begged their ass to do what they did before, just one mo time, and they said Yes, they would, and now I am back . . . *on* the fukkin track!

Plus, as I have told you, and because I think it is important in connection with what all went on, I *am* goin to give you a little teaspoon sip ever' now and then of some of that googah Leland Shaw wrote in his *Notebooks.* Then, in *PART TWO* of this book, you will be able to see a bunch more of it that Brainy was getn ready to have published by them coksukkas out in Califukkinfornia.

For one thing, when you see it, it'll help you keep in mind how fukkin crazy Leland Shaw was and how even more crazy them *threaters*—or that *threater*—was for wantn to kill anybody over it. Kiss *my leg*! I just can't feature it. Anyway, from time to time, I do promise to hand you some of Shaw's wild-ass stuff.

Funny thing, though, it's like *the threaters* didn much care if Shaw was nuts; they just wuddn in favor of *tellin* anybody about it. That right there told me it was most likely a woman or more than one of em. In addition, I guess that's why it has always looked to me like the up-standin people who were supposed to be in their right minds are, a lot of the time, crazier than a Sugar-Ditch lizard.

Now, one other thing, and this is super-ass important: Some-body—I ain' gon say who—said to me the other day, *"Junior Ray, you've got to make certain you craft a tight, flawless plot line in your next work."* That's word for word what they said, and of course that person did have a point. That individual would be right on the fuk-kin money IF I was gon be write'n an actual *g'novel* with a made-up story and such. But, as some of you well know, that is not the case with what I "talk" about in my books, because, bygod, I aint makin none of this up. I'm just tellin you the honest-to-God, Gospel-ass truth about what happened, in the best way I can. And if it sounds like it's something that's been made-up, then I guess that's at least part of the point of me tellin you about it. You wouldn want to hear about something that was ordinary, and when you know that what I am tellin you is the swear-on-the-coksukkin-Bible, undiluted fingerfukkin *facts,* then, sumbich, you understand the place and all this they call the Mississippi Delta. That's mainly my objective.

So, fuk a tight-ass plot. Hell, anything with a *plot* IS made up! Life aint got no plot . . . though most of us end up in one.[4]

AW-ITE. IF YOU'RE LIKE me, and I reckon you might be, then you're always up for sumpm to eat, so check out *this* book's "first" of my famous recipes, which you can add to those you already have in your family-ass edition of *The Yazoo Blues*:

Junior Ray's Famous
Mississippi Delta Catfish Delux!

You cook this up with a ground sirloin slab-ette, sawtayed in olive oil, garlic, & black pepper, topped with a real thin layer of pure white grits covered very lightly with grated, sharp-ass Vermont cheddar, over which your Mississippi Delta Catfish fi-let—likewise sawtayed but in canola oil, cayenne, & basil—is laid and topped with (1) mushrooms that's been sawtayin along with your ground sirloin slab-ette, and (2) a piece of fukkin parsley.

---

4   Attributed to H. R. Williams. —ml

CHAPTER TWO

*What Caused the Problem—The Notebooks of Leland
Shaw—A "Tweety-Tweet" Excerpt—Letter to the Chickasaw—
Poets Are Buttholes—Junior Ray Wrote a Poem, "Gollee
Moses"—Dyna Flo's Littlest Girl, MiniVan—Recipe No. 2:
Junior Ray's Famous Game Pie*

R ight here is a little sniff of what's caused all the problem—
and why young Mr. Brainsong was getn them death threats
through the U.S. Mail. If you're like me you won't be able
to figure out why anybody would want to kill a sumbich over the
following, which is what Brainy's got as a beginnin to his forth-
fukkin-comin "Sailing to Alluvium: The Notebooks of Leland Shaw."

You're about to read something that only a bunch of gotdam
tweety-tweet women, possibly up North, and probly a few alcoholic-
ass queers in probly New Or-leans would ever even want to look
at. And after you see it, I have some more things to tell you—stuff
you might not want to believe could come out of a human head
. . . cause frankly it was, and is, the gotdamdest thing I ever saw or
heard of. Anyway, here's what I was talkin about:

Leland Shaw, from Ledger No. 2: Letter to the Chickasaw

Therefore, I feel I should write a letter, as a matter of courtesy,
to the Chickasaw, which will allow me explain who I am and how I
happen to be here. But that is a fatuous proposal. Though I know who
I am, it is not entirely clear how I got where I am. Even so, I seem to
be compelled to constantly imagine I have to explain it all, and all of

it is funnier still when I realize I am writing to myself and not at all to the Chickasaw who, frankly, would not now be interested in the subject. I am sure my great-great-grandparents would be amused. I know perfectly well there are no Chickasaw nearby, except in Volume "A" in the Chancery Clerk's office and, lost but loosely adrift, in the blood of some of my fellow Celts.

Did you, O noble autochthonoids, know we came here expecting quite a lot? Yet, what did we find? There you were, having already met and admired the British, quite comfortably adapted to our ways, planting cotton and corn and listening to the slaves sing about Jesus, in Chickasaw of course.

Where was the mystery? Where was the exotic? There was more to life than cotton . . . somewhere else.

And so I am compelled to ask the question: Could you not have retained something of your ancient origins far beyond the Bering Strait? Were the caribou worth it after all? Were the giant sloths aclaw, acreep, when first you found your foot in the Land of Colonel Reb? I think not. You were the new ones, and all those others ran off and disappeared with the waters, swift disease, mastodons, and the last glaciation. I always say, if the polar cap fits, wear it.

> *Nevertheless,*
> *I have discovered your timeless ways*
> *as they were before the taint of contact*
> *with your unfellow man.*
> *And now I know how to walk like thought*
> *across the naps of popular girls—swift,*
> *barely visible,*
> *and indefinite.*

You could have been the communicator. We would have been the receivers. You could have called. We might have answered. I see it all so clearly now. Communicators like to say the words. Receivers love to hear them. The division is basic to our species. Normally, of course, I would rather speak than listen, but ancestrally I am certain the reverse would have been true, if only for a moment. And, as I am sure you know by now, moments are everything. They seem to be all I have. The question is where to spend them. "How" is not an issue. But "where" is of the utmost importance, which is why I am trying so hard to find my way home.

> *It is only by night*
> *that we see your darker bodies shining in the starlight*
> *as night and stars and cold fall all around to cloak me*
> *as I move*
> *in search—in search of searching I sometimes think,*
> *though I call it by another name: the search for home,*
> *where, desperate as I am to find it, I cannot say*
> *what I shall do once I'm there . . .*
> *seek to leave it, I suspect,*
> *for the sake of more adventure.*
> *Oh, like the sailor who longs for the shore,*
> *once he's seen Spanish Marie,*
> *he feels again*
> *the hunger for the sea.*

This is what will happen to me; thus, I will stick with the quest for high water and the way home. I am a vibration of firm resolve. Energy matters. (ha ha)

There is one thing, however, of which, lately, I have become convinced. They do not make the skin of Chickasaws in rubber.

Conditions improve. The weather is exceptional. There are so many bright, cold, *cold*, clear days, so many stars by night, possibly a number of extremely distant galactic pinpoints and magellanic mist, and, I might add, planets by dawn and evening twilight. Indeed, were I not consumed with the matter and energy of escape and evasion, I might well be content to linger here for a while behind the lines.

But that cannot be. I am among foreigners, and I do not mean the Chickasaw or, of course, the Choctaw of the lower Delta and, to some degree, of the greater part of the known Muskogean world. From any contact with these Amerind beings, one might well be up a Creek . . . the sure-enough Muskogee to the East along with the *Alabamo* bound.

So much for anthropottery and shard habitat. My people were the latest of the Late Mississippians unless we say the title belongs to the Italians and the Lebanese. Oh, bury me not on the lone praline.

O Masters of Muskogee! How is it that our lives became so intertwined in these winter fields beneath the hawk? We, you and I, thought we were the panther but understand at last we are the mouse. And the killer bird is mostly circumstance; it is the night that flies by day . . . and not a creature at all in the most important sense.

The enemy is not tangible; therefore we cannot grapple, cannot "come to grips" with its murderous mass. Indeed, its beak protrudes from our frontal lobes; its talons are hidden in the folds of our underpants. We carry the monster. Flea bite us. Goddee smite us.

> *Now I find there are jungles in the memory,*
> *jungles of deciduous trees and still water among the cypress.*
> *Dark life moves unseen between the tupelo*
> *and beneath the green softness of the duck moss.*
> *Things are devoured, and things are born.*
>
> *Bad enough there are hawks above and hawks*
> *below that fly upward, fast, like feather rockets*
> *to knock the stuffing from the goose.*
> *And, then, there are the "thingamabobs"*

beneath the surface of the slough.

You Chickasaw are not here at this Barmecide feast in this pre-posterous Potemkin village, this improbable hallucination that my captors have presented to me as my home—which partly also was your historic home and the home as well of so many of your Okla Falaya, Potato Eating, and Six-Town Choctaw brothers . . . and sisters.[5] So, except for the rubber skin worn by the enemy, I can say to you the emperor is naked.

I am never taken in by it—even though, I will admit, often I am tempted to think I may be wrong about everthing, but then I breathe deeply two or three times and, ultimately, say to myself: "Leland, re-member who you are," and, immediately, I know, without any doubt at all, that whatever it is I am, *I am not whatever it is they are.* And, so, in that way, I keep my perspective, my balance, and my hold on truth.

With rubber skin they look
like those I've known before,
both white and black, but,
underneath,
I know they are Germans.

And all the while I look for the land of *mingos*[6] and Mandingos—although, ha! . . . I forgot. You rascals were insatiable slavers. So much for the Mandingos who, I am certain, just had to shuffle their feet and say yassuh or whatever the Chickasaw equivalent of that might be.

---

5   The three Divisions of the Choctaw before the Removal were the *Okla Falaya* [Longtown People, i.e., long people/far people], the *Ahe Apat Okla* [Potato Eating People), and the *Okla Hannali* [Six-Towns People]. The word *Okla* can be translated as *people, nation,* and also as the third-person-plural pronoun, *they.* Further, in Chickasaw *Okla* can mean town. Chickasaw and Choctaw are very close, rather like two dialects of the same language. —ogbii

6   Chickasaw-Choctaw for chiefs . —ogbii

But that's okay with me. I know about time. However, when others find out what went on and what happened later with the Chickasaw Freedmen, I'm afraid there'll be skunk stew for Sunday brunch.

Mind you, I'm not down on *you* any more than I am down on *my ancestors*, and that is because the future perspective—along with the various forms of modern ignorance—was not there. They did not have the privilege that comes with retrospect. And, also, lest we—and ye—forget too much, the Mandingos had a hand in it as well—a two-hand grab in fact. When it comes to human history, no one is innocent.

The long and the short of it all is that you stood in the way of our wealth, and we had to frighten you. We had to cheat you. We did it all for ourselves! We had to believe you were not like us . . . my folks, the *true human beings* with golden souls, beloved by God, and endowed with the right of avarice and empowered by a license to take. You trusting Indigenes never stood a chance. Never had a prayer. We were enormous germs who came to attack you with our newly minted modernity. Indeed, that you survived is remarkable and certainly not part of our original plan. We do not like to feel bad about the wrong we do. Thus, your continued presence reminds us, reminds us of ourselves and of the wickedness we merely make into cookies.

We were—and are—a bad lot, O Mingos out of time. We have eaten you. And still, somehow, you allow us to say grace. It is difficult for me to realize that the land I hold so dear is the world we ruined for you. But if your enemy is me and my kind, then, I must say, we are on the same side and share a common cause.

Sincerely,

Leland Shaw

THERE IT IS. AND it's just what you'd expect from a gotdam town *sissy*. You know what I'm talkin about. You've seen em—those kind of tall, willowy, wafty-ass coksukkas people always says is "tho aR-tith-tic" and can "play the piano, oooooeeeee!" Plus, they'll always make it a big fukkin point to mention: "And he was so good to his *mother!*"

Course, Shaw wuddn all that tall. He wuddn wafty neither. But he did live in the fukkin town. I cannot seem to ever get over hate'n his ass. That don't bother me, but I can see maybe it ought to.

The other thing about it is, people sometimes talk about how Shaw's write'n is so "*beautifully-ass* poetic." Fuk that. Poets are buttholes. On the other hand, I wrote a poem one time, too, and even sent the sumbich up to Nashville cause I thought it would be a big hit as, not as a' actual song but, you know, like a "resuscitation," on the Grand Ol' Opry. But I never did hear nothin after I mailed it up there. Fukkum. I coulda been world famous.

Anyway, the real reason I wrote what I'm gon show you is because, you remember my girlfriend, the one over near Sledge, Dyna Flo McKeever?—One of her daughters at that time was havin trouble learnin her Bible stories in Sunday School, so I wrote a song—although, as I just said, it's not so much a song as it is sumpm you *say* instead of sing. Anyhow, I wrote it up in order to help the child get the hang of all that ratshit about Moses. Course, I do know that stuff even though I don't believe a gotdam *word of none of it. And never did.*

Anyway, here's what I come up with for Dyna Flo's little-est girl, MiniVan—I called it "Gollee Moses." Later on I sorta thought I might re-name it "Holy Shit, Muthafukka," so it would have more of a chance of bein a hit, but I guess I wanted little chirren to be able to hear it, and that's why I had to call it what I did, to make it be nice. And just so you know: I can *rhyme* up a—that's right, you guessed it—a gotdam storm! It aint nothin to it. Anyhow, this is it:

GOLLEE MOSES
It all got started back a long while
When Pharaoh's daughter was swimmin in the Nile;

She looked in the bushes and saw a little chile
And said, "Gollee Moses!"

One day the Lord said Moses, you're the man
To lead all the Chillum to the Promise' Land.
Well, Moses struck out with Pharaoh at his heels,
Moses on foot, the Pharaoh on wheels.

When they got up to the Red Sea waters,
The chillun ast Moses, "What we gon do?"
And Moses told the Chillun, "Orders is orders,"
And the Chillun of Israel walked right through.
Well, Gollee Moses!

Weeelll, the army of Pharaoh followed after Moses,
But just fo' the waters covered up their noses,
The whole army said: Gollee Moses!
Moses on a mountain top thinkin very hard,
Long come a cloud, and out jumped God,
Well, Gollee Moses!
The Lord put the Law in Moses' hand,
Said, Moses, tell the Chillun they better understand,
If they don't do what these things say,
I'll wipe out the world in half a day!"
Well, Gollee Moses!

Moses told the Lord, "It weren't none a me,
Just a big epidemic of iniquity!
I gave the Chillun your Ten Commandments,
And they come up with the First Ten Amendments!"
Well, Gollee Moses!

Moses come down bout an hour'n a half,
Found all the chillun round a golden calf;
He said, "Chillun, Chillun, what's goin on?"
They said, "Laughin, dancin, singin a song!"
Well, Gollee Moses.

Moses told the Chillun, "Y'all make me mad,
jumpin round and actin bad,
But I'mo tell y'all one thing now:
You gonna get rid of that golden cow!"
Well, Gollee Moses!

From then on down to this very day,
When folks don't know just what to say,
They open their mouth and bug their eyes,
They take a deep breath and say with surprise:
GOLLEE MOSES![7]

It musta worked because when MiniVan got to be eighteen, she took off across the Miss'ssippi River and went to be in one-nem whatchacallit communes over in the Ozark Mountains, near *Your-Eeka* Springs, wherever the fuk that is. Arkansas, I reg'n, which is too far Out West for me. Anyway, the next thing we knew she was workin with a bunch of long-haired sumbiches, makin cheese. They was all born-againers. But I have to hand it to em—they worked

---

7   I admit I have had my doubts about whether Junior Ray actually wrote the above. It is true he possesses a strange talent for rhyming and indeed for rhetorical timing. Without convincing proof to the contrary, I shall have to take his word . He did pop out with a few lines once, just after I had come back to St. Leo. They rather startled me, to wit: *Way back in the Garden of Eden, Adam had it easy, didn do no weedn, but it came to an end one fateful day, when he bit into the apple and he heard himself say: Woman is a woodpecker, Man's like a tree, I got a hunnud-pound woodpecker peckin on me.*—ml

hard and did pretty well, and their cheese company is called: *Wholly Goats Christian Cheese Company.* Plus, on ever' one of their labels it says *God Works in Mysterious Wheys.* I reckon God will forgive their spellin. ChrEYEst!

You can probably find some of MiniVan's company's cheese if you ever go to a health food store. It aint my kinda cheese, which mostly is bout what you'd expect, that country-store big old yellow hoop. But, MiniVan and the born-againers send their stuff all over everywhere. So you are apt to bump into it if you go anywhere at all, and I mostly don't.

Anyhow, I believe the girl is happy and lives in somethin called a yorp,[8] or some such thing, in one big room with a lot of other Christian cheese makers. Plus, Dyna Flo is okay with it all. She always just says MiniVan is doin church work, and leaves it at that. I guess I would like to think it's possible my "song"—my *"resuscitation"*—mighta had something to do with MiniVan's spiritual development.

Dyna Flo's other two chillun—two boys—is in ever' kind of trouble you can think of, and it'd take more'n old Jesus and an extra-virgin Mary to get em out of it. I'm talkin about everything from killin deer outa season to tree rustlin—and oh hell yeah!—to makin Crystal Meth on a party boat in Pompey Ditch. You can always figure on seein one or the other of them totally tattooed little shitheads cutn grass and pickin up trash on the side of the highway, in a pair of *aw-inge* coveralls. I don't have nothin to do with their asses! And one neez days somebody's gon shoot em.

---

8   A yurt. —ml

Junior Ray's Famous Apple-Black Cherry-and-Grape-(All-at-the-Same-Fukkin-Time) Game Pie!

1. Go get your Browning Sweet Sixteen, and blast the crap out of the game: namely, quail, dove, duck, deer, tweety birds or whatever as long as it's in season and you're willin to eat it—and remember you can't just use one kind of anything: you've got to use at least THREE DIFFERENT wild meats—but that don't include fish. (You can use all the fish you want, some other time, in my *Junior Ray's 9-Step Fukkin Fish Soup*, which you can easily find all laid out in my second book, *The Yazoo Blues*, which, sumbich, if you don't already own a copy, you need to get you one, at a *real* bookstore.)

2. Parboil it all—then pull off the best and most tenderest little pieces and th'ow em in a big bowl so you can take your hand and kind of mash all of it together against one another while you . . .

3. Pop it good with salt and pepper. And as you know I prefer cayenne.

4. Then add the fresh chopped (peeled) apples, sweet seedless green, if possible, Thompson grapes, and those frozen black pitted cherries you read about in the name of this dish, above, and continue to mix up the whole shootn match with your hand—or if you know you ought not to use your hand, get a big-ass spoon or sumpm.

5. And while you're mixin' all that, add a good dose of Mad-Dog 20-20 or M.D. 20-20—which is why down here it is sometimes called *Eye Doctor*—it's a right popular hip-pocket wine better known as Mogen David 20-20. But any half-ass-decent cream sherry will do. Plus, yes, you can use bourbon whiskey, or cognac; that just depends on you—hell, th'ow Co'-Cola in

the sumbich if you want to. I don't give a fuk. But don't put in no gotdam actual sugar that you can *see*!

6. When you've done everything I've told you to, above, or are just wo' out with foolin with it, dump ever' bit of it in one-nem ready-made pie crusts. Then set another ready-made pie crust on top of it for a top, and shove it all in the oven on the middle rack at 350 degrees for an hour or until the crust is brown and nice and the smell is ir-refukkin-zistable. You might have to check on it from time to time. Go by your nose.

CHAPTER THREE

Tombo Is Dead as a Muthafukka—Shot with a .410—Turkey Season—The Evans Place—The Visitor's Tree—Farley Trout Is Dead "as a Busted Balloon"—Steele "Froggy" Waters Swallows a Gig—Miss Attica Knew the Territory—Old Euster Draynum "Was Lazy as a Winter Turtle"—Miz Potts Is Eaten by Beagles—Merigold Is Suspected—The Letters Are Mailed from Clarksdale—Recipe No. 3: Junior Ray's Famous Valentine Special

They found Tombo Turnage dead as a muthafukka, setn bolt-upright underneath the so-called Visitor's Tree out there in the woods on the other side of the levee, out on the Cut-Off[9] on the Evans place, the first day of turkey season.

He was shot just once, right smack in the middle of his chest, with a shotgun, which shouldna been strange but was, *because,* by the number of pellets they found in him—which was No. 7½ shot and sure as shit wuddn no turkey load!—and also by the small *size* of the gotdam pattern the blast looked to have been from a .410[10] three-inch shell, and *definitely* not from no twelve-gauge, nor no .20 or .16!

Plus, whoever done it squeezed the trigger facin DI-rectly at him, right in front of his ass, and, by the look on Tombo's face when they lifted up the mosquito net he was wearin—like every other sumbich out there in the woods that day—you didn have to

---

9   An oxbow lake "cut off" from the Mississippi River in 1942 by the U.S. Army Corps of Engineers and nowadays sometimes called Tunica Lake. —ml

10   .410, a small-gauge shogun, usually pronounced "four-ten." —ml

be no Sam Spade to know that when ol Tombo seen the shooter it didn cause him no concern at all.

As for the turkeys, I'm confident that you know you hunt them ugly buzzard-headed fukkas in the spring, in April usually, so there's always a lot of fukkin bugs to contend with. One other thing is that—if you was the murderin-ass shooter—you couldna told for certain if it was even Tombo or not you was shootn at. It's like the killer just walked up to him, said, "Good mawnin, Tombo," and blasted him in the chest point-blank, dead-center, kablam. Like I indicated, above, you don't have to be no *valefukkindiktorian* to figure *that* out.

Anyway, all this is mostly what got me to thinkin, because there wuddn nobody on this earth that woulda wanted to shoot Tombo Turnage. That's a fact I know for absolute certain. So, I figured the shooter musta thought Tombo was somebody else . . . such as young Mr. Brainsong II—Brainy!—*because*, see, the Evanses had invited Brainy's citified ass—while Brainy was still in Califukkinfornia—to come out and go turkey huntin after he got to the Delta. Only Brainy had to call em up at the last min- ute, really just as he was tryin to leave Lost Angeleez, and ast em for a raincheck because he had done caught the fukkin flu and probly wouldn get to St. Leo in time to go on the hunt. And it was the truth, too, because Brainy does not lie. So, a little later, the Evanses *then ast Tombo* did *he* want to come out, and Tombo took em up on it quick as a drive-in fuk.

THORNTON EVANS, THE SUMBICH Tombo had gone huntn with and who owned the land, found Tombo's dead ass right around eleven o'clock that mornin, setn there in the woods, already surprisin'ly cold considerin how hot it was, propped up against the Visitor's Tree, about five hours after he heard what he thought was Tombo's shotgun go off. Thornton said sumpm about it give him a funny feelin because it seemed to him the shot was not as loud as he believed it ought to have sounded.

Anyway, when Thornton left the woods hissef, thinkin Tombo woulda hiked on back to headquarters with a turkey, Thornton got back to his commissary on the dry-side of the levee and seen Tombo's car still parked there. Something about that bothered him big time, so Thornton went back over cross the levee, drove as far as he could in his jeep, then walked the rest of the way to where he'd situated Tombo, down under that big white oak Visitor's Tree. Thornton had put Tombo there a good half-hour before daylight, in the hopes that his "visitor" might get hissef a gobbler. But, as it turned out, Tombo was the one that got *got*. And there he was, his gun layin' crosst his legs, the safety on, and hadn fired a shot.

Miss Elsie Palmer told me a long time ago that Thornton was a Chickasaw, or at least his great-granddaddy was one. I believe it too, cause Thornton, that sumbich, is dark as I don't know what. Yet he don't never mention nothin about him bein a' *Inyan*. Hell, I would.

Anyway, it was April. There it was, hot as a "*big*-dog," and what air there *was* was already fulla mosquitos. So, natchaly, it was turkey season. And, as I am sure you know, that's the time in the whole fukkin Delta when every good ol' boy—and every gotdam Planter, banker, and preacher, and even one or two niggas—drops ever' thing they're doin' just so they can spend mornins before sun-up and late afternoons sweatn their butts off deep in the woods, mostly across the levee in a swarm of wild-ass bugs whilst they set still as a toadstool, chirpin and sqeakin and squawk-assin on them goofy little turkey callers, in a cross-eyed concen-fukkin-trated attempt to impersonate a red-hot-to-trot *turkey-ette,* out there in the wilderness, *putt-putt-puttn*-out artificial turkey phone-sex in the hope that *they*, them gotdam fat-ass female-turkey impersonators in camouflage, might trick a fifty-pound, love-crazed, buzzard-lookin turkey gob-bler—all fanned out and pant'n, with his eyeballs big as a couple of Frisbees, and his tongue hangin' out like a red necktie—into strut-assin toward em out of the bushes just so some sportsman-like *lethal potbellied drag-queen,* who's good at talkin turkey, can shoot the shit outa him. Then that hero—a local good ol' boy or maybe some Meffis businessman—will take the po' coksukka home to put him in the freezer, or to the taxidermist to put him on the wall.

That's the way it is. What usually happens is that the shooter and his family will somehow chomp around on that big-ass bird for three days and *simulfukkintaneously* have the taxidermist fix up the po' bird's head and his beard, which is extremely important in the turkey-huntn world, and of course the tail as well, into a kind of artistical combo on a plaque, so it can hang on the wall in the TV room, between the coyote's head and the singin big-mouth bass.

I never could see it. Like I said a while ago, in the face a turkey and a vulture looks just about the same—even though, of course, their personal hygiene is quite different and a turkey don't stink the way a buzzard does.

Anyhow, in the Delta, turkey season was a bigger deal than any of the other huntn seasons put together. Shorter, too. There wuddn a whole lot of time to realize your wildest turkey dreams. And maybe, in part due to the rush, people got shot fairly often, possibly as much or more than they do durin deer season, because, see, there in that April thicket, some super-excited sportsman would be in the woods all camouflaged and hid, just a'callin away, often slunk down behind a log, and soundin just like a fukkin *turkey hen* sayin: "Hey, big boy, come gobble up some of this wild-ass turkey pussy!" Then, uhn-hunh, Mr. FieldandfukkinStream would stick his head up over the log to look around to see if any gobble-gobble loverboys was comin his way, and that's when some *other* sly hunter, hide'n right there in the woods real near the caller—shoot, the two fukheds mighta gone into the woods together! . . . plus, both of the muthafukkas woulda-shoulda knew at least generally where each of em was supposed to be setn—and STILL that other sumbich I'm talkin about would—wo'-out with the bugs, the humidity, the heat, and with April as well, and happy as all get out to bag hissef a hen—aim straight at what looked like a fine fat female to him and shoot his turkey-callin buddy square in the gotdam face, convinced when he done it he was finally gon bring home the wild-turkey version of Marilyn MONroe.

It was a datgum mass phenomenon. But you wouldna never caught me setn out there—if I wanted a gotdam turkey, I sure as shootn wouldn BE one in the bargain. I'd go somewhere and buy me a live one, let the sumbich run around the yard on a line for a day or two then say, "Okay, muthafukka, I guess you're bout as wild as you're gon get." Then I'd chop off his head, pluck his ass, clean him, and stick him in the stove. Fuk setn in the woods. Especially in the gotdam Delta. In April. ChrEYEst.

A FEW WEEKS AFTER they found Tombo, somebody come up on FarleyTrout, and him dead too as a busted balloon, slumped forwards over the steerin wheel of his car, out in front of his antique store down in Shelby. It's called *The Antique Shop*. Which really was a pretty sensible name for it when you think about it. And I am glad he didn change the gotdam "The" to "Ye" and call it a gotdam "Shoppe."

Anyway, there that sumbich was, cold as a French fork, dead in his car which—and I'll say this just once—was the *same kinda car* as Brainy had . . . a 1996 Ford Camilla!

One nem little silver letter-openers was stickin out the back of Farley's neck, which the woman who helped him run the store told the police was a "rose-patterned Kirk *raypoosay*." And I said, "Kirk, my ass. It was a gotdam dirk."

Then, about two weeks later, in May, there was "Froggy" Waters, face down and gone to Heaven in Beaver Dam Brake with his own gig stuck in his th'oat. He was out there with two or three of his buddies, and they're the ones that found him when they was on their way back to their vehicles.

His real name was Steele . . . Steele Waters. People called him *Froggy* on account of how much he loved to go frog giggin, even though he coulda got all he wanted to eat and and all he ever wanted to look at from India or gotdam Japan, up at one or two of the fancy-ass grocery stores up in Meffis. But Froggy just had a thing about waden around giggin bullfrogs—even though they wuddn as plentiful, or maybe even as healthy for you to eat as they was a long-ass time ago . . . you know . . . before there was all them *chemicals* and such. But I reg'n that didn matter too much to Froggy. It's a funny thing, but I have found that when people want to eat somethin, they don't let a lot of health concerns—like death—get in their way.

Anyway, the thing that turned your blood to Kool-Aid was the fact that Froggy *had invited Brainy* to go with him, and Brainy was pretty excited about it and was all ready to go and everything, and had talked about it for a week, especially out at the Boll & Bloom, which, if you ast me is the world's first fukkin internet. Whenever you want to spread some news, just whisper it once at the Boll & Bloom, and it'll damm near be on the Rash Numbaltz Show and all over the gotdam Meffis TV before you get your butt back home. So, in one sense, it wuddn like Miss Attica couldna knowed about him bein ast to go wade around in that big-ass swamp. Plus she knew exactly where they was gon be giggin because her and her husband, Euster Draynum, had been out there with Froggy and nem a buncha times before.

Let me just say this before I say anything else. Miss Attica's husband was ol' Euster Draynum because Miss Attica never did want to give up her family name, especially for the likes of *Draynum*. She wuddn about to. Even though she wuddn no gotdam

Democrat and in fukkin fact believed every other woman that got married ought to take on her husband's name, Miss Attica woulda rather been dead and in hell with her back broke in Arkansas than to give up her Rummage name for a po-ass sumbich like Euster . . . even though, as people said, Euster *had been* really sumpm to look at when he was young and could charm hissef into anything and and talk his way out of it as well. Yet and still, the sumbich didn never amount to nothin. People said he was lazy as a winter turtle, and I guess that suited Miss Attica just fine because she could do whatever she pleased and still have him for company. Which, I believe, everybody *further* said was the way she wanted it to be: namely, when she was a girl, she played with dolls, and when she got to be a grown woman, she played with Euster.

Euster, though, did have the gift. He coulda been successful at just about anything. And for a while he worked in Meffis and was one of them, whatchacallem, "Bond Daddies." You know, with the gold chains and all. But the story was he got in some kinda trouble, which, natchaly, nobody ever says what it was, so that tells you right off the fukkin bat it was about somebody else's money.

Anyway, ol' Euster, that muthafukka coulda sold a hat to a headless bat. On the other hand, people just never do fit in the suit you think they ought to wear. That's how it was with Euster. And now the sumbich is getn old like the rest of us. Oh, well.

Back to the killins: You know how plans is. Brainy had had to back out of goin frog-giggin with Froggy at the last minute because he got a letter from the I.R.-fukkin-S. and had to go up to Southaven to get it took care of. So, basically, I guess, somebody—like, fuk, *God*—was tryin to send another message to young Mr. Brainsong II: namely, that he'da been dead now if he'da gone frog giggin then.

WHAT YOU HAVE TO realize is that nobody else at that point knew what Voyd and me and Brainy knew. So most people just thought, dang, there sure is a lotsa killins goin on. But, as I say, at that point they—the general public, I mean—didn know nothin about the threat letters nor about Brainy havin been invited to turkey hunt and go frog giggin, nor did they see that Farley Trout's car was the same as Brainy's and that Farley, hissef, more or less was the same as Brainy too, if you get what I mean, and they had become, you know . . . *friends*. Although, actually, that aint got nothin to do with any of it.

But, Son! There was some stuff happenin! And to top it all off, old Miz Potts was also found dead in her flower bed by the meter-reader, done in with the hedge clippers, and half et up by her own two old beagle hounds, which that Worthless Nigga Ezell used to call "beaverhams," and the po-lice pretty much thought Miz Potts's daughter, Merigold,[11] done it, because, for one thing, nobody could locate her. I knew, though, there wuddn no connection in Miz Potts's death and them others. And there wuddn.

Anyway, there he was, young Mr. Brainsong, out there in California, tryin to come up with a real important book all about Shaw's googah and, in fact, had done signed the contract and every-thing—not with no company outchonder in Califukkinfornia as I had formerly believed but with thissun rightchere, NewSouth, over in Alabama. Alabama, I hope you understand, unlike the Delta and possibly the whole rest of the state of Mississippi, is where a lot of very famous white men is from, like Hank Williams for instance. Plus you can look at a road map and see it's pretty much a straight shot from Alabama right on up to Nash-ville and the Grand Ol' Opry, and everything. Most people, of course, in the Delta was black when I was comin along. And most of the music was that "Woke up this mawnin" kinda crap for which, now, there's a gang of so-called festivals havin to do with it all up and down Highway

---

11   Merigold Potts was named after her very distant "great-great cousin" Merigold Benoit; see *The Yazoo Blues.* —ml

61. I guess I ought to mention, too, that there's that off-the-wall Africanistic Miss'ssippi drum and fife stuff you find amongst them blacks up over in the Hills a little ways. And it's crazier than a cowgirl on a jumpstick.

But back to what I was tellin you about young Mr. Brainsong. It was like, kablammo, outa the gotdam smog—I aint never been out there, but I have heard em talk about smog on TV, and it's generally always in Lost Angeleez, and they show you a picture of it, like a huge-ass automotive fartcloud hangin over the city, so that's why I said it—he gets that first letter from Clarksdale, Mississippi. It's from some nameless sumbich that says that he, young Mr. Brainsong, deserves the fukkin death penalty for: One, helpin me do my first book; and, Two, for even imaginin he was goin to publish anything that featured Shaw's crazy-ass *notes*.

That all just beats the doggy-do outa me. Aint nobody sent me no death threats. Especially from *Clarksdale!* Fukkum. Gotdammit. Ass'oles.

But young Mr. Brainsong—Brainy!—iddn like me. He believes them sumbiches mean to kill his ass, and he aint ready for it. There-fukkin-fore, that's where I come in. And I decided I'd call on every swingindik, maybe a blue-haired old bat or two, and all the worthless-ass niggas I could think of to hep me get to the bottom of this and save Brainy's life.

Junior Ray's Famous Valentine Special!

Get three pounds of chicken hearts. Boil em a long time till they're soft. Add salt and pepper, and lay em gently on top of a bed of egg noodles. Then stir the crap out of em. And that's my Valentine Special. You can always use brown rice—That's my favorite, and it's pretty good for you. I learned that from the hippies down at Clarksdale, you know, the ones I told you about, in my second book, who opened up little vegetarian restaurant on the side of the Sunflower River right after the shoutn had stopped when the Civil Rights thing was over, back before I become a' historian.

Note: You can do the same things with gizzards—but remember to boil em a long time so they'll be really tender.

CHAPTER FOUR

*An Old Cracklepoot, Miss Attica—& Her Sibling, Miss
Laconia—Clubs—Junior Ray in Little Texas—Mr.
Garfischbein—The Aunty Belles—"Sisters, Do Your Duty!—
How to Control Your Man—Mad's Letter—Gene LaFoote's
Gull Friend—Mad Finds Enliss Roux—Poem: "Oh, Sail
the Eliot-Elliot Waves"—Recipe No. 4: Junior Ray's Famous
Banacamoley Dip*

It was that old cracklepoot Attica Rummage that first popped
into my mind when young Mr. Brainsong showed me those
letters. Miss Attica didn live in Clarksdale; she lived right here
in St. Leo, but she had a sister down there—Miss Laconia—who
though she never said much a-tall could let you know by the way
she raised her eyebrows and pruned up her mouth that she was
just as godawful as Miss Attica was, 'least from my point of view,
which is the only one I've ever had.

Oh, both them old society hens—course you know we're all
about the same fukkin age!—anyway, them old cluckers would smile
at me, and Miss Attica would say, "Hiyew, Junor Ray, whatchew
been doin?" But when I'd try to answer, they'd be lookin away and
not payin no 'tention and start to wavin at some other old fart-
depositer 'cross the room. So, I just said fukkum a long time ago,
and I smile and act friendly, too, but, just like Miss Attica and her
persimmon-mouthed sister, Miss Laconia, I'm not.

Anyway, if there was ever anybody that could kill you for little
or nothin, besides myself, of course, it'd sure as hell be Miss Attica

Rummage. And her Clarksdale sister, too, I reg'n. And they was both of em in them women's clubs: you know, the Garden Club, the Bridge Club, the Daughters of the American Revolution, the Colonial-gotdam-Dames, and the United-ass Daughters of the Confederacy, alias the *UDC*, which, by god, to give the Devil his due, way back, awarded my ass a fukkin "scholarship" one year when I was livin out beyond Little Texas and tryin to come into town to school without no shoes. It didn cost no money to go to school, so the scholarship was simply that they bought me a shirt, a pair of shoes, and a warm coat with a hood on it from Mr. Garfischbein's ready-to-wear, up on Main Street, in St. Leo. And the truth is I have appreciated it to this very fukkin day. I aint got nothin bad to say about the UDC.

Mr. Garfischbein was a funny old sumbich and a dyed-in-the-wool Delta Jew.[12] He never said much to nobody, just run his dry-goods store and spent a lot of time standin in the doorway, especially on *Sair'diiz*[13], lookin at the folks on the crowded street, mostly Niggas of course, walk back and forth on the sidewalk. His store was there on the west side of the railroad tracks, right next to the *Palace The-ater*, where the black folks could set in the balcony.

12   There's no such thing as a "dyed-in-the-wool Delta Jew." The relationship between Delta Jewry and the Goyim varied from town to town. One community might not admit them to the "country club," while another would. Most Delta Jews began as merchants and, overall, remained merchants. But there were many others who, while they held onto their stores, usually dry goods and ready-to-wear, also entered the professions, acquired cotton land, went off to conservative, traditional Southern colleges—Washington & Lee, Vanderbilt, Tulane, as well as (absolutely, definitely a destination for bright Southern boys) Princeton—and thus became "Planterized," as much so as a Polk or a Pemberton. Indeed, acculturation was always the present danger. Still, socially, in the Delta, when it came to the issue of "acceptance," suffice it to say that if "Big Daddy" and the Gentiles needed money for a project, frivolous or otherwise—the Confederacy would always stick out its hand and welcome the Jews. —ml

13   Saturdays. —ml

Then, there was another pitchashow right across from there, on the east side of the railroad tracks, called the *Savoy*, which was for Niggas ONLY, and didn no white people never go there.

Overall, though, back in the forties and the early fifties, when you think about it, back then, in a' odd way, things was pretty mixed, and nobody thought too much about it. I mean there weren't very many white people in the first place. Them Delta counties was all ninety-somethin-percent black. But that wuddn the way it was over in the Hills. Anyhow, there was such a crowd of folks, mostly black of course, in and out of the stores in the little Delta towns back then—especially, as I sorta indicated a minute ago, on *Sair'diiz*—you couldn stir em with a stick.

Anyway, sometimes, after I was out of school and had begun workin as a deputy for Sheriff Holston, I'd pass on foot by Mr. Garfischbein on a Sair'dy evenin, and when I'd get up even with him, I'd hear him say, real, real low: "Jeezus Schmeezus," then I'd look over at him and both of us would laugh. It always made me think him and me and the Jews knew sumpm the Baptists and nem never was able to catch on to.

Now YOU MIGHT WONDER how a sumbich such as me knows about the women's clubs, like the ones other'n the UDC. I know about em because the town is teeny-ass. It really only has a population of around fifteen hunnud people inside the so-called city limits, which is a little bit *not* the whole story but also not too far from it.

Anyway, *one* of them clubs in particular, and one I did not specify, above, was very different.

Every so often the Rummage sisters, and some of the others pretty much like em among them gotdam Planters, would organize a big-ass meetn. They'd call it a fukkin "convention," and there'd be women from all over the Delta and in the Hills, too, that would come to St. Leo and be put up in people's houses for two and a half days, usually a Thursday and a Friday, with a gigantic-ass "brunch" on Saturday, in a tent with a wooden floor, set up in Miss Attica's side yard.

Sheriff Holston and, later, Sheriff Brown and, even later than that, Sheriff Moundtemple would ast me to be available to the visitors—and of course to Miss Attica!—just in case they needed any help with anything, which they pretty much never did and mostly just looked straight-ass through me like I was sumpm they didn want to have nothin to do with. Still, from all the yip-yap, that was one way I got to know about ever' one of them fukkin clubs, all of which, I can tell you, except for me, didn allow no pekkawoods anywhere near em. Anyway, this one I'm tellin you about now has come to look like—way back and all along—it might be at the core of what all was happenin.

They was the *Aunty Belles*! That's what Miss Attica and nem called their club, the gotdam *Aunty Belles*. And though I guess you could say they traveled here to Mhoon County from all over the deep South, most of em was from—or was closely connected with—the Miss'ssippi Delta. I do know that. Plus every one of em was *Planterized* in some fashion or another. Weren't none of em pekkawoods.

I also knew "Aunty Belles" wuddn the official name of the organization, but I never could get an answer on that whenever I'd ast the question about the name of the thing. And you can bet your great-granddaddy's balls every one of those old cheerleaders was all *Delta Daybewtaunts*. Some of em had even made their *day-bwew* in Meffis at the Meffis Country Club, and if you listen to them tell it, that's about as high class as a sumbich can ever get.

But, see, here's sumpm important, only under normal-ass conditions *I wouldn have knowed it was*. I heard Miss Attica makin a speech at one of them so-called conventions they used to have. The women that come to attend would stay, as I told you a minute ago, in some of the houses here in St. Leo and out in the country, but what I did not mention was that a whole bunch of em would go to Meffis and check into the Peabody, then drive down to the meetings here in St. Leo. Yet that wuddn no problem. Highway 61 is a short shot and only takes about forty-five minutes.

More-gotdam-over, I happen to further know, one way or another, that a fair-sized gaggle of em would make it a point to get to Meffis a day early, usually on Wednesday mornin, so they could go over to Confederate Park at the fukkin stroke of noon and cluck up around an old corroded-lookin plaque that has the followin words wrote on it:

PALMS FOR THE SOUTHERN SOLDIER;
CROWNS FOR THE VETERAN'S HEAD;
AND LOYAL LOVE AND HONOR
FOR OUR CONFEDERATE DEAD.[14]

Then, when they'd finish bowin their heads, holdin their hands over their hearts, and their farts was all gone with the wind, the whole flock would ruffle and strut down Front Street—on the fukkin sidewalk of course—to the Little Teacup where they'd fill up on grits and gravy, and quail fried with Crisco and coffee in a big-ass iron skillet. And after that day-early coop-full was th'oo, they'd order up a double slice of lemon icebox pie. I know all this cause I seen em, more'n once, at the park . . . but McKinney told me the rest.

Anyway, on that day I was tellin you about when I heard Miss Attica makin her speech, the women was all gathered in the old Community House across the street from the north side of the Courthouse—you know, where the Rotary Club and sometimes

---

14   Placed in the park by the Confederate Dames, Tyler Chapter, 1909. —ml

the Boy Sprouts meets. And on that day, as Miss Attica was finishin up, she ended with more or less this:

And so, dear Sisters, we must do our duty even though it might sometimes seem, perhaps to our spiritual and our community leaders, not quite the thing we should do. Nevertheless, we remember our oath, and we are guided only by our purpose! Remember—the *Four Patriotic Infinitives of Power*: namely, To Preserve! To Protect! To Punish! and . . . To Prevent. So, *Sisters*, do your duty!

That's the gist of the thing. I may not have give it to you word-for-fukkin-word, even though I can imitate it pretty good; plus, I got McKinney to give me a leg up on it with, you know, how it woulda sorta sounded Miss-Attica-rized. But I believe you and me, both, get the flavor of it.

You might want to know this, too, about Miss Attica. One story is that it was her who gave *instructions* to every generation of new brides-to-fukkin-be on how to maintain control of their dum-ass husbands-to-be and, therefukkinfore, have a perfect Marriage. Suppos*ably* everybody up and down Highway 61 knew what Miss Attica told em. She'd set beside em real close on that big old couch in her livin room. Then she'd take ahold of both their hands in both of hers, and she'd tell em: "My dear, if your husband is ever cross with your ass, just look at him with those big, beautiful brown, blue, green, black beady-ass eyes of yours, and say to him—'How can you talk to me that way when I love you so!'"

As you can probly tell, I didn give that to you word for word neither. But, accordn to Miss Attica, her special-ass fool-proof advice would do it, and the whole idea was, after knowin what Miss Attica had told her, the bride-to-fukkin-be immediately had the pussy power to put some po' sumbich in the trick and grab his nuts before he even got a chance to really use em. And, later, after she'd sweetly sqwooshed his unsuspectin ass, she could whip out Miss Attica's secret weapon of mass-ass destruction, turn it around, and use it on her chirren.

I WROTE TO MAD[15] about the *threaters* and how it seemed to me the letters, which, remember now, was all mailed from *Clarksdale*, was wrote by a *woman*. I explained the whole scene to him, includin them findin ol' Tombo Turnage shot to death beneath the Visitor's Tree out in the woods, over the levee, along the bank of the Cut-Off, on the Evans place. Mad wrote me back the gotdamdest thing I ever read, and when I showed it to Brainy, both of us said, simulfukkintaneously, more or less, somethin that seemed to come out like: "Ho-lee Cogdukkin Hogdrool!" I honest to god don't know what it was, but it upset Brainy a good bit because he never did use no cuss words and always blinked a lot whenever I did, which of course was all the fukkin time.

Anyway, here's what Mad said in his letter:

June 22, 2009
Okhatachito Parish
711 Nostalgie de la Boue
Blanchedelacarte, Louisiana 70300

Dear Junior Ray,

I have always wondered if this subject would ever come up. Let me tell you something my mother and her sisters—my three aunts—told me when I was still very young. In fact, it seems to me that when they first brought it up and I first heard it, I was quite little! Yet, fortunately, I have a prodigious capacity for recall. But

---

15   James Madison "Mad" Owens, in The Yazoo Blues. —ml

let me hasten to say that this topic—this odd organization—was in fact addressed on many occasions throughout my formative years, both in my house and at my grandmother's. Indeed, just for the record I should mention that my grandmother was born in 1869 and therefore was a little girl during Reconstruction! The point is that from childhood to manhood I heard a lot about the Aunty Belles, usually in the late afternoons and early evenings on my grandmother's side porch where my mother, my grandmother, and my mother's sisters sat in big wicker chairs, jingled glasses of bourbon full of ice, and talked with their friends . . . and as they spoke, . . . doves mourned and white oaks[16] swallowed the falling sun . . . while those waning days began to race away in the dusk . . . and rush from their moment . . . into a darkening world . . . and the distance of another time.

In any case, even then I knew they did not approve of those they discussed—whose names, in fact, they did not always reveal.

Apparently, after the Civil War, an organization of Southern women was formed at exactly the same time the Ku Klux Klan came into being under the leadership of General Forrest and, indeed, through the co-leadership also of my great-great uncle, Robert Clell Dismukes, of Gallatin, Tennessee, whose family, much earlier, had arrived in the area and then, a little later, around 1849, migrated into that relentlessy peculiar land of yours and mine there in the Yazoo Delta—which we all refer to as the Miss'ssippi Delta, though it is a long, long way from the actual embouchure of the Mississippi River, below New Orleans, where that great ditch debouches into the Gulf of Mexico.

For one thing, almost all or a heck of a lot of the Scotch Irish who settled our part of the South came from Mecklenburg

---

16 Very tall, large, old trees that are called "white oaks" locally—here in our little Mississippi Delta town of St. Leo, in Mhoon County—but are really swamp chestnut oaks aka cow oaks. —ml

County, North Carolina, near Charlotte. More specifically, my kin on that side were from a tiny Presbyterian community called Steele Creek. The majority of the whites who developed the Yazoo Delta were descended from *Lowland* Scots, *Borderers* mostly, and *Reivers* to boot, who left left Scotland and went to Ireland then, later, got asked to leave and came to America. The point is that's why so many of the towns in the Delta have Scottish names. They don't come much "Scottier" than *Panther Burn*.

However, by the time the work of the Klan was finished, the original brotherhood had been infiltrated and polluted by what even General Forrest, I think, referred to as some "very bad men." Therefore, the older, more established, better educated and formerly landed gentlemen put away their robes forever and officially "disbanded."

But the women did not disband. And their secret sisterhood in its original form thrives to this very day—it exists so secretly, in fact, that only a very, very few women at the present time even know of its existence . . . or ever knew that such a thing had existed in the first place.

When the sorority was formed, after "The War," each member swore an oath in blood that she would—and this is according to my Aunt Del, who said she heard it from one of her teachers at Miss Timlow's Academy in Washington, D.C., in 1909—"remain vigilant and ever ready to root out any harmful element that would—deliberately or accidentally—do damage to the glory and nobility of their culture and the Cause."

Although that might sound harmless on the surface, underneath they were blood-bound by that oath to *kill* if such "rooting out" became necessary. Thus, a sinister swarm of potential assassins was born. All this I got from my mother and my aunts—who for some reason also always felt they were obligated to include a reminder that the punishment for revealing Masonic secrets was death. It was hard for me to imagine any of the men I knew back then who were Masons killing each other over "a secret," but after I grew up I realized, of course, that nothing is too preposterous.

The connection was not entirely clear, but fortunately I never knew any Masonic secrets or God knows I am certain I would have let them slip long before now, and I suppose I'd be lucky to be alive, even deep as I am in the coastal marshes, on the left bank of Bayou Nantasanah,[17] here in Southwest Louisiana.

Apparently in the present day, the girls who are chosen for membership are all descended from the founding members and, like their foremothers, are trained in the arts of Lucretia Borgia and Catherine de Medici, as well as in those of Madame de Pompadour and Madame du Barry, all of whom would no doubt agree that "For beauty, men must suffer." But subtlety and finesse were their watchwords and the mark of their art, and that is why I am a little surprised at the *shotgunning* of Tombo Turnage even though, from what you have told me, I do think there could be a connection somehow between Tombo's death and the mission of this hellish and certainly most exclusive sorority. Generally their methods were said to be so subtle, so genteel as it were, that they were undetectable, even at those odd times when the local authorities might have been inclined to detect them. Yet, there were those few who knew—always knew what had taken place and why.

They call themselves "The Confederate Daughters for Truth, Justice, the Southern Way, and Light in our Name"—or *CoDa-TruJuSoWaLION*—more often just *CoDa*, which of course is Latin for "the tail." The tail, in this case, is the "Light in our name," the acronym for which is l-i-o-n, *lion*! That "lion," naturally, had been, collectively, the men who organized the early Klan.

---

17   Choctaw/Mobilian Trade Jargon: Nanta / What + Sa / I + Banna / Want + Bayou = "What I Desire Bayou." —ml

Thus, *Codatrujusowalion* is the women's secret password, according to my mother anyway, who believed they may have wanted it to be a longish tongue twister to make it more difficult for a member to reveal if she were among strangers and drunk in a public setting.

I believe, also, that the older members like to refer to themselves as the *Aunty Belles*[18] and that it is thought that a strain of unacknowledged fanaticism may be quite alive within the current membership, albeit a militancy mainly concentrated in those members who reside in or who are from the Delta.

Also, I don't want to be talking out of school, but I seem to remember there was something lurking in the shadows of the things my mother and my aunts imparted to me, and it is that there may have been, and there may not have been; there may be—and there may not be—a connection between the *Aunty Belles* and the Deep Southern branches of two of our modern-day sororities the Chi Omegas and the Tri-Delts. Further, that there could be a kinship of some sort between the Delta Debutantes and the Aunty Belles strains the imagination, but, still, the notion was squarely planted in my mind. And such a thought is not far-fetched. Indeed, far-fetched is only far for those who live in places where there is nothing to fetch.

On one hand I cannot be surprised at the possibility of even the most absurd or even the most monstrous truths. But, on the other, I find myself saying, "Oh, for heavensakes!" Even so, I felt I ought to mention this, just in case. If I had ever said any of this as I was growing up, my mother, and her sisters—and my uncles and my grandmother, too—would merely have laughed and declared that I was "the most imaginative boy they'd ever seen"!

Now though, to continue, it was long thought that Attica

18 Here Junior Ray interjected: "Me and Voyd already knowed that, remember?"—ml

Rummage, who has always lived in her grandparents' house, had been taken into into the fold of that toxic feminine relic of the early post-bellum South. Miss Attica's family had been in the Delta, and had lived along the banks of the great river that helped to make that peculiar alluvial plain, since the days before the Chickasaw and the Choctaw agreed to relinquish their control of it. Miss Attica's family name, way back, was French. It was *Ruemarché*, with an acute accent over the "e" on the end; but over time, being as far north as they were, there in the Yazoo Basin, the tongues of their Scots-Irish neighbors had too much difficulty with the gallic phonetics of the name, and so the family simply let their name become what so many around them seemed to think it was: Rummage.

The Rummages were, however, not so distantly related to the old families of the Gulf Coast, the Gauchees, the Plauchees, and the Beauchets, but *not ever* to the O'Sheas—and most emphatically not to the Mangiacavallos and the Rosatattuzzis—all of whom the Ruemarches, now the Rummages, looked down on and still do, but publicly deny it, to this very day.

Frankly, my Aunt Xylda was not at all impressed with Miss Attica's pedigree and once remarked in the sweetest voice possible that Miss Attica never was as "nice" as she thought she was. And, by that, my Aunt Xylda implied she and my mother and my Aunt Del all knew something about the Rummages they weren't ever going to say.

For one thing, we were kin to the O'Sheas and to the Schmattermans as well, by marriage of course, and when my mother found out the new "country" club being built down the road at Okataktak was not going to admit the Habibis, who were from Lebanon, she refused to give any more money to the Presbyterians, and when she ate out, there in St. Leo, she would only go to the Boll & Bloom Cafe, on the side of Highway 61, and never accepted an invitation to dine with any of her friends at the new "country" club, just a few miles south of town. In fact, whenever any of her ladyfriends mentioned the *country club*, my mother loved to ask them: "What *country* might that be?"

Lache pas la Patate,[19]

Mad

PS: Gene says to tell you hello and that he has found . . . a *gull* friend.

PPS: It is not the "why" of existence that concerns me, and it is not the "how"; it is the "that" of it which seems the most mysterious. yffjmo

PPPS: I, too, have found someone to, shall I say, fill up my life. She is beautiful, seems to want to be with me forever, and her name is Enliss—Enliss Roux.[20] Indeed, Junior Ray, I believe she is the "one." Today, as you might imagine, I wrote a poem for her. It goes as follows—

For Enliss

Oh, Sail the Eliot-Elliott Waves

by James Madison "Mad" Owens

It is imperative, categorically

Never to say Kant

And miss the chance of voyage or jaunt

As one who loves

And sails the sea.

---

19   "Don't drop the potato." —ml
20   Is Mad our Shropshire Lad? Is Mad a man of Kant and Cannes, living in T. S. Eliot's linguo-eclectic land laid waste? Or does he trade commodities according to Ralph Nelson Elliott's theory of waves? Has he found the Golden Ratio in Louisiana, south of Houma? —ogbii

A "Wasteland" Eliot, c'est moi, and an Elliott marketeer aussi
Who rides an Eliot-Elliott Wave because I Cannes.
I'm also a true seaman sitting in the nave,
With steady hand to steer, grab an oar and leave the shore
As captain and as slave.

Now, If sailor he be blind abaft,
He has no contrast fore and aft.
There is nothing there he thinks to ask;
Thus never can a future be, for if he has no memory
And if he's lived no past; then ¡qué lástima! Alas!

Some say the ocean's but an empty door
For him who's left an empty shore;
Therefore,
Not so for me, and this is true:
I have found the joy I never knew
And find life filled with Enliss Roux.

When Mad wrote that letter, he didn know, and neither did I, that there would soon be two more killins besides ol' Tombo. Anyway, I'd say Mad's poems is improved a good bit, just judgin by that one, which is a whole lot better, it seems to me—and consider'bly deeper as well—than them he used to write to Money Scatters[21] before he had to leave her and go south, you know, at first down to Horn Island and then, now, down into what I call the "white space on the bottom of the fukkin map."

Still and all, as far as poems and books and other such crap-ola as that is concerned, I might not be no certified expert in littertour, but bygod I have seen a helluva lot of it since the day young Mr.

---

21   The object of Mad's failed ability to love perfectly, in *The Yazoo Blues*. —ml

Brainsong—Brainy!—showed up at my door and wanted to take a look at all those ledgers Leland Shaw left behind in the silo. And then, Lord knows, there was the *zillion* others we found years later when Miss Helena Ferry, damn near on her death bed, and Sheriff Holston, who by that time was long retired and walked slower than a fieldhand in July, got the county to donate some inmates from the Mhoon County Penal Farm to go clean up Leland Shaw's mama's empty house. Miss Helena was kin, you know. And the convicts, I don't even think none of em took nothin they shouldna have, neither, but they sho as hell found a truckload more of those gotdam ledgers, and every one of em was full of Shaw's googah.

Anyhow, if things ever chill-ass out around here, I guess I'll have to go down to Luzianna and see Mad one of these days and meet Enliss. She sounds okay to me. And, if Mad likes her, I am sure I will too. Shoot, I liked Money. And she liked me. But I have a strong feelin me and Enliss'll always be strangers to one another. I don't have to *fill up my life* with nothin. Mad's different though. And that's okay. Plus, he's older now, and accordn to him he don't *lose his necktie* no more, "God knows where," like he used to.

Junior Ray's Famous Bananacamoley Dip!

Bananacamoley Dip is real simple. Mash the fuk out of a bunch of bananas and add, you guessed it—Home-made *my*naise! What a lot of people don't never realize is that home-made *my*naise takes care of a lot of seasonin and texturizin problems. See, people don't know what they're actually eatn—They think you've laid some kinda wootydooty fancy-ass recipe on em, when the truth is that what you've put in front of em and what they're gobblin up could be nothin but butterbeans, but they can't tell it because the home-made *my*naise makes whatever it might be taste like sumpm they'd have to buy in Meffis. Especially if you get some nem English crackers to go with it.

I forgot. You can add nuts. Fresh nuts, not salted ones. I recommend puh'kahns, walnuts—both English and the regular Miss'ssippi kind, and you can use pis-gotdam-tacios, too. But I do not recommend ahmonds or filab'ts[22] cause they're too gotdam dry. Plus—ChrEYESt!—yes, berries as well if you want em, as long as they are ripe enough so they don't pukka up your mouth like a green persimmon, and I guess I ought to include sweet seedless grapes as well. The truth is only a shithed would th'ow in sumpm he knew wouldn taste good, so I aint gon worry about it no more. You're on your own now.

NOTE: Listen, sumbich, don't try to fix none of this if you're unsupervised or fulla beer!

---

22 Almonds or filberts. —ml

CHAPTER FIVE

Understandin Delta Women—Planter Women Made the Fukkin
World—Co'-Cola—The Rosedale Christmas Dance—Always
a Nigga Band—The Ole Miss Hop—Th'ow the Pekkawoods
in the River—Family Names—Sunflower's Daddy Married a
Pekkawood—Daybewtaunts—More about Delta Women—
Shotguns—Colleges—Grin, Shoot & Dance—Recipe No. 5:
Junior Ray's Famous Old South/New South Chocolate Pie

I t aint exactly news that Mad had a tendency to get off the
fukkin subject, but that was all right. We—me and Voyd and
Brainy—got the nut of what he had to say, and I thought it
was gon be useful.

Also, a lot of times you just *know* somethin is somethin, only
simulfukkintaneously you don't *truly* know if it is or it iddn. Then
along comes a thing like Mad's letter and lets you see flat out you
was right about what you thought and that there really was somethin to what you was suspicious about. I'not gon say that's the
way things turn out one hunnud percent of the time, but it does
happen a good bit, and this is one of those times. Mad laid it out
like, I suppose, I aint surprised he would.

You have to understand Delta women, and I am talkin here
mostly about those that belong to the big shots, you know, them
gotdam Planters—and by that I don't mean all of em has to be actual farmers; it's a class thing if you know what I mean, and people
can be in it without ever plantn a gotdam weed or a cotton seed.
Anyway, plantn or not plantn, all emm sumbiches comes from it,

and every fukkin one of em would claw through corrugated tin to keep from fallin out of it—except for a few of em who marry some of *us*, and then it's their mammas and daddies who has a lifelong piss-fit about that. ChrEYEst. I would too.

First of all you can forget about any kind of notion that Godalmighty made the world. He didn. Them dadgum Planter women made it, and they made it to suit theirsevs, only they have had to spend a lot of time patchin it up and getn the spots out because Old Re-fukkin-Ality keeps rippin the stitches and spillin the chili on it. Anyway, these gals wouldn blink even once if they thought they had to do away with your ass for them to have things the way they want em to be. And that's a fact. They learn that in their grandmamas houses, and then a lot of em become expert ball-surgeons over at the University—or the fukkin *Dubbya*.[23] So that's it in a nutsack: these women tap the tune and say what's what. Which, around here, is how it's always gon be.

The trainin begins when they are born. Their mamas hand em over to a Nigga woman so, even as day-old baby girls, they can start bein the boss right off the bat. Plus they'll have a special name for the Nigga woman—Bessie, Lovey, Georgeanne, Bertha, Sarah, BigMammy, Flossie May, Ideelia, Queenesther, Eutoria, Earleen, Hambone—and the whole fukkin family will always be goin on about how they LOVE IDEELIA, and how, yassuh, even though she is black as a barrel of burnt-ass oil, uhn-hunh, IDEELIA is "like one of the fam'leh!" Bullfart. And *Ideelia* knows it too. But that's the shape of it, and it's where and partly how these Planter women get started bein the smilin, sweet-tongued, mad-dog viscious, ballchewin bitches they eventually becomes.

They leaps outa the startn blocks with tea parties when they are little girls; only it aint tea, it's fukkin Co'-Cola. Then, long

---

23   Mississippi State College (now University) for Women. —ml

about when they're round twelve or so, they has the little dances
where all of em is a foot taller than the little fukhed Planters' boys
they're two-steppin and fox-trottn with, and all this is just to get
em ready for the main act which would be the big Daybewtaunt
blow-out down in Greenville and also up in Meffis, cause, as you
already know, a whole gang of all them high-class sumbiches down
here in the country does also belong to the Country Club up in
Meffis—which, you may or may not know, in modern times aint
no longer nowhere near no fukkin country. All that is beyond my
ass. I have never figured out the right way to think about it or
come up with a way to look at it that makes any sense, and I am
fairly certain it aint no use in tryin. I'm just tellin you the way it is.

But the big number, before the change come and everything,
was the Christmas night dance in the courthouse down in Rosedale.
Man, that was sumpm else, and all them Delta bigshot girls—and
those of the same-size shot from over in the nearby Hill towns, like
Lexington, Como, Carrollton, Hernando, Coldwater, Sardis, and
Senatobia—all them is included in this batch as well—but there
never was much of em that come from places in the state farther
away in the Hills, you know, like over at Columbus and Tupelo
and such, cause I guess they had their own thing goin. Hell, I don't
know. I just know what I know about where I am.

ANYWAY, AT THEM DANCES, all the beauties, and I have to say right
now, that every fukkin one of em was a gotdam beauty and that
aint no lie—these Planters girls wuddn, and aint, like them big
old women I seen pictures of from up North that look like they
could knock down a squad of NFL-ers. No-suh. Even though I
aint got a lot of good to say about Planters and bankers and such,
I do have to own up that their women are about the best-lookin
I guess in the whole fukkin world. I'm just guessin of course, but
I'd put money on it.

Plus—and the way I understand it is that it has been this way for at least three generations and more—when these women danced, they never stopped. From the time the Nigga band—it was always a Nigga band, and a generation ago, back in the twenties, they tell me it was old W. C. Handy hissef! . . . these Planters woulda th'owed Hank Williams out the fukkin door!—started up till they played gotdam "Goodnight, Irene,"[24] these women, once they hit the dance floor, they didn never check-up and danced their hair-do's lopsided non-stop till, as I say, the last fukkin tune; and, durin the whole time, all them little fukhed Planters' boys would be steady breakin in, and sometimes one of em would no more'n catch a girl's hand when another fukhed would be right there on him, tappin his ass on the shoulder!

Now, bear in mind an important fact: all this was always all mostly in the winter after the harvest, which meant, in a good year, all the money was settled up and there was plenty to go around; but even if the agricultural year had been a gotdam disaster, that never stopped these sumbiches from dancin. It was sumpm. I seen it.

All of the fukheds would come in their tuxedos and, if the dance was to start up after nine o'clock, then they'd show up in their white-ties and tails . . . and it wouldn be long before all their coats was off, and they and the girls would all be boogiewoogyin' and sweatn like a store window. Listen, I was over at the coksukkin University one time in what they called the Grill, and them sumbiches was in there by the jukebox boogyin and woogyin at eight o-fukkin-clock in the mornin. They called it the Ole Miss Hop!

My people never heard of such carryin on. Hell, back then, we was lucky to ever hear of anything. What *Ole Miss hoppin* we mighta done woulda been from cotton row to cotton row draggin a fukkin pick sack that was longer than Avalon Holcomb's dik and

---

24   Traditionally, the last song of the night. —ml

heavier than a wagon load of pigs. Fuk a bug! I got another tale to tell you about college kids later.

Anyway, while them Planters' girls and boys was dancin, we was workin our ass off in the dirt. And one time I even heard one nem highclass little diklikkas tell another'n—and the two of em didn think I could hear em—but I could, and I was lookin straight at em, too. The first one said: "Chah'z Royal, they ought to th'ow every single one of those redneck pekkawoods . . . you know, *all* of em way out there east of Highway 61, around Six-Mile Lake, on the edge of the Delta—Chah'z Royal, I'm sayin right now *somebody* oughta throw the *whole batch* of em—every man, woman, and any of their sorry excuses for a child!—into the Miss'ssippi River."

Then the *other* seersukka pink-cheek muthafukka said, "Uhn-hunh. Every last one of em. I agree. They really are a subhuman species. Those no 'count sonsabitches are lower than the Niggas, and my daddy says he's sorry we ever let the first one of em ever come here."

And then he hollered out: "Hell, Harper! You tell Cary Stoneville and Ben Lomond I'll take *one* Nigga over a hunnud po-white *Hill* trash any day!"

I aint never forgot it. Fukkemm bigshot sumbiches.

I have got to tell you some more about these type of people, so you will understand what happened and why it could have. I know you might be askin who were all these girls; what was their families' names? Well, they was who you might expect: They was the Farfields, the Sylterses, the McRiverses, the DeJabalettes, the Lanyards, the Kinnells, the Kingstons, the Sandersons, the McGheehees, the Meaultons, the Carrolltons, the Quitmans, the Issers and the Queeners, the LeFlores (yes, Sunflower did come from them gotdam Planters, but she fell out of the fold because her daddy married a pekkawood and never did recover), the Bolivars, the Bilsons, the Lobdens, the Slawtts, the Lumners, the Colcombs, the Klipstones, the Shermonsons, the Saxtons, the Purdines, the Neeks, the MaGleans, the Longshards, the Stivelles, the Shortasons, the Irwinlowes and the Pillowtemples, the Blackingtons, the McBerryoakes, the Boggsides, the Falconshaws, the McClarkels, The Dattelmores, the Glenwoods; then right next door you have to add a buncha others—even though they're technically in the Hills, but it's that special kind of Hills, the kind I mentioned a minute ago with them towns: Como, Hernando, Carrollton, Sardis, Senatobia, Lexington, and Coldwater; and all them girls from those places, who get included in the high-toned stuff down in the Delta, are from the same kind of folks I'm tellin you about—and they would be the Boynters, the Tedges, Seaseys, the Cutters, the Lessers, the Bookers, the Nellises, and a branch of the Bilsons, plus a whole lot more, like the Renskews over there just at the bottom of the bluff.

Course the truth is all the Delta bigshots come from the Hills, too. I mean, you got to come from somewhere, and didn nobody come from the fukkin Delta itse'f . . . except snakes and painters[25] and gotdam alligators.

That's right. They're all cut out of the same big-ass cotton snake.[26]

So . . . them *daybewtaunts* might look like they aint got a brain in their heads, but, lemme tell you, most of em is smart as a starvin rat, and every last one of em can hunt and fish and jump fences, ride'n in them skimpy-ass saddles, straddlin them gotdam long-leggity horses. Therefore you better not sell em short. And I don't.

I mean you take any dove hunt and a helluva lot of goose hunts—and I guarantee you, on the bird-dog field trials—them daybewtaunt women are there right in with the men, except of course in a real sho-nuff deer camp, but then the kind of men I'm

---

25 Local dialect for panthers. —ml
26 Samples of cotton to be classed were shipped to Front Street in Memphis, and were called "snakes," and were laid out on long tables in the offices of the cotton buyers on Cotton Row. —ml

talkin about don't go to that kind of a camp; they got a spiffy-ass "lodge" built back in the woods that has everything they could ever want includn indoor plummin. And that's the sort of place in the woods them women goes so they can hunt with their husbands and all and don't have to go pee on a tree. Shoot, I think that's one of the reasons some of them fukhed boys marries em. Well, that aint the onliest reason, but I do think these highclass, superclean sumbiches admire their women for bein, at least in some repects, like theysevs but without the beards, which the women, as you know, *allow* the men to grow durin huntn season. And I do mean allow, cause any coksukka that grows one without a permit is fukked for the year. If that sumbich gets any pussy at all, it's gon have to be imaginary. But that's marriage in a walnut, iddn it?

Mostly these Planter women likes to use double barrels, and about half of em prefer the overs and unders, and the majority of em likes those expensive brands: Berretta and Parker and such, and a few, some years back, was partial to the Browning semEYE-automatic Sweet Sixteen. But Miss Attica loved to use that lillo light *Ithaca*, full-choke four-ten pump. She even carries it duck huntn and does all right. Goose, though, that's another story.

Now, BACK TO WHAT I was talkin to you about a few minutes ago. When it comes time for these girls to go to their colleges, I have already mentioned a couple of the places their mamas and daddies sends em off to—the University and also, as you know, to the fukkin *Dubbya*—but a lot of these Planters' daughters also goes off to Gulf Park down on the Mississippi GuffCoas', right smack on the GuffaMexico, and a good many of em gets shipped way-ass off up to Virginia . . . and I know the names of some of those fancy schools because, livin here in the midst of these rich-ass muthafukkas I have heard those Virginia places talked about so fukkin much its comin out my ass; anyway, they are: Hollins College, Sweet-ass Briar College, Mary-gotdam-Baldwin, and Mary-fukbutt-Washington, and there's some who even go way, *way* up the country to two famous female schools in particular, one called Smith and the other by the name of Bennin'ton. (I have noticed that if one neez girls does go up there that far away, they generally don't never come back. And I've always thought it might be because they learned sumpm.)

The question, though, is that if some of the older women in the group really are more like Miss Attica and really, really might be up for killin folks in order to protect the image of something that don't even have a gotdam image in the first fukkin place, and I'm talkin about the dumb-ass idea of Southern manhood. First of all what Southern man are they thinkin of? Cause if the image has got to be some rich-ass ootchy-scootchy big-shot ookydooky kind of thing, then these murderin-girls fukked up a long time ago when they didn exterminate ever' one of my gotdam relatives. I don't think our ignunt asses have done much to improve the image. I know I habm.

But here's the key and the thing to remember. With all I've told you about how fukkin capable and smart these *daybewtaunts* is, they're like a lot of Deep Southerners: they don't ast a lot of questions, they just do what they're brought up to do, and that's it, while at the same fukkin time—and here's the big joke—they like to think of themselves as rebels. Rebels? *Billy Macon's third-extra ball!* They aint ever rebelled at nothin in their goodlookin waited-on-hand-and-foot lives. Hotfukkindam. Hoddydadgumtoddy!

So, see, they really could smile at your ass, shoot your cousin in the head, and want to dance all night with you after they done it. I am tryin to tell you, you are not dealin with the average American here. You're dealin with a sixth-generation Mississippi Delta Planter's daughter.

Junior Ray's Famous
Old South/New South Chocolate Pie

A. Get a ready-made pie crust, and th'ow it in the oven. You'll want to cook the crust before you add what you're gon put in it.

B. Get some fukkin chocolate: You can use them little boxes of pie fillin you find in the grocery store, or you can do what I normally do. I go buy a pie. I take it home, and scoop out the fillin, which I put in a bowl. If the pie has m'rang on top, I remove it and put it in another bowl and set it aside. The main thing is you have to find out what chocolate pies have the kind of fillin in em that you like—the best one I've ever found is Mrs. Jebel-Nassour's. She and Mr. Jebel-Nassour—they're some nem Lebanese down below Lyon—have a restaurant on the side of Highway 61 where you can get A-rabb food, which I like but aint gon go into now. Anyway, whenever I want to make my Old South/New South Chocolate Pie, I get in my Explorer and ride down the road, and I just buy me one or two of Mrs. Jebel-Nassour's chocolate pies and take em home. That way you've got the fillin, and you don't have to do nothin to it except spoon it out and put it in your already baked, ready-made pie crust—the way I'm tellin you to.

C. When your pie crust is baked and brown, put it on the kitchen table and fill it up thissa way: in one-sixth of the pan, put some of Mrs. Jebel-Nassour's chocolate on the bottom, and put *creme fraiche*—and, yes, gotdammit, I do know what that is; I aint that gotdam ignunt—on the top; then you do the reverse in the next wedge, and so on, up and down, back and forth, so one "slice" has the white stuff on top, and the next one has the dark stuff on top. That's it.

WARNIN': Before you jump into all that, above, take one

nem sheets of cardboard the laundry puts in your shirts, and cut it longways into strips about one-inch wide. Then take the strips and arrange em inside your baked pie crust so you get six wedge-shaped pie sections. Once you do that, you can put in your chocolate and your *crème fraiche* the way I told you to.

D. After you add the fillin, and you've got it all sectioned off, keep the cardboard strips in the pie. Cover your pie very, very lightly with some plastic wrap, and run it in the Frigidaire. Be careful and don't mess up the fukkin pie.

E. Leave the sumbich in the icebox over night, then pull out the cardboard strips. Keep the pie in the Frigidaire—or the coksukkin icebox, whatever you want to call the sumbich—till right before you want to serve it.

F. Take the m'rang, and if it aint all dried out, put it in a little bowl and set it on the table beside your pie. It won't hurt nothin and it tastes good. Aint no sense in waste'n it. I call it *shifoffa*—like in that song one nem famous Niggas used to sing.[27]

---

27 The famous singer was Nat King Cole, and the song was "Frim Fram Sauce," lyrics by Redd Evans, music by Joe Ricardel, and in the sheet music it's chafafa not shifoffa: "I don't want French-fried potatoes, Red ripe tomatoes, I'm never satisfied / I want the frim-fram sauce with the ausan fey, With chafafa on the side." —ml

CHAPTER SIX

Cousin Lombard Stuffs His Family—Hand Rule Helped Him—
What Miss Attica Was Like towards Voyd & Me—The Street
Car—Jesus & Rabbits—Calhouners & Black Hats—McKinney
& Mad's Folks Were Exceptions—McKinney Tells More and
Mentions Danger—Recipe No. 6: Junior Ray's Extra-Famous
D.U.I. Hunnud-Proof Fruit Toppin

I t aint like Miss Attica's family hadn never had no 'tention
drawn to it. She had one first cousin, Lombard, on her mother's
side—the Abernathys—and Lombard did sumpm even the law
couldn figure out what to do about. So, they never did nothin at
all. Lombard lived with his grandmother, two of his aunts, and one
of his uncles in an old house south of Saint Leo, back off Highway
61. It was in the middle of, I'd say, fourteen acres and all hid away
by a woods so full of white oaks very few people had ever seen what
the house looked like. And those same few plus, once in a while,
somebody deliverin a package or a piece of mail or sumpm were
the only few that had *ever* been back up in there at all. And me;
as you know, there aint no place a deputy can't go. Anyhow, we all
knew Lombard loved all his family and, really, each and every one
of his relatives a whole lot. That's why it always had seemed so odd
that, whenever one of em died, Lombard never did seem all that
tore up. But one day, lord god, everybody knew why.

Right before I retired, the new sheriff at the time, Charlie
Cargood, ast me to go down to Lombard's and see if he was all
right, because hadn nobody seen him in town for a while, and his

phone was out of order. He was getn on up in years.

Anyhow, I drive down there, and I turn off the highway onto that narrow, half-assed gravel driveway that winds back up in there to his house, which had been his grandmama's. I pulled up in front of it, cut the ignition off, and got out. It didn look like anybody was at home. Well, it did and it didn, if you know what I mean. Anyhow, didn nobody come to the front door when I knocked on it.

I was about to just get back in the patrol car and go on back to town, but I decided to walk the extra mile and step round back to see if by some chance old Lombard was there. And he was.

I come up to the steps of the big screened-in back porch, which was high up off the ground and run the whole width of the house, and I seen Lombard setn up on it, glide'n back and forth in the swing, smokin a Lucky Strike. I knew it was a Lucky Strike because me and everybody else knowed that was all he ever smoked.

"Hey, Lombard!" I said.

"How AH yew, Junior Ray?" he said.

"Fine," I said. "Are you okay?"

"Quite well," he said. "Come on up on the po-ich, and let's have us a visit. I've got some *Polk's Stand Fast* and a bucket of ice to go with it."

Fuk. I hated the smell of Scotch whiskey, but I said, "That sounds good to me." I put my left foot up on the bottom step, looked up, and that's when I seen—clear as I'm talkin to you now—right through the screen, ol' Lombard wuddn alone. The whole fukkin family was there: his grandmama, his mama, his daddy, the two aunts, and his uncle Robert. They was all setn there on the back porch with Lombard. He had had em stuffed! Like Robert E. Lee's horse!

I said "Hi" to *everybody* and set there and talked with Lombard for a reasonable amount of time, then I drove on back in to the sheriff's office and told Charlie Cargood all about what I had found. He said, "Holy Malathion!" and got a'holt of Ardmore O'Keefe, the undertaker, and he met Ardmore down at Lombard's. Ardmore brung his two helpers and they loaded up the *amba'lance*—which was also a hearse—with Lombard's kin and hauled em back to the funeral home in St. Leo where Ardmore and nem wound up havin to once again set everybody up in chairs, this time around the walls of the visitation room because there wuddn no space to put em anywhere else. Plus, they really did not need to be refrigerated because they was stuffed. Anyhow, that's where they was gon keep Lombard's loved ones till the sheriff could decide where else to put em. And I was hope'n that would not be the jail.

They was all SUPPOSED, of course, to have been buried on Lombard's property, and there was a tombstone out there for every fukkin one of em—it's just that none of em had actually ever been inside the caskets! Lombard had always preferred to conduct "private" ceremonies. He used to say he was like the Jews when it come to funerals and wanted to get his loved ones in the ground pronto-ass quick. And he wuddn gon have no embalmin done. Lombard claimed his aim was to have those that was his and that he loved "restin in the arms" of their Mother Earth as quick as gotdam possible, and that is exactly what he always did. Or appeared to anyway.

He did not allow no talk of Jesus and of risin from the fukkin dead or, as he called it, any other superstitious crap like that. A handful of friends and cousins would be present, and Lombard performed the service hissef. He'd say the Lord's Prayer, the Twenty-Third Psalm, and, without mentionin ol' Jesus, read through the Sermon on the Mount. Then, right on the spot, he'd pick out two or three random-ass passages from the Book of Ecclesiastes and read them sumbiches, too.

Further, he always donated a generous wad of cash to the Freedonia Abysinnian Methodist Episcopal Church choir from up in what we in St. Leo called The Sub, which is now referred to as *North* Saint Leo, and the choir members would sing a couple of mournful but rockin-ass good hymns. After that he'd sploosh out a little water around the grave for his dead kin, so, as the black folks always said when it rained at a funeral, the Lord could "wash their footprints off the earth."

The big question was where did he keep all of the *loved ones* till the rest of em was all "dead and gone"? The answer to that is Ruleville!

LOMBARD'S BEST FRIEND WAS an old sumbich who lived farther down in the Delta there at Ruleville. His name was Hand Rule. By now you may have figured out that a lotta these Planter muthafukkas set up their own gotdam towns, and that's the reason a lot of em has the same name as the town they live in, even if they don't no longer actually own the gotdam town. My people never owned no towns. Didn many of em ever live in none neither.

Anyway, among other things, Hand Rule was a taxidermist, and you can figure out the rest of it. Hand would come get the bodies from Lombard, and Lombard would lock up the caskets tight as Dick's hatband and have the graveside services. Then, Hand would stuff the aunts and nem, wrap em all up, and store em in a special air-conditioned room in his place of business. It was simple as pie. When the last one of em finally died, which was about three years before I found Lombard up there on the porch, Hand had trucked everybody up to Lombard's place , and him and Lombard had arranged em around in chairs on the screened-in *po'ich.* And that made Lombard about as happy as he ever wanted to be. I guess that's why he never did look all sad and everything whenever one of his *immediate* own passed away—to *Ruleville*! Ha ha. That's a further joke, sumbich.

Anyway, I know what you're thinkin. But the UPS and nem nor nobody else wouldna never gone around back of the house.

And I guess nobody else ever even went up to Lombard's house at all. So there you are. If I hadn paid him a visit, everybody'd still be setn-nair on the back *po-ich* with Lombard drinkin gotdam Scotch Whiskey.

A lotsa people think Miss Attica knew about all this but didn want to say anything because Lombard was her first cousin, and she did not want her family name involved in nothin of that peculiar nature. Somebody swore that for a while she went around claimin she and Lombard was "second cousins once removed," which was a coksukkin lie, and Lombard never forgave her fat ass for it. Hell, I'll take a sumbich who has his dead kinfolks stuffed and sitn around the house over a lyin, mean-ass, overbearin—and I believed MURDERIN—shithed any dam day of the week. But when it all came out, Miss Attica sure as succotash could not escape the fact that everybody knew she and ol' Lombard was not just cousins, but fukkin *first* gotdam cousins. And that was that. It would take a dadgum genius-kiss-my-ass-Ologist to keep it all straight.

Rummage, of course, was Miss Attica's daddy's family's name. Her mother's mother was a Cabuttler, and her mother's oldest sister, Hernanda Rose Cabuttler—Miss Attica's *ahntee*—had married Bateman Abernathy, who was Lombard's daddy. People called him "Scooter." Anyway, as far as the Abernathys was concerned, there wuddn but one of them around no more, which was Lombard. And that sumbich is barely-ass alive now and in a fukkin nursin home in Marks.

McKinney told me the rest of them Abernathys was all up in Middle Tennessee, around Pew-lasky,[28] but Bateman Abernathy's branch of that family had been in Mhoon County here in the Miss'ssippi Delta, ever since before the gotdam Indians got shoved across the river by you know who—the coksukkin Planters and their

---

28   Pulaski. —ml

kind! She went on to say that some people believed old Scooter's folks mighta been Chickasaws, but she pointed out that her mother told her that Scooter said they wuddn, they was just plain old white folks, even though, he claimed, he woulda liked to have been a' *Inyan*. Accordin to McKinney, the Abernathys was Scotchy Irish to the core and come through North Carolina to Middle Tennessee, and from there, two brothers, one of which was Lombard's great-great-granddaddy, made it down to the Delta. Which is the way it was with a good many of these Planter muthafukkas. And that's how it is. I wish I was a gotdam *Inyan*. Hell, I drutha be anything than just a fukkin pekkawood!

Miss Attica's aunt Rose *married up,* "they" say, because "they" also tells it that Miss Helena Ferry[29] would roll her eyes whenever anybody ever mentioned the "Cabuttlers." Miss Attica almost never said nothin about the Cabuttler side of her family, and McKinney told me Miss Attica always claimed not to know much about em and that she "was plainly more influenced by her papa's side."

I have already given you a taste of what Miss Attica Rummage was "like" toward Voyd and me, but the truth is she didn never have much to say to neither of us or to many folks at all that was in any fashion connected to us. Mostly, even when she was younger, she spoke to people like me and my kind through somebody like that Worthless Nigga Ezell or through Berta, the black woman that seemed like had been in that house and had been the same gotdam age as long as I can ever fukkin remember. Niggas are strange.

I used to observe Miss Attica, of course, and through the years it always just looked as though she went about her business in a way that told the whole world she was abso-fukkin-lutely en-gotdam-tirely certain to the bone about everything she was doin—and about everything you was doin too.

---

29 Appears in *Junior Ray* (NewSouth 2005). —ml

That's how them Planter people behave. You know, like they own everything. Which they do. And I guess they act that way because they was raised up to believe that no matter how anything else was, if they didn approve of it, they could just change it all to suit themsevs. Whereas my folks didn have shit, and had to eat it as well. Plus, I reg'n we was supposed to feel good and thankful when them Planters' wives and the people in the town bundled our smelly asses up and brung us outa the gotdam woods into the *Methodist Sunday School* to sing about how Jesus just LOVED the little churrens.

Fuk 'at noise. Even when I wuddn but nine, I knew it was a load'a pig spit. But I really kinda enjoyed it later when the *Presbyterians* went up to Meffis and brung back an old broke-down streetcar and set it off the road out there in the middle of nowhere between the ass-end of Little-fukkin-Texas and the Yellow Dog,[30] really just as you got into Dooley Woods, which, as you know, was a' actual woods that used to be right around Savage, by the Coldwater River. Anyhow the point is they put it there for us to use as a church and a Sunday School. It was like that caboose, later on, them Piscob'ls had set up down there at Slab Town before po' Preacher Flickett blowed it up along with all them pitiful shacks in that so-called town.[31]

First of all, though, our streetcar wuddn far from where we was livin, and I got to carry my gun with me when I went off to the Sunday School. I'd hide it behind a log; then, after all the prayin and Jesus'n, I could rabbit-hunt my way back to the house, I mean, if you could call what we lived in a house. Anyhow, as far as I am concerned, Jesus is a fukbump.[32]

But now I want to say something else, about Voyd's people.

---

30 A famous Delta railroad. —ml
31 See *The Yazoo Blues* (NewSouth 2008). —ml
32 A "pimple." —ml

Them sumbiches come down into the Delta out of the Hills from up around *New Abdera*.[33] My kin, as you know, come from up around Clay City, which I do believe is a cut above them coksukkas from New Abdera. Anyway, Clay City is not too far from Calhoun City—and aint neither one of them places any kind of a fukkin city whatsoever—and so, for some reason or another, we was all, way back, referred to as "The Calhouners." And it was not a good thing to be called that. At least not in the Delta. And them Planters and their folks was bad about it. Some of them called us the "black hats." Even the Niggas called us "The Calhouners"—like they was better'n us.

Which I think they was. Lookin back at the whole situation and all, I can kinda see how they coulda come to that conclusion.

BUT WHAT ABOUT McKINNEY's people, and what about Mad's folks? There are families amongst them Planters that apparently did not have nothin to do with that gotdam lethal-ass traditional crapdoodle. As it was explained to me, a bunch of them Planters, right after the Civil War, said, "That's it. We aint havin nothin to do with no more killin—Yankees, Niggas, Scalawags, Whoever! We aint doin it!"

"Plus," they said, "we got to be extra careful not to run the Niggas off, cause we can't be Planters without em."

McKinney indicated that there was a part of her growin up that always seemed somewhat secrety and that one or two times some of the women had invited McKinney to join in on something, but her mama always told them McKinney would not "be able to attend" on account of she'd be out of town or some such flippityblip as that. McKinney said, back then, she didn quite

---

33 Abdera was an ancient Thracian city whose air was thought to make people stupid, a bit of classicist trivia that must have been unknown to New Abdera's founders. —ogbii

understand what was goin on, because she knew goodn well she wuddn gon be out of town, and when she'd ast her mama—Miss Babydoll—Miss Babydoll would just say, "It's nothin, dear, just some *things* those ladies bring up once in a while, *things*, dear, in which your grandmother and I chose long ago not to participate; yet, we never want to be impolite, so this is the way we handle it." And McKinney said she never really understood what "it" was. Later, though, after McKinney was pretty much growed up, she said—"I began to hear rumors, rather wild rumors, and I thought to myself: That's the craziest stuff I ever heard of! But then I said, nope, nothin is too crazy for where I come from, and I am goin to stay as far away from any of it as I can."

So she did, but, unlike most of them I told you about who does go way off up the country, McKinney come back. Thank-fukkin-God.

Mad and McKinney, and Miss Helena and Miss Sadie Hamlin[34] and a few others is and was the exception. What I'm tryin to say is that some of these Planters is different from the bulk of em and are more like regular fukkin human-ass beins. On the other hand, from my side of the fence it's pretty simple: I like Mad and McKinney and anybody connected to em, mainly, because they like me. And that's the long and the short of it.

But you need to hear the horse from McKinney's mouth. Listen up. Here is part of a letter she wrote to Mad after I showed her his letter[35] to me tellin about the Aunty Belles:

> There are some things you don't talk about, and the possibil-
> ity that every woman around you with a cucumber sandwich
> in one hand and a Co'-Cola in the other could be a potential
> murderess is one of them. I never knew, in all those years, who

---

34   Appears in *The Yazoo Blues* (NewSouth 2008). —ml
35   This was obviously not meant to be part of this book, but Junior Ray insisted. —ml

was who or exactly what was what, but I did know there was that *thing* my mother and my grandmother tried to shield me from and that they would not discuss. Still, one hears things.

Thus, I never knew what the truth really was, whether there was something about the Chi Omegas, who were certainly Southern to the core, or whether there was a dark secret attached to the *Deep* Southern wing of the Tri-Delts—whose origins were not Southern at all. Nothing was defined, only rather hugely hinted at, tantalizingly implied, like what was it about the KDs? Or, for that matter, all those old blue-haired UDCs, who, frankly, were the ones most suspect. But I knew "they". . . "them". . . whoever they were . . . were there nonetheless and no doubt sitting right next to me in the dormitory bathroom—not the UDCs, of course—during that one semester I attended at Ole Miss! However, because of what I was perhaps programmed to believe could be real danger, I have had to ask myself if the publisher might want to edit all this out of Junior Ray's book. I would not want to *endanger* the reader. I mean, if there is any danger at all; I frankly don't know.

I expect you could not help but notice, again, the names of them two girls clubs—the *tchEYE Omeegases* and the *Try-ass-Dultresses.* I didn know much about all that, but if Mad talked about em and McKinney brung em up, then I had to pay attention. I just hoped conditions wouldn get no more complicated than they probly could be.

Anyway, about McKinney's letter to Mad, she said a helluva lot more to him but it was mostly a carload of highly pers'nl stuff concernin her life; you know, some things she'd did and some she hadn, but either way it looked like she had loved every minute of whatever she got herself into—and out of as well. A good bit of what she said defeats the Ditty Wah Ditty outa me. I just don't know exactly what nor where she is talkin about most of the time. Still, I thought if you could see it you might get sumpm out of it. I mean, this bein littertour and all, McKinney ought not to mind; so I am putn the whole hindquarter includn the hoof in the back of the book as a ApPENdage.

Now THIS IS SUMPM no civilized muthafukka can do without:

Junior Ray's Extra-Famous D.U.I. Hunnud-Proof Fruit Toppin

This is easy. All you have to do is throw a lot of fruit, canned or otherwise, into a quart jar, pour in a lot of sugar; after that, fill up the sumbich with *Jack Daniels* and let it set in the cupboard and soak for a year or so, then haul it out and glop the contents on top of vanilla ice cream, and it will knock your ass plumb off.

CHAPTER SEVEN

*Mojack—Old Don't Mean Old—Tombo Was Mistook for
Brainy?—Number 7½ Shot—Authorities Have No Answer—
Junior Ray Is Not Satisfied—The New Sheriff Is a Dum-
ass—Voyd Wants a Badge—Feefees Not Feces—"Palms for
the Southern Soldier"—Recipe No. 7: Junior Ray's Famous
Forbidden-Fruit Plum & Hot-Ass Pepper Jelly*

So, anyway, one day, one day fo' we even knew we was gon be
diktectives, Voyd and me are out *investigate'n* over 'cross the
levee in the Evanses' woods at their little screened-in summer house by the bank of the Cut-Off. And then I seen it, and I
couldn't believe it. "Gotdam, Voyd," I said. "I *seen* 'im."

"Seen who, Junior Ray?" said Voyd.

"*Him*," I said. "Mojack."

Voyd's eyes got big as two fried eggs, and he said: "Gotdam.
Gotdam. Got-da-um! That old Nigga, I know, has died three fukkin
times and maybe more since I been born; then, he pops up, and,
if you say somethin' about it to anybody, especially to them black
sumbiches, they just laugh and change the fukkin subject. Yet, *everybody* keeps on talkin about the muthafukka like he's really real."

"Niggas *is sumpm*," I said, 'cause I couldn think of what else
to say. For one thing I never did believe a word anybody ever said
about no "Mojack." Hell, there wuddn no Mojack, and there never
had been. Or . . . was there and always had been? I felt I needed
to add, "Yeah, just when you think you understand em—Niggas,
I mean—sumpm happens, and you know you never did." Which

is true, but mainly I wuddn feelin like engagin in no colorful-ass discussion because I was havin a little trouble getn ahold of mysef.

"Let's just go," Voyd said, and he started walkin off toward my Explorer. I hollered at him to come on, even though it was *me* that was tryin to catch up with *him*. Right then I did not know which was the most terrifyin', Voyd or an old Nigga fairy story.

See, *Mojack* was supposed to be around when I was just a little squirt, and he was always part of Mhoon County, mostly in the wild everday standard-ass bullshit that the Niggas and even most of the white people carried on about, ever since I can fukkin remember—even after he theoretically died the first time I recall, not to mention the second and third times. And those times was just more times piled on top of the time a hunnud or so years ago when anybody probly first said anything about him. Plus, didn nobody appear to know when this-here *figment* was born in the first fukkin place.

Story or not, I don't know if he just wuddn as old as people thought he was or whether, accordin to the tales, he'd disappear for a while and word would get around that he'd done died. Most people, the ones I guess who believed in him, always thought he'd died, and then, when he kept comin back, they just sort of got used to that, too. It's like, down here, things don't have to be definite.

However, the last time I heard he died was in November of 1999, and the New African Baptists, back over on the west side of St. Leo, across the Sugar Ditch and kind of behind where the old City Equipment Barn used to be, had a big—I'm talkin fukkin huge—gotdam funeral for him, and buried his ass, so they said, right out northeast of St. Leo over by a little slough just to the east of Highway 61, and north of the Nigga school. Well, it's actually just a regular school now, legally, but it used to be the *Nigga* school, legally, and I still think of it that way, mainly 'cause, you know, there aint nothin but Niggas that goes to it. Legally of course.

Mojack, though, *was supposed* to have lived for the longest time up in the middle of Hollywood Brake a few miles above Tunica. But back in the fifties, when the lumber companies come in there and cut out all the cypress, he left, they said, and people begun to see him mostly out in the deep woods down thissaway over 'cross the levee. Everybody, mostly Niggas but some white folks as well, was scared of him because they thought he could do sumpm to you if he wanted to. Sumpm, somebody said, *unworldly* like. And I thought, hotsnot, how fukkin more unworldly-like can you get than the Miss'sippi Delta? So I never believed none of that sheepdip.

I thought there was just a series of crazy old Nigga hoodoo doctors who liked to live by theysef and make their livin huntn and trappin and bringin in game once in a while to sell to a few of the white families in town that didn have no men in em that hunted and fished but who liked all that wild-tastin stuff just the same yet wuddn gon ast nobody to give it to em. It was mostly just rabbits and squirrels but raccoons, too, and sometimes just regular, plain lillo tweety birds—especially ones like I mentioned in *The Yazoo Blues*—feelarks and robins and snipe, maybe a few redwings, and a hawk or two before shootn em got to be a sin. Well, fuk, I wouldn want to shoot em either, gotdammit, but I'm warnin your ass not to repeat that!

Lemme correct mysef real quick: I said a snipe was a plain lillo tweety bird, but it aint. Believe it or no it's a fukkin bonafide-ass game bird—dam near a semEYE-type-of-waterfowl, since it's usually a wet field you scare em up in.

Anyway, along with only three or four white sumbiches in the county, Mojack, if of course there really was a Mojack, probly knew more about the woods, on both sides of the levee, than any of em. I don't know, though. That's a hard thing to judge. I guess it'd be more accurate to say Mojack was just more mysterious than the other sumbiches. But he had the edge on that: because a muthafukka really can't be white and mysterious, yet a Nigga can be both, If you know what I mean.

Suddenly, Voyd and me, both, seen him. There he was, stannin over by a big sycamore lookin at us, with his hands in his pockets. He appeared to be about sixty, and he was dressed in overalls, a light-tan canvas huntn coat, and rubber hip boots with the tops rolled down. His hair was real short. It was gray, and he was wearin one nem baseball caps that said DELTA COUNCIL on it.

"Are you Mojack?" I ast him.

"Is I what?" he answered.

"I'm astin you if you're that Nigga that lives in a tree in the woods and has been doin so for the last one hunnud and eighty-five years," I said. And he come back with, "Man, you outa yo mind. I is a Nigga, that's fo sho, but I don't live in no tree, and I aint a hunnud and sumpm years old. My name's Wilson, and I works for Mister Thawnt'n."

"You're sho you're real?" Voyd ast.

"Fuk yeah, I's real—whatchewtawkinbout!"

"Listen," I said, "my podna here and me is . . . is . . . *diktectives*, and we're tryin to find out who shot Mr. Tombo on the first day of turkey season underneath that big oak they call the Visitor's Tree."

He didn say nothin for a minute, like he was studyin on the question; then he said, "It wuddn but one shot, from a lillo four-hunnud-and-ten. A big woman come up the bank, off the Cut-Off, shot Mr. Tombo and clumb back down the bank; she got in a boat and went off tw'ohd the camps. It was a boat wif one nem big 'lectric motors. I couldn tell, from where I was stannin, if she was by hersef or if there was some mo wif her, down in the boat. I couldn tell, but it sho coulda been.

"How come you aint told nobody about that?" ast Voyd.

"Aint nobody ast me," he said. "Y'all's the first diktectives that come around me wantn to know sumpm."

"You're sho it was a woman?" I said.

"It was a woman all right, but I couldn rekanize her on accounta she had her head all covered up wif one nem skeeta nets. She was kinda on the big side."

Now, that sure sounded like it coulda been Miss Attica. Course, we still couldn prove nothin even though what Wilson told us, I guess you could say, bulked up what we already believed anyhow. Voyd and I looked at each other like we was both thinkin the same thing, but when I turned back to ast the Nigga another question, the sumbich wuddn no longer there.

I ast Voyd where the fuk—*"Where'd that Nigga go!"*—and Voyd was in the middle of one of them kinda starin straight-ahead glassy-eyed spells he sometimes gets and he said, "I didn know he went nowhere."

Well, "Wilson" sho as hell wuddn *nowhere* to be found. Both me and Voyd looked around the immediate area hard as we could, but we couldn turn up no trace of the sumbich. The weirdest feature of it all was that after everything was over, and the mystery was as solved as it was ever gon be, I mentioned to Thornton Evans one day Voyd and me talkin to "Wilson" out in the woods, who worked for him, and Thornton just looked at me with a blank-ass look and said he didn have no Nigga named Wilson who worked for him and never did. He said Voyd and me must be fukkin mistaken. But, bygod, I'm here to tell you we wuddn. ChrEYEst. That made hairy bugs run up my ass.

Anyway, this was the first time I had just flat out claimed Voyd and me was diktectives. But the whole idea caught on, and Voyd was really hot for it, and I was too.

HERE IS A FUKKIN flashback. Bear in mind it come as shock when I mentioned to Brainy that old Tombo Turnage—

One second, now! I got to clear sumpm up: *When I say a*

muthafukka is "old So and So" it don't necessarily mean he was old;
you oughta know that, and, if you don't, then I just do not know what
to tell yo ass.

Anyway, back to "old" Tombo—the ol' sumbich had been found
shot to death out across the levee turkey huntn with Thornton
Evans, and Brainy told me he, hissef, was supposed to have been
huntn with Thornton Evans but had to back out because his sinuses
was actin up.

He further said the Evanses had always been very helpful to
him whenever he'd been in town and that the Evanses had been
longtime good friends of his uncle, Mr. Brainsong—God rest his
fukkin soul—for whom Brainy was named. Anyhow, before Brainy
left California, he had phoned up the Evanses and told em he was
comin to St. Leo, to, as he put it, "wrap up a few loose ends" but
. . . *had not told them* about the letters he'd gotten from the threaters!

It was, of course, while he was talkin to Thornton that Thornton
invited him to go turkey huntn, and Brainy thanked him and said
he would and that he was certain, in his words, "that it surely could
prove to be a most important experience that might be useful to
him in his work in the future."

But, as I told you some time back, the day before he was to
catch the coksukkin plane from Lost Angeleez to Meffis, he got a
bad case of the flu, so, as you know, he telephoned Thornton and
ast him could he have a rain check, and Thornton told him that
was okay. Then, it wuddn long at all after that conversation that
Thornton and his wife saw Tombo Turnage at the Boll & Bloom
and ast him did he want to go turkey huntn, and you know the rest.

The thing is, when Brainy turned up on my front steps lookin
like hammered shit, it wuddn just because of the threaters but was
mostly because he hadn got no sleep because he was still kinda puny
from the flu. In any case, the point is no matter how you slice the
gotdam head cheese, he wuddn the one setn underneath the Visi-

tor's Tree the day Tombo got shot and killed. I didn say nothin, but I was thinkin a *whole*-fukkin-lot.

I coulda almost predicted what was gon happen, and it did. The sheriff, who—let me make this crystal-ass clear—was NOT the new po-lice chief who I will in fact get to in a little bit—declared Tombo's death was caused by foul play, only he said he couldn even imagine what that would be. And he certainly did not have no answer for how Tombo coulda got blasted with *Number 7-1/2 shot* from—as it was decided—what looked to have been a gotdam lillo four-ten on the first day of turkey season. Didn nothin about any of that even begin to add-ass-up. The problem is that a lot of people, professional and otherwise, will just let a thing drop if they can't figure it out right off the fukkin bat. But I aint like that, and I don't spec you are either.

Anyway, there it was, and it looked to me like there wuddn no more to be said about it. And even the very fukkin idea of *not knowin* seemed to suit just about everybody concerned, except me of course, bein an experienced law enforcement professional, but I still aint opened my mouth about nothin yet.

As you might imagine the silly fukkin notion that Tombo kilt hisself "cleanin his gun" was all over the place and which of course was not only not true but tee-totally fart-brained. *First of all* most sumbiches who knowed him knew Tombo never cleaned his fukkin shotgun. Plus, he wouldna been cleanin it setn there under the gotdam Visitor's Tree while he was huntn turkeys. He had his back up against the trunk of that big white oak; his legs was crossed like a Inyan chief, and he was holdin his old-timey, square-back, big-ass twelve-gauge Remington semEYE-automatic shotgun in his lap. Tombo wouldna never carried one nem little extra-lightweight sissy-ass Ithaca four-ten pumps. And he sho didn own one!

But strap in, sumbich. You now know who did: Miss Attica Rummage! She only owned one shotgun that I happened to know of, and it was that Ithaca four-ten pump she'd had ever since she was a girl. I used to run a rod th'oo it and oil it up it for her when she'd send it along with her daddy's pistol over to the Sheriff's office to get *maintained*. Plus, she loved to try to shoot doves with it. And that's hard to do because a four-ten just can't get on out there like a twelve-gauge can. It dont th'ow out as big a pattern either. Now, all this I'm tellin you is important, and it's something I recommend you keep in mind.

Second of all, the whole so-called official investigation wuddn worth a number-nine can of goat shit. That new sheriff and his boys didn know sqwut. And didn do sqwut neither. What I saw and heard let me know sumpm was not right. Googah like this never woulda happened when Sheriff Holston was alive and runnin things! Those ol' sheriffs might notta been trained, but they was sho as hell professionals.

ChrEYEst. Now, though, see, they got a fat-ass ignorant old pekkawood sumbich that don't know his dik from a bean pole and owes ever' coksukkin crook in this part of the Delta a gotdam favor. So, yeah, that country-ass white muthafukka'd say *anything*. Dumbastuhd. I remember the *idjit* a few years ago when he was a deputy. The jackass looked at a circular hole in a glass panel of the side door to Miss Chizza Lowe's house and said, "What done 'at?"

Holy Dee-fukkin-ldrin!"[36] I thought. This cooty-brain duddn even know how burglars cuts glass with tape and a glass cutter to get their arm in through the hole so they can unlock the door from the inside. Gee-fukkin-ZUHSS! Where did that sumbich come from? And how did he get 'lected sheriff of Mhoon County? I sure as a chifferrobe don't know!

ANYWAY, MOVIN FORWARD, VOYD said if him and me was gon be

---

36   Dieldrin, a banned agricultural insecticide. —ml

diktectives, he wanted us to ride up to Meffis to what he called Guns and Blammo—but which was really a serious-ass gun store called Gun City, up in North Meffis, east off Highland, on the south side of Verano Avenue—so we could get us some Private Investigator badges and some *IDs*. I figured it could be possible we might have to use something like that before all this whatever-it-was was over, so I said, "Fine." And we got in my Explorer and I drove us up there to the gun store.

Fortunately, in Mississippi, you don't have to have no license or nothin to be a private *dik*tective. You do in Tennessee, but I decided we'd cross that legal ditch when—and if—we come to it. And I wuddn worried a-tall about Arkansas, 'cause I knew we wuddn gon go over there nohow. FukKEMM ignunt-ass Out-West sumbiches!

So we got our badges and little leather badge holders that looked like wallets, which I told Voyd we could whip out and flop open if we wanted to identify oursevs as private-eyeballs. See, when you opened the little wallet thing up, there was a place for your badge on one side and, on the other, was a clear plastic little window you could put your *picture* ID in, once you got the picture, of course, and pasted it on the official blank ID card that come with the holder. Nachaly, we decided to use em as our *regular* wallets. That way we could flash our badges ever' time we went up to any kind of a counter to pay for sumpm or, if we was ast to show our driver's licenses. I mean, there wuddn no sense in havin' what woulda amounted to *two* wallets in our pockets at the same fukkin time.

But Voyd remained upset 'cause, as he put it, "Gotdammit, Junior Ray, what good is it for us to have our badges and official IDs if you and me's in the fukkin woods all the time where there aint nobody to show em to!"

"We aint gon be in the gotdam woods all the time," I told him.

"Well, it's near 'bout the same everywhere else," he said, "because we might as well be in the woods as out there in the coksukkin country tryin' to show our badges to a buncha pekkawoods and Niggas."

You have to understand that Voyd don't notice a lot, especially how things has changed, and that it was getn pretty difficult to find either a pekkawood OR a Nigga, so I didn say nothin to him right then; plus, he was about to start up whinin like a gotdam tittybaby. "Well, just whut-th'-fuk do you suggest, Voyd?" I ast him after a few beats.

And he smart-mouthed back at me with, "I *sug*-fukkin-*gest* we go to a gotdam CITY!"

He did have a valid point. The problem mainly was where we was gon come up with a city in the Delta. *There aint none.* I mean it's an old sayin' by, I'm pretty sure, some queer who was a friend of a fellow I knowed down in Greenville, that "the Delta starts in the lobby of the Peabody" hotel up in Meffis, but, sumbich, it really don't. And somethin' was tellin' me that our gotdam investa-*fukkin*-gation just flat wuddn gon take us up to Meffis, except of course to get supplies, whatever the fuk they might happen to be.

It turned out I was wrong. But I'mo tell you about that later.

Still, I kept thinkin about the issue. Miss'ssippi has Jackson. It aint in the Delta, but I guess you could call it a city, though to my mind that'd be stretchin' it. Oh, I know it's done growed a lot, and I hear people is livin in the suburbs and in some fancy-ass housin' developments with a buncha fast-food joints and motels of one sort or another all around em, but, the core of the place, as I remember, aint much of a city. Hell, I been there twice. 'Course, only *one* of those times was for any more'n just a few minutes. But it was e-fukkin-nough for me.

"Voyd," I said, "I know you're right, and I feel the same exact-ass way, but we're gon have to use our gotdam imaginations." I went on to say that if we was in Clarksdale for him not to think about how broke-dik it was and how small it was—even though it was a shitpot-lot bigger'n St. Leo—and, if he could, to try and focus straight at who we was talkin to and not pay no attention to the fact that we wuddn in some big-ass city, and that if he could make hissef do that I thought he'd be able to get into the swing of things and enjoy bein a gotdam private diktective.

He said he'd do his best, and after that Voyd lightened up so he didn look like he was on the verge of whinin. I just used psychology on his ass. I picked it up from Sunflower, you know, his trouble-in-a-bubble wife who had been like a cat on a roach runnin his little white rat's-ass around for years.

Anyway, he was fine, he really was, as far as I was concerned, but it is hard for Voyd to ever let anything just drop, so the next thing I know he's comin out with: "And I reg'n when we go up to Meffis, we could go by to see the *feces*."

What do you say to a fool like that? I about lost it, and I said, "Not *feces*, Voyd! It's *feefees*, you ignunt sumbich!" And I told him, "Voyd, I was talkin' about the *feefees* which is what them Frenchies in the movies calls all good-lookin women."

"I don't know no French," said Voyd. "I just always heard you say back yonda you was goin' up to that nekkid club[37] up in Meffis, to see the feces.

"Gotdammit, Voyd," I said, "in the first place I wouldna had to go all the way up to Meffis to see feces; and why, Voyd, in the name of Gravel-gotdam-Gertie[38] and Lena the fukkin Hyena,[39] would I or any other muthafukka want to look at *feces*?"

"Hell, I don't know," the little shitbird said. "I guess don't nothin surprise me these days. It coulda been some kinda fertilizer for all I knew. Anyway, I just took you at your word and didn't think no more about it."

---

37 The Magic Pussy Cabaret & Club. —ml
38 comic strip character in Dick Tracy , by Chester Gould. —ml
39 comic strip character, 1946, in Li'l Abner, by Al Capp. —ml

"Feces was *not* my word," I told him. "My word was *feefees*."

"Junior Ray, it don't make no difference," he said in that kinda high-ass voice the Niggas use when they're tryin' to lie and make it look like they aint, which in fukkin fact is what every one of us does down here whenever we've got our dik in the dirt. One way or a-coksukkin-nother, all white folks, especially in the Delta—on a bred-in daily basis—*talk like Niggas*. I mean, sometimes you can't tell the difference. That's just the way it is. I guess it must be natural.

"What*ever* you want to go look at in Meffis," he said, "is ooohkay with me—that's *yo'* business."

By then I was thinkin' about shoot'n that little coksukka right smack up the nose, but I tried one more time: "Voyd," I said, "I promise you I wouldn never drive up to Meffis—or anywhere else—to go look at a buncha *feces*. Now, I want you to hear what I'm sayin, *'cause it's important to me that you understand what it was I said and that you believe me.*"

"I believe you, Junior Ray," he said. "And I'm right with you; I wouldn go up there to see no feces—nor no feefees—neither."

"That's good," I said to him. "That's good, Voyd."

"I know," he said, "cause I wouldn't want to get em mixed up."

Junior Ray's Famous Forbidden-Fruit Plum and Hot-Ass Pepper Jelly

Use whatever fruit you so desire, as long as you steal it. That's a must. And, of course, don't forget the pepper. To do it right, you need to grind up some of them fresh green holler-pain-yos and th'ow them sumbiches in with the boilin fruit while you're cookin it down, before it turns into jelly.

Now, this is a minor thing, but, if you're like me and don't know how to make actual *jelly*, you need to give Tuckahoe Gwynne a call, up in Meffis. He'll fill your ass in on it, because he cooks up pepper jelly just about every duck-bustin year of his life—like he learned from his Uncle Pete. I'm tellin you, Tuckahoe knows. Plus, he is just about the best meat cook in the whole coksukkin Mid-South. He learned that from his Uncle Pete, too. Anyhow, call him up. He lives right there in Meffis, off Central Avenue in one nem "gated communities," you know, where you need a gotdam number to get your fukkin ass inside. Yellin won't do no good. I reg'n all that's designed to keep the Niggas out. Or—ChrEYEst, I don't know!—maybe to keep em in.

Chapter Eight

The Letters Was Wrote by a Woman—Mailed from
Clarksdale—The Whole Heart-Stoppin Idea of Pussy—The
Yoknapatawpha Book Store—Voyd and Me Discover Bop-
a-Lee—The Five Dollar The-Ater House—Two Nekkid
Professoresses & a Skeleton—Voyd Knows the Secret
Handshake—Junior Ray's Famous Ole Miss Cutie-Frutie Pie

Bein a private diktective caused me to have to think a lot more than I had planned to. For instance, what was it about the nature of the letters that led me to think they was wrote by a woman? The write'n was pretty. Of course I know there's a few men who write all fancy and neat, too. Brainy was prone to it and to some degree I think Mad was as well. Anyway, as I say, there was *just sumpm* about the whole gotdam nature of the letters that made me think, uhn-hunh, a woman wrote this thing. Plus, just for the record, they was *all three* mailed from Clarksdale.

And, see, Clarksdale, dikinthedirtrundown as I have already mentioned that it has unfortunately become—albeit with a slim-ass hope of revival—has a fukkin *country club*. And I have found that wherever you come across a gotdam country-ass town—one that's sitn smack in the middle of a JYE-mongus cotton field—and that town has a country *club* . . . you can bet *women* is rulin' the roosters on that ranch. Lemme tell you, don't nothin of any importance, good or bad, happen in such a place without women bein at the bottom *and* the fukkin top of it. But, hell, *any* sumbich knows that. And if he don't, he aint very smart.

Yep, country clubs. Some sumbiches joined em. But, I never coulda—wuddn, you know, educated enough. And I knew it. Yet some of my kind—and you'll rekanize who I'm talkin about—*some* of em by hook and crook and hard work, too, got to be genuine Delta Planters themsevs! And one of em right now that I'm thinkin about is in a coksukkin country club!—as if that sumbich coulda got to be any more country that he already was. And I further aint sayin where that country club is either, on account of state and federal privacy issues . . . and also that particular country club would have a Sunday *boo-fay*[40] fit if they knew the sumbich I'm talkin about was in it. Oh, hell yeah. In the fukkin country club! But, you know, I have to admit that the muthafukka worked hard, bought up distressed land and bygod made it! Me, though, I knew I wuddn smart. I just wuddn, and while them other pekkawoods was out there *suck*-ceedn, I was busy runnin around hope'n I could shoot somebody. That's the difference, mainly.

Anyway, so as not to be outdone by Clarksdale and some of the other little Delta—and Loess Hills!—dales and villes, St. Leo built *itsef* a "Country Club," too. Hep me, Hannah! It wuddn much and still aint, and most of the clubbers kept on lope'n the road to the one in Clarksdale. I guess it stands to reason that a country club is a place *to go to* if you want to get away from just the ordinary everyday non-country life, whatever this day and time down here that might be. Anyhow, St. Leo's Country Club is located around three miles south of the town down Highway 61; you turn left on Highway 4 and drive bout a mile and a half east, then south again, for a little way along Limerick Road. The truth is you won't be getn away from anything if you go to it. I mean, once you're there, you're still right here.

However, Clarksdale was the place to go—even though some of

---

40   Buffet. —ml

them Planters here, the big ones anyway, is, as you already know, also members up at the Meffis Country Club and/or at the Chickasaw Country Club; plus at another cocksukkin place called the gotdam Uni-fukkin-versity Club. It's right smack in the middle of Meffis and don't even pretend to be no country club. They don't do no golfin at it. The members there just bebops them tennis balls around and swims in the swimmin pool and guzzles down whiskey in the bar. Shoot, that all sounds okay to me. Except I don't give a shit for tennis. And I sure as sheetrock wouldn pay to do it. So I guess I can see why I don't belong to no club like that. The only club I ever really enjoyed was the Magic Pussy Cabaret & Club where Money Scatters was the star. Nobody ever said a discouragin word, and all the girls was nekkid. You can't beat that with a tennis racket.

Of course, when it comes to country clubs and tennis balls and stuff like that, I don't want to be too arrogant. I expect there are a lot of things I don't know but I don't know what they'd be, and I don't much give a dog fart.

The big question is why would a little country town want itsef a country club? It never did make sense to me, but then I drutha be dead and in hell with my back broke in ARKANSAS than swat little balls 'cross a pasture or over a fukkin fishin net.

Although I have to tell you: I *do* like them little short skirts the women wears when they're playin tennis. It always makes you think you're about to see something you aint never saw before, which, if you really think about it, would have to be something you never would and never *could* have ever thought about in a million fukkin years. Even if you tried your best to come up with something, you couldn. But, natcherly, you know and I know that's what the whole heart-stoppin idea of pussy and what it can do to a sumbich is all about. I doubt anybody will ever get to the bottom of it.

Anyway, back to the death threats and them letters: The question is what woman was it, there or here or *anywhere* in the Delta—or in the whole state of Mississippi for that matter—that would have such a non-stop bee in her butt so bad about how people everywhere else thought about the fukkin South that she would want to actually get rid of some sumbich? And by that I mean: *kill his ass.* I had to start thinkin again.

It was gon have to be a woman—one who knew her way around the woods—and there was two or three I could come up with who I knew liked to hunt doves at the end of the summer. Plus, they also hunted ducks and quail. And two of em liked to get on horses, jump fukkin fences, run after bird dogs, and chase foxes. I couldn think of none who liked to hunt turkeys, but that didn necessarily matter that much because whoever it was only had to know about the woods—and I'm talkin about the Evans' woods in particular; they'd have to also know how to get in and out of em without bein seen by nobody.

It could have been Miss Sadie Hamlin, but it wuddn. She was dead. And had been for a while. And wouldna give a crap about what anybody thought about the gotdam South. Still, I'm here to tell you. I wouldn put nothin past them type of women. I kept thinkin and thought about the possibility that the threat-writer and murderess could have been Miss Elsie Cooper. But she didn give a cootpoot about how anybody wrote about the South either. Plus, she mostly went to Ireland to hunt, and she fished over there, too. I remember way back, after a good year, she and old Cap'm Cooper bought em a sho-nuff castle over there for little or nothin. And from what I understand, them Irishmen was glad for the Cap'm and Miss Elsie to have it.

I met one of them Irish muthafukkas once. He was a helluva sumbich, and I liked him a whole lot. He stayed out-chonda along White Oak Bye-oh with Miss Elsie and the Cap'm. They put on a big fish fry for him and bygod invited me. So that's how I got to

know him. 'Cept for the way he talked, I couldn see a whole lot
of difference between him and me. That Irish sumbich hated the
gotdam Englishmen almost more'n I hate Planters and Niggas and,
of course, *bankers*; only he said he and his buddies would borrow
Miss Elsie's car and drive it up north of wherever the fuk they were
and th'ow a stick of dynamite across the state line between his
Ireland and what he said was the other one that still belonged to
the fukkin English. That was the first I knew there was two kinds
of Irelands. Anyway him and his buddies meant business.

At least that's what dynamite says to me. I aint never blowed up
nothin with it except a beaver dam. And that aint hardly the same
thing—although them beavers is smart, and you can say industri-
ous, too, plus cute. But the little bucktooth bastuhds is arrogant!
They're just too gotdam full of theysevs and five thousand acres of
trees to suit me. One thing those flat-tailed giant water rats does is
they drown out all the hardwood by keepin the trees underwater
all year. So if a landowner don't blow the dams and get rid of the
beavers, which in fukkin fact he just about can't, the trees is doomed
to become nothin but a watery-ass moon-yard waste of dead snags
that even the quackflappin ducks don't want much to do with.

Also it coulda been Sugsie[41] Crawsthbrake. She grew up in
the woods and could hunt up a storm. However, I guess I knew
she wouldna spent no time write'n a buncha threat letters. She'da
just shot the sumbich and been done with it. Besides, I truly liked
Sugsie, and I liked Miss Elsie Cooper and the Cap'm, too. So, I
can tell you flat out I wuddn gon spend no time suspectin people
I liked. Fuk that.

THE *threaters* WROTE *another* letter. But it wuddn to Brainy. Yet
it was Brainy who told us about it. He come over to the house

---

41　Pronounced *Shoog-zee Cross-brake.* —ml

one eve'nin'. Voyd was there; him and me was watchin' *Columbo*. And Brainy, soon as he was inside and fo' we could say, "Sit yo ass down," he *announcified*: "A fourth threat of homicidal violence has been delivered!"

I ast him where was it, so Voyd and me could see it, and he said, "It's in Oxford."

"The letter," he said, "was received by the manager—who is an old friend of mine—at the Yoknapatawpha[42] Book Store, right there in the middle of town."

"The what . . .?" I said

"The book store, Yoknapatawpha," he said.

"Yahkna p'fahffa," I said.

"No, Yoknapatawpha," he told me.

"That's what I said," I told him. "Yahkna p'fahffa."

"Yeah," Voyd chimed in, "The Yahkna-tawfa Book Store; I been there."

"That aint it," I said. "It's Yahkna p'fahffa."

"Yoknapatawpha," said Brainy.

"I'm just gon call it the fukkin Oxford bookstore," said Voyd.

But I looked hard at his ass and said, "I'm callin' it what Brainy says it is, you little shitbug."

"Yoknapatawpha," Brainy said.

"Fukkin 'A'," I said. "It's the gotdam Yahkna p'fahffa Book Store."

Natcherly, bein professionals, we followed the lead and *went*

---

42 Here, with a deep genuflection in honor of the truth of William Faulkner's obvious genius, I must tell the reader that Faulkner was wrong about the definition of Yoknapatawpha. He believed it meant "'slowly moving water' or 'water flowing slow through the flat land . . .'" [Please see Thomas S. Hines's wonderful book *William Faulkner and the Tangible Past: The Architecture of Yoknapatawpha* (University of California Press, 1996), p. 149.] It does not. Actually it is two real words from Choctaw/Chickasaw, namely: Yakni (earth) + Pataffi (ploughed, ripped, fallowed). And Yoknapatawpha is the original name of the Yocona River. I like to translate it as "the plowed ground." —ogbii

way-on over there in the gotdam Hills to the unpronounceable
bookstore, and we got the letter—but that was only because Brainy
was with us. That sumbich manager looked at Voyd and me like
we was a couple of possums that had waddled into the livin room.
But, he shaped up somewhat when Brainy told his ass I was the
R-ther of the book he, Owen G. Brainsong the Second, had been
the interviewer on. The news hit the fukka kind of strange, and I
could tell it was because somehow or another he had thought Brainy
had wrote that book, *Junior Ray*, which you and I know is not the
case. Brainy just *wrote it down*. It suited me to let it go at that and
we didn get into no discussion about the other book.

Anyhow, I thought we was gon come straight back to the Delta,
but Brainy said he had some more of his *brainy-kinda* friends he
wanted to say *hi* to, especially Professor Jonathan Piddlesby, who
owned in a big ramblin house over on the edge of the campus at
the University; and that's where we took Brainy and parked the
car. He told us that's where he'd be, even if at some point he went
off to say hi to somebody else, meanin he'd be comin back to be at
Professor Piddlesby's old-timey, *hine'ty*-lookin[43] house.

Brainy ast us if we wanted to take the car. We told him that
was fine but that whilst he was doin his visitin and sayin *hi*, Voyd
and me b'lieved we druther walk around and see what the gotdam
uni-fukkin-versity looked like, and so we hiked on off even though
it was getn late.

Old Professor Jonathan Piddlesby, you see—*not*, as you mighta
thought, Brainy's uncle Mr. Brainsong, who, as you fukkin well
know, verified to Miss Florence that Voyd and me had in fact
found a German submarine and, further, hepped me become a
historian[44]—was what brung Brainy into the Delta in the first place

---

43   "Hine'ty"—rhymes with "ninety"—is dialect for "haunty," or "haunted." —ml
44   In *Junior Ray* (NewSouth, 2005) and in *The Yazoo Blues* (NewSouth, 2008).
      —ml

and had told him about all that had gone on with Leland Shaw and everything. Plus, Doctor Piddlesby, we come to find out from Brainy, was the world's leadin-ass authority on anything a-tall havin to do with—aw-ite, here goes—*Anthropological Philolo-fukkin-Ology*, or some such lappidoodap, which as you know was Brainy's field of speci-AL-ity. Plus, to bring your ass even more up to date, Brainy had come to know about Piddlesby through the Doctor's books on the subject, which Brainy had read the eye-wax out of while he was studyin here and there all over the country in them big famous uni-gotdam-versities, getn to be a *Doctor* hissef—you know, the kind that can't cure your ass of nothin.

SPEAKIN OF SPECIALITIES, I aint never figured out how a sumbich can just decide to concentrate on just one fukkin thing and get up every mornin and go deal with it, you know, like a lot of them doctors and dentists and re-search signtists and a whole gang of other sumbiches does.

I mean, spose a muthafukka was to become, say, a *Toe-Ologist* and didn do nothin except work on *toes* all day long, every day of the week and once in a while on Sair'dy if there was an emergency. I just can't understand it, even though, bygod, I am thankful that there *are* individuals out there that does—and that *loves*—them specialized jobs. But, what would it be like for a fukkin *Toe-Ologist?* Every footsukkin moment of his life would be dedicated to *toes*— which is what you'd want if you was to have a problem with one of yours. But what about him? Here's how I see it. One day the *Toe-Ologist* comes home from work, and he's smilin to beat the band:

"Hi, dahlin," says his wife. "Did you have yo-sef as good-ass day at the office?"

"You betchum, Mumba Jean," he'd say back. "Today I seen what I believe is the perfect fukkin *toe*. And I got a gotdam *Polaroid* of it in my pocket to prove it."

"Oh, heavens, Sweetheart," she'd say. "Can I see the sumbich, too!"

"Yes, you can, Honeybun," he'd say, "only not just yet!"

"But, precious Diksicle," she'd say. "How come I can't look at the *perfect toe* this very fukkin moment, *rat* now?"

"Cause, Mumba Jean," he'd say, "I'm savin it for the *unveilin!*"

"The unveilin?" she'd say. "Goodness fukkin gracious!"

"That's right, Lovebunny," he'd tell her. "The *unveilin* of the perfect-ass toe!"

"But . . . but . . . where will the unveilin take place?" she'd ast him.

"It's gon be up at the *National Toe-Ologist Convention* next week in Meffis! We gon ride up there in a *toe*-boat. And *you*—my little pussypudd'n—are gonna be stannin right there beside me to share in the big-ass honor!"

"Oh," she'd say. "My dearest Dildo, you've worked so hard for this. I just cannot wait for the *unveilin!*—so I can stand beside you and see the perfect coksukkin *toe.* I am so dikslurpin thrilled!"

"I couldna done it without you, sugarbutt," he'd say. And then they'd amble on back to the kitchen, eat their low-fat supper, hop in the bed, and watch *Law and Order.*

ANYWAY, AFTER A WHILE me and Voyd come up on a row of some more big houses, only they was all pretty new-ish-lookin in comparison to the ones *off* the campus, and one of these new ones, which was three stories high and sported a buncha colyums all across the front, was thumpin up off the ground with music and there was lotsa what looked like *town-sissies* jumpin around in khaki pants and them blue shirts with the buttons on the collar; so we said, "Day-um" and went inside.

Right outa nowhere, while we was stopped dead-still, there, in the front hall, some super-scrubbed well-fed little shithead with a face fulla fukbumps pops up and hands both'a us a bottle'a some kinda beer I aint never heard of that had a picture of two grinnin white sumbiches in short pants, with each one holdin up a foamy glass of beer, like it's what you was supposed to do if you was to drink that brand. Fuk that. But, just the same we told him we appreciated his hospitality, cause the truth is we did, and sometimes I wish I wuddn so fukkin hard on people, even just behind my eyes, but I aint gon get into that now.

The place was jam-packed with college students, I reg'n, dancin and drinkin, and there was some stair steps that everybody was hangin around on and goin back and forth up and down on. Anyway, from the looks of things, the party had been rockin at maximum strength a pretty long time, and it turned out that it was some big celebration they had over there every year called "Bop-a-Lee."

"What's goin on?" Voyd ast a lillo girl who come skippin around the corner from the livin room, headed toward the stairs. She had on Daisy Dukes, a T-shirt, and a pair of low-cut basketball shoes.

"Bop-a-Lee! YAY!" she said and grinned a big-ass grin.

Voyd jumped back and said, "Day-um"; then he looked at me and come out with: "Holy Shit on a Cane-Pole."

"YAY!" the lillo girl said again.

"Thank you, sweetheart," I said.

I have to tell you it was only after we had finally got back home that I later found out that the school had changed the name of the celebration—you know, they changed it when the gotdam *Americans* found out about us, and the Niggas got to come to the school—anyway the sumbiches at the college had to think up a new name that wouldn piss nobody off, which meant they couldn no longer call their old-time traditional big-ass springtime blow-out for the students *Dixie Jubilee*. Now, it was just plain old *Bop-a-Lee*. I guess everybody over there at the university figured the name Bop-a-Lee wouldn raise no smoke like *Dixie Jubilee*—which, kinda sideways, referrin to the old slave-ownin rebel Confederacy, mighta done.

Fukkum. My folks didn own no slaves, and they didn give a shit about the Confederacy neither.

Whatever. Anyhow, them kids didn give a *hoddy-ass-toddy* what it was called as long as they could have a gotdam good time where they could get in all the boppin and hoppin they wanted to do.

"YAY! You welcome!" the *lillo* girl said—now I'm callin her a "lillo" girl but you do realize she coulda been thirty fukkin years old for all me or Voyd could tell. ChrEYEst! We didn know nothin about college students then—and don't now! . . . although Voyd does have two granddaughters that graduated from Meffis State. But I always say, "Who the fuk *hadn?*"

We just kep stannin there, so did the girl. She was pretty as a popsicle. Then another one came up and stood beside her, and both of em was lookin at me and Voyd and just smilin from both ears like a gotdam advertisement.

"YAY!" the first one hollered again.

"YAY!" the second one said.

"Do yawl live here in this house?" Voyd ast em.

"No," said the first one, and then the fukkin noise ratcheted up a mile or two, so it was hard to hear what she was sayin, but it sounded like: "This is the Fi . . . D'l . . . Ayter house"—which seemed to me she was sayin we was in the *Five Dollar The-Ater House*[45]—and then she said, "They're *baw-weez!*"

"YAY!" the second said. "My boyfriend is a FLY ON THE PIE!"[46] And then the two of em looked at each other and both of em hollered, "YAY!"

I have to tell you that if we was in the *Five Dollar The-Ater* House, it was the *best* show I ever seen.

"I'm a KYE-OH," said the first one—and when she said that, wham, I seen the words on her T-shirt, up on the left side of her

---

45   Phi Delta Theta. —ml
46   See footnote 45. —ml

chest. There they was: *TchEYE Omeega*. And right with those words was a capital X and a gotdam *horseshoe*! That's why, later on whenever the subject come up, I called em the *Ex-horseshoe* girls.

She was definitely one nem TchEYE Omeegases Mad and McKinney had wrote about. I never did hear how the words was s'posed to sound from Mad. I only saw the words in his letter. I did *hear* McKinney say the words, even though that don't make a helluva lot of difference. I still called em the way I saw em: *TchEYE-fukkin-Omeega*. Gotdammit.

"I'm a Tri-Day-ult," the other one told us—course she had to holler over the fukkin noise. "A *Tri-Day-ult*?" I thought. And she showed us a thing hangin around her neck that looked like it was triangles made of di-monds, and I said, "Oh, you one nem *Three-Arrowhead* sisters." Then, bygod, it hit my ass: She was one of them *Try-ass-Dultresses*! Both them lillo girls was *both* the two things Mad had mentioned in his letter, and McKinney had said sumpm about as well.

"Unh-huhh," the Try-ass-Dultress said, "I gay-iss." And she held up the di-mond thing and squinted at it, and said, "*Ah-Ha'hn.* That's right: *Day-ulta, Day-ulta, Day-ulta!*"

There it was—Voyd and me was stannin there, drinkin beer, and lookin point-blank into the eyes of two possible death-dealin *Aunty Belles in-trainin*!

"Naawww," I said to mysef. "Naaawww." It was just too hard to believe that them lillo pretty things could ever in their lives be persuaded to gig some po' sumbich in the mouth with his own frog gig! "Naawww," I said to mysef. "Fuk, no."

But, I suspect, because we had become diktectives, Voyd and me knew at, that very fukkin minute, when the second little co-ed said, "Day-ulta, Day-ulta, Day-ulta"—and I have to tell you she also added on: "Kin I hay-up ya, hay-up ya, hay-up ya?!"—we knew sure as Sugar Ditch that there had to be some connection with the coksukkin Delta and with sumpm about the South we hadn never knowed nothin about nor ever imagined. The question, of course, was "What the fuk was it?" I mean it wuddn like Voyd and me had growed up hearin about no killins goin on all along havin to do with protectin the so-called image of Southern fukkin manhood. That's sure as shit a gotdam *Lost Cause*! However, three muthafukkas was dead, and there was some kinda ungodly connection between them killins and Southern women. We was suspicious.

Anyway, Voyd and me was just stannin stock still there in the entry hall lookin at them two college girls, with our tongues hangin out like red neckties—and I'm talkin about red as a fukkin fox's ass in pokeberry time! Then quick as a' unplanned churchfart the two little possible future Aunty Belles give us a big ass hug, said, "Bye, yawl!" and zipped off down into the room where all the dancin was goin on. And that's the last we saw of the Ex-horseshoe and the Three-Arrowhead girls.

But there was a lot more lillo girls flittin here and there and boppin up and down, and every one of em was, I b'leeve, the good-lookinest females you could ever even imagine, next to the ones, of course, in *Hustler* Magazine. ChrEYEst. Me and Voyd was havin oursevs a time! And we did not want to spend no more of it right then bein gotdam diktectives! We was takin a break.

THERE WE WAS, AND, by then, evenin had come on and it had got dark outside. I stuck my head *thoo* the door and looked both ways up and down the street, and it seemed like every one of the houses was havin a Bop-a-Lee party. You never seen such carryin on in your whole fukkin life! Them little sumbiches . . . and some *mighty big sumbiches* as well, that I judged to be possibly on the football team! . . . yassuh, I mean to tell you . . . every fukkin one of them college boys and girls was havin themsevs a TIME! Son! If I hadna knowed where we was, I'da thought we'd run up on a buncha holy rollers, what with all the gotdam hoppin and boppin and leapin about and everything.

And then we understood what it all was: We'd done stumbled into one nem "frat" houses you hear about and see on television. Maybe it wouldna seemed like no big deal to some other folks, but I guarandamtee you Voyd and me and hadn never been inside one of em in our whole po' piddiful-ass lives. Whoo! Fuk a gotdam federally protected migratory waterfowl!

But you know how it is when you're young. Them college boys, every fukkin one of em, was sportn a full tank of that whatchacallit . . . *detesterone!*

Then here come one more of them little co-eds. Course she wuddn especially all that little. And thissun was a redhead and, like all the rest, could result in instant-ass death if a sumbich was to look at her, drink a Co'-Cola, and puff on a Camel cigarette. That combination right there woulda kilt any grown man I know. It was dam near unbearable. I couldn say what them *campus cuties* was full of, unless I guess you could call it *GodBlessTerone!*

Anyhow, here is the picture you need to keep in mind: There is more human beins, more noise, and more jumpin up and down per square-fukkin-inch than me and Voyd has ever been witness to. We didn know whether to grin or piss on the floor. It was like we was in the middle of a gotdam popcorn machine—with all the little "kernels" red-hot, oiled-up, and bouncin around hollerin "Hoddy Toddy!"

Anyway, this dynamite lil' trick who just come up to us looks at Voyd and says: "Hey, are you a teacher?"

Voyd looked at me, and I looked at the girl. Voyd was about to say, "Fuk no," but before he could manage to get out the, "Fuh'. . .," I told her, "Not exactly. We're private investigators."

And she said: "YAY!" But then she followed that up with, "Oh, my Gaw-wuhd, are we in truhh-buhl?"

"Nome," Voyd chimed in—I mean he WAS the one she was talkin to in the first fukkin place—"Nome," he said, "Yawl aint in no trouble whatsomever. You see . . ." And then I looked at that lillo girl, and she had done took off her T-shirt, blippity blip, just like that, and was stannin there pointn her tits at me and lookin at Voyd. Then she said, "I just luhhhhhv older mee-in! YAY!"

I didn know whether to holler Thank You Jesus or Holy Poley, so I said, "Hot Fukkin Tit Mouse!"

And Voyd said, "Thank yew!"

She grabbed ahold of my hand, looked up at me, and said, "Come on, let's dance! . . . YAY!"

"Are you one nem TchEYE Omeegases or Try-ass-Dultresses?" I ast her.

"Unh-uhn,"she said, "I'm a *Toyota Toy*. My boyfriend is a *Delta Yo'r To Cap Her*, you know, the *Dee-Eye-Kays*—they're next door to the *Fly On the Pies*! But the *Dee-Eye-Kays* are rollers, and the *Fly Or Pies* are just, well, too, you know, ookie-tookie!—like, you know, campus leaders, *Beemoseez* and everything. Anyway, my roommate is an *Alfalfa Cigareema*!"[47]

And then—you got it, Sumbich—she said, "YAY!"

I found out later that a BMOC is a "Big Man On Campus." There aint no way I'da known sumpm like that. Didn none of them names of things mean nothin to me—except the ones Mad and McKinney had made mention of. And maybe there was some fukkin link tween them two things and the Aunty Belles, only I was findin it pretty hard to see it. On the other hand, anything them

---

47   In Junior Ray's defense, the noise level was so high inside the Phi Delta Theta house that he could hear only parts of what the girl was saying. Most likely she was referring to, respectively: the Tau Iota Tau sorority, affection-ately known as the TITs; the Delta Iota Kappa fraternity, i.e., the DIK's, pronounced Dee-Eye-Kays; the Phi Omicron Pi fraternity, also called the Phi O Pi's; and the Alpha Sigma Sigma sorority. *Beemoseez* is how he heard "BMOC's," or Big Man/Men On Campus. —ml

Planters might have their hand in I wuddn gon discount one fukkin bit, but, like I said a minute ago, Voyd and me was havin oursevs a gotdam good time, and, I was thinkin some words to mysef sorta like old Clark Gable said to Scarlet-ass O'Harris: "Frankly, my dear, neither me nor Voyd gives a water-squirrel[48] fuk nor a football fart right now, cause we're gon whoop it up at Bop-a-Lee in the *Five Dollar The-Ater House!*" That, of course, might notta been word for word the words I was thinkin, but I expect you get the flavor of it.

The cute little redhead grabbed ahold of my hand and hauled my ass out of the entry hall and into the middle of the thickest crowd of movin objects you mighta ever thought to be possible this side of the big cricket-box at Tooter Tait's Bait Shop—on the Cut-Off, over in the Delta, 'cross the levee, just west of St. Leo.

Anyway, she and I commenced boppin up a storm—*me* without no sense, and *she* without no top, so, right about then, I guess you could say I was the one that wanted to holler: "YAY!"

You could just call my ass *Bop-Along Cassidy!* But now bear in mind Voyd and me is past sixty—a whole helluva lot past it. However, didn none of that seem to make the slightest bit of difference to the Bop-a-Lee *hoppers* and *boppers.* It looked to me like you coulda been a gotdam stray dog or a barnyard animal, or even a fairly large bug or a '57 Buick, and them little sumbiches woulda offered you a beer and ast your ass to dance. Further, you do realize, too, that a lot of that fukkin hospitality twit-spit comes from the way them fukkin Planters think things ought to be. It don't necessarily mean all that much, but I grant you it is nice to have. So I s'pose I can't cuss their ass if I'm drinkin their liquor and dancin with their women.

I was havin a gotdam good time and had done completely forgot all about Brainy and even why we was over there in the first place.

---

48   A beaver. —ml

Kiss my leg! I forgot about Voyd as well until all of a fukkin sudden I realized I did not know where that little fukka was. That always did worry me, and it worried me then, so I 'scused mysef and went back up into the entry way, but he wuddn there. I looked thissaway and thattaway, and no Voyd. I went th'oo the house and out the back door, but no Voyd. Then I walked around again to where I'd been and looked at the stairs. College boys and co-eds was still setn on the steps; then there was some who was comin down em, and there was a bunch that was goin up. Something inside, and not too deep neither, told me to join the crowd goin up.

So, I got on the steps and kept on steppin till I got to the top, where I wandered around and looked into rooms and shit like that, hope'n to find Voyd, but all I seen was arms and legs and underpants. And a carload of empty whisky bottles.

Plus, there was another fukkin floor. The gotdam house had three gotdam-ass whole, full-size floors! And, as it turned out, there was a' attic as well, which coulda been considered a fourth floor! So I climbed the narrow little steps up to it. When I come to the top of those stairs, I seen that it wuddn a whole lot of space just right there but I spied a closed door directly on my left, and anuddn, just as directly, on my right.

I opened the one on the right, and it was darker'n a muthafukka, but I could see it was fulla trunks and lamps and card tables, and random lumps of stuff, so I shut that door and turned toward the other'n. That's when I heard the whisperinn and the gigglin. Well, it was whisperin, but it was loudish. And the gigglin didn scare me like it did way long ago when Voyd and me was out in the woods near the Coldwater River lookin for Leland Shaw.[49] Fuk knockin, I thought, so I just gave the door a good-ass push, and, whoosh, it opened right up! I looked straight into what appeared to obviously

---

49 See *Junior Ray*, NewSouth 2005. —ml

be a big meetin room, and at the far end of it I seen Voyd. There that little butthole was. This time he wuddn setn there nekkid in no country-ass Nigga juke-joint, playin strip poker. Nope a'Nope a'Nopa. This time he was setn there nekkid in a gotdam black, wooden, cheap-ass coffin with three Bop-a-Lee partners—and they was nekkid, too. They was all twined up together like three gotdam telephone cords. Anyway, Voyd and *two* of his partyin' pals looked at me and said, "Come on in! Get in here with us! We're havin our funeral now, so we won't have to have one later!" And they all fell out laughin, drunker'n shit.

So there was Voyd, in his silly-ass sixties, scrunched up in a coffin grinnin like a hung-up hound, with two good-lookin nekkid fully grown-up women. One introduced herself as a professor of *Partnership and Agency* at the Law School. She had a head full of that real good-lookin kinda gray hair you see on some older women who look better'n a whole lot of younger ones. The other gal reached out like she wanted to shake my hand and told me she was the *Assistant Tennis Coach;* then she made, I hav' to say, a pretty good joke that it took "balls" to be that, and I agreed it did.

And the *third* sumbich, snuggled up there with em in that coffin, was a gotdam skeleton! And he—or she—didn have much to say one way or another. I couldn hep but get the idea the po' bastuhd was just one nem muthafukkas that don't never like to leave college, like Mad Owens's *uncle Jossum* who, they say, hung around a' extra year or so up in Virginia at *W-and Fukkin-L* where he volunteered to hep coach the football team just so he wouldn't have to come home. Fuk. That's fine. I can see it. I might notta wanted to leave neither . . . if W-and-Fukkin-L was anything like Bop-a-Lee. I don't know about the goin-to-school part. But, I had already seen that even if I was to en-roll somewhere, I wouldn be talkin about no gotdam *Junior* College. I doubt any of them little skimpy joints *has* a Bop-a-Lee.

Anyway, ChrEYEst, for all I know that skeleton coulda got hissef locked up there in that gotdam room and didn nobody find his fra-gile ass till a year later. Then of course it was too fukkin late, and they probly just didn have the heart to tell the sumbich to leave. Fuk, I don't know. That's a joke. Here, pull my finger![50]

Anyhow, just sizin up the way the room looked and all, I judged the gotdam skeleton somehow or another to be a necessary part in whatever it was that fraternity needed to do from time to time to be a coksukkin fraternity. They're bound to a'had secrets, like the Masons. Only, possibly in a college fraternity, unlike the Masons, the secrets might notta been all that nailbite'n important, not enough anyway for em to kill you, I mean, if you was to let a few slip. Fuk if I know. I was just guessin.

Voyd, I suppose you could say, had done pretty much defiled the secret meetn room of the national *Five Dollar The-Ater House* Fraternity, which, as I found out later, was the tip-top one in the whole gotdam school. See, them boys' daddies was all Planters and doctors and lawyers and bankers and such, which, of course, *is why* the gotdam house had three—and dam near four—fukkin floors! So, it was a good thing I got Voyd—that little burpa-cola—out before anybody could give a yeehaw cowfuk if we was ever there in the first place, which is what I did.

"Get up from there, Voyd," I said, "and put your clothes on before I arrest your ass for abuse of the elderly." The law teacher didn pay no 'tention to that, but the Assistant Tennis Coach gave me a big frown; then she and the lady Law Professor commenced to kiss. ChrEYEst. Take me out, Coach!

By the time I finally got Voyd more or less into his clothes,

---

50   I did not pull Junior Ray's finger. He does that all the time, and I just ignore it, although he really doesn't need his finger pulled to fart. He thinks it is hilarious, and he did it all during the "talking" of his first book with young Mr. Brainsong II, who eventually had to seek professional help. —ml

and we was goin out the door of the meetn room, the two women had done sunk way down outa sight into the black wooden coffin, and there was only the skinny-ass skeleton setn up there for us to wave 'bye to.

"Bye, Slim," said Voyd.

"Rock on, Mr. Death," I said to that college skeleton's old bony sef. Then, for some reason—I can't say why—I pointed to Voyd, who was totally shitfaced, and I spoke again to the skeleton and said: "How do you like your blue-eyed boy?"[51]

At that, the brittle-ass coksukka winked at me and said: "Fuk you, Junior Ray. I'mo see yo' ass later!"

But I told the sumbich, "That aint sumpm I'm dyin to do." Ha ha. That's another joke, muthafukka. Here, pull my finger.

VOYD PASSED OUT BEFORE I could get him back to the house where we left Brainy, so I shoved him up underneath a juniper bush on the side of that main-ass buildin with the fukkin colyums on it. I walked on to Professor Piddlesby's old ramblin-ass house and found Brainy up on the po'ich smokin a see-gar with one hand and holdn what he called a "snifta" in the other. The professor had long gone off to bed, and Brainy said he knew Voyd and me—or one or the other of us—would show back up SOMEtime, so he decided he'd just make hissef comf'table. Which he did. And that's where I found him, *sniftin* away.

"We ought to head back to the Delta," he said. "But where's Voyd?"

"I left him under a bush back yonder at the school," I said. "But we can drive in there and I'll tho'w his drunk ass in the car."

Brainy said that sounded just fine, and that is what we did. On the way home to St. Leo, Brainy wanted to know where we'd been

---

51 Has the mind of Junior Ray somehow collided with the soul of e. e. cummings? —ogbii

and how Voyd got so fukked up, so I told him all about *Bop-a-Lee* and me dancin up a storm and, then, about findin Voyd in the coffin with the two women professoresses—or one professoress and a coach*esse*, hell, I don't know—and I told him about the skeleton, too.

Brainy said he knew about the skeleton because, the fact was, he had been a *Five Dollar The-Ater Houser,* hissef, and his "friend," Chumly, had been a FYE OMICRON PYE—like them little diklikkas in the house that was next door to where we was—way back when both of em had first went to college, up in Ohio. It's a funny fukkin world.

"Dang," I said. "I be dog!" I mean, what else could a sumbich say?

Anyway, I was drivin, and it wuddn long before Brainy popped off to sleep, too. So there I was, all a-fukkin-lone, with Brainy asleep and Voyd passed-out, drivin through the dark of night outa the gotdam Hills and back home down into the fukkin Delta, thinkin about the skeleton.

FOR A WEEK AND a half after that little blow-out I could not get Voyd to stop goin on about how we was in a fraternity house over at the Uni-fukkin-versity.

"Lemme show you the handshake, Junior Ray."

"Gotdammit, you little fukhed," I said. "You don't no mo' know a secret handshake than if you was a jaybird. It's a good thing, Voyd, you never did get to go to no college, or I truly don't believe I'd be able to stand it."

"Fuk you, Junior Ray," he said.

And I said to him: "That is the last time I am ever takin you with me over to Bop-a-Lee *every* again! I cannot depend on your sorry ass—and I aint gon let you show me no coksukkin SECRET HANDSHAKE."

Plus, I told him: "You coulda got both of us in trouble, old as we are, boppin around with them co-eds—and then I have to hunt all over the gotdam place and finally find you setn up in a coffin, nekkid, with two of the professoresses and a grinnin gotdam jackalant'n!"

"They was nekkid, too," he said. "And the skeleton aint gon say nothin."

Junior Ray's Famous Ole Miss Cutie-Frutie Pie

Ole Miss Cutie-Frutie Pie is a fukkin pie, made with peaches, apples, cherries, blue berries, pears, and some PECANS—because, as you know, them Ole Miss Cuties is nuts. Ha Ha. That's a joke, gotdammit. Anyway, here's what you do:

1. Get two ready-made pie crusts—(a) one for the bottom, and (b) use the other'n for a top, and (c) this is not as easy as it sounds.

2. Sweeten up your fruit and pecans with honey or brown sugar.

3. Dump in the mixed-up fruit and pecans.

4. Cook it in the oven.

5. Eat it with low-fat ice cream or frozen yogurt. I learned about yogurt from the Hippies, although folks used to eat it when I was a little boy, only they called it clabber. It mighta been a little different but not all that much.

CHAPTER NINE

River Rats—Junior Ray Is Not Perry Mason—Shaw Longs for
High Water—The Threater Was Unafraid—Little Quitman
Tait's Hand-Ripened Tomatoes—Recipe No. 10: Junior Ray's
Famous Forbidden-Fruit Peach P'zerves

Over the levee, the Evans's woods, as some of you know, were a good mile south of where that family of river rats used live. I aint got nothin against river rats; I just don't know what else to call em. Anyway, their shanty boat stayed down at the foot of the levee on the wet side at the edge of the woods till I swear it flat-out went back to the fukkin earth. It was all just planks and wuddn no metal in it a-tall. And in the Delta if you take your eye off sumpm for half a gotdam second, it'll rot. And that shanty did exactly that and rotted away to just a' outline on the ground.

But it sat down there forever, and once some Boy Sprouts, I reg'n, rigged up a sail on the thing with a big two-by-four and a bedsheet. A lot of times the Sprouts' mamas and daddies would carry em out there and drop em off, and the little sumbiches would camp out there a couple a hunnud yards away from that old shanty boat, where they'd fuk around for about two days on the side of a bar' pit[52] and play in the quicksand, which right there

---

52   "Bar' pit," pronounced "baah" pit, is colloquial for "barrow" pit or "borrow" pit, the name given to the numerous scooped-out, square and oblong depressions over on the wet side of the levee that were left when dirt was excavated to build the great earthen two-hundred-mile dam put there to prevent the Mississippi River from flooding the Mississippi Delta, a peculiar alluvial plain of legend and song, a.k.a. the Yazoo Basin, as it did in 1927. —ml

wuddn but about two feet deep. Dumb little fukkas.

Anyway they tied the two-by-four to the front end of the cabin with what looked like it coulda been several hundred yards of clothes line, made into one long-ass piece from four-million lillo short sections knotted together. I aint never seen anything like it. Me and Voyd had noticed the line back when we was chasin around after that crazy sumbich Leland Shaw. I didn think much about it at the time, but I recall that a good while later two or three ladies in town phoned up Sheriff Holston to say somebody—and they figured it was teenagers—had took down their clothes lines; and one lady said whoever done it had also stolc a couple of her bed sheets.

Defeats me. Anyway, we didn pay much attention to it at the time, and we still didn connect the shanty with the ladies' phone call. For one thing, the ladies was all in town, and the old home-made houseboat was outchonda on the other side of the gotdam levee. I mean, I was just a deputy, not no fukkin Perry Mason.

ALMOST ALL OF THIS current problem with the murder and the threaters' letters to Brainy has to do with Leland Shaw's "Notes," which is, as far as I am concerned, mostly goat pills, pure-dee old rabbitcrap, which as you know don't amount to nothin neither; and it galls me to even be associated with it, although I guess I *am* and somehow aint never not gon be.

Hate is a funny-ass thing. Mad's write'n duddn bother me none, but that crazy Leland Shaw's stuff does bother me, just the same as he, hissef, has always bothered me—I mean it's the very fukkin *idea* of him even bein on this earth that bothers me. I can't hep it; it chaps my ass. Why the fuk I still tolerate bein anywhere near it is the biggest gotdam mystery there is, if you ast me.

But whoa Jackass! Speakin of Shaw, that sumbich shoulda been a major league pitcher 'cause he can sho th'ow a gotdam curve. If you recall what I just said a minute ago about that old empty, mostly rotten shanty boat me and Voyd took a look at over cross the levee, you'll want to take a big ass look at this part below—it's gon be in Brainy's "publication" of Shaw's "Notebooks." Now bear in mind, Shaw never believed he was home after World War Number Two, and so he spent his en-tire insanity on tryin to get back to Mississippi even though he was hidn out in the Delta the whole time.

FROM LELAND SHAW'S "NOTES":

Never a coastal citizen, I knew only a little about sailsmanship. I know about tacking. I believe I could tack. And that bit of mariner's knowledge should serve me well enough when I find the high water and, of course, a boat, but I don't anticipate a problem . . . and, if there is one, I shall construct a craft and install a mast.

My God! How can I have been so oblivious? If I am to take advantage of the high water—whenever and wherever it shall be—I must have a boat. And as I have no talent for machinery, I will most certainly have to fashion a sail.

I know just where to go first. Right on the other side of the levee, at the very bottom of it and to the left of the road that goes out to Bird-o, which, of course, is spelled "Bordeaux," there is an abandoned fisherman's shantyboat. It was Troy's house, where he lived with his father and mother and three little sisters.

Troy. Where is he? Where is the family? Where are any of the fisherman? Where are the fish? Where, oh, where am . . . I? I am not six anymore or ten, and I have long passed through Mhoon County Elementary, long gone, too, from flash cards and long division, far removed as well from recess and boys against the girls, mumblety-peg, marbles and tops, no more softball, touch football and tag. Swallowed up. Swept away. And Troy with it.

But his old home-made floating house is still there. *But*, for Heaven's sake, I have been here in this grand facsimile now for fourteen years.

I should know there are no more commercial fishermen living out across the levee, and no Troy either, because I am not where this is. Or, more accurately, THIS is not where I am.

In both cases it is all a huge illusion on an enormous scale. I do not get it. The why of it is incomprehensible. I only know the "it" of it, not the where or the when or . . . its reason for being, unless the it-ness has something to do with me. There are too many "its." And I have an impulse to swat them.

Thus, am I to assume the abandoned houseboat is a trap? That is too much. A trap within a trap. Yet one cannot assume the best or that all is well in a place where people run around in rubber suits, impersonating Negroes.

However, the question of a vessel is answered, and if the shanty-boat has no leaks, the next piece of business is to find the sail and a mast to mount it on, and I am going to have to acquire some tools. But maybe not.

There are some very long two-by-fours on the west bank of Nahollotubbe Bayou,[53] right by the bridge, on the way to the levee. Aha! Yo-Oh, Heave HO! Sails are available on every clothes line, and I can use the clothes line, too, to lash the mast to Troy's buoyant former home. I knew I could depend upon the buffalo,[54] and I bless their dangerous bones.

Yes. *In medias res* was what it is. Away from field and thicket, gone past slough and sluggish stream, beyond the knees of cypress trees, then in The River and on to the salty pond, and, by that, I mean the Gulf of Mexico, a name which I have always thought was somewhat arbitrary when, in fact, that great body of magnificent slosh might just as legitimately be called the Gulf of Mississippi.

I shall put in "Two Years Before the Mast," rivaling the achieve-

---

53 From Choctaw/Chickasaw: *nahollo*, white man + "t" for elision + *abe*[ubbe], killer = White Man Killer Bayou (pronounced: bye-oh). —ml
54 A large freshwater fish with infamous bones. —ml

ments of Sir Joshua Slocumb. All I shall need is my ship! . . . a knife and a blanket and, most certainly, a strong line and a few good hooks. An adventurer has to eat.

The beauty of entering the channel of The River is that I won't require a sail at all but can ride southward swiftly on the hydrologic power of the nation. I see myself upon the deck scanning the course ahead, as I and my craft pitch forward, roll, and yaw a little in the cool clear air and the bright brilliance of an early spring sunshine, and I shall imagine I am as unassailable as a Southern Baptist.

The contradictions are unavoidable. For example, how am I to know The River is actually *The River* and not merely a clever extension of my imprisonment? In other words how shall I know it is real? I cannot see around every bend, and for all I know, the thing that appears to be The River may in fact stop and go nowhere at all around one of the bends to the south.

That is to say, why would the Mississippi River, here, be real if the bank I stand on is not Mississippi? The answer to that is simple. It's a matter of time. When the high water comes, then, I will know The River is real, and I can know that even though the dry land around it *is not*— That's just it: the dry land won't be around it when the flood comes. But the core of the truth is that no matter where a person is, it is the high water that connects him to all there is on the earth, or at least to the edges of it and right up inside a large measure of it, near enough to all things to put all things in range, so to speak.

Mu-tha-fuk! That defeats the doodah out of me. But I want to get back to the fukkin isssue at hand, the *threater letters*. Even though everybody involved in the investigation was not a professional like I am, we could tell pretty much the letters was not wrote by different people—and, as I have also emphasized, it seemed to be pretty obvious that that one person was a gotdam female, mainly from the sissified look of the handwrite'n and all. That was the easy part.

But, *why*, I ast your ass, *why*, when you think about it, *was it* the *threater* her-probable-sef done the letters in hand instead of scissorin out the words from books and magazines and such. That was puzzlin as a beavergator at first until I realized it didn make no difference. The woman was certain she wuddn never likely to get caught. Even if she *was* caught, wuddn much likely to be said about it! She knew that as far as killin men is concerned, most women down here figure there is always a good excuse for doin that. So there it is. Her ass was covered.

For one thing, look at it thissa way: Just the letters themsevs didn do nobody no actual bodily harm! Second of all, there really wuddn no connection that you could hands-down out and out *prove* between the threater letters and those three po-ass sumbiches that did get killed. I am not countn Miz Potts.

I don't even think no famous dicktectives, even ones as good as O'Grady Quinton up in Meffis was—and that list includes Dick Tracy, Sam Ketchum, Mike Hammer, and Sam-fukkin-Spade— there-bygod-fore, I hereby fukkin say none of them sumbiches, neither, coulda tied the *perpertratess* in this case to them three murders. Not with no square knot anyway.

I mean, slick as all them sumbiches are that I just named, I don't think they coulda handled the situation here in the Delta. And, yes, I did give some thought to goin to Meffis to see the F-B-ass-EYE. But I didn believe they'd be able to get the job done neither. That's when I realized it was up to me an Voyd to crack the case.

There was actually a total of ten letters all together, and ever fukkin one of em was mailed from—you got it . . . *Clarksdale* . . . That's one of the main reasons I couldn hep but suspect Miss Attica because she was all the time runnin down to the Clarksdale

Country Club for one little thing or another, and, of course, remember, she had her sister down that way, Miss Laconia, who, fortunately for the deceased, was a widow. She had been married[55] to one nem big-ass bourbon-drinkin Planters a little north of Clarksdale, between there and Moon Lake, right off Ranjel[56] Road, over toward the river.[57]

Later on, Miss Laconia contracted *Old-Timers* and didn have no mind whatsoever, so they put her in a nursin home. She'd lay there like a dead bug. But you wouldna known the difference. Somebody said she was kinda like one nem Egyptian mummies, only when they fed her she could eat a gotdam Cadillac. She was a teenyweeny thing, and they said she could suck up peas and carrots and mashed potatoes like a fukkin four-row cotton picker. It must be sumpm to own twelve thousand acres and not know it. Shit, it must be sumpm to *be alive* and not know it, although I expect more folks than a' average sumbich might imagine are runnin around *uninformed*. Anyway, as a diktective, it was hard for me not to keep thinkin about Miss Attica. Just something about her was hard to get away from. So, old Voyd and me set our sights on her and her alone.

BUT RIGHT NOW, SINCE you've heard me talk a lot about Clarksdale, I have *got* to tell you some more about Little Quitman Tait. You remember[58] he was a part owner of the Magic Pussy Cabaret & Club up in Meffis without none of his immediate or even any of his distant kin knowin nothin about it. Plus, you know I mentioned he further had a notion he would like to open up what he called

---

55   In the Delta, even married women were referred to as "Miss," followed by their first names. —ml
56   Hernando de Soto's private secretary, 1541. —ml
57   The Mississippi. —ml
58   Junior Ray is referring to his second book, *The Yazoo Blues*, NewSouth, 2008. —ml.

the Quitman County Bathhouse, out in the middle of nowhere, as a place for rich people from Meffis to come to and take baths, and get involved in a whole lot more besides. Little Quit was a pistol-ball even when he wuddn no older'n twelve or thirteen. And since then, I can tell you he has had hissef a time! Anyway, I know him fairly well, for a lot of reasons, and I couldn't let you go on no longer without hearin what I'm about to tell you.

First of all anybody who is even barely-ass acquainted with the little sumbich knows he can get away with just about everything, mainly because he can talk anybody into anything. He can sell you your own gotdam front yard if he decides to. Anyway, he's a helluva sumbich, and I have always liked him, even if he is one nem Planters.

He growed up in Clarksdale, down in Coahoma County, but he and his family still has a few acres—of-fukkin-*course*—over in Quitman County, more or less next door. They even has some bottom land up in the Hills, in *Tate* County—see, *Tate* County is named for the Tait side of their family, however, because of some hoohaw they had among em, some of the Taits and the Tates changed how they spelt their name, and I don't know if it was the Taits or the Tates who done the changin. But all that's another story and not what I want to talk about now.

When Quit was in high school they sent his ass up to Chattanooga, TENnessee, but he'd come home in the summers. And one summer he took a notion to see if he could make some money on his own, so he decided to sell tomatoes. He didn grow em, but he didn have to. That little sco'fa went out and around and persuaded a' old black preacher and his wife to let him have a shot at sellin *their* tomato crop—they usually had two or three acres of em every year, and people in Clarksdale always bought the old preacher's tomatoes, but every year there was a lot that did not get sold and had to be th'owed away, or give to somebody's hogs.

Anyway, Little Quit talked to the Fed-Ex guy—there was a truck that come to Clarksdale every day and—I guess you could say *alerted* the driver to what he, hissef—Little Quit—was up to, so he had that nailed down, along with his weights and costs and times and things; then he put a' ad in one nem rich-ass sumbich magazines—*Money & Country*, or *Elegant-Ass Livin*, some such as that—which a lot of well-heeled muthafukkas up North apparently all like to read, and his ad *said*:

Direct to you—
Legendary Mississippi Delta Hand-Ripened Tomatoes!
Hand-Ripe Gardens
1609 Red Panther Lane
Clarksdale, Mississippi 36476

And as you might imagine, he did not wait till he got home for the summer that year to set a lot of that up. Anyhow, the little scownbooga got all his ducks in a row, and the next thing him and his whole family and the old black preacher and his wife knew, wuddn none of em getn no sleep at all for havin to fill orders and ship em out. Little Quit nearly give his daddy, his mama, his little sister, his cousin Hopson Burdine, and the preacher and his wife major heart attacks on account of the stress—and his daddy, Big Quit, swore that if he could hep it he wuddn never gon let that little diklikka ever try to make no more money the rest of his smart little, wild-ass life.

However, the preacher and his wife was happier'n a sow eat'n sorghum. That was one thing about Quitman, he was straight as a' arrow. Even though he *was* one nem Planters, his people had a reputation for bein good to their labor, black or white, and they was all mostly like Little Quit was, so, as you know, I have always made exceptions when a' exception was due. He wouldna cheated nobody—except maybe those fart-heds up North—to save his life.

Yet, there it was, the phone calls and the letters was comin in, with people sayin how they had to have some of them "hand-ripened" tomatoes; and after a while the people, them mostly up North, who handed Little Quit that crokersack full of orders, all swore they'd never tasted nothin like them Miss'ssippi Delta Hand-Ripened Tomatoes and they was dyin to have more.

I thought: "Mercy on my ass!" How could those fukkadukkas up there in wherever the doodah they are and who won the Civil-Gotdam-War be so ass-kickin dumb? How, I ast mysef, did they think a tomato, in the Mississippi Delta or anywhere else, got ripe in your gotdam hand?

Later on in the fall, after he'd done gone back up to that military school in Chattanooga, the FBI come to see him. His daddy went to the outskirts of Heartattack City again, over that! Sumpm about inta-fukkin-state commerce and false claims. ChrEYEst. They got Lawyer Cutrer[59] on the case, and he telephoned Senator Stimson and Congressman Alcorn Smith, and between the three of em they managed to keep the whole thing quiet and got the U.S. Government to let little Quit alone if he would promise not to sell anymore tomatoes.

Like Lawyer Montgomery, a long time ago, in St. Leo, if you had Lawyer Cutrer, down in Clarksdale, on your case, *none of it never* went to trial. It has always impressed me what them Mississippi Planters could do on a national scale. And some of it I approve of, mainly because I hate pissy-anty systems and standin in line and signin my name and dipshit stuff of that nature. The Planters all seem to be able to do things the old way, and the truth is I do like that much better than the way things generally has gotten to be. It is also true that maybe the old way has not always

59   Pronounced Kew-traire. —ml

worked in my favor, but I know it would have if I had ever needed it to and had ast the right muthafukka to step in. My problem was I just never was big on askin nobody for sumpm. Fukkum.

And them Planters: You can't touch'em! You just fukkin cannot touch emm coksukkas. It don't matter how *right* you are or how dum-ass *wrong* one nem sumbiches is, you aint ever gon touch their ass.

The whole thing really pisses me off, and I can't hep thinkin' about what Quitman told me one time. Bein part of that Planter crowd, he goes to huge-ass blowouts every whipstitch up at that biggest and oldest of all them so-called *country* clubs in Meffis, which in fukkin fact is setn right smack on the edge one of the biggest and oldest Nigga sections up there. It's called Green Pastures, and I guess all them Planters and old rich cotton business coksukkas up there that built the club put it where it is so they'd be snug up next to a steady supply of cheap hep and trusty-ass straw bosses.[60] Hell, I don't know. Fukkum.

Anyway, Quit says he's seen plenty of screwin bumpin up and down in what they calls the Scarlet Room. He says it goes on there in plain sight when the room is plum fulla people, all drinkin Scotch whiskey and havin' theysefs a helluva time. He claims it's easy if your date's got on one nem big-ass hunnud-dollar party dresses and aint wearin no panties. Quit says all she's got to do is set on your lap. Frontways of course. So you can kiss, too.

He never told me nothin about no dope there, other'n Scotch whiskey and such, but it coulda been present all the same, already inside the folks, who mighta got it from their doctors and then popped it before they walked in the door. To my mind, though, if a sumbich has all that much money to be hangin out at a place like that, and a glass of good whiskey, he don't need no powder to

---

60   A black in charge of a plantation's workforce would not be referred to as a "manager." He was called the "straw boss." —ml

make his ass feel no better'n it already does. Plus, the po-lice aint gon raid the Scarlet Room. They couldn get past the gate.

Now, SUMBICH, IF YOU want to add another "forbidden" fruit recipe to your kitchen skills, try the one called:

Junior Ray's Famous
Forbidden-Fruit Peach P'zerves

Step One: Hire you two or three lillo boys to sneak over some evenin into Scrap Nelson's peach orchard right when them fuzzy sumbiches are fallin off the trees, and . . . you get the fukkin pitcha. The p'zerves are forbidden because the fruit belongs to somebody else.

Step Two: See if you can find a Presbyterian lady to make the p'zerves for you.

Step Three: Label the jar.

CHAPTER TEN

Why Brainy Comes to Live in Mhoon County—Brainy
Has a Friend—Cholmondeley (Chumly)—Brainy Is a
Queer—A Family Thing—Sunflower Opens a Store—The
Obzhay Boodywoowoo—Areeva Drtchi—Ms. Drtchi
Recommends Stethoscopes—We Spy on Miss Attica—The
First Surveillance—Beneath the House—"Wipe Yo Foots,
White Man!"—Recipe No. 10: Junior Ray's Famous
Supersonic Oyster Stew

Course the letters—well, three of em—started droppin in on Brainy while he was still livin in Cali-fuk-assin-forn-ya, at about the same time he had done made it known he was movin to St. Leo and had already rented an apartment up in the north end of town, in that triplex I guess you'd call it. He told me later on that, if he could afford to, he wanted him a house made out of rough cypress boards, and he said he might want it to be located out in the country on the side of a slough. And I thought to mysef that ought not to be too hard to do because, as you know, sloughs are one of our major features here. Show me a house by a slough, and I'll show you a snake in the kitchen cabinet. Plus a mosquito as big as a gotdam crow. Yet, all in all, I suppose that is part of the charm.

Why, you might ask, did young Mr. Brainsong want to come to live in St. Leo, here in Mhoon County, after havin what seemed like such a hard-ass time bein around me—even though you know all that changed, and him and me and Voyd is now damm good friends. And I have come to like "Brainy" a helluva lot because I respect his ass, and because, well, I tend to *like* a sumbich who *likes* me. That's my definition of a worthwhile muthafukka.

Anyway, more on the word "like": Brainy told me the decision to move to the Mississippi Delta just come to him one day, out there in Lost Angeleez. And here's what I mean. He said he was ride'n along past where they made the movies, and he said it just suddenly struck his ass that wuddn nothin out there anything in itsef, but, instead, it was all just sort of "like" somethin, and he made up his mind then and there that he did not want to live and die in a place where things was only "like" somethin and not actually sumpm in themsevs. He wanted to be in a place that *was* somethin, not *like* somethin.

So, he said he couldn think of no place he'd ever seen that was more *unlike* any other place he could think of than the Mississippi Delta. There it was, kablam, and he set about getn ready to move that very afternoon.

ChrEYEst. He went on to say that people out there all worked extra hard to tryin to be "different" but that people in Mhoon County didn have to try at all. They just flat-ass couldn help bein like nothin else on this fukkin earth. When he told me he was movin here, I said for him to come on—and to fuk them sumbiches out there. If he didn want to be around em, I figured I wouldn have no use for em neither, with the exception of maybe Randolph Scott, and Johnny Mack Brown. And, of course, Dale Evans. Abbott and Costello was on my list too. Even *I* know you can't just ditch the whole wagon load on account of a few million bad apples.

Anyway, we kep' on a talkin:

"I have a 'friend,' Junior Ray," he said.

"Fine," I said, "I got one or two mysef."

"I mean," he said, "I . . . have . . . a . . . *friend.*"

"Well, fuk," I said. "That's good."

He didn say nothin for a minute; then he come out with, "His name is Chumly."

Later on he showed me it was spelled "Cholmondeley" and was a name some sumbiches here and there had over in England, only this sumbich was from Cincinnati, and him and Brainy had started out in college together as ass'ole buddies back up in Ohio. Anyway, it did take a minute or so for me to see what I was lookin at, and then I caught on and thought to mysef: ChrEYEst! Brainy was one of *them*! And so is the other sumbich!

"Mu-tha-fuk!," I thought. "Brainy is a queer!" For another minute or three, I didn know what to do, but then it come to me: It was a family thing. And that was it. Just like his uncle, Mr. Brainsong—*Mr. Brainsong*. So that settled the whole issue, and I said, "Well, hell, Brainy, I think that's just fine. What's the sumbich do for a livin?"

Brainy looked like somebody'd just lifted a fukkin truck off his ass, and he said, "He's a writer, Junior Ray. Chumly is a very wonderful—and splendidly sensitive—writer."

And I immediately thought: Great. The world needs another fukkin writer like it needs another coksukka from Arkansas.

Anyway, Brainy got hissef a friend, and . . .

Chumly turned out to be a sight. That sumbich liked to run around Brainy's apartment in light purple pajamas with pictures of pies and cake printed all over em. And he wore big fluffy pink house slippers. I liked Chumly. Hell, he was always nice to me. I didn care if he was a queer, except I mostly always would walk over to their place so nobody would see my Explorer setn outside it. That's one good thing about a little town. People who walk are invisible, kind of like Leland Shaw was. Don't get me started on that. ChrEYSt.

BUT BACK TO BRAINY. "Damm," I said. "If you're getn death threats mailed to you from Clarksdale, Mississippi, why in God's name did you move from Lost Angeleez over to here in the Delta where the fukkin threaters is?"

"I know," he said. "It doesn't appear to make much sense."

"No, it don't," I told him.

"Well," he said, I simply had to decide which death was worse."

That lost my ass, and I said, "Hawnh?"

"Junior Ray, have you ever been to Barstow?"

I told him I hadn and also didn know what or where the fuk it was, and he said if I ever did go there, I'd know in a flash what he was talkin about. However, I did ast him if the whole shootn match was like Barstow, and he said, "Yes, it is, in one way or another."

And then he explained that some parts of Califukkinfornia had trees and that, once in while when there wuddn no smog,[61] you could see em. But he said, where he was at, even though it was in Lost Angeleez, it was all pretty much like Barstow.

He did make it a point to tell me that things was somewhat different and a whole lot better in Northern California but that the main problem he had out there was what he called "anonymity." That meant out there he didn have no kinfolks—plus, nobody else had none neither. And he laid it out to me that, bygod, he did not want to die "anonymously."

I told his ass I agreed with him one-hunnud percent, even though I did not have the "smoggiest" idea what the fuk he was talkin about.

SUNFLOWER GOT HERSEF A store in Meffis. And it is somewhat *connected* to this whole episode and to Voyd and me's diktective skills. Anyway, it aint exactly a store; it's a gotdam booth, and it's

---

61   Junior Ray has established his familiarity with smog in Chapter Three. —ml

in one nem so-called antique malls that have done cropped up all over the fukkin place.

And as you might imagine nothin would do but that Sunflower had to give her booth—which she calls her *store*—a funny-ass *Frenchy-fied* name. I don't know what it means or even how to say it cause I don't know no fukkin French. And she don't neither, but the closest thing to the name of Sunflower's fukkin boo-teek is sumpm like *Dez Obzhay Boodywoowoo*. At least that's what I call it. Anyway, fuk all that foreign crap. When you get beyond a pile of skinny-ass fried potatoes, that's about it for me as far as French is concerned.

But that's not why I brought it up. Voyd said the woman that has the "store" *next* to the *Obzhay Boodywoowoo* is, or was—hell, he don't know—*also* a private diktective!—who had worked in the East Meffis area many years and had therefore dealt with more ungodly carryin-on than you could shake your dik at—mainly because East Meffis had now got to be so full of people from the part of Meffis known as Midtown—which as you know is just TROUBLE spelt with a capital "M"—and that she could maybe hep us some to find out who's sendin those death-threat letters to Brainy.

Anyway, Voyd said Sunflower ast him if we wanted to talk with "Areeva," who, I guess, was originally some kind of fukkin foreigner because her last name is *Drtchi*.[62] But Sunflower assured our ass it aint no gotdam Eye-talian name neither; it's sumpm worse. But I don't give a tunafish fingerfuk about that.

Miz Drtchi was a big old girl and a lot of help. She wuddn half bad lookin neither, so one afternoon when Voyd wuddn with me, and Sunflower had the day off, I went up to Meffis to see Miz Drtchi. She talked to me a long-ass time because I guess the antique business was a little slow that day. Miz Drtchi provided me with

---

62   Junior Ray pronounced it *Duhr-chee*.

several useful ways to obtain information on the sly. Course I do have considerable law enforcement experience—and I guess you could say Voyd does too—but that experience was mostly with actual sumbiches, right up on em, if you know what I mean, and th'owin their ass in the back of the patrol car and haulin em to jail. We was more like a SWAT team cause we didn have to fuk around and prove nothin. So I figured her *diktective* tips could come in handy.

For instance, she recommended I get Voyd and me some gotdam stethoscopes!. . . as well as a tape recorder and a wind-up alarm clock.

In addition, Miz Drtchi told me we might want to have a spyglass, and a camera, too, with what she called a "zoom" lens. Plus, she reminded me that we needed to have our vehicles in tip-top shape at all times so we wouldn never break down and not be able to leave un-noticed from a stake-out, and she emphasized that bein un-noticed was the biggest thing to keep in mind and, she figured, was goin to be hardest thing of all for me and Voyd to do. Last, however, she said Voyd and me had to per*fect* the art of "tailin." In other words, if we had to follow a suspect from St. Leo down Highway 61 all the way to Clarksdale cause we thought the suspect—well, Miss Attica—was gon go there to mail a letter, it was *e-fukkin-sential* that the su*s*pect not sus*pect* we was behind em. Me and Voyd had already covered that, but, never-the-gotdam-less, I looked at Miz Drtchi, blinked, and said: "Oh."

Anyway, even though I am a seasoned law-enforcement professional, stayin concealed on Highway 61 would be pretty hard to do, because if you've ever been on Highway 61, you know there aint nowhere to hide, nowhere a-tall, and if you have to stay far enough back so they can't see you're there, then, sumbich, you aint gon be able to see if *they are there!*

Things wuddn gon be easy. Yet I was determined. So, without sayin boo-turkey to nobody, I got the stethoscopes. But I didn buy none of the other stuff.

I DROVE THAT VERY day, after my talk with Miz Drtchi, to the store right in there on a corner near the Baptist Hospital on Madison where the nurses and doctors buy a lot their gear, and I come back home with a couple of fukkin stethoscopes. But, maybe it was because I was getn into bein super-secretive I held off tellin Voyd, and I also did not inform his ass about my conversation with Ms. Drtchi, mainly because I wanted him to think that usin the stethoscopes was all my idea. Fuk . . . a . . . duck.

Voyd come by my house on a Monday evenin so we could watch *Crime Solvers Incorporated*, which as you know is about a company of private diktectives that gets to the bottom of *haynus*-ass crimes the police aint able to do nothin with. He looked at the plastic sack and said, "What's in the sack?"

I didn give him no answer and said, "We're gon spy on Miss Attica."

"But, how do we spy on an old fat woman, Junior Ray?" Voyd ast.

"We have to use *stealth*, Voyd," I said. "We can't never let her think we are anywhere around. We got to be invisible."

"Bull-fuk on *that!*" said Voyd. "That's just bull-fuk. How in the hell are we supposed to be invisible, Junior Ray? You are about as invisible as one nem L'Turno super-earthmovers."[63]

Then I pulled the stethoscopes out of the sack and laid em on the coffee table.

"Here, Voyd, take one of these h'yeahn."

"What are those?" Voyd ast.

"Those, muthafukka," I said, "are stethoscopes, like the doctors uses on your chest to hear your heartbeat."

"What are we gon do with em?" he ast.

"We are gon spy on Miss Attica with em, that's what," I said.

"Are we gon listen to Miss Attica's chest?" he ast.

---

63   R. G. LeTourneau invented famous massive earth-moving equipment. —ml

"No," I told him, "We are goin to listen to her *house*."

"Her house!"

"That's right," I said, "her house. Plus, at other times, we'll put on disguises. But, before we get into that, we'll use these!" And I grabbed the two stethoscopes off the coffee table and held em up for emphasis. Then I told the little sumbich that there wuddn no such a cussword as *bull-fuk*.

He still didn get it, cause he don't really pay attention, so he come on with, "How we gon use them things? Are we just gon walk up to her ass and tell her to say AHH!?"

Voyd thought that was funnier'n a four-legged guinea hen, so I said, "No, ass'ole. We are gon go up under her house!"

And that's exactly what we did.

We waited till the weather was just right, dry and not hot, not too cool, and after it got dark, Voyd and me walked north up School Street—cause we didn want nobody to see either of our vehicles parked near Miss Attica's—and we tipped up to the back of the house, which sets there on the southwest corner where School Street runs into Flossie Lane. It was gon be our first real surveillance as private diktectives.

IN ADDITION I THINK I should tell you that we knew from Sunflower that Miss Attica had told her she was gon come up to Meffis and go by to see Sunflower's "store" before she drove back to St. Leo. And we had it all worked out with Miz Drtchi, who, as you know, owned the booth next to the *Obzhay Boodywoowoo*, that she would try to conversate with Miss Attica and, through her special skills as a trained interrogator, attempt to see if she could learn anything about Miss Attica's havin anything to do with *CODA* and the Aunty Belles. This is the kind of stuff that if you told somebody about it they wouldn believe your ass. But that's cause they're the kind of silly sumbiches that thinks they live in a sensible world, which they don't, only they aint insensible enough to know it.

Anyway, finally there we was. And I was whisperin. I explained to Voyd again how we was gon do it and that we was gon go up underneath Miss Attica's house and listen through the floor. And by that time we was stannin in the dark by the openin that was used by ol' Did-by-Dave, the Nigga plumber, whenever he had to crawl th'oo it so he could fix a leak or unthaw Miss Attica's pipes.

"But, Junior Ray," he said, "what if we was to get caught? What the fuk would we say?!"

"Voyd," I said, "we aint getn caught, but if we do, we'll claim we was up under there scope'n out roaches so we could go back and trap em and sell em to the sumbiches from Meffis who fishes out over the levee at the Cut-Off." Hell, Casco Boggs and his brother, Bibbs, used to go up under the City Drug Store all the fukkin time and get tons of roaches. You used to be able to see their lights shinin through the cracks in the bricks. There was a shit pot of a lot of roaches up under that soda fountain; plus there was the Help Yourself Grocery right there in the same block.

Then Voyd come back with, "Well, what is Miss Attica gon say about us sayin she might have thousands of fukkin roaches under her house? She aint gon like that one damm bit."

"Easy," I told him. "We'll say bygod there wuddn one fukkin roach under that house and that it is the only house or buildin in this whole gotdam town we been under that don't have a single bug. And that ought to make her real happy."

"Still," said Voyd, "we was under her house."

"Don't worry," I said. "People *love* apologies, if you've noticed, especially on the news, and so we'll just say, 'Yes'm, Miss Attica, we know we shoulda ast your permission, and we're sorry as a couple of muthafukkas we didn do it, and we won't never not do it again.' And she'll say: 'Why, that's all right, Junior Ray and,

and, and Mr. Mudd; I accept your apology, and I am just very pleased that you did not find any roaches under my house.' Then she'll go up the next day and ast em at the *St. Leo Times* to put it in the newspaper.

"Go on," I said, and Voyd more or less melted away through the access and disappeared underneath Miss Attica's house. Then I did the same thing, only it was a little harder for me because I am bigger than Voyd, who is small and weaselly.

After we got up under there, it wuddn so bad because Miss Attica's house is built up pretty high off the ground—not as high as the old "telephone" office by Miss Helena Ferry's old house, but it was high enough so Voyd and me could sit up without havin to scrunch down. It wuddn bad a-tall. Anyway, we scooted on all fours over to where we knew Miss Attica and Euster's bedroom was. We wanted to hear what they had to say before they went off to sleep.

"That horrid ma-in!" That's what the old sow said, and both Voyd and me picked it up real good with our stethoscopes which we was holdin up against the floorin, and I knew she meant "me" because I had heard her say it before, way back a long-ass time ago, in the courthouse when I was a deputy. The old blue-haired blimp thought I couldn't hear her, but she didn know how sound carried all through the rooms on that first floor of the courthouse—where I was, you know, before everything changed and they built all that new "facility" over on the side street. Fukkum.

Anyway, old Euster kinda mumbled sumpm, and that was pretty much it for our first official surveillance.

PLUS, I GUARANTEE YOU, that high and mighty way she had toward people like me was part of everything around her. Even her fukkin car at one time, a big old 1957 Buick LeStream, didn care for me and used to backfire any time the motor mighta been runnin and I got near it. Worse than that, one day when I went up to her front door to take her back her daddy's pistol—and, also, her little Ithaca .410 pump, which I believe her daddy had in fact give her for a Christmas present when she was real young, and so, as I have told you, ever fukkin-ass year for the longest-ass time after her papa passed away, she always sent both them guns over to the Sheriff's office to get all cleaned and oiled up—anyway, on that particular occasion, her gotdam Nigga man, O. G., who had worked for her mama and nem and then, in his fukkin eighties, was workin for her and Euster—who apparently didn know doodly about guns, which is sumpm I aint yet figured out—come to the door. I'm stannin there with the guns in my hands, and that old black sumbich, O. G.!, looked straight at my ass, right smack in my eye, and hollered: "Wipe yo' foots, white man!"[64]

I wiped em. But bygod I'da shot that coksukka on the spot if I'da thought for one minute I wouldna lost my job. Only, you know, though, Sheriff Holston was one nem Planters, too. Good to me as he was, still, he was part of em! And those ass'oles wouldn stand for the likes of me messin' with their Niggas. Gotdam muthafukkas. The Planters, I mean.

Anyway, the funny thing is, too, that if I didn know almost for a coonfart fact that it was Miss Attica that was sendin them threater letters and, further, that it was her who shot Tombo Turnage, letter-openered Farley Trout, and gigged old Froggy Waters out there in Beaver Dam Brake, I'd still consider putn an air hose up her butt, sellin tickets, and watch her rocket off to Big Shot heaven, wherever the fuk that might be. Meffis probably.

Another thing, whenever Miss Attica walked in anywhere, she took up the whole fukkin room. I don't mean she was fat, like one neez women—or, hell, some neez fukkin men—that makes you immediately think of a huge-ass pile of tremblin jello with a

---

64   William Faulkner's "Barn Burning." Coincidentally that is exactly what Major DeSpain's Black butler says to Ab Snopes. —ogbii

hunnud-pound fillin of *you-know-what*. I mean it aint so much you could say she was *large*, she was just *big*.

Miss Attica was big as a modern-day combine and twice't as viscious, I always thought. Plus, more or less like the comment about Miss Attica made by Mad Owen's aunt Xylda, I remember Miss Helena Ferry one time said about Miss Attica that, "She is a lot to look at but not much to see." I aint never forgot it. I always thought Miss Helena's attitude about Miss Attica come from the fact that she knew her when Miss Attica was a girl and that sumpm godawful musta happened that put her on Miss Helena's bad list. That coulda been. Or maybe it was that wild-ass business surroundin Miss Attica's crazy cousin Lombard. But all of a sudden, bygod, yonda's a light at the end of the fukkin culvert, and I'm thinkin what Miss Helena said back then about Miss Attica mighta had somethin to do with the Aunty Belles!

Now, as they say, the grits thickens.

Junior Ray's Famous Supersonic Oyster Stew

There aint nothin to it. Get the freshest shucked oysters you can find—If I was you I wouldn use none that wuddn at least ten days away from the sell-by date, because shucked oysters don't hold up long, I don't give a shit who packs em. And the small containers don't have as long a shelf life as a big gallon jug does.

Anyway, once you get your oysters, select a big-ass pot. Pour a lot of the oyster juice in the pot, and a lot, you see, won't really be all that much. Then grate up some celery. After that, put the celery in the pot with the oyster juice, with some salt and pepper, and sort of saw-tay it. That tenderizes the celery and flavors the juice.

At the point you think the celery is pretty tender, dump in all your oysters along with the rest of whatever juice is still with em, and cook that for minute or so—but not too long. If them oysters start to crinkle up, that's when you need to come on in with the fat-free SKIM milk. Th'ow that in the pot and let it come to a scald—NOT a boil . . . just a scald. You'll see the milk start to stick to the sides of the pot and bubble there a little on the metal.

When that happens, check your oysters. You'll want them crinkled a little bit, but not too much, because, then, they start to shrink, and they lose that cooked but still juicy, fresh texture, which is really what you're shootn for. So pay attention to what you're doin.

At the point you believe your supersonic oyster stew is just right, cut off the fukkin fire. While the stew is setn there on the stove in the pot, fix your bowls you're gon eat out of. That means get the bowls out, grab a handful of fat-free saltines, and make a fist. That will crumble your crackers for you. I'd recommend two handfuls for each bowl.

CHAPTER ELEVEN

*Underneath Miss Attica's House—We See a Monster—It
Was Merigold Potts—Kilt Her Mama with the Hedge
Clippers—We're Caught by Secundus—His Daddy
was Judge Justiss—Lyberia Shipp Was His Mother—
Primafaysha (Justiss) Shipp Was His Sister—Secundus Is
the Po-lice Chief—"Yes suh," I said—Secundus Enlists
the Services of That Worthless Nigga Escll—We Break
Our Promise to Merigold—Recipe No. 11: Junior Ray's
Famous KKKobbler*

O ur second official sub-flooral surveillance did not last long
because of what happened. While we was underneath
Miss Attica's bedroom with our stethoscopes plastered
up against the planks in the floor, I glanced-ass over at Voyd who
is lookin straight at me but also NOT at me; it was more like he
he was lookin on past me, over my right shoulder, and his lips is
movin a mile a minute, but aint no sound comin out except for
a low, low kinda *uuhhhhhh*. His eyes was big as clay pigeons, and
he was a-thrustin his little flashlight back and forth, stabbin the
air. I turnt myself around so I could see behind me and near bout
shit a Buick.

I was lookin straight at a gotdam monster! And, sumbich, you
know I couldn holler, cause Miss Attica hearin the ruckus and then
catchin us up under her house woulda been worse than bein et up
by a muthafukkin monster.

"Hi, Junior Ray," the monster whispered.

"Hi," I whispered back, and then real low, of course, I come out with "Fuuhk-ah-*Duuhck*!"—because I seen the monster was Merigold Potts.

Voyd was froze. By that time, though, I had the situation under control. "They're lookin for you, Merigold," I said.

"I know, Junior Ray, but I needed to get away for a little while without actually havin to leave, if you know what I mean."

Voyd was still froze, so I continued my whisperin with Merigold. "They say you kilt your mama with the hedge clippers."

"I did. But I only wanted to kill her a little bit."

"A little bit!" I said.

"Yeah, you know, just a little bit, Junior Ray, not all the way, only enough to put her in a better humor. You know how she was."

"I do that," I said. Miz Potts possessed one of the worst fukkin dispositions any human bein could ever be credited with havin. I mean, wuddn nothin ever done right, said right, or thought right. I guess the truth is I could more or less see Merigold's point of view and understand her position. In a way in Merigold's mind it wuddn murder because she never intended for the old woman to stay dead. It was more like, maybe, "corrective" action.

Anyway, hard as it was to do, I looked at Merigold and said, "You mean you been down here underneath Miss Attica's house for the last two weeks? What have you been findin to eat?" I aint even gon tell you how bad she smelled. She musta been over on the other side of the house, up at the front, when Voyd and me crawled under. It was a big fukkin house.

"Bugs do fine," she said. "Occasionally I get one that doesn't taste so good, but most of em don't have any taste at all, except the ants, and I suppose they've been up in the sugar. I like the ants—want one?" And she stuck her finger out with some little flecks on it, which I took to be mashed-up ants.

"No thank you," I told her. It wuddn the ants as much as it was the fingers, and I'm sure by then you know I had a few more questions about Merigold's fugitive survival skills.

"You won't tell on me, will you, Junior Ray?" And she followed that with, "Hi, Voyd!"

Voyd and me looked directly at one another; we looked up at the floor, and then we looked back at each other, and setn there lookin eyeball to eyeball, him at me and me at him, both of us at the same time said: "Fuk no."

And I added, "Shoot, Merigold, we aint the official law no more, plus we don't know nothin about what happened, other than they found your mama in the flower bed et up by them two beagle hounds y'all have; other'n that we don't know a datgum thing about none of it, and you can rest assured . . ."

And here, Voyd unfroze hissef and chimed in with, "That's right, Merigold, rest *A*-Sured"—then I finished up by tellin her: "We aint got a dog in this fight." I hoped me mentionin the word *dog* hadn hurt her feelins.

"Not one single dog!" Voyd said.

"Thank you, Junior Ray. Thank you, too, Voyd. It was nice seein y'all," she told us, and she begun to move back into the dark, and we couldn see her no more, nor hear her neither. Voyd and me figured that was the end of our stethoscope spyin operation, so we headed-ass on all fukkin fours, stealthily, of course, fast as we fukkin could!—over to the hole in the underpinnin we come through, and I was the first one out.

I COME SCOOTN THROUGH the access head first and into the yard on my hands and knees slap between a pair of big-ass legs. The legs belonged to Secundus J. Shipp. And I said, "Oh, shit."

Now, I'mo have to explain about him:

Secundus is a unusual sumbich. He is the chief of St. Leo's

police department, and his jurisdiction is only over what goes on inside the town, not for the county around it. Plus, he is big as big as a dump truck, and he is black, but he is also the son of Judge Russell "Rusty" Justiss, who, of course, was a white man—the "J" in Secundus's name is "Justiss."

Somehow or another Miz Justiss—Amanda Idella Justiss, who was called Miss Dell—never caught on to the true employer-employee relationship she and the judge enjoyed with their long-time cook, Lyberia Shipp—with *DUBBYA-AITCH'-fukkin-OOOM* the judge fathered two chillun, a girl, named Primafaysha, and, of course, a boy they called Secundus because the Judge and Miss Dell already had a son, themsevs, named Russell "Rusty" Justiss Jr., who, in fact, is our number-one judge around here now. His daddy and his mamma have been gone a long time.

Anyway, about Secundus, I remember when he was real little, and I more or less watched him grow up. He and his sister and his mama, Lyberia, lived in a little house behind the Judge's, over on the east side of the railroad tracks across from the Baptist Church. Everybody in the whole town seemed to know the story except Miss Dell, who, smart as I am certain she coulda been, I think was maybe one of those women who only know what they want to know and shuffle stuff around to make it all go the way it suits em.

People thought Miss Dell was just a silly Southern-ass woman who didn know nothin about nothin and didn want to know nothin. But I have always believed that silly old women aint silly at all and know plenty and that it aint ignorance that keeps them from ever sayin anything about stuff but, instead, it's a kind of smartness the average shit-heads aint in tune with.

Anyway, if it suited her not to know, then it suited me. And the judge, he was a gotdam good judge in my opinion. He was who he was and was pretty good at bein hissef, which is more than I can say for a lot of other sumbiches.

WHEN IT COMES TO you know who, and I am talkin about black folks, I have found that it is fairly fukkin easy to be a racist—till, of course, you run into the worst of your own kind and meet the best of theirs. And I guess I coulda looked head on into the eyes of the worst of my kind just lookin in the gotdam mirror, but people aint born bein able to see theirsevs, and it takes a while to do so. And, at least in that respect, I aint no different from most other sumbiches.

Anyhow, I do have the fukkin sense to know the good from the bad and the best from the worst, and can't nobody deal with Secundus J. Shipp and not know he is the gotdam best of the best, and, if you want to know the truth, I think he is that, not in spite of the fact that he is somewhat black, but bygod beCAUSE of it. And, I know, just me sayin such probly makes my ass some other other kind of a racist, but, hell, I expect whatever type of racist you or any other muthafukka could name or come up with, I'm sure I'd qualify.

You don't have to be a fukkin genius to figure out how Secundus had a lot of advantages not many of the other black chillun around here had—like him getn sent off to a private school in Indiana and then goin on to West Point later on. He also went to Vietnam as a lieutenant and come back pretty shot up, because I guess bein a' MP didn mean you was just directin traffic all the time. Plus, they give him some medals. One of em was a silver star.

Funny, iddn it, when it comes to two different veterans. I wanted to shoot the shit out of Leland Shaw and hated him for almost no reason I could put my finger on, except his bein part of them Planters; yet, here is Secundus who I dearly-ass love and admire, and he's black! I can't figure it. I have laid my ass awake at night tryin to make some sense out of it, but I have not been able to nail it down. I mean, Shaw didn do nothin to me. And I'd be the first one to admit he did not deserve the way I felt about him. It's just

that I couldn't help it. Anyway, I suppose I have improved, even
though it was not intentional.

Just to cut it short, Primafaysha growed up and when she
graduated from the Mhoon County "black" school she moved up
to St. Louis and lived with her AHN-tee. The story was she went
off to college in O-gotdam-hio, married a lawyer—who they said
was largely white like her—and has lived all these years in a town
called Westerville, which I am told is up near Columbus, wherever
the fuk that is.

Secundus, though, come up later through the early, semEYE-
integrated school system that was in place down here for about
one short-ass stutter-step, but when it was clear that wuddn
workin out, he got sent off—by old Judge Justiss, of course—to
some kinda private Quaker-oats school up in Indiana, and after
he graduated, that sharp muthafukka, as I have told you, went to
college at *West Point!*—stayed in the gotdam Army forever, in the
MPs, then he retired as a bird-colonel and come back home here
to St. Leo to live. Also, he was, so they said, a' expert in logistics,
whatever the fuk that is. At first he had some kind of management
job with the HotSlot Casino folks, but it wuddn long before St.
Leo hired him to be the police chief, after another sumbich who
had the job went to do prison time, down at Maxwell Air Force
Base over in Alabama. It's the same-o-same-o: you name it, that
other fukhed done it.

St. Leo got the deal of a lifetime when they gave the job to
Secundus. I mean he's a hometown boy that really did turn out
well, if I do say so myself. I guess it's because, you might say, he
had good parents.

Anyhow, there are four fukkin "officers" workin for him. All
of em is white, but one is a big old girl named Frances who used
to be a telephone operator here till the dial system was put in, and

it's Frances's job to deal with the women who get hauled down to the jail. Frances is pretty well on up in years, but that don't seem to get in the way of her bein able to knock the shit out of any wild-ass heifer that won't do what she wants em to.

Now the jail is, as you may know, run by the sheriff and owned by the fukkin county AND our lillo town combined. Anyhow, this day and time, what with the sheriff's department and the [*haw-fukkin-haw*] "city" po-lice, St. Leo does have some semEYE-modern law enforcement goin on. And that had to happen because of all these casinos we got up in the north end of the county, along the river. Ho-lee Sheet-rock! At night, up in the sky, part of Mhoon County is full of searchlights and lighted-up four-lane parkways snake'n out across the gotdam cotton fields to where all that Alice in Fun-derland crap is—yeah, where I used to work, too—and where all the po-ass sumbiches come and lose their fukkin paychecks every Friday and, then, all durin the rest of the week, lose what they've had to borrow. Most of em are Meffis ass'oles, but truthfully they're from all over the country. And I have to say, if what I'm seein out there is America, then we don't stand a Chinaman's chance. Plus, like I was getn ready to tell you, after the sun goes down if you turn your head to the west off Highway 61, you'll see what looks like the Meffis Cotton Carnival and the coksukkin huge-ass Mid-South Fair all at once! Hollywood, too, I reg'n. Or Lost-gotdam-Vegas! Which I aint never been to and aint gon go. Fukkum.

But, back to what I was tellin you before I told you that: This big, black sumbich, Secundus, who—I guess you'd say, aint really all that black, but, you know, he didn have nothin to do with none of that—is possibly one of the finest-ass men on this earth we was ever fortunate enough to have want to come back here. And that includes this time in question when I sludd out from under Miss Attica Rummage's old house. I am not kiddin. And I've got to say, experienced as I am as a law-enforcement professional, I couldna done what I set out to do, even with Voyd's help, if it hadna been for Secundus.

NEVERTHELESS, THERE I WAS, on the ground lookin up at him, and I was scared spitless I wuddn gon be able to talk me and Voyd's way out of whatever kind of mess we was in.

"Junior Ray," he said, lookin down at me there on all fours, like a gotdam Pekinese, "What might you be doing?—and I suppose that is Voyd Mudd peeping out of the hole behind you; am I correct?"

"Yes-suh," I said, still down in the dirt, strainin to look up at him. "That is correct."

"I have a feeling you two have an interesting reason for crawling around under Miss Attica's house, and I certainly would like to hear it—I have not informed Miss Attica . . . yet."

"Oh, shit," I said again. And then I come out with, "Chief, if we can talk, I'll lay it all out, because, frankly, Voyd and me should have run this by you in the first place."

We went over with him to his vehicle. I sat up front with him, and Voyd ducked into the back seat and sat sort of humped over, forward, like we was gon have a three-way conversation, which, of course, we wuddn. Plus, he was nervous, because, as I am sure you know, you cannot get out of the back seat of a po-lice car.

Secundus got in the driver's seat and, looking straight ahead, said, "I saw your flashlights shining through the cracks in the bricking of Miss Attica's underpinning. I didn know what was up, and I knew it wasn't a couple of raccoons or Floyd Brunson trapping roaches to put in his bait shop, so I decided to see who—or what—came out . . . and here y'all are."

I told the chief all about the letters—and I did let Voyd hop into the discussion once or twice, and that made him feel a lot better. Anyway, I especially told Secundus about the three threater-letters that was penned by the same hand and mailed from Clarksdale.

And we let him in on what Mad had said in his letter to me about the secret s'rority of the Aunty Belles and about their long-ass password as well.

It took a while. But we, mostly me, natchaly, filled Secundus in on how we had decided to become diktectives and that was how come we had the stethoscopes and why we was up under Miss Attica's and all that. We give him our findins, too, on how each of the three dead muthafukkas—who, of course, did not include Merigold's mama, Miz Potts—was connected by one-ass common denominator, and that denominator was young Mr. Brainsong and his forth-comin publi-fukkin-cation of some more of that crazy sumbich Leland Shaw's "Notes," which as you know I think is nothin but googah and not worth killin nobody over.

But I guess it's the *googah-ness* of it that has the threaters so upset. McKinney said she thought the threaters would like it to be more on the order of what she called the "poetic prose and delicate poetry" that coksukka down in Greenville used to write. Beats the shit out of me. Far as I'm concerned, if it's not Conway Twitty or Roy Orbison, it aint poetry.

We told the whole fukkin thing. And we had to own up to the fact that in the two times we'd been lisnin in on Miss Attica and ol' diknose Euster from under Miss Attica's house, we hadn heard nothin yet that was incriminate'n. But, still, I said I had high hopes that them stethoscopes could hep us to solve the case. My position was that just because our stethoscope-ical tactic hadn worked out on the first two tries, or might not for-fukkin-ever, that didn mean it wuddn worth it, cause I b'lieved it was. A sumbich don't have to be one-hunnud percent successful to do a good job! If that was the case, half the muthafukkas on earth would be outa work.

Anyway, after we filled Secundus in on everything we knew, he looked us both in the eye and said, "Y'all have done a good job. It's worth lookin into. Here's what we're goin to do. We will enlist the services of our worthless friend Ezell, who owes me and the town of St. Leo a long list of favors."

See, Ezell, since he no longer could live at the jailhouse, had become Miss Attica's show-fer,[65] and I don't know why Voyd and me hadn thought of getn him in on what we was doin, but, well, I guess him just bein Ezell is what caused me not to consider it. Anyway, Voyd and me said, "Yeah!" and both of us was finally able to release the vise-like grip our ass'oles had on our underpants.

Secundus had known Ezell all his—Secundus's—life. That's because Ezell was a lot older. Anyhow, Secundus wuddn no more like Ezell than a fox is like a pet mud-turtle. There was a heap of difference. And in a way, I guess by some kind of comparison, I mysef am a whole lot more like Ezell than I am like Secundus.

Just like me, Ezell's daddy was a field hand, while Secundus's papa was a fukkin judge. Course, there again, you could say Secundus and me was a good bit alike in that we was both law-enforcement professionals.

"By the way," I said to the chief, "Merigold Potts is livin up under there," and I pointed to Miss Attica's house, "in case you was wonderin where she was. Voyd and me was worried that if we told anybody, she'd tell on us, so . . ."

"Don't worry," he said, "I'll take care of that." And I knew he would.

---

65   Chauffeur. —ml

Junior Ray's Famous KKKobbler

This dish belongs to what I calls my after-thoughts, like what you might think about after you done eat your ass off and are cravin sumpm sweet. Brainy says it might be classy to Frenchify the thoughts and call em *Apres*-Thoughts, but I don't know; I aint never ate nothin French except the fries. Anyhow one of my after-thought dishes would be as follows. This is fairly simple to prepare. Pay close attention to the five easy-ass steps:

1. Buy a frozen cobbler.

2. Bake it like the directions tell you to.

3. When it's done, take it out of the fukkin oven, and cut a coksukkin cross on the top crust.

4. Pour bourbon where you cut the cross, and light the sumbich.

5. There you are. Put it on the table.

CHAPTER TWELVE

Merigold Is Lured from under Miss Attica's House by Bobbakew—No, a Black Man Did Not Kill Miz Potts—We Ast Secundus about Mojack—Dreamed up by White People— Junior Ray Would Like to Be Like Secundus—Crazy Baines Died on the Job—He Pulled the Fire Alarm—Ezell Brings in an Unmailed Threat Letter—"We Know You Are But a Disgusting Sodomite"—Voyd Does Not Want to Wear a Dress—Limericka Rhodenweeds—Voyd Comes Close to Getting Stabbed— Recipe No. 12: Junior Ray's Famous Deputy Special BIG BREFFUSSammidge

The next day, around noon, while Miss Attica had done gone off to Meffis, with Ezell at the wheel, Secundus and one of his officers lured Merigold Potts out from under Miss Attica's house with a big tub of steamin-ass hot bobbakewed pork shoulder. The smell of it had her zoomin out from under there like a gotdam hell-I-don't-know-what-kinda-gotdam . . . *thing*! I mean she musta been hungrier'na muthafukka, livin up under there for weeks like she had and eatn mostly bugs. Lord! Anyway, a bobbakewed pork shoulder is hard to stay away from when you aint starvin, much less when you are.

It was perfectly fukkin clear Merigold kilt her mother. Some people, if you can believe it, tried to say a black man did it. But that was crap. Black men don't kill old blue-haired women with no hedge clippers, and even if they did, they wouldn't just do it and go on off; they'd take somethin for their trouble, a gotdam stick of baloney or sumpm, but they wouldn't just kill a sumbich for nothin and leave em in the flower bed to be et up by a couple of beagle hounds. That's the kinda thing white people does.

Merigold done it, all right. I mean, she said so to me and Voyd underneath Miss Attica's house, but you still have to think it out cause Merigold, bein Merigold, you wouldn never just want to take the first word that come out of her mouth. Course we all knew she was crazy as a sugar-ditch rat, but nobody woulda thought she'd kill her mama.

And I was really glad we was able to tell about seein Merigold to Secundus because I truly was uncomfortable thinkin we wuddn ever gon be able to say nothin about seein her when we was underneath Miss Attica Rummage's old house.

I guess you can see why Voyd and me could not keep our promise to Merigold. I just don't even want to think what Secundus mighta did to us if he had found Merigold hide'n underneath Miss Attica's house and we hadna told him she was. It was a gotdam double-clutch-fuk . One, if we hadna got caught by Secundus, then we might notta had to go back on our word to Merigold even though, two, I have to tell you, I'da worried a whole helluva lot that she mighta spilled the shit-soup later on and our ass woulda been johnson grass. So, like I said, we pretty much had to tell on Merigold after we got caught by Secundus when I raced my ass outa that access to get the fuk away from her and Voyd was behind me, with his mouth open, half-way through the gotdam hole. We didn have no coksukkin, bug-eatn choice.

Of course, when Voyd and me tried to talk to Secundus about Mojack, he wouldn have nothin to do with it and said there wuddn no such thing as Mojack and that Mojack was just a gotdam "invention" dreamed up by white people to make black people appear more different than they actually was—and Secundus did also say he thought blacks and whites WAS different but that there wuddn no fukkin mystery involved. After talkin with Secundus about Mojack, I swear I come away feelin like I was closer to them Planters than I had ever imagined I was or woulda ever planned on bein, at least as far as believin in Mojack is concerned. On the other hand, I do have to say the temptation to believe the unbelievable has always been a fukkin issue with me, I guess cause it's so fukkin easy to do. Anyway, the truth is, I know for a fact that if I had to be like anybody I can think of, it'd be Secundus. That sumbich is a helluva man. Fuk my mangey-ass kin and the rest of them ragtail ass'oles back over in the Hills. He's got MY respect. Them pekkawoods never did know nothin about Niggas in the first place, cause they was too gotdam poor to own any.

One OTHER reason we got caught by Secundus was because my look-out, Crazy Baines, didn give me the signal, which was that he would call my cell phone, which I had put on "meeting" so there'd be just a teeny-ass little boop and I'd look at the lighted-up window on my phone and see his phone number, and that was to be the warnin that somebody was out there near the house, and then we wouldn't go bustin out and get caught.

But the sumbich died on the job.

You didn know nothin about that! I shoulda told you before about Baines, but I'll tell all about him—and what happened—in just a little bit. I didn inform Voyd neither, and it pissed him off. But that don't bother me none. I don't tell the little pea-weasel about lots of stuff, like when I went up to visit Miz Drtchi. And I am sure you can figure out why. I mean of-fukkin-course the little turd-tapper IS my best friend and my oldest runnin buddy, but, *Son,* I learned a long-ass time ago that whenever things get thick and important enough to pucker up your ass'ole, it's best not to fill up his sparrow-size head with too many fukkin dee-tails. So that's why I done a private deal with Crazy Baines. Secundus said he would take care of getn Crazy Baines funeralized and buried.

Which he did. I truly felt sorry for ol' Craze. It's funny. Every time I thought about him, I thought about me. ChrEYEst.

We just called the sumbich "Crazy Baines." He came down to live in the Delta from up in Meffis because what he done to hissef by doin what he did . . . was just too gotdam much for those sumbiches up in Tennessee to handle. But I aint got no problem with what he done, and I think he ought to do it every fukkin day cause he was right.

Ol Craze had been a college professor at that big-ass junior college up in Meffis for nearly twenty years. Then, one day, for no reason at all, he pulled the handle on the fire alarm in the hall outside his classroom—just pulled the muthafukka and that was that.

There wuddn no fire, of course. Plus, there was a camera in the ceilin of the hall, so Baines was right there on the big silver screen, calm as a cabbage, walkin over to the little red box on the wall and flippin the switch. It was white.

When they ast his ass why he jerked off the fire alarm, he said, "Well, I was alarmed. I have been alarmed for several years, and I just thought it was time to ring the bell." After that he didn say nothin more for about a year, then they fired him and he wuddn a professor no more, at least as far as the folks who run the college was concerned.

For a while he worked as one nem "greeters" for a Big-Mart out on Shotwell Boulevard, up in Meffis, but that didn last long because he kept askin people why they wanted to shop in a store that was, as he put it, the "American Dream gone b'zirk." So, natchally, Big-Mart fired his ass, too. Some shitfinger from a half-ass so-called "Senior Center" took his place. You could shoot me right now a hunnud gotdam times before I'd put on one 'nose little red vests they make you wear. Fukkum.

That's how, basically, Craze come down into the Delta to live among us in Mhoon County. And he got along okay, with some work here and there heppin out the funeral home at funerals, answerin the telephone out at the Ford dealership, keepin the parkin lot clean around the Boll & Bloom Cafe, out on Highway 61. He made enough to satisfy him, and he didn mind doin whatever it took to do it as long as, he said, it was honest labor. So, I didn think the sumbich was crazy one damn bit. Personally, I thought he was the way a man ought to be.

Just to sort of round all this out, what Craze was "alarmed" about is actually sumpm the school and in fact the whole gotdam country should have been alarmed about. He said it thissaway, which I'm fidna to show you. The sheriff and nem and the undertaker, who is also the County Corona, found it all wrote down inside the house he'd been livin in when they went over there to gather up his possessions, which wuddn much, so they could take em down to the courthouse and try to find out if he had any kin. It turned out he didn have none. And that may be the saddest part of the whole thing, *you* know—his life and then, of course, *his death*.

What ol' Craze had wrote was really kinda sumpm. First of all there was a lot of it, and it was writ down in long-hand on the backs of un-opened en-velops, you know, the kind that always says Prsrt up in the right-hand corner where the fukkin stamp is s'posed to be. And the en-velops wuddn all jumbled up, neither. They was stacked in colyums clean up to the top in a cardboard box from the likka store, and as it turned out they was in abso-gotdam-lutely the right-ass order. Well, the sumbich was, you know, one-nem super "neat" type of folks. He didn never even wrinkle his shirt. Anyhow, natchally I was curious about what was on those en-velops; so, after the sheriff and his little helpers got em back to the courthouse and dumped the box, along with a buncha other stuff Craze had, on the floor of a certain back hallway that don't nobody even go in no more and that leads to a back door that don't nobody never make use of, I eased th'oo there and snatched the sumbiches, went out that fukkin back door and took the box and them en-velops over to Miss Minnie McDonald's and ast her to type up what she saw. Which she did. Furthermore I didn put her in the trick by tellin her what it all was or where I got it. Plus, I never heard one coksukkin word about that box. I'm tellin you, it woulda set there on the floor of that dingey-ass hallway till all the Baptists in Bobo started dancin. If I didn know nothin else in this gotdam world, I knew not one single shithed would ever give that box a thought and wouldn never miss it.

Craze didn say nowhere that I could see who he was write'n to or who he mighta expected to read it. He just wrote it and stuck in the Mad Dog 20-20 case-box. Anyway, here's some of it—not the whole string'a red weenies by a long shot—but this'll tell you why he pulled the fire alarm:

I was alarmed! Our educators have become prostitutes. And our so-called colleges have become retail outlets. But our teachers have remained for the most part fairly true to the profession. I like to think there is a great difference between what one likes to call an "educator" and the peculiar individual who is called to be a "teacher."

I was alarmed! It seems our educators have ceased to have any interest whatsoever in education and now focus upon merely appearing to have an interest in education. "College-For-Everyone" has turned post-secondary schools into a very large "businesses" whose main objective is merely to keep their doors open in order to preserve a multitude of livelihoods. Indeed, the goal is no longer to teach nor even, really, to learn but simply . . . to graduate.

I was alarmed! The administrators now call my students "our customers"! Am I a salesman? Will my name soon be put up on a large board as one among a roster of others with gold and silver stars stuck beside their names? Will there be a "Salesteacher of the Month"? I was told we we are to focus on how to keep our students—Nay! "our "customers!"—physically attached to the school. The administrators referred to it, inelegantly, as "butts in the chairs." In Latin that is retention. It means, as an economic necessity, ignorance has replaced excellence.

I was alarmed! Apparently each student represents about $5,500.00. And there was the constant whisper within our unhallowed halls and ivyless walls that our hope must be that more of our "customers" might ultimately walk proudly across our questionable-college's stage at graduation. Proud of what I might ask? Certainly not of having done very much. However, that does not seem to get in the way of being proud.

I was alarmed! Many of my "customers" could not read the textbook, even when they happened to have acquired one. There were often at least two or three "customers" who lived in our city and had gone twelve or thirteen years through the Public School System, yet had no idea what state lay on the other side of the river that runs by the city, or even, in a few cases that there is even a river at all. I am speaking of the Mississippi.

I was alarmed! The level of student skills and their stock of expected, general knowledge appeared to sink lower year by year. Finally it became as though I were teaching children, middle-schoolers, who whined and complained at every assignment, which, alas, most of them would not do, and some would not even attempt to complete the work. They shuffled their mental feet and walked into to class slower than sleepers on a dreamless street. Alarmed? Oh, yes . . . like one finding a tiger in the driveway. So one morning I decided to do something about it. Learning was dead. And it wasn't for lack of vitamins. The problem is lack of fire. I pulled the switch.

I was alarmed!

I knew the po' sumbich wuddn just write'n about the Niggas and that he was talkin about the whole colorful ballgame down here in the Delta and up in Meffis. Even I know how unfair things was in the old days and how hard life for the black folks most generally is known to have been. And I aint sayin that bein po means you got to be black. Fuk that noise. But, the thing is, that, in the old days, and now as well, there is more black people where we are than there is white ones, so, arith-m'-tically, if the p'centages of rich and po was to be the same for both bunches, then because there is and was way more of *them* coksukkas than there is of us, that means, just number-wise, there was and is more po blacks than there is and was po whites. In fact, down here the Mississippi Delta, the black sumbiches outnumbered the white muthafukkas near-bout ten to one. Which is why bein around black folks don't really bother me none. It aint like that over in the Hills.

Don't get my ass wrong and start thinkin I'm some kinda kiss-ass lib'ral. Whatever the fuk that is. I'm just tryin to say that in this po-ass section of the fukkin country, the history of po blacks and po whites, apart from *them*—the blacks, I mean—bein slaves and all and, later, bein made to set in separate rooms and havin to say "Cap'm please" all the gotdam time, is pretty much the same. And the attitudes that come from that kind of hard-ass time took hold on all of us and don't get shook loose very easy.

However, you have to recognize, that for the Niggas things was different in one very important-ass way; namely, they was held down by the law, and so it was harder for em to move up out of the gotdam Delta dirt and improve their situation, whereas—of fukkin course—*my folks, po as they was but bein white*, coulda gone up to Meffis and into the Walgreens Drug Store and et a hamburger at the lunch counter, which didn none of em ever do because the sumbiches didn even know where the fuk it was and wouldna give a shit if they had. Still, the point is, if they hada give one, and if theyda had the money—and if theyda wanted to spend it thatta way—they might have and *could have.*

But the Niggas didn have that choice. They just flat out couldna et no hamburger at the Walgreens lunch counter, cause if theyda tried it, theyda got their ass arrested. So I've always thought crap like that and more besides held em back, even if, like us, they didn give a sorghum shit about goin to Walgreens in the first fukkin place. Well, you get the gotdam pitcha. That's the way it was and how yesterday is still with us. Yassuh. The past don't go away, that mean sumbich is nappin in our bones. But it is bad that some-neez little shitheds can't even read a' eight-page fukbook.

As for Crazy Baines, a lot of what people get called aint nothin a-tall like what they are, and I think that was true of Craze. Folks mighta thought it was crazy for him to pull the fire alarm, but, as you know, I don't.

SECUNDUS TOLD EZELL NOT to say nothin to nobody, or, if he did, he would not never be no trusty again in Ezell's—or anybody else's—lifetime . . . if he, Ezell, should ever get thowed in jail and that they—Secundus and Judge Justiss Jr. and nem—might send his worthless ass down to Parchman as a habitual no'count sumbich.

That seemed to do the trick, and two weeks later Ezell showed up in the chief's office with an unmailed letter he had slipped in his pocket the day before when he had taken Miss Attica to the Clarksdale Country Club and she had told him to run into Clarksdale and mail some letters for her. She handed him a stack with a rubber band around them, and he drove on in to town to the P.-fukkin-O. where he looked through the packet and saw that one of the en-velops was addressed to Owen G. Brainsong II, 131 Northside, Apt. B, St. Leo, Mississippi 38709.

He put it in his pocket and here it was—and the handwrite'n was exactly the same as it appeared in the other three Brainy had received, cause, natcherly, I'd seen em. Plus, when the chief opened it, it said: *"You shall be fortunate if all we do is "steer" you, "barrow you," geld you, and take away forever your useless manhood!! We know you are but a disgusting sodomite!"* I looked at it and said, "ChrEYEst, there it is again!" And thinkin about them three unfortunate ass'oles that got kilt, I am glad didn none of em get their nuts cut off.

Lord! That woulda been awful. I don't think Judge "Rusty" would go easy on Miss Attica or nobody else if they'da done sumpm like that. It makes my skin crawl like when you scratch your fingernails acrosst a blackboard. I mean, killin is one thing, and maybe them Aunty Belles was upset, but I sure can't figure out why anybody would want to cut Brainy's, or anybody else's, nuts off just for pub-lishin a book full of Leland Shaw's insanity. Hell, it aint *that* bad.

Anyway, Secundus told Ezell he done good but that what we needed was a letter *that was actually mailed and had a postmark on it* and that if Ezell could tell him when he thought that might have took place, he would then see about getn the letter out of the hands of the U.S. Post Office before it was put on the truck.

AFTER THAT AND IN the meantime, I knew Voyd and me had a train-load of work ahead of us if we was to get the goods on Miss Attica—OR on whoever it might turn out to be. We had to establish all that shit about "beyond a reasonable doubt" and "probable-ass cause," and Secundus warned our asses to be careful and not to fuk up the investigation by being as stupid as we usually are, which baffled my ass because I was not clear on exactly how stupid we was.

So I said, "Voyd, you're gon have to wear one of your fat-ass old grandmama's dresses, and we can buy you a wig, these days, damn near anywhere," and then I told him I was gon locate me a beard and one nem *blind*-man's white walkin canes, so wouldn nobody recognize us. At the time I didn really see how we could call ourselves diktectives without doin none of that.

I do have to admit I had some misgivins about it, but as long as it was Voyd who was gon dress up in women's clothes, I didn really give too much of a shit. The point is if we was gon follow Miss Attica around up in Meffis without her noticin us, we was gon have to be incon-cotton-ass-gotdam-spicuous, if you know what I mean.

Voyd did not carry on about it and truthfully did not appear to mind dressin up in women's clothes all that much, which bothered me a little bit because I expected him to th'ow a gotdam fit. It just goes to show that don't nobody really know nobody no matter how long they've known em. Plus, you can usually bet on the fact that what something looks like now aint what it's liable to look like later.

Anyway, the deal was he was gon have to hang on to me or vice versa because I was supposed to be blind. That caused me some concern, too, about the whole gotdam thing. But I said to myself, gotdammit, if a sumbich is gon be a diktective, then he's gotta be a fukkin diktective and do what a diktective has to do. Which is what we was doin, and that's all in the coksukkin world it was.

We knew we'd have to be careful because any time anybody tries to get away with anything in Meffis, they always wind up doin whatever it is they aint supposed to be doing right smack in front of the very last-ass sumbich they'd ever want to be knowin about what they was doin. It was gonna be tricky.

However, the idea was, like I said a minute ago, that Voyd, dressed up like an old lady, was going to be leadn me around, owin to the fact that I was makin out like I was blind. That way I could keep an eye on Miss Attica the whole fukkin time, thoo my dark glasses! So, the truth is I'd be leadn Voyd. That was the plan. It's complicated.

And then there it was. He done it. All of a sudden the little shitbird pipes up with, "Fuk you, Junior Ray! I aint gon be no gotdam old lady even if it is in my own grandmama's dress—you be the old lady, you sunnavabitch!

"Voyd," I said, "She was *your* grandmama. I can't be wearin *your* grandmama's clothes. That's against the gotdam law—and the Bible too! Hell, man, there's just some things a sumbich just don't do, and one of em is wearin another muthafukka's grandmama's clothes." It took a lot of persuade'n, but in the end I got him to do it.

And I was glad, too, that I didn't have to worry no more about him bein a partial queer.

PLUS, HE KNEW IF he didn I might tell Sunflower about him trottn over to the courthouse all the time so he could flirt with Limericka Rhodenweeds, the mostly white—but not entirely—secretary who never did shit but drink Co'-Colas and fuk with her fingernails all day long in a little office next to the County Board Room. She looked like she ought to be smart, being largely white an' all, but she was dummer'n a gotdam sack of peanuts. 'Course that aint why Voyd liked her. Deep down I think he has always wished he was black.

I don't believe Limericka *wished* anything much, and if she did, I don't think it went much further than the Coke machine. One time her car broke down, and the County Clerk ast Voyd if he would take Limericka home to where she lived, down around White Oak subdivision. They didn get there till seven-thirty that eve'nin, and Voyd near bout got stabbed. Like what took his ass so long to go seven miles?

Sunflower never knew about it. But I did. The door on the driver's side has a two-inch-wide knife hole in it where some black sumbich jabbed a butcher knife right after Voyd pulled the door to. I had to explain to Sunflower that sometimes a truck can come along and park beside a car, and if it's a truck that has a lots of tools on it, one of them tools once in a while can jam into anything that's parked next to the truck. I told it so it sounded like it made perfect-ass sense, which, of course, it didn. Anyhow it satisfied her.

Voyd kept his little .25 automatic in his pocket for six fukkin weeks. And, as far as I know, he aint ever been back to the court-house and ducks down in the vehicle whenever we drive past it.

Junior Ray's Famous Big Breffus Sammidge

Hunnud Percent Whole Wheat Bread, Peanut Butter, Banana, Microwaved Egg, Soybean Mynaise—Plus a Split, Uncured but Fully Cooked TurkeyWeenie

And that's pretty much it.

CHAPTER FOURTEEN[66]

We Follow Miss Attica to Meffis—Ezell Is Part of the Team—
We Go to Goldsmith's Department Store—Voyd Is Hit On—
Stalked by Strayhorn Crockett—Ezell Breaks the Case—The
Threater Letter Is in the Mail—In Clarksdale—Secundus Has
Big Connections—Multiple-Agent Eagle Swoop—Miss Attica
and Euster Have Sex—Voyd and Me Listen—Miss Attica Does
Sumpm to Euster—Junior Ray Remembers a Funny Thing
Mad Wrote About Sex— Recipe No. 14: Young Mr. Brainsong's
Famous "Hi-Tee Treat"

P retty soon we knew Miss Attica was plannin to go to Meffis
again, and she was gon get Ezell to drive her up there, because
he told us. Also, although Ezell was not by no means an
official diktective, now that he was part of the investigation task-
force natchaly he was clued into exactly what Voyd and me was
gon be up to. However, I don't believe he ever woulda imagined
what Voyd might look like in a dress.

So, anyway, when the time come, Voyd and me got in my truck,
wearin our fukkin disguises, and we followed Ezell and Miss Attica
out of St. Leo, turned left at the Boll & Bloom Cafe, and motored-
ass on up Highway 61 to the big fukkin city.

Ezell made it a point to tell us he would be careful and make
sure he did not run off from us and leave us not knowin where
they was. Bear in mind he didn necessarily give a shit about me

---

66   Junior Ray refused to have a thirteenth chapter. —ml

and Voyd, but he was scared dikless of Secundus. Anyhow, after just a little more'n an hour, there me and Voyd was, trackin Miss Attica!—followin around after that old pootballoon—who really aint much older'n I am—out east on Poplar at the Oak Court Mall, and she had not showed even the slightest sign that she mighta noticed us, which, if you want to know the fukkin truth, surprised the doowah out of me.

Now I have to say, there aint anything about Goldsmith's department store that I do not know. I am familiar with it back'ards and forwuhts. On the other hand, I guess, who aint? Plus, as you may remember Goldsmith's used to be downtown on Main Street before Meffis became a fukkin suburb of *itsef* and Main Street turned into the Mid-America Mall that didn have no roof on it and without there bein very many Mid-Americans. But lately it has gotten somewhat better.

Mainly, however, I was always afraid at some point Miss Attica was gon notice me and Voyd back-ass behind her all the time; only the truth is she never did turn her head and look around, which, if she had, she'da seen me lookin like a blind man and Voyd lookin like a gotdam mattress in a wig.

Here's the thing though: One, we knowed *she musta kilt them sumbiches.* Two, all in the hell we was tryin to do was see if there was some place she went, somebody she saw, and/or some-*thing* she might do that would indicate that there could be a gotdam hook and eye between her and them death letters—or even between her and the killins themsevs.

Anyway, after a while, right as she was leavin Goldsmith's, and headn out into the big-ass so-called Mall that connected Goldsmith's and that other fukkin store, Twillard's, I caught sight of a sumbich behind us, and he went everywhere we went, so I said to Voyd: "Hey, muthafukka, do you see that butt-hole back yonder by the dummy in the striped bikini?"

And Voyd said, "Yeah, I do, and you know who it is, too."

And I said, "Oh, shit, it's Strayhorn Crockett from Sarah's Bottom!"

"Unh-huhn," Voyd said.

"Gotdammit!" I said. Lem'me think what to do—you spec he knows we're us?"

"I don't really think so," Voyd said, "cause he don't appear to be payin no 'tention to yo ass, but he sho is inter-rested in mine."

"Gotdammit!" I said again. "You know they had to talk to that fool last year because he was hangin out at the Senior Center up in South-fukkin-Haven,[67] and the women got upset about the way he'd just sort of sit around and drool at em and not never do none of the *group activities.*"

"Oh hell yeah, I know," said Voyd. "Monty Hardy came up from St. Leo in a fukkin po-lice car and snatched his ass back down to Mhoon County. I mean, that sumbich Strayhorn aint but forty-something, and there he is chasin around after these old gals up in their sixties and seventies . . ."

"And fukkin eighties and nineties too," I added, and then I said, "Muthafuk!" cause I knew I was gon have to hit that coksukka in the head with my white-ass walkin cane before he found out Voyd was Voyd and the object of his lust. I mean, now, what can you do about a sumbich like that?

Luckily, I did not have to hit the muthafukka. By that time we was hustling to get out of Goldsmith's and into the Mall to follow Miss Attica on down to Twillard's. I guess you could say we was actually runnin, and, when we got on out of the store and into the Food Court, I turnt around and could not catch sight no more of Strayhorn. That was a fukkin relief to me, but I could tell Voyd felt a little let down.

---

67 A suburb of Memphis just across the line in Mississippi. —ml

Before it was all over, Miss Attica had to visit every dum-ass store in East Meffis. We was all over Oak Court AND across Poplar into Sears and all them other gotdam ladies shops—include'n a coksukkin art gallery and a kiss-my-ass fukkin bookstore! I won't get into that although, as you know, I already had a whole different opinion of bookstores in general and that one in particular because when my first and second books come out, they put em on their shelfs and ast me to come up and sign the sumbiches. Which I did. I'm just glad as hell they didn recognize my ass when I was "blind" and holdin hands with Voyd.

One thing, though, had me confused at first. When Voyd and me was cutn a trail outa Goldsmith's into the Mall and the Food Court, tryin to keep up with Miss Attica with Ezell taggin along behind her, I noticed everybody stoppin and starin at us with their mouths hangin open. As I say, at first I was confused. I figured it was because Voyd looked so fukkin unappealin in his grandmama's dress. But that wuddn it.

"They was starin at your ass," Voyd said.

"Fuk you, Voyd," I said. "Why would them sumbiches be starin at me?"

"Cause," he come back with, "you was bustin outa that store in front of me, is why.

So fukkin what?" I said.

"Junior Ray . . . ," Voyd said.

"What? Gotdammit!" I said.

Voyd didn make no sound for about half a second—I don't even think he was breathin—then he looked straight at me and said, "Dumbutt! You was a blind man! Remember?" And he pointed out: "Yet there you was, runnin ever' whicha way, this way and that, out through the fukkin food-court, in your dark glasses, dodgin tables, and whackin at the air with a white stick! You scared the crap outa half-a Meffis."

"Oh," I said.

And that was the first time in my life I did not have nothin to pop back on Voyd.

Anyhow, overall, me and Voyd pretty much enjoyed surveillin the sus-spek even though we come up empty-ass handed as far as evidence was concerned. But I think both of us knew a sumbich has to have patience to be a good diktective, and I guess we had some. However, it wuddn long before everything changed.

EZELL DONE A GOOD job! Not too long after our surveillance in Meffis, he come over to the house early one evenin about eight o'clock. It was dark. And it was a Friday. He knocked on the door. I opened it and looked at him stanin there just a'grinnin, and he said: "She done it, Junior Ray! Miss Attica done it!"

"Done what?" I said.

"She done mailed one nem letters to young Mr. Brainsong at the Clarksdale post office!" he said. "I seen the letter, and I axed her when she got in the car did she want me to go by the St. Leo pos' office and mail the letter she had in her hand, but she tol' me *no*, that she'd mail it when we got to Clarksdale. And she did."

Then Ezell said, "But, she didn. Miss Attica was gon mail that letter and a little stack of some others, but all of a sudden she axed me to do the mailin. She handed me the whole stack. And I got out of the car and went inside the pos' office and put all them letters in the box! That was around seb'm o'clock and wuhn't nobody there. We was on the way home."

I guess you could say Ezell broke the case. We didn have no time to lose. I don't know why that worthless sumbich didn tell Secundus 'fo he told me. But, neverthefukkinless, I guess I did the same thing, because I called Voyd. He was there at my house in about six minutes, then him and me and That Worthless Nigga Ezell rode around town and caught up with Secundus, who really did more "night watchin" than the folks he had working for him. We, and mostly Ezell, told him what had happened, and the Chief said he'd take it from there. And then he ast us why the fuk we did not *call* him sooner! I didn have no answer for that. It just seemed easier to go look for him, and frankly I believe it was. Anyway if I'da called I'da probly got his coksukkin voice mail.

I HAVE TO TELL you bout Secundus, the sumbich has some connections. Big ones I think. And *one* of em was a strange muthafukka called Multiple-Agent Eagle Swoop, a spindly little sort of hiccup of a man who mostly you'd see every now and then sitn—wearing dark glasses—drinkin coffee in the Boll & Bloom Cafe out on Highway 61 in St. Leo, or doing the same thing in Clarksdale at the Ranchero and sometimes setn all by hissef at the Rest-Haven Restaurant. Both of those are on 61, too. I don't know what it is about that road, but there is a hell of a lot more on it than just cars.

All I ever really knew about him was that he was awfully special and that didn nobody else seem to know much about him neither. Plus, he didn never talk to anybody. And his dark glasses was a whole helluva lot darker'n the ones I was wearin when Voyd and me was surveillin Miss Attica up in Meffis. Far as I know, Swoop worked for the FBI, or was supposed to, or used to, or sumpm, but the sumbich was the one who was able to get the letter from the folks in the Clarksdale post office! Now how the fuk he did that I do not gotdam know unless he in fact *is* with the F-B-Fukkin-Eye. And when I quizzed Secundus about him, all I got was that Eagle Swoop had something to do with protectin voters. And when I said, "Protect em from who?" Secundus just looked over at me and said, "You know who," and that was the end of that.

I used to think I knew just about everything there was to know about down here, but I could see right then and there I was out of touch and hadn realized it. Damm.

So, the next day, around two o'clock in the afternoon, Voyd and me and Ezell was waitn with Secundus who was stannin by his po-lice car outside the "City Hall," which is new and wuddn there way-ass back when I was comin up, and for one thing, it's setn on top of what was the railroad track, and even though there aint no more train or no more track, every time I drive in front of it, I look both ways.

Secundus had said, "Junior Ray, if you and Voyd and Ezell have a moment, I've got something to show you—it'll be here in a few minutes."

We said, "Fuk yeah," and I guess four minutes after that, a serious-lookin black 2000 Ford LTD with a spotlight on the driver's side, right above the side-view mirror, pulled into the parkin lot; the door opened, and that strange skinny lil sumbich I was talking about—around five-feet-nine in his black-ass dark glasses and his customary skinny-ass black suit—got out. Secundus walked over to him and shook his hand like they'd done knowed each other for a thousand fukkin years. Then him and the little fukka walked over toward us.

"This is Multiple-Agent Eagle Swoop," Secundus said.

"Hidey-do," Voyd and me said. Ezell didn say shit cause he don't have much home-trainin, but we was all three wonderin what the fuk this sumbich was. And he didn crack a smile for none of us. It was the first time I had ever been that close to him, so to speak, and we hadn never been innerduced.

Swoop had a GI haircut and no hat. He took them dark glasses off and gigged our asses with two burnin-hot high-voltage blue eyes that looked straight th'oo your skin and bones and, for all I know, seen *tomorrow*! The closest I can come to describing his eyeballs is that they reminded me of two super-ass intense little pilot lights on sumpm that might explode. I felt like I had said hello to an appliance.

We looked at Secundus, and he knowed what we was askin even without us havin to say nothin, so he said, "Eagle and I have been friends for a long, long time, and he agreed to do us a big favor." At that, the skinny little sumbich reached in the left inside breastpocket of his black suit-coat and whipped out a' en-vellop. His arm out shot out fast-forward, and he gave the en-vellop over to Secundus and said: "Here's some more." And, from the opposite pocket on the inside of his coat, he pulled out the *rest of the letters*, the "stack" that Ezell had put in the mailbox down in Clarksdale for Miss Attica. And that really cinched the whole ball game on account of all of em was *addressed in her handwriting*, as was the threater letter—except, unlike the others, it didn have no return address. I reg'n Miss Attica was tryin to be slick.

But it did have a fingerprint—on the back of the threater-letter where she'd pressed down at to make sure it was sealed. Secundus was able to find out that it was in fact a "jelly" fingerprint of her left middle "digit"—he found that out because, later, when she come in to see Judge Justiss, Secundus more or less formally arrested her and had her to make her fingerprints. Anyway, the jelly print was somewhat smudged, but a print nonethefukkinless! We come to find out—well, when we was speculatin on the left-hand-middle-digit print—Ezell told us that Miss Attica liked to eat muskydine[68] jelly she made from the vines in her own backyard, and so that mornin, before they went to Clarksdale, when she was at the breffus table, she had some of it on her fingers, which she had not licked thoroughly-ass off before she started fukkin with her stack of stuff to mail. So there it was.

Multiple-Agent Eagle Swoop looked at the threater letter that Secundus was holdin in his right hand, then, with them dark-ass glasses and pointn to the letter, he looked over at Voyd and me and

---

68   Muscadine; a wild grape native to Mexico and the southeast U.S. —ml

Ezell and said, "I don't have the slightest idea what is in it, and I don't want to know. I'd go crazy if I let myself become involved in the personal goings-ons of you folks down here in this Godforsaken swamp—drained or undrained."

He turned around and quick as a goodbye fart he was in the big old LTD on his way out of the parkin lot—but as the vehicle come up even with all of us standin there watchin him leave, he stepped on the brakes, his window come down, he whipped off them dark glasses, aimed them eyes right at us, and said: "On the other hand, everything down here is personal, iddn it?"

Then *Zoop*! before you could say "Fuk yeah!" his window was up, and he was rollin off eastward out of town to Highway 61. And we had the goods on Miss Attica. Well, sorta. But it was sure as Shuqualak[69] beyond a reasonable doubt.

BUT I DO HAVE to tell you this: After me and Voyd got caught by Secundus up under Miss Attica's and we had the talk, Secundus told us we could do our surveillin some more, and I for one was pretty proud of that because it said to me that Secundus had some faith in our professional ability to gather evidence, *but he told us to be careful not to get caught*, because, he said, if we did, he was gon figure out sumpm "unpleasant" for me and Voyd to have to deal with. Keep bearin in mind that Secundus wuddn no ordinary sumbich. Besides bein black, he was, like I told you, a gotdam West Point U.S. Army MP bird-Colonel, and you just don't get no higher'n that. I don't spec there was ten of em in the whole fukkin U.S. of A.

Anyway, right after that when Voyd and me was conductin our third high-tech stethoscope-ical diktection, we was down under

---

69   A Mississippi hill town, pronounced like "sugar lock." Some say it means "hog wallow," but according to Mad Owens, the name is from the Choctaw for "where beads are made." Junior Ray just likes the sound of it; he has never been there. —ml

Miss Attica's house lisnin away th'oo the planks in the floorin, and we're hearing mostly what seemed like just a lot of chit-chat between Miss Attica and old Euster. But then things got quiet for a minute or two, and we heard Miss Attica say: "Have some more elderberry wine."

Now, we heard this just as clear as the cellophane on a pack of peanut butter crackers. See, it had took a little while for Voyd and me to get a good fix on where Miss Attica and old Euster was so we could tune in on em, but after a while, the two of em stopped movin from one place to the other and we was able to stop crawlin all around under the house, and finally we had our official stetho-scopes plastered up against the bottom of what we already knew was Miss Attica's and Euster's bedroom.

They'd done et their supper, fiddle-farted around in the house for a little bit, and was then up in the bed watchin TV, which appeared to be Hawkeye an' nem on *MASH*. Anyway, we could hear the tube plain enough, and you'da thought the *Rest-o-tronic* or whatever and the bedcovers woulda soaked up what the two of them, Miss Attica and old Euster, was sayin to each other, but it didn. That told me sumpm important about how secure what a sumbich said in a "bed" situation might and bygod might not be. Just in case, I mean, you know, like if I was to ever find mysef in a simyoola set-a circumstances, nohmsayin?

Then *MASH* went off, and there was some music comin out of what we figured was still the TV, but it wuddn none I recognized right off—I mean, I did and I didn. However, it wuddn but a rabbit-fuk minute before *that* changed as well, and, when the light-bulb, so to speak, come on, I looked at Voyd, and he looked at me, cause both of us had heard *exactly* the kind of music it was plenty of times before—you know, that goin-nowhere-doin-nothin-no-words background type of music—and along with it we could hear: "Oh, Oh, Oh, Oh, Yes, Yes, Yes, Yes, Oh Yes, Oh Yes" . . . you've heard it,

too, unless of course you're just teetotally dickless and trickless—
It was a *gotdam porn movie they was lookin at!* Son-of-uh-bitch!
That's the way it is, iddn it? You just don't never know what the
fuk people do even when they're people you wouldn think would
be doin the stuff you'd think they wouldn be doin. CHREYEST!
I expect you get the pitcha.

All of a sudden, though, it wuddn no longer the television we
was hearin. It was them! It was Miss Attica and old Euster rollin around in bed havin some kind of sex, right there in front of
the tube. My first thought was, "Holy Shit. God, don't let them
sumbiches reproduce!"

"Atty-watty," we heard old Euster say.

"Euster-booster," Miss Attica come back with.

"Fuk!" Voyd and me whispered, simultaneously.

"UmmmaNummma-n-ummm," one of em—we believed it was
Euster—said, and the other'n—had to of been Miss Attica—chimed
in with, *"Unh, unh, unh, ooohooo."*

Granted it was hard to know precisely what they mighta been
doin, but it was pretty easy—well, for the most part—to tell their
sounds from the ones on the TV. Me and Voyd have been around
Euster and Miss Attica all our bad-ass lives, so we do know what
them two fukheds sound like. Miss Attica sounds like a talkin watermelon, and Euster's voice resembles the strain of a difficult shit.

But what I've told you aint all there was:

"Have you got it on?" Euster ast Miss Attica.

"Oouuuhooouumh," she said in a way that made me picture
her as a giant-ass edible bird.

"It's so big," Euster gargled.

"Oouuuhooouumh," Miss Attica said again, and, then, "You
love it, don't you, Eusty-boosty?"

"Awnh-Hawhn," he said. "Did you put the KY on it?"

"Yessy-Wessy."

"Well . . . I don't know . . . "

"Mine's bigger than *Yoh-wuhz*," she sorta sang. "Here goes."

"I don't know, Atty . . ."

"Hold still," she told him.

"YOW!" he said.

Voyd and me was stunned. If we heard what we thought we heard, we aint never heard nothing like it; although, out in Cali-fuk-assin-forn-ya, I believe, it might be more common than it is here in the Delta, whatever the fuk it was. And what I think it was, was Miss Attica fukkin Euster in the butt with one nem strap-on diks the girl queers likes to use on one another. So my most immediate question was, what did that make Old Euster and Miss Attica? Reversible queers? It was definitely some kinda enter-course. Well, at least, I believe Miss Attica was havin sex . . . but Euster was getn screwed

I GUESS, TOO, YOU might be wonderin if Miss Attica and Euster ever heard us when we was lisnin in on em. Well, they did.

All of sudden, one night, Miss Attica said: "Eusty, I believe we have another raccoon under the house."

And he said, "Gotdammit. T'hell with that 'Spare-a-Varmint' trap; next time you hear the thing, call me, and I'll just shoot through the floor and kill the sunavabitch; then I'll get that no-count Ezell to go up under there and pull him out. We'll ask Deltoria to cook it for us."

"You'll do no such a thing!" said Miss Attica. "No suh, Mister Man. I do love raccoon when it's properly prepared, but you will not shoot your pistol through my mama's Hereez!"[70]

And we heard Euster say, "Okay, dammit. Okay. I'll just get Ezell to crawl around under there and get it out however he can. I'll give him five dollars and the coon."

---

70   Heriz. —ml

"That's better," said Miss Attica, "But tell Ezell he is not to shoot all over the place when he is down there."

And Euster said, "Yes'm."

As you might well imagine we was quieter than a muthafukka after that. Cause we knew ol' Euster might get drunk and shoot th'oo the floor anyway. But here's sumpm I probly ought not to tell you about, cause it'll tell off on me, but what the fuk.

Them two old fukheds was amazin. Plus, it sho is true that a sumbich don't never know what goes on behind closed doors unless of course he's got a fukkin stethoscope and can lisun in from the gotdam crawl-space under the coksukkin house. So, sumbich—OR sumbichette—you aint gon believe this: Voyd and me was well into, I think it was, our sixth sub-housal expe-fukkin-dition, and, Son, we thought we knew everything a muthafukka could know about the gotdam world till we found out we didn. Well, maybe we found out it was me who didn. Anyway, there we was with our stethoscopes, tappin into the sound waves from up in Miss Attica's bedroom and after a while here come a buncha gotdam fiddle music. It was the soft dreamy kind, not loud a bit, and we heard Miss Attica say, "Ooo, lamikin, here's my big ol' breast; I know you are just ache'n to take a bite of it."

And then Euster come back with, "I want your sweet juicy thigh, too, Atty-watty, but, honey-love, take a look at my giGANtic leg!"

"Law-wud! Law-wud, Eusty! My law-wud, it's so biiiG! I'm gon have to call it, Mister Leg! How can you manage all that?!"

"Your little Eusty is a big man."

"I know he ee-iz—Put that dee-licious thing in my mye-outh!"

"Open wide, dahlin—wait, love-bunny! Let me dip it in charlotte russe! So you can lick it first. Is it good? Suck it!"

"UmmmmMummmmmm, yayiss, yayiss, yayiss! Mo-wuh, mo-wuh! I want some mo-wuh, Eusty Boosty! Charlotte russe is sooo goo-wud! Put some on my thigh!"

"I'll do it with my fingers! There we go; lemme bite it!" Euster said.

"Ouuuuuuu," said Miss Attica, "Bite it, bite it, bite it, BITE . . . IT! Bite-that-thigh!

"Come ON charlotte rssss! Here she is! I'mo dip that big juicy leg and I'mo dip that sweet thigh! Look! there they go—yeeoow—in an' out, in an' out! Whoh-hoh, Look at that! I got charlotte rsssss all over em. Les us taste'm both—together!"

Holee Tickledik! I thought, how the fuk was they gon do that!? Course I know and you know, when people is havin sex, they think they can fuk on a motor-scooter. Plus, I kep thinkin to mysef, them old senior fart-hoppers got em a threesome goin on with somebody named CHARLOTTE! And up to that point, sweet Charlotte aint said nothin, so I figured she was just setn on the bed, or lyin there, or godknows what, letn Euster and Miss Attica dip parts of theirsevs in her whatchamacallit! And I thought: "Shit, Charlotte, say sumpm!"

I was bout ready to pass out, till Voyd chirped up and said: "Fuk, Junior Ray, them two buttholes is eatn fried chicken and swabin it around in charlotte rooge. Lissen."

And right then Miss Attica gargles out in that vegetational voice of hers: "Gracious, I am full to the brim!" Then ol' Euster followed that with, "Me, too, dahlin. I'll put the chicken and the charlotte russe back in the ice box—let's see what's on the Tee Vee."

And Miss Attica said: "You just watch anything you want, Eusty; I am so wo' out I am goin straight to sleep."

"Okay, sweed-aht," he said.

And that was that.

I hadn never heard of charlotte rooge before, much less dippin chicken in it, but Voyd said his grandmama used to make it every Christmas and that it was good as a bowla pussy. He claimed charlotte rooge was his favorite-ass dessert. Fuk, I thought. Gotdammit.

The whole thing seemed like it was a whole lot more than it was, and I sure wanted it to be. But even though Voyd and me never did come up with any evidence by lisnin in on Miss Attica with our stethoscopes, I did learn a helluva lot about what a sumbich can do with a chicken leg.

I DON'T KNOW WHAT it is about sex that people think is so gotdam awful, when at the same fukkin time, sex is all they seem to really care about even if they claim they don't. It's like them gotdam Republicans—always doin stuff with their weenies and tweenies they don't want nobody else to do and, further, tryin to make people think God, hissef, don't want em doin none of that neither. Worse than that, I guarantee, while I'm talking to you right this tock-tickin minute, one nem so-called Tea-Party coksukkas in Congress up-air in Worsh'nun DEE-cee is busy as a beaver in Belzoni leapin up on the back of a whatchacallit—intern—and flappin his arms wildly, you know, like the muthafukkin cockadoodledoo-to-you that he is. . . . Plus, I'll make you a nickel bet that for a solid half of them other flag-waggin, necktie-gaggin balltuckers, just another boy for Jesus and a plain ol' cock'll doodle, too. I seen it on the news. And so have you!

But, carin or not carin about sex, it's the same thing. It's like when you go on a diet: food is still the issue, only instead of spendin all your time thinkin about eatn it, you spend all your time thinkin about *not* eatn it. And that's the way it is with sex. Either way, you got your eye on it.

Mad Owens pretty much summed it up with a thing he told me when we was on that island.[71] We was just setn around, and Mad said, "Junior Ray, I wrote something funny about sex." I practically remember the whole thing word for word—but this is your

---

71   Horn Island, at the far edge of the Mississippi Sound, in the Gulf of Mexico: See *The Yazoo Blues*. —ml

lucky day because Mad mailed me a zeerocks of it, so here it is—it's sorta like sumpm from the Bible, and this is how it goes—listen up while I read it to you:

IN THE BEGINNING, the Lord made everything, and then he added a rather bland, not-quite-finished creature called Man. Unlike most of the other animals, which were divided sexually into males and females, there was only one Man, and it was neither.

There was nothing to distinguish one kind of Man creature from another. In specific, the Lord had not provided Man with sexual parts of any sort, mainly because, at that time, the Lord wasn't sure Man ought to have any. Angels didn't, though gorillas did. It was more a problem of classification than anything else.

Finally, the Lord decided to give Mankind a distinguishable, if not distinguished, set of sexual characteristics. He called an angel and said: "Take these things down to Earth and attach them to the creature called Man." And he gave the angel a diagram and an instruction sheet with numbered steps to help him put the parts on right.

"Remember," said the Lord, "put these on the males and those on the females. Then He held up an example of each item so the angel could see which was which. "And," said the Lord, "be sure nobody gets more than one."

"Don't worry," said the angel. "I know I'll get the hang of it."

Just as the angel was leaving, the Lord called out and said, "Oh, wait a minute. Take some of . . . uh . . . these . . . "

"Bosoms," said the angel. "They're called bosoms."

"How do you know that?" inquired the Lord.

"I saw some once when I worked for another religion," replied the angel.

"I might have known some polytheistic gang leader would beat me to the idea," grumbled the Lord. "Patented too, I suppose."

"Very likely," replied the angel. "They were more or less standard equipment."

"Goddamnit," said the Lord.

So the Lord told the angel to give the bosoms to the females. "Be sure they match," He said. "And," He added, "don't give any to the males. It might make them boastful."

Then the Lord continued: "Tell Mankind that I have sent them these new attachments just to break the monotony and that I hope they enjoy them, but they are not to use them."

"Not to use them, Sire?" responded the angel.

"That's right," said the Lord. "They are not to use them."

"That doesn't seem fair," said the angel.

"I don't have to be fair," answered the Lord.

"Why?" asked the angel.

"Because I'm the Lord," said the Lord, "and you're just an angel."

When the angel returned from Earth, the Lord inquired how Man had received the new attachments, and the angel said, "Very well, Sire. They seemed delighted to have them and were quite happy just wearing them around as ornaments."

"That's great," said the Lord.

"But," said the angel, "things changed when I told them you said not to use them."

"Oh," said the Lord, "so they were unhappy because I forbade them to use their new equipment?"

"Oh, no, Sire," said the angel. "Your forbidding them didn't bother them in the least. They got upset because they couldn't figure out how it worked. They insisted I tell them, but, being an angel, I didn't know either."

"Well, that's good," said the Lord. "If I don't give them the instruction manual, they won't ever find out. Right?"

"I'm not sure," said the angel. "When I left, they were experimenting like mad. They said if they didn't catch on by Thursday, they would call in a consultant."

"Shoot," said the Lord.

And so, by trial and error, through persistence and with perhaps a little help from the Devil, mankind's forefathers and foremothers learned how to use the new attachments given to them by the Lord.

Regardless of what anyone may say about the new parts, their greatest virtue seems to lie in their remarkable *durability*. For, in all this time, mankind has never been able to wear them out.

And that's it, sumbich.

Young Mr. Brainsong II's Hi-Tee Treat

I wouldna never knowed about sumpm like this, but I have to tell you it is de-gotdam-licious and tastier than a mutha-fukka. See, Brainy's been to England, so he knows stuff a lot of people don't have no idea about, and this recipe is one of em. Course it's just a' everyday thing to them diklikkas over in England. And this is what it is:

Sourdough bread, with orange marmalade and stilton cheese on top of it, all toasted up in your toaster oven. But remember to spread the marmalade on the bread first, then lay on the stilton. That's so the cheese'll woozle down all over the marmalade on the sourdough bread. And make the thing big. Don't be like them thinny-skinny Prez-ass-p'terians.

You can't beat it, especially if you also drink a cup of hot fukkin tea fulla hot-ass milk along with it. You can put honey in the tea, too, or sugar . . . but personally I like the honey. Plus, it's better for you. I think.

Anyway, this aint sumpm you're apt to get at the cok-sukkin local-ass BizzyBee-type cafe, the likes of which such meat'n'three places you may no longer find in these lillo dead-ass broke-dik Delta towns. And I guarantee you will not come across nothin like young Mr. Brainsong II's Hi-Tee Treat over on the other side of the gotdam Miss'ssippi River in Arkin-fukkin-saw. So, go grab a gotdam teacup, stick out your pinky finger, and have a good time.

Chapter Fifteen

*Merigold Is Sent to Parchman—The Unthinkable Is
Not Abnormal—We Go Dove Hunting—Voyd and Me
Trade Lead with Miss Attica—Miss Attica Confesses to
the Killings—No Crime Was Committed—Ham You
Rob It—Recipe No. 15: Junior Ray's Apres-Hunt "Dove
Lovey-Dovey"*

M erigold was sent down to Parchman, you know, in the
middle of the fukkin Delta right there on the side of
Highway 49 West, just north of Drew. Well, hell, she
kilt her mama with the hedge clippers!

Her lawyers did a good job of layin it out how she was crazy
and everything, which she is, and the jury agreed that she was but
that they just didn think she was crazy enough. So Merigold did
not get put in Whitfield, which is the state *IN*sane asylum, but is
gon spend the rest of her life in the state penitentiary at Parchman,
where she is right this minute, in the women's section—which
used to be the cannery. But that's all okay. It's a shame of course
that any of what she done, and has to pay for, ever happened in
the first place, and that she has to be locked up in Parchman. But,
at least it's somewhat close to home, and I expect that makes her
feel a little better.

Merigold is truly crazy, and I frankly do believe her when she
said she just meant to kill her mother "a little bit." Yes, I do. And I
feel fukkin sorry for Merigold because somethin in me just won't
permit me to feel hard toward her. On the other hand, I feel sorry

for her mother, Miz Potts. But, all things considered, I feel sorrier for them dogs that et her.

The truth is, Miz Potts woulda been hard not to want to kill on a daily basis. Some people are like that and she was one of em. You've seen em, always walkin around like that *Lil Abner* fellow Joe BIT-SPILK.[72]

Furthermore I don't know if they still do any cannin in the Women's Prison, which as I mentioned is where it was done back in the days when the prison was just a big-ass plantation and the guards with the guns was in fact the prisoners themsevs—they was the trusties, and was called "the shooters," and each of em carried a nickel-plated, lever-action .30-30; plus, some of em lived alongside Highway 49 with their families, and the stripes on their britches run longways down their legs as opposed to the ordinary sumbiches in the camps whose stripes run round and round. Anyway, even the roughest, toughest, meanest muthafukka penned up on that reservation wouldna never wanted to eat nothin Merigold mighta put in a can.

There's one other thing. Merigold told the court that sometimes her mama was not really her mama but a "bagga'ster." She said a bagga'ster was a thing that had eighteen tentacles and that the tentacles come out after you in sets of threes; plus, each one nem tentacles had a fishhook on the end of it, which, if it ever grabbed ahol', you couldn never get loose from it, and that mostly was why she had to pick up those hedge clippers and chop up her mama.

Them twelve fukhed jurors still did not feel she was crazy enough to be crazy. Course I can kinda understand it, but I don't think the rest of the country could have.

But that's just it, iddn it? Most of what I consider to be "General America" likes to believe that the godawful unthinkable-ass

---

72 Joe Btfslk, Al Capp's contagiously dark-clouded sad sack. —ml

things is abnormal, while, down here in the national crotch, we don't. About the only thing *abnormal* down here on any given day would be a sumbich that didn like football and, if he was white, was a gotdam Democrat! That'd be abnormal. The bulk of the rest of human and non-human activity is thought of pretty much as *standard operatn procedure*.

WE NOW HAD CAST-IRON proof that Miss Attica was sendin them threater letters, but we still did not have no hard evidence to tie her to the actual killins—even though Secundus, with me and Voyd's help of course, was more or less able to put her at the scene of all three of the killins.

Plus, of somewhat major-ass importance, Miss Attica only had the one shotgun that I knew about, and it was that Ithaca .410 pump. In addition to which, we also knew she had a fondness for three-inch shells and number 7½ shot, which she had sprayed me an Voyd with for near bout two hours that time she invited us to go dove huntn with her out at Silty Harrow's sorghum field. Silty was Miss Attica's cousin. Singletree Hames was, too. ChrEYEst! All emm sumbiches was kin!

Her invite'n us was just outa the blue and wuddn sumpm we or anybody else woulda ever expected her to do. Voyd and me figured she might be on to us. Anyway, we thanked her and said we'd love to go dove huntn out there on Silty's place. Miss Attica was bubblin with smiles and runnin over with marshmellas and molasses. It didn feel right. You know every one nem *Planter*-women can shoot. All of em has a gotdam gun!

The day come, and Voyd and me drove out there. It was in a field real near the levee about halfway between the Tait place and the Evanses. And it was easy to get to. We just drove out the west side of town, and once we crossed Bailey Bye-oh, we hung a sharp left onto a turnrow[73] and went south for almost fifteen hunnud yards and there we was. Voyd and me pulled up beside Darby Sherds's old *hoopdy-ass* Buick, got out, and walked about three hunnud feet to the fukkin sorghum field where Miss Attica—and I expect twenty more of them *Planter* sumbiches—was standin around talkin about who did and who didn make a lucky big-ass lick in the commodity market.

She wuddn the only female there, neither. Miss Lucia Newell was present as well. So was her daughter Dee Dee, who was getn ready to marry Singletree's nephew, Noel Towns, down at Perthshire on Highway 1. And Sugsie Crawsthbrake[74] was out there, too, and I knew she could shoot the shit out of a twelve-gauge cause, one time at a skeet-shoot south of St. Leo on the Mangum place, by Lake Josephine, I seen her squeeze off one shot and break two clay-pigeons right as they crossed.

Anyhow, out on the dove field before and even during the hunt and all the shootn, Miss Attica was *Miss Super-Ass "One of the Men"*—while also being super-ass womanistic at the same time, as was all them other "Planter" women, whose over-scrubbed husbands owned six thousand acres of the best class-one soil in the Delta and rented ten thousand more from the fukkin Bluedential Insurance Company as well as from the usual platoon of blue-haired old widows.

Then there was me an Voyd. "Oh, hi yew, Junior Ray!" some ass'ole'd say and be off like a shot out of his own gun. Voyd and me stood around mostly, lookin here and there and all around over the field, like we was sizin it up, which we wuddn; it's just that none

---

73 A "turnrow" is that part of a cotton field—or of any cultivated field—where the tiller turned his mule or mules—or tractor—around at the end of the row. The "turnrow" evolved into a narrow dirt road upon which one might ride a horse or drive a truck or car to inspect the field . . . or park for sex. —ml

74 See footnote 41.

of them other muthafukkas didn no more want nothin to do with Voyd and me than a gotdam jaybird wants a BB up his ass. And we knew it, so we tried to look like we was doin just fine, which we was, but you know what I'm talkin about.

Pretty soon we was all headn into the field, and everybody was directed to where they was to stand, and Miss Attica told Singletree to put Voyd and me directly across the sorghum field from her so that we was lookin straight-ass into the setn sun, and she, then, had the late-afternoon September sun to her back and a clear view of us.

Well, you know, it aint that we was in any type'a danger. I mean even if Miss Attica had shot point-blank across the dove field at us, the gotdam pellets outa that little pop gun wouldna done nothin at the distance we was at—but there hadn been no distance in Tombo's case.

I have to admit somethin I do not like to own up to, and that is I always wanted me one of those sleek-ass little shotguns. You just can't imagine how fukkin light they are. I don't know how them Ithaca people does it, but they do. Plus, as I mentioned earlier, it is very unusual for anybody to hunt doves with a four-ten. But that did not appear to bother Miss Attica, and she managed to get her limit.

Voyd and me got our limit, too. And I believe so did everybody else. As the sun sank lower and lower, them birds come zoopin and zoomin into that field faster'n you could say bullseye. It was a lotta fun, and, I have to tell you, if you have never eat a dove, you need to try some.

But the whole fukkin afternoon, when them speedy, dumbutt little birds'd flap their ass across the field, Miss Attica rained down lead on us, which, though it wuddn dangerous, was pretty dadgum annoyin, if you know what I mean.

The onliest thing we could figure was that she had not invited us there to do no dove huntn. Unh unh. We dam certain knowed that. So we supposed, and I think rightly fukkin so, it musta been because she wanted to send us a message, which, frankly, we further supposed we had already received a good while back: namely, that Miss Attica knew she was a sus-spek.

I mean, whuht tha fuk, we didn know nothin for certain a-tall. I guess bein a diktective can make a sumbich be suspicious of just about anything. On the other hand, we coulda been right.

Anyway, we th'owed some shot back at her. Even when there weren't no birds.

Wuddn none of that gon stop us from bein diktectives, and wuddn nothin gon keep us from findin out the exact truth, or at least the next best thing to it. And I could tell, just from Miss Attica's manner, after the hunt was over, and we were on our way to our vehicles, that she knew Voyd and me was relentless muthafukkas, cause she didn hardly speak to us nor, really, even look at us. She just got in her car, where Ezell was sleepin, and that sumbich woke up and took her back to her house.

ALSO, WE COULD DEFINITELY put her in Shelby around about the time Farley Trout was stabbed with the little silver letter opener because Ezell had drove her down there and had let her out at the Oil Mill where she had some business she had to discuss because she owned a big chunk of the stock. And when Ezell come back later, from fukkin around in the cafes, that's when he saw the highway patrolman's car, right in the middle of town, with the lights blippin and blappin, and a little crowd stannin around Farley Trout's car outside Farley's shop, in there on the west side of the railroad tracks setn amongst all them other, empty, boarded-up stores.

Miss Attica was stanin there, too, minglin with the onlookers, and when she seen Ezell with her car, she got in the back seat, told him to put his show-fer's cap on, and then mumbled sumpm about havin made "an awful mistake." Ezell, at the time, just figured she had fukked up at the bank somehow or another. Anyhow, he said she seemed unhappy all the way back up Highway 61 to St. Leo and didn say a word the whole time.

I don't think it woulda ever been possible to have tied Miss Attica to Froggy Waters bein gigged in the th'oat with his own frog gig. That was a hard one. Still, we believed she did it, and we knew bygod she certainly could have did it! We also knew she would have did it, too, because them letters left no doubts she was out to stop young Mr. Brainsong II, lucky little fukka, from publishin Shaw's write'n. So if any of that was true, I mean if she wrote them letters, well, there you are.

As you already know, Secundus did not go over to Miss Attica's and arrest her. He and Judge Russell "Rusty" Justiss Jr. got together, and the judge called up Miss Attica and ast her to come to his office because he had a very important matter to discuss with her. So she come over there the next afternoon, and Secundus formally and politely, and more or less privately, arrested her big old butt right there in Judge "Rusty" Justiss Jr.'s office, where they also held an "arraignment."

But here's what happened—Judge "Rusty" Jr. put it thissaway: He told Miss Attica, there in the presence of her husband, Euster, along with Secundus, and me an Voyd, too—although him and me wuddn actually inside the judge's office but was listening at the door with our *stethoscopes*—so, anyway, *the judge told* Miss Attica that her just having mailed *even one* of them death threats was enough to send her to federal fukkin prison, that what she done was a very serious-ass federal crime—and also just a plain old *crime* crime as well—and even though she might not have to spend a whole lot of *time* locked up in a *federal* prison, he said he could definitely arrange for her to *go* to one—over in Atlanta, Georgia—even though he hissef was not a federal judge. Still, he told her, it *was* a federal offense, one bygod in fact which, he said, he was prepared *not to even mention* if she appeared to listen to what he had to say and do what he told her, and Miss Attica swore to his ass, yes, holy-jesus, that she was willin to do that and anything else he wanted her to besides.

He also informed Miss Attica that she had been arrested not necessarily for the *federal* crime of scarin the crap out of people through the U.S. mail, but that she was to consider hersef now in custody mainly on the basis of what he and the police chief—that's Secundus—believed to be what the amount of evidence at hand appeared to warrant as "probable cause." In other words, he explained, it sure as shavin cream looked like she had either killed Tombo Turnage, Farley Trout, and Froggy Waters outright or at the very least had had a helluva lot to do with it.

Judge "Rusty" Jr. flat out told Miss Attica that no matter how a person looked at it, it was pretty clear to him she had done a whole lot more than just *violate a few sumbiches' civil rights.*

Judge Russell "Rusty" Justiss Jr. let her know they were ready to test the scatter pattern from her .410 and send the little silver letter opener AND the fukkin frog gig over to the state crime lab at Batesville and that there was a good chance they would find some of her DNA on one or the other, even if she used gloves—and she did love to wear pretty white kid gloves whenever she went out of the house. But he told her that wouldn make no difference at all and terrified the livin shit out of her—so much in fact that she commenced to confess to the whole gotdam thing, which is what the judge and Secundus had in mind in the first gotdam place.

Miss Attica teared up and boohooed and said she was so sorry and that she never meant to harm, much less *murder,* none of them three dikheds, and Judge"Rusty" Jr. said, yes, he knew that. She laid out what she claimed was "exactly" how she done all three killins, but some of what she said, I thought, did not hunt worth a fish-fry fart, and I think you'd agree that the "x" in "exactly" don't always mark the gotdam spot. Anyway, Miss Attica told the judge that she had intended to do good overall but that she had simply been mistaken when she done what she did to the three deceased. The judge said he had taken it into consideration.

So this is what Judge "Rusty" Jr. come up with as a solution to the whole thing—bear in mind the judge, Miss Attica, even her attorney, Lawyer Tippendale "Tip" Draughon, was part of them Planters, and they had a way of dealin with things, which, I have to say, more or less got the job done without loadn the situation up with a buncha complicated complications. Secundus, now, even though he was black, was you might say because of who his daddy was and, of course, because that made him a half brother to the judge, was really part of them Planters too!—at least in the way he seen things, even though wuddn nobody ever supposed to mention none of that because the Delta wuddn like I hear Luzianna is, with all them Frenchies, where what-is *is*. Unh-unh, up here in the Miss'ssippi Delta what is *is* of course, but people are more likely to pretend what is *aint*.

First, the judge said the case would be "continued *sine die*," which I am sure you know meant it was to stay on the books but that there wuddn no date set for doin anything more about it. Bear further in mind, that basically, by this time, everybody setn there in the judge's office, and even Voyd and me just outside the gotdam door, is involved in commit'n one kinda crime or another as far as the State of Mississippi would be concerned, which I am happy to tell you it wuddn, because *nobody* who was there was gon say a gotdam word beyond that time and place. Or at least, right then, didn intend to.

Anyhow, Judge Russell "Rusty" Justiss Jr., who, I think, is some kinda genius because, him havin an *en*-tire fukkin *society* as well as the most peculiar-ass part of the coksukkin world to consider, he worked it all out in the following six easy-to-understand reasons, and I've got em here for you:

1. That, as far as he was concerned and at least for the time bein, Judge "Rusty" said, "No crime has been committed!"

2. There wuddn no crime because there wuddn no intent, or as the judge put it in proper lawyer terms, there wuddn no *mens rea*, which meant bygod that

3. All three of them killins was simply a big-ass mistake—"A tragic mistake, Yes!" the judge said, "Unquestionably, but no crime" . . . because

4. He empha-fukkin-sized that Miss Attica *had meant* to murder young Mr. Brainsong II—absofukkinlutely!— but, instead, she had *mistakenly* kilt them other three po' sumbiches *while not havin harmed young Mr. Brainsong II at all* one gotdam bit. So,

5. Since she had not done nothin whatsomever to Brainy yet had *done-in* them other fukkas purely by mistake, then, see, there it was—all just a coksukkin accident, clear as cow piss. And,

6. As any sumbich knows, it aint a crime to have a' accident. That's why it's called a gotdam accident.

The judge added to all that I just handed your ass by saying he believed his opinion would be admired by some long-dead fukka named *Ham You Rob It* and that it would be approved of by another dikhed he called *So Long*, or sumpm of that nature, and, likewise, he said he was more confident his landmark rulin woulda been "perfectly understood by Draco," whoever the fuk that was, and that his—Judge "Rusty's"—*commentary* on it was surely-ass gon be "immortalized in maxims by a latter-day Wingate." Finally, he b'lieved if the whole thing hada took place up in the city, he woulda made a killin—no *pum* intended, he said—and my ass was lost again on that one. Anyway, Judge "Rusty" added on, what he done most definitely woulda been "applauded" by some Eye-talian coksukka he referred to as "Judge Cardozo," who I guess lived up in Meffis—although, I'm sure I told you, them Eye-talians is all over the Delta as well. And that's because they fukked up and thought they was comin here to a farmin paradise. And then, of course, it turned out to be *us* . . . and the Niggas . . . and, oh, hell, . . . the Jews, the Chinamens, the gotdam A-rabs, and one or two Greek muthfukkas, and so then there we was, all of us, under the chubby pink seersukkin thumbs of them Planters and bankers. But I reg'n them Day-goes did all right, and, I spose, so did everybody else. And by that I mean all them foreign-ass muthafukkas, us Pekka-woods, and, natchaly, the Niggas. And I hate to think how them sweet-smellin, shoe-shined, new-car-drivin, just-hopped-outa-the-fukkin-bathtub, Panama-hat-wearing Planter muthafukkas have racked up . . .

Course I had no more idea than the gotdam man in the moon who any of them dilikkas Judge "Rusty" Jr. named was. But I didn give a hooty-owl holler because my main concern was pretty much a done-deal, and that was *havin Miss Attica Rummage know that her ass had got caught.*

Judge "Rusty" Jr. also declared that: "In some respects the situation, itself, might not be that unusual from an historical point of view and maybe could even be construed by other jurists as simply a personal if not in fact merely a local matter, although," he went on to say, "in the present case" three fukkin homicides did "more or less eliminate that possibility."

I got the pitcha. Three killins was about two over the line. But Judge "Rusty"Jr. saw he could handle it.

That's when I seen it. Suddenly everything about law and judging became real clear. It's like this: Say you was to go the Mhoon County Bank and rob it. "Stick-em up," you'd holler, and the sumbiches would hand over all the cash you could carry. Then, let's further say the sheriff and nem caught up with your ass. Here's what you could do. You could claim you did not mean to hold up that bank but that you had meant to rob the *other* bank—the St. Leo Planters Bank. Thus, see, you hadn had no fukkin intention whatsoever of robbin the one you robbed and that you robbed it by mistake.

There you are. No gotdam crime was committed. And you're off the fukkin hook, k'whap, just like that, like a big old gar in the floodgate on the old levee out at Freeman's Landin. I seen it all clear as water in a sandboil that day when Judge "Rusty" Jr. had his talk with Miss Attica. And I said to mysef right then and there that bein a lawyer and a judge aint hard once you get the hang of it. And I believe I could.

Junior Ray's Apres-Hunt Dove Lovey-Dovey[75]

Section One: Dealin with the doves.

You can't use nothin but dove bosoms. To get those, you have to know how to flipm outa the bird. And this is how you do it:

A. Grab one of the doves you or somebody else has shot.

B. Cut off the wings with a sharp-ass knife, or just ripm off—but, whichever, be sure you remove'm from right at where they're attached to the body of the dove.

C. Hold the bird face-up with one hand, and ram the fingers of your other hand up inside the body cavity just below the pointed bottom of his—or her—breastbone. It's easy to do, like skinnin a rabbit, and . . .

---

75 Caveat cookor. —ml

D. Get hold of that breastbone; use some muscle and pull it upwards quick and back over the dove's head, like you was tryin to take off a bird T-shirt. Separate what you're grippin from the rest of the bird. Your dove bosom will then be "flipped" out. There won't be no feathers nor no skin, and normally you don't have to do nothin more to it but chunk it in a large bowl which you will have on the table beside you—but if there does happen to be a smidgen of skin attached to the dove breast, it's not hard to get rid of. Plus, th'ow all the rest of them dove carcasses out the back door so the coyotes and the coons and the possums and the bobcats and the foxes can get to the in-nuds and everything durin the night.

E. Be prepared to "flip" for quite a while because you are goin to need a lot of dove breasts to fill up . . . your bowl.

F. Dump in a whole lot of garlic powder on top of em and mix it all around with your hand. Then wash you fukkin hand.

Section Two: The actual cookin part

1. Get out your iron skillet. Put it on the stove.

2. Coat the bottom of the muthafukka with pecan oil. Plus, set out your salt and cayenne so you'll know where it is when you need it. And you will need it.

3. Be heatn up two cans of condensed golden mushroom soup in a big-ass saucepan—DON'T ADD NO WATER . . . but do th'ow in a fully-loaded cup of Mad Dog 20-20, or just a cream sherry, not none of that dry or medium kind.

4. You're gon need a "bed" for your dove bosoms to rest on, so plan on havin a huge amount of Miss'ssippi brown rice already cooked. Don't fuk with none of that Arkansas crap. Or—and this is always a winner—do the same with a potful of the littlest new potatoes you can find at the gotdam grocery store . . . cause I know you aint gon grow your own. Me, per-sonally, I suggest you boil em. Some individuals will use toast

as their "bed," but I do not recommend that. As far as I'm concerned, toast, no matter what type it ever was, never had much to say for itsef.

5. The rest is simple. Get your pecan oil hot, and dump in the dove bosoms. Stir 'em round and round for half a minute or so whilst they are searin and brownin a little bit. And add some cayenne—but watch out, don't over do it.

6. Add more garlic powder, too. You can't overdo that.

7. When you have sawtayed the dove breasts in the pecan oil and garlic and cayenne for a few minutes it's time to toss in your condensed golden mushroom soup which you have already mixed with a cup of Eye-Doctor, that is to say: Mad Dog 20-20 . . . or the al-fukkin-ternative I suggested, above.

8. Let all that simmer for a while so all the various juices and sundry flavors can marry. You can add a little salt. But be extra careful about add'n it because the condensed golden mushroom soup is fully seasoned as it is. Still you are gon need a little extra salt to give some taste to your Miss'ssippi brown rice or to your tee-nyney new potatoes which, if it was me, would be boiled, but they're your taters so you might wantm sawytayed, baked, microwaved, or otherwise. They're goin in your mouth so it's up to you, Chilidog.

9. When you feel you've cooked long enough on your dove breasts and condensed golden mushroom soup mixed with a hip-pocket wine, have your chosen "bed" p'pared and setn there; then pour everything you got in the skillet out on top of your rice—or the tiny taters, and . . .

10. It'll be ready to eat. Do it, Sumbich. Don't fuk around and let it get cold.

Chapter Sixteen

I Coulda Been a Judge—Judge Russell "Rusty" Justiss Jr. Orders the Disbanding of the Aunty Belles—Me and Voyd Are Told Not to Never Say Nothin—Shaw and Heisenberg's Uncertainty—Southerners Was Born Asleep—But What About the Niggas?—Recipe No. 16: Junior Ray's Famous Fancy-ass Scallops, Shrimp & Mushrooms

Yep, I could see it. Until that moment I had never realized how fukkin easy it was to be a lawyer and a judge. It all made perfect sense to me, and I thought, "Well, I be dog'! I coulda been a judge AND a philosopher AND a historian AND a gotdam preacher all at the same time if only I'da know'd what I know now a whole lot sooner!"

As you might imagine, all this that was goin on in Judge "Rusty's" office made Miss Attica feel a lot better. And she was setn there noddn her head up and down in the af-fukkin-firmative. And old Euster looked greatly relieved as well. The judge, though, made it clear that if she carried on any more of this death-threat crap, and if any more people died under suspicious circumstances, he was going to revive the whole thing and lock her ass up.

"Furthermore," he said to her, "I fully expect you to see that this club you belong to, these so-called Aunty Belles, is disbanded forever, and if I so much as even get a hint that you are involved in any manner in any kind of organizational activity apart from the St. Leo Garden Club, the Bridge Club, or the Presbyterian Church

Circle, I will have Secundus come and haul you off in front of God and Dollar Bob.[76] There is no statute of limitations on murder or the accessory thereto!"

Miss Attica swore to do all the judge demanded, and she also expressed concern for the families of the three sumbiches she slew. The judge told her he would handle that, which meant he wuddn never gon tell none of them folks what we all had found out, but he was gon tell them that the county had a special fund which it used just for families that had lost loved ones in such a dark-ass unsolved way. And, some weeks later, Secundus informed my ass that each family was given two hundred and fifty thousand a piece, tax free. And he said for me to keep quiet about it, or he'd find somethin—and plenty of it!—to charge me and Voyd with. Plus, he said, even if we did tell all about what happened, nobody would believe a fukkin word of it. And he was right about that. But I wondered how many more things there was we might not be sposed to say.

See, Mhoon County was by then becoming one of the richest counties in the whole United States because of all the fukkin casinos that built big-ass gambling halls there, so, truthfully, that money they give them people wuddn nothin. When the local government didn have nothing special to do with all the money they was getn from the ten or so Lost Vegas enterprises, they'd pave somethin. ChrEYEst, those muthafukkas have paved everything that would hold still. Way back, electric lights was one thing, but now they're just fukkin up the whole gotdam place with the cosmetology of progress! It made me wish Miss Attica hada shot me! Well, you get my drift. Plus, a sumbich would just about have to be a *somebody-sumbich* in order for his family to get a big hunka dough like that.

---

76 A long deceased, ubiquitous town character who ran errands, bore burdens, and carted away unwanted things but charged only a dollar for his service.
    —ml

I am fairly sure the county wouldna been payin out like that to no pekkawoods. Even though there is more of us than they used to be.

See, except for Multiple-Agent Eagle Swoop bringin the threater-letter and them other letters to Secundus, plus him, *Multiple-Agent Swoop*, sayin he didn want to know nothin about what was in it—nobody in the whole fukkin country of America knew a gotdam thing about what we knew, which is why Judge Russell "Rusty" Justiss Jr. had the upper hand.

Funny thing about Miss Attica and all them old—and, I am fairly certain even though I can't never prove it, *young*—killer day-bewtaunts: they don't none of em mind profanity, but they can't stand insanity, yet they've got more actual craziness to deal with on a daily basis than they do of high-cussin sumbiches like me. So, I mean, you'd think they'd be used to the gotdam insanity. I guess it just goes back to them losin the war and all. Plus they probably know, too, that if they was to send a muthafukka like me a threater letter, I'd just tell em to go pee in their purses, cause as you well know I am not a gotdam gentleman.

Right now you might be thinkin, "Yeah, but they weren't one-hunnud percent sure about that"—about who they *could* and who they *could not* scare the diks—or maybe even *the tits*—off of. You know, I'm talkin about who they b'lieved they could bring to heel and who, on the other fukkin hand, might turn out to be a crazy-dog that wouldn stop huntn and runnin around the sorghum field and wuddn never in this world gon come back to the truck. I spec you know what I am talkin about. So I want to show your ass sumpm that Shaw said about how even really smart people aint always certain about what they're doin, yet, at the same time, it don't stop em from doin it. I do have to admit once't in a while that everything the sumbich wrote down wuddn just a handful of goat pills. Here it is:

SHAW:

"The more precisely the position is determined, the less precisely the momentum is known in this instant, and vice versa." —Heisenberg, *uncertainty paper*, 1927

Mr. Heisenberg was certainly certain about uncertainty, and, after I read about his principle, I gave it a lot of thought, especially after we got overseas and were living so much of the time in holes, and in the snow. It was during that experience that I knew, once and for all, uncertainty was for me, and now here it is again and could not be clearer. However, I have not precisely determined my position, and my momentum is only as fast as I can walk about.

If only I had done better in algebra! But even long division was impossible, particularly with decimals. Next to war, in which I saw what should never have been looked at and did what should never have been thought of, grammar school was the most difficult experience I have ever endured. But wait:

Goes now the hunting harrier
Ancient marsh hawk
Who strikes low along the ditch.
I will emulate your flap and glide
By holding out my arms at thirty-five degrees
Above the horizontal, and I shall leap
Into the cold clean air and
Try my best to remain
In flight.

That muthafukka was wild wuddn he? I left that poem thing there on the end of it just to show you how wild. But what all that tells me is that knowin somethin and bein certain about somethin are two completely-ass different pieces of business. As I see it certainty is like somethin you adopt. And I think most people probly do. Otherwise they'd all fall out and foam at the gotdam mouth. The point is when all this chasin after Miss Attica was goin on, I'd say every one of the players in the game—which was mainly Miss Attica and some of them Aunty Belles, me and Voyd, Secundus and Judge "Rusty," and, I guess, Multiple Agent Eagle Swoop, and yeah, hellfire, even that gotdam Ezell—was all certain about whatever they was doin without actually knowin whether what we was up to had much truth in it—or enough at least for us to be spyin and investigate'n up a storm the way we was. I mean how many times has a sumbich thought he seen truth when there wuddn no truth at all to what he thought he saw? None of us knew what was really beyond the fact of them letters. And it turned out what we did find out was basically just the result of a good guess. Now, wouldn none of this bother Leland Shaw nor that Heisenberg sumbich.

Anyhow I s'pose the best example of certainty would be that there aint nothin more certain than a lynch mob. People cannot get no certainer than that. I mean every one of them yobobs is entirely certain that the po sumbich they're putn a rope around is guilty as shit and that they, every pekkawood in the lynch mob, is doin the gotdam Lord's work! Halla-fukkin-luya. And then, natchally, sometimes one or two of them po—and I believe you will always find—white grits-guzzlin shitheds will find out the sumbich they hanged didn do what it was they hanged him for, and that mizzabul pekkawood comes to realize a day late and twenty-five cents short that he shouldna been part of the gang of them righteous super-certain muthafukkas that strung the po sumbich up. Yet, Oh Hell-o Bill! . . . you cannot call a muthafukka back from the dead! But it aint just pekkawoods that gets into that kinda trouble—look at Miss Attica and all her uppy-uppy lady friends! And by the fukkin way, the whole truth still aint come out about all that.

But back to the important gotdam question of knowin versus

just bein perfectly-ass certain you know sumpm, I am prepared to say that nobody knew what-was-what even in the case of Merigold, bless her off-the-wall-bug-eatn heart, nor about her Barky-Munchy-Pet-Treat mama, Miz Potts, who got scarfed up by the beagles—but who in fact for all I know mighta been the best old woman you ever knew in your whole life, although now of course it is too coksukkin late to find out, even if it was ever findable outable in the first fukkin place. So off we went, *certain* as a car-loada Cub Scouts but largely, in fact, totally fukkin uninformed. Anyway, here we are, still not knowin the whole story about none of it but *certain*—and this is what I now clearly see, we are certain—because we don't know doodly. And I defy your ass to tell me that aint so.

Certainty don't depend on knowin. Certainty is mostly just believin, and of course, as I pointed out in my second book—*The Yazoo Blues*—believin is mostly what Southerners do. I tell, these muthafukkas will believe dam-near anything as long as somebody else they approve of does. That's another thing about Southerners, they aint prone to single action. That's why, when you find a Lone Ranger down in Dixie, you got sumpm.

Uncertainty is for folks who are wild about *knowin* the real truth of things. These are the individuals that wind up givin us all the doodads and the comfuts we love to possess—and they found them things because they was *uncertain* and kep a'lookin. Certainty, though, is for shitheds who are "believers" and you got to watch out for them sumbiches, cause they'll just walk through a gotdam wall without botherin to locate the door.

I THOUGHT I WAS the most ignunt sumbich alive until I realized sumpm else. One day it came to me like it did to old Tombo, with a full-choke blast of BB's, that them gotdam Planters actually lived on a whole nutha level of ignorance not here-to-fukkin-fore recognized by the experts. And what made it all so awful was that those coksukkas used to control everything about my part of the world. They don't no more, but it wouldn't do no good to tell em that. They, theysevs, has refused to this day to understand the nature and complete extent of their unrealized handicap. Thus, bygod, in a way, you see, they still DO control everything in this part of the world. It's crazy. Which, here, means it aint.

You have to know right off the bat that bein a Southerner is like being in the grips of a drug. It's so powerful that after a while a sumbich can't tell the difference between livin and dreamin. We think we're *really* livin, but the real truth is we're dreamin. All of us down here, them sumbiches the Planters and my people, too, was born asleep.

It's just that most of us didn have much say-so in the way things was run. By "most of us," I'm talkin' mainly about my folks and, of course, the Niggas.

The gotdam Planters, of course, they're the ones that brung the Niggas here in the first place; then, by God, they hauled in the Chinamens and, later, tricked the shit out of the EYE-fukkin-talians and lured *their* ass here into the Delta, and once all emm sumbiches was here, then—OH Hell-o-Bill, *THEN*—here come the Jews and the gotdam Lebafukkinese openin up stores in all these little towns to sell stuff to the whole shoot'n match—and if that wuddn enough, *more* Jews and *more* Lebafukkinese piled in all the time off the trains to sell stuff to the ones who had the stores, and of course, natchally, just like them Planters, to have sex with the Niggas. It was just an unfortunate chain of serious events.

Anyway, as a class the Planters is goin' strong even if most of em aint no longer in the cotton business. You'd think somethin as soft as cotton wouldna had such a hard history and caused so much misery to folks. But that aint the way it was, and I can't change none of that now.

BUT WHAT ABOUT THE Niggas? You almost have to rely on the sumbiches, and I don't mind that, really. Hell, white people in the Delta don't know no other way. But there *are* some problems.

First of all, white folks forget how fukkin mean they was to those black muthafukkas, so whites now tend to think: Oh, hell, our white-ass-sevs is just the nicest things since a sack of marshmellas. Plus, they've managed to arrange it in their heads so's it's easy—and more comfortable for em—to believe the blacks are doin all the bad stuff—which they are and *always have* amongst themsevs! But see, *now* they're doin it to some of the whites, especially up in Meffis. Oh, shitchyeah!

Accordn to what I hear, it almost seems those black coksukkas is robbin and killin white folks up a storm there in the city. Plus, they aint let up a gotdam bit on themsevs neither. That's why I always carry my pistol. It'd be a shame to shoot one of em—as you know, I've always much rather'd to shoot a white man—but sometimes you just aint got a choice.

The problem is knowin when them sumbiches, and, ChrEY-Est, a lot of em is just teenagers, is gon to come at you. Plus, I tell you, when they get into it and get to goin with all that gimme-yo-money-muthafukka-gimme-yo-money-NOW-I'mo-blow-yo-head-off crapola, it's hard, in the middle of them circumstances, to talk em out of whatever they've got in mind to do to your ass. You're lucky if you just got pistol-whipped.

Of course we can't control none a' that now. Times have changed, and we can't no longer just go out, like I heard Sheriff Ketchum used to do in St. Leo, back in the 1930s, and hang a few of them sumbiches from the light poles. The downside of that, so I've heard, was that *it upset a lot of the Planters*—and especially their wives—damm near as much as it did the Niggas; so the "town" *de-sheriffized* old Ketchum's ass, run him outa St. Leo some way or another and put a gotdam Planter in his place, which right then and there turned a lot of them Delta county sheriffs' offices into a gentleman's business—with men just like Charlie Cargood, who was, I have to say, one of the most decent sumbiches I ever knew, next to Sheriff Holston. I only got to know Charlie later, when he was real old, a few years before he died. I reg'n I was one o' the few sho-nuff pekkawoods he ever had a fondness for.

He said people on the passenger trains comin through town had complained, too, when they'd look out the windows of the dine'n car and see one or two bodies swingin in the breeze over on the main street, in front of the drug store.

I have to say that woulda been a little bit too fukkin extreme even for me. And you know me, I normally don't give a shit about most things. Anyway, I guess by the time I get it all figured out, I'll be just about dead. Gotdammit! Aint that a hell of a note?

Now lissun, keep all this under your Cotton-Was-It Delta Council baseball hat. I wouldna wanted none of it to get back to Secundus, although I don't reg'n he'da thought it was a fukkin news flash. I guess I wouldn want Ezell knowin about it neither, but I aint too worried, cause that sumbich don't never read nothin.

Anyway, he's comin over to the house tonight to eat supper with Voyd and me cause he likes to watch *Seinfeld*, mainly on account of he thinks white people are funnier than a couple of dogs stuck-together tryin to have sex in the middle of the street, and his TV is broke. Plus, he seems to like my cookin. Hell, you can't fill his ass up! But, you know, them sumbiches is like that. Fuk. He'll want pie, too.

Junior Ray's Famous Fancy-Ass Scallops, Shrimp & Mushrooms Saw-Fukkin-Tayed in Olive Oil With Basil, Garlic, & Cayenne (over Angel Hair Spaghetti)

That just about tells you what it is already. However:

1. Buy fresh unpeeled shrimp, from the Miss'ssippi GuffCoas'.

2. Buy your angel hair spaghetti, and get to cookin it. Add some olive oil to the water to keep the angel hair from stickin together. And add a little salt as well. It won't take but a few minutes to cook, then, drain it and set it back in its big pot. You do not have to keep it hot. You can let it get to room temperature, because, when you finally pour what you'll have in your skillet on top of it—all that hot olive oil, scallops, shrimp, and mushrooms—your spaghetti will warm right up.

3. Buy the biggest scallops you can find, because they tend to shrink when you cook em. Even gotdam so, if you want to, cut the sumbiches in half.

4. Get fresh mushrooms, too, big muthafukkas. Be sure you wash em, and also you might want to chop em up just a little bit. That's your decision.

5. Peel the raw shrimp and set it to the side.

6. Drain the liquid as best you can from around the scallops—otherwise your skillet will fill up, basically, with scallop-water, mixed with the gotdam olive oil, and then you'll have to pour all of that off while it's all still cookin, and it'll be a coksukkin mess. But if you don't then you'll wind up boilin everything, and you'll want to avoid doing that at all fukkin costs, because it would be the gotdam end of the whole masterpiece.

7. Put your olive oil in your skillet. Then shake in a ton of basil-leaf pieces and a car load of garlic powder. Fuk the fresh stuff. You do not need it. Also, add a good bit of pepper—be

careful, though, because you can overdo that. I'm just warnin your ass.

8. Fire up the skillet and give all that seasoning a jolt; then, when it's bubblin up a storm th'ow in the scallops. You'll want to start em to cookin a little bit before you put in your shrimp. If you're like me, you do not ever want to confuse a tender scallop with just an out-and-out raw-ass scallop, and, even if the scallop is not all that raw, it can still feel a little bit, in your mouth, like it's on the raw side unless you cook it till those tiny little cracks begin to appear on it. You know what I'm talkin about. You've seen em.

9. Put in the shrimp. Cook it so it's fukkin done. Check it.

10. Add more basil and more garlic powder.

11. Th'ow in the mushrooms.

12. Keep cookin, and keep lookin. And, when you know what you've got in there is ready . . . cut the fire off, take the skillet off the stove to where the angel hair is setn in the big pot, and pour the whole hot, super-delicious shootn match on top of the pasta. Then stir the shit out of it with a big wooden spoon. If you have nerve damage, you can use your hand. But that's optional.

13. Eat it up.

CHAPTER SEVENTEEN

Redneck Vampires in Arkansas—Brigham Mounds Rises from the Dead—L'Oshunya Screamed—Baseball Is Too Slow—Voyd and Junior Ray Are Uninvited by the Rotarians—Is There Such a Thing as a Fartologist?—People Have Trouble Believin the Truth—But They Can Believe in Methuselah—"Some" Want Me to Stop Cussin, Gotdammit—Lucky Dogs in the Quarter—A Happy Woman—Recipe No. 17: Junior Ray's Famous Own Personal Favorite Late-Night Sammidge

I've been hearin about all emm redneck vampires and country-ass zombies, or whatever you call em, over in Arkansas. Well, Son! That's Arkansas for you. We aint got none of that over here on this side of the Miss'ssippi River; I don't care what they say about New Orleans. But don't get me wrong. I'm not just out and out sayin we're better'n nose Arkansas sumbiches. I'm just sayin *our* pekkawoods have better things to do than run around suckin on people's necks.

I guess the closest thing to the walkin dead and all of that we might of ever had was once when Brigham Mounds was pronounced dead around five o'clock in the mornin outside a cafe in the alley behind the stores on main street, and they put him in one of those body bags and zipped his ass up and took him to a black funeral parlor up in the Sub[77] and left his ass there for the staff to tend to when they come in at nine. He'd been shot in the head with a

---

77   A black subdivision on the north side of St. Leo. —ml

.22 short. The only thing was, Brigham *wuddn* dead. Plus, he was black and not no redneck.

He come-to inside the bag up on the table where they'd left him in the funeral home. But he was still zipped up in the bag and couldn get out. However, he swang his legs off the slab and was able to stand up,. By this time it was probably 8:45 in the mornin.

So there he is, confused as hell and standin up in a sack, yet he did not panic. He commenced to hop around, hope'n, I suppose, he'd find a door or somethin. Anyway, at nine o'clock, Cleon Fishmon, one of the owners, and L'Oshunya Johnson, who was in charge of the housekeepin, come to open the place, make sure it was spiffy, and get everything ready for a whole slew of family and friends to view the body of Cat-Iron Parker, who died of just regular old age at a hunnud and one. Cat-Iron told somebody once that the secret to his long life was Co'-Cola and young women, both of which, they say, he bought by the case.

L'Oshunya went straight to the embalmin room, and when she opened the door, there was Brigham, zipped up tight in his big black sack, hoppin across the floor toward her. L'Oshunya screamed till up in the evenin after she run outa the funeral parlor to her house a tenth of a mile west, back toward old Highway 61. Cleon didn know what the fuk was up when he seen L'Oshunya hollerin her head off and cutn a trail up the street, but it didn take him a minute to do the same thing and follow on after her the second he caught sight of Brigham hoppin out of the embalmin room into the hallway, and, then, once Cleon lit out, it didn take Brigham long either to get to the front door and into to the street hissef, where, by that time, two sheriff's deputies was drive'n by and seen the black sack hoppin up and down.

It wuddn so scary out in the daylight. They stopped their car, got out, and heard Brigham sayin, "Hep me, gotdammit! Get my ass outa this thing!" And they did. They unzipped the sack, and

Brigham looked at em and said: "Muh-thuh-fuk! Where am I?"
And the deputies said, "They thought you were dead and gone to
Heaven, Brigham, but don't worry, you're back in Hell." They took
him into St. Leo to the emergency room at the new little hospital
and fixed him up. The bullet had hit him square in the back of the
head, but it could not git through the hard-headed sumbich's skull.

I KNOW THIS AINT got anything to do with being a diktective, and
you might not think none of this has nothin to do with anything
at all, but you're fukkin wrong. It does, and it's got a name, too. I
learned it from Mad Owens. He heard me goin off to the side like
this one time and said, "Junior Ray, there's a philosophical term
for what you often do in your books."

"Dang," I said. And I ast him what the fuk it was, and he said:
"Well, it's what the experts call the *Full Inventory of Furniture in
the Existential Showroom.*"

"Dang," I said again, "I like that a lot, and I didn even know
I was doin it."

"That's the beauty of it, Junior Ray," he said, "because if you
knew you were, it would seem beside the point and it wouldn't get
done." Then Mad went on to explain that all book writers and of
course book talkers have to pay attention to "form," and he said mine
was like a fukkin tree, so that meant I could branch out whenever
I seen the necessity to do so and that was what made the gotdam
tree the tree. That makes sense to me. So all of what I'm gon to
tell you in this chapter is, in my view, things you need to think
about if you're gon do any thinkin whatsoever about the Miss'ssippi
Delta—and I mean the real fukkin Delta, the Yazoo Basin, not
that crap over in Arkansas or down there in Luzianna across the
Miss'ssippi River from Vicksburg, goin over toward Tallulah, and
it's not that gotdam delta way-ass below us where the Miss'ssippi
River runs out into the GuffafukkinMexico. I'm talkin about the

official *bonafide* Delta, the one of coksukkin legend and song. It's the one that got to be famous, and those other deltas, bygod, did not. The Delta where I live is what it is and there aint nothin nowhere like it, but mostly—even more than how it looks—it's what goes on in it and, to some degree, out of it but around it up in Meffis and over in the Loess Hills. However, if you don't want to know none of that, I don't give a crawfish fuk. Go get yoursef sumpm to eat and look at the big flat-screen TV. You can jump back in later if you feel like it; it don't really matter where, cause, you know, it's a tree. But just remember, sumbich, I'm givin you the cheeseburger super-dee-lux.

Anyway, if baseball is the all-American sport, then I guess I aint a All-a-fukkin-American. I don't have no apologies to make about it. Personally I get more out of watchin a field full of lespedeza[78] than I do lookin at the World Series, which, I have to say, seems to go on longer than a night in jail or five minutes in a gotdam church.

I don't mind football. As you know, I love to see people knock the shit out of each other and, of course, I like to look at the cheerleaders. Plus—and this does not mean I am a gotdam queer—I really like it when the band plays and marches all around out there on the field, and of course you know I *love* to watch them majorettes jumpin all over the place. I have often wondered why their daddies didn say somethin to em.

Once, me and Voyd thought we had made our way into bein buddies with the big shots. You know, apart from ol' Voyd and me becomin diktectives and all, if you live in a small town, there's just some things *you* do that aint really got much *to* do with nothin except just bein there, and one of those things is tryin at least a little bit to be good citizens, so that's the way Voyd and me thought of

---

78   A common agricultural ground cover in the American South, restores nitrogen, holds on to the top soil, and makes hay while the sun shines. —ml.

oursevs when one day we got invited to eat lunch with the St. Leo Rotary Club—with all them Planters and whatever was left of the rest of Mhoon County's movers and shakers, cause, since the end of hand labor, there aint hardly no merchants left in the town no more. I'm surprised, rilly, there's any a-tall.

Anyhow, every Thursday all the men in St. Leo who was anything to speak of and a shit-load of them Planters—near bout every fukkin one of em—eat lunch at the Rotary Club, which really is not AT no *club* a-tall but just in the little Community House, which I have told you about, located across the street from the north side of the courthouse, which I have further told you about, is where the ladies of one church or another or the fukkin Garden Club or somethin of that nature feeds all emm old sumbiches a meat and three[79] and gives em cobbler for dessert.

So Voyd and me went. And we went a bunch more times after that. But after one of those lunches in the last part of that July, we couldn never go again because of what that little dikhed Voyd did. And not being able to go no more meant it was gon to be just that much harder for us to find out who was sendin the threater letters—because, you know, at any kind of gatherin you always hear sumpm somebody ought not to say that can kinda cut you a path in the direction you need to go. If, of course, you're a good lisna like I am.

But Voyd fukked it up when he let loose a loud one the week before, right when we was all singing "R-O-T-A-R-Y That Spells Ro-Ta-Reee" and simultaneously givin each other the Four-Way Test.

Voyd thought there was gon be another verse and that he could just fart and nobody would hear it, but Miss Isabel stopped playin

---

79 Through time and tide there have been some changes, but it was almost always the ladies of the various protestant churches who fed the Rotarians, usually a meat and three veggies followed, of course, by dessert. And, yes, along with other Dixie dogma, macaroni and cheese is allowed to be a vegetable. —ml

the piano after the first chorus, and Voyd ripped one off right at
the end of "Ro-Ta-Reee." That was it. They all knew it was Voyd,
even though he stood there in the room lookin around like he,
bygod, wanted to know who done such a terrible-ass thing, but
evv-rybody knew it was him, and the next week was when he—
which meant me, too—got ast NOT to come back to the Rotary
Club lunch no more.

Here's how they done it. They got Brother Brotherton, the
Methodist preacher at that moment—I say "at that moment" cause
as you know none of them sumbiches stayed around for more'n
two or three years, which, as you further know, is the Methodist
"way"—anyhow, they got Brother Brotherton to take Voyd off to
the side that next Thursday while we was all standin in front of the
buildin waitn for the word from the *ladies* to come in, but just when
the wife of the new County Agent appeared in the door, Brother
Brotherton caught Voyd by the arm and held him back. He told
him they all loved him but that they was extremely-ass worried
about his health and wanted him to see a specialist.

Later Voyd ast me if there was such a thing as a fart specialist,
and I told him probly they was called fartologists.

Anyhow, Voyd swore to Brother Brotherton that he would try
to get cured, and that's when Brother Brotherton smiled one nem
preacher-smiles I guess they learn in "preacher school," then he
flicked out his *fork-ed*-ass tongue, stepped backwards inside the
Community House, and closed the door; and when Voyd reached
up to turn the knob, it was locked up tight.

Lemme just say this about Voyd. Course he's my friend, but
Voyd is the kind of sumbich that'll come up right beside you in a
restroom when you're tryin to pee in one nem yernals, and start
peein too—and *also* want to talk to your ass while he's doin it. What
makes a man like that? What kinda mama did he have? Didn he get
enough of pissin down the middle of the street all over town way

back when he and a gotdam pekka-posse of other little diklikkas used to walk along peein up a storm, seein who could pee out the farthest—and the highest!—when he was five-fukkin-years-old?! What's the matter with that fukhed?

It defeats my ass. You can't pee no more, with him standin there slap up next to you! The only thing you can do is play like you was finished, shake it off, zip up your gotdam britches, and get the fuk out. And, as you are well aware, that is hard to do.

MOST PEOPLE THINK STRANGE out-of-the-way things can't happen or can't *be* because they're too gotdam strange. But most people are wrong. Them things can be, and I'd lay money that they mostly always has been. For example, most people wouldna never thought a buncha daybewtaunts and blue-haired old women would consider goin around killin folks, but bygod they did consider it. And one of em we now know of did it, too, somehow or another. Wuddn none of that hard for me to feature.

Yet, people seem to have trouble putn any kind of faith in what I tell em. And that they have a problem with that is, to me, the strangest thing of all, because they don't have the slightest difficulty swallowin all that stuff about Methuselah and Moses and Jonah and Jesus. But here I am relate'n just everyday goins-ons, and they're laughin and sayin, "Aw, naw, Junior Ray, we aint got no time for your fukkin foolishness." I mean, you tell *me*, how can a muthafukka believe in Heaven and Hell but can't handle the kind of things I try to inform their ass on? Lord! They don't have no hesitation a-tall believin three Wise-asses followed a coksukkin star. You ever try to do that? Puh-fukkin-leez.

On the other hand, that we—or anything whatsoever—is even here in the first place seems pretty outlandish sometimes to me.

GOTDAMMIT, FUKKIT! THE MUTHUFUKKAS are makin me clean up

the way I talk, gotdammit. Here's the deal: If you don't see a cuss-word in here when you need one, it aint my fukkin fault, sumbich.

Some suit-wearin coksukka's wife raised hell about it, because she said she couldn read my books out loud to her tight-ass book club that mostly likes to set around and fart "Jesus Loves Me" to each other about how fukkin lovely the autumn leaves is. Any-way, the pressure was on, and kiss my ass I said "Okay," I'd tone it down. So now you can put your own muthafukkin cusswords in wherever you want, or up your polite, bigshot, fishbelly-white ass for all I care.

Plus, they said I can't say too much in this book like I did in the other'n about anybody's lips being "like a little perch tryin to swallow a corndog." I aint supposed to cuss no more nor say none of that in here now the way I did in *The Yazoo Blues*, you know, about nice historical ladies sukkin a sailor's dik on a boat in the Tallahatchie River. I guess I'll have to change up my words. For instance:

I won't no longer say "fukhed." I'll say "duckhed."

I won't be sayin "shit-hed" neither. I'll say "sh'theed."

And for "Redneck muthafukka," I'll just say "turd brain" and won't use no new, improved version. Which means I won't be sayin it much.

No more "coksukkas." From now on they are "clodsukkas."

Gotdam's gon be "Hot-Mam!" And maybe also "Gnat-Dum."

"Muthafukka" will turn into Mexican and be "muh-ThER-ro fuh-KER-ro."

You won't hear "sumbich" ever again. It's gon be "snubbitch."

"Pussy" can be "poolala." I kind of like that better anyhow. It seems a lot more polite.

"Nigga" is gon become "Nizzly." And "Pekkawood" can be "Paykawoofa."

"Dik" will here-after be referred to as a "deeb." Or maybe a "deeber." There was actually some little town sissies that used that word back when I was a "Vuggin" boy.

As you can see, instead of Fuk, I'mo say "Vug." And "Vuggum." You get the "Vuggin" idea.

Can I do it?

FUK NO. On the other hand, I'd be lyin if I kep on sayin everything's changed except me. The fact is, I've changed a helluva lot. I'll give your ass an example: It don't bother me one little bit that we now got black football players on the Miss'ssippi University football team. Plus, it don't bother me none that one of my supervisors is black, neither, where I work parkin lot security part-time up at the Lucky Pair-O-Dice Casino. For one thing that sumbich is more like me than those Yankee ass'oles we both work for. Fuk *EMM* sumbiches! Truth is, I don't think black anything woulda bothered me that much, because, as you know, it's the gotdam Planters and the fukkin Bankers I got a bone to gnaw on with. But I am not gon get into none of that now.

On the other hand, that's not the whole truth either—about them coksukkin Planters and gotdam Bankers, who, as you know, are the same ass-rippin thing!—because I wanted to get back onto what I said earlier about how you can't touch em. And that is one thing that aint changed. It will change, but it hadn yet, and maybe, in some kinda way even I cannot understand, I don't want it to. There's some other stuff that people think has changed but it aint. For instance I could say, oh, down here it's the same dirt and the same old sky, but that's not so one bit.

Back a long time ago the mud was mud, and that was it. Some of it was buckshot, and some of it was what's called class-1 soil, which is that light, sandy-looking shit that dries real well, and it's that kind of dirt down here—and *not* the real dark stuff that you'd ordinarily think would be the best for farmin—that produces the big-ass cotton yields. That dark dirt, the buckshot, the Tunica-Alligator-Sharkey clays, is class-3 soil, and it's a gotdam clayfoot mess. You do not want to try to walk around in it when it's wet, or you'll get back to your vehicle with the en-tire field stuck to your boots, if your boots aint still stuck in the field! And that's why they call it "gumbo." But what's different now *overall* is that all that dirt is full of fukkin chemicals you definitely would not want your babies to go runnin barefoot in.

Anyhow, back to the way I talk: Like I said, I aint supposed to cuss anymore. *They* said I can a little bit, but not as much. *They* who? *Them!* Gotdammit!

But, ChrEYEst, I been lyin all along. There wuddn no national movement by the forces of Jesus and tight-ass decency comin up against me and expectin my ass to stop cussin, cause it aint gon happen. Fukkum. Course I mean that in a *nice* way.

It was McKinney and Brainy that was on me to cut it out. That's all. There wuddn no ladies' church group or nothin. Shoot, I'm just glad Mad aint here to jump in on my ass too; although he might not. He'd probably just say, "Cuss away, Junior Ray. Cuss away." Hell, they said I cuss like a gotdam Army sargeant, but I told em I did not need no lessons on how to cuss from the gotdam government. They'll get over it.

Anyhow, I ast young Mr. Brainsong—*Brainy!*—and McKinney—hell, I know they're right, but it's way too late to do much changin—I ast em how the *crapolotomus* I was gonna say anything worth a *porkdik* ever again.

They declared men didn mind cussin but that women had a hard time with it. I said, ChrEYEst, fukkum. I gave em recipes in the last book! Plus, the fact is some women do not mind cussin, and one of em—I will not say who it was—got to likin it so much she took to doin it, and her dum-ass husband couldn't make her stop; only before he knew it, she didn give a chipmunk fuk and left his fat ass before he could th'ow her out. And she went down to New Orleens.

Last I heard she was sellin Lucky Dogs in the Quarter and was shacked up with a black cabdriver in a room over Metasacci's Bar way up near where the French Quarter runs out at that double-ass street. I been there. I been down to New Orleans now a couple of times, late in life you might say. I don't know a helluva lot about the place, but I do know somethin. Anyway, I seen it. The fukkin French Quarter, I mean. And I seen where I'm talkin about. It is hard to tell east from west and north and south in that city. I swear I can't do it. No matter where you are, it feels like your ass has crossed the Miss'ssippi River, and it hadn.

But the woman I'm tellin you about told Sunflower she was happier'n she ever was and wuddn never gon come back up to no Tri-Delt reunions. You know, that's them Try-Dultress. Anyhow, I guess I can see it. If you got a hotdog cart and a cabdriver, what else do you fukkin need?

Junior Ray's Famous Own Personal Favorite Late-Night Sammidge

Made With: Creamy organic peanut butter, large-curd cottage cheese, lettuce and soybean or some kinda reduced-fat mynaise, on extra-fresh one-hunnud-ass percent whole wheat bread. Or you can cross over to the wild side with the same kind of peanut butter, soybean or other mynaise, and sliced-up green olives that are stuffed with pimento. It does not sound good, but it is. However, if you elect to go with the wild-side version, you'll want to be sure and ditch the cottage cheese.

But whichever sammidge you decide on—and I recommend one of each, don't forget to *mash down* on the sammidge or slap the muthafukka real hard before you eat the sumbich.

Note to the Eater: Always make two, or four if you're combinin the versions, so you won't have to risk spillin your quart of Panther Burn Beer if you had to get up out of the Barcalounger to go back to the kitchen to make another one.

CHAPTER EIGHTEEN

A Message From Voyd and Me's Good Buddy Owen G. Brainsong
II—Brainy!—"Sumbich" Is a Term of Endearment—St.
Leo Named in Honor of a Thief—Leo Laufengeld—Shaw
Can Hover—A Bird Explains How the Submarine Got to
Mhoon County—The Baron Fensucher—Spring of 1942—
Oberleutnant August Sommer—Friedrich Jaeger, Became Fred
Hunter—Recipe No. 18: Junior Ray's Famous Ice-Gloosh

I thought about letn you in on this right at the beginnin of the book, but I had to tell you all that about Voyd and me and Miss Attica first. Anyway, you will want to hear somethin important Brainy has to say, so, by God, this is from Voyd and me's new good buddy and a gotdam good-ass sumbich, Owen G. Brainsong II:

A Message from Owen Glyndwyr Brainsong II:

Dear—and I hope!—Constant Reader,

Allow me to say I am, as it turns out, most pleased to be once again part of Junior Ray's literary efforts. Time is a splendid medicine, and once enough of it had passed between my first experience with him and the present, that and a circumstance of common interest have brought us together again, brought us indeed together as friends, and I am sure he is as much surprised by that turn of events as I was. In short, I was threatened with imminent death, and Junior Ray became my champion and protector.

The fact is that Junior Ray is not a bad person. He is merely a product of his environment as we all are, and once one can get past his unfortunate habits of speech and his often barbaric attitudes toward, well, perhaps, almost everything, one finds him to be a true friend and, I have to say, the most genuine of individuals. Certainly the tale he is telling you is, for the most part, about what he and his friend Voyd have done in the interest of my safety and general well-being.

I have informed my therapist—and, yes, also my Unitarian minister along with my . . . *companion*—of this remarkable change in my feelings toward Mr. Loveblood, or now more familiarly, since we have in fact become friends: Junior Ray. Forsooth, I have learned an important lesson from him: namely, *I like those who like me*, and that guiding principle is precisely what my association with Junior Ray has—I won't say "taught" me but, more accurately . . . "given" me.

It is entirely through this unlikely situation that I have come to know America for what it really is. It is without question the land of the free. And Junior Ray not only epitomizes that claim; he is the veritable apotheosis of it. He cares not a fig what others think of him. Our Mr. Loveblood is not burdened with the normal array of social qualms, nor is he hounded by any inner need that even remotely requires self-examination. His responses are quick and uncomplicated: If others should complain that he is a racist, Junior Ray will reply forthwith that they are "shitheds" and then amble off to dine upon a "kew" at the Pokey Porker, just north of St. Leo, on the side of the highway. Junior Ray is why the First Amendment was written. I have even learned that "sumbich" can be a term of endearment.

However, the most important thing to remember is that all the events relative to Miss Attica and the Aunty Belles took place in the recent past, more than a decade after the first casinos appeared—although, for the sake of absolute clarity, the story he tells has very little to do with any of those glittering, jingling, artificial atrocities. It's just that not long following their arrival Junior Ray had retired and had been hired by a gaming club in the vicinity of Mhoon's Landing. The establishment was called the *Golden Gar*. Later, along with many shifts in the county's balance of "big licks," that minor pleasure palace moved some few miles to the north and became the *Lucky Pair-O-Dice*, with which, as most of his readers know, he is professionally associated to this very day.

In any case, as Junior Ray puts it, "Most, but not all, of the sumbiches—and sumbich*ettes*"—he talks about are long dead and gone. And, as he further explains, a number of those that remain are too old and/or too "nutty in the head" to care or to know whether they themselves are dead or not. I did caution him. But prudence is not a Junior Ray virtue.

Owen G. Brainsong II, BA, MFA, D.Hum., Ph.D.

Professor of Philological Anthropology & Hidden Works

Department of Investigative Studies

Northern Pacific College of Broader Knowledge

P.S. The other day I received something remarkable. When I opened the door of my little apartment at the north end of our little town of St. Leo, on the east side of the now-defunct Illinois Central Railroad tracks, a manila envelope had been placed on the concrete slab that serves as my porch. I took it up, went back inside the living room and opened it. The package contained two *pieces* of writing: one of these specimens is written recognizably in Leland Shaw's hand, on pages torn from a ledger, exactly like those in which all of his work thus far collected has been written; and the other composition is in someone else's calligraphic penmanship, though whose I cannot say!

I do not know who brought the packet to my doorstep. Junior Ray most certainly did not put it there and said so. Indeed, I don't have to tell you that, if Junior Ray says it, *it is* so, or at least he would believe it to be so; thus, I am at a loss to know from whom and whence the envelope came.

McKinney was not the bearer, either. (She and I have become great friends, quite close in fact, and talk all the time. I have found that the world is full of wonderful individuals and that most of them live here in the Mississippi Delta. Who would have thought I would ever make such a statement, but I confess, much to my amazement, I have begun to learn a number of surprising things since that first time I was here, just a few years ago, when I was quite confident there was little except access to Shaw's "Notes" that I could gain by having come to Mhoon County, here in St. Leo—a community renamed as you may know to honor a man who, as president of the town's little bank, ran off and disappeared around 1915—indeed, rode out to O.K. Landing, caught a river steamer, and puffed away down the Mississippi—with the entire cash accounts of several of the town's citizens, then later he returned for a visit and was received warmly and appreciatively by others to whom, prior to his thievery, he had extended one sort of extraordinary financial kindness or another.

And it was those grateful and then influential townspeople who changed the name of the little town from its aboriginal designation, *Pontashto*,[80] to that of *Saint Leo*, in honor of Leo Laufengeld, the felonious absconder who lived out his life peacefully and freely in New Orleans and never reimbursed even so little as an Indian Head penny to the vulnerable widows and other trusting souls he had so easily robbed.

---

80 Chickasaw: big borrower. —ml

But now, regarding the envelope that appeared at my door, here below is the type-set rendition of the specimen:

OCTOBER 6, 1949—I SAY *EN GARDE!* TO GRAVITY

It was in the mid-afternoon, in the backyard, at Mama's house, there, in St Leo during the fall of 1949. The trees had turned; the weather was neither cold nor warm but rather warmer than cool, and the town smelled like the piles of burning leaves, tended by Negroes with rakes in their hands, completing the little municipality's sensory dimension that since I could remember defined and marked that time of year. So I decided to give *it* a try.

We always think we believe that whatever we put our minds to, we can do. Certainly I have always found the notion acceptable, and that is absolutely why I have restrained myself many times from putting my mind to one thing or another. I felt I did not need to accumulate any more expectations on the part of other people or for myself OF myself than I could comfortably deal with at any of those unfulfilled moments.

Even so, I decided, finally, to try *it*—to hover! Yes, the "*it*" was "to hover." And I more or less knew I might be able to do so because in dream after dream after dream, for the longest time, I had practiced and had been successful. I saw no reason to make a distinction between dreams and not-dreams, and, indeed, at some point, right before we left Oran, in North Africa, for what turned out to be Sicily, I knew I could hover if I in fact put mind to it, but five years passed before there, in my backyard, I made the first attempt. And I was successful.

Here's the way it works. A person has but to create just the right amount of isometric tension in his body—it has to be a considerable amount—and somehow a release is produced between the earth and the person, and up one goes—not far, just off the ground a bit, but with practice the height can be increased. More practice, I have to add, is needed for forward motion and for general control. Yet, in terms of simple levitation—I prefer to use the word "hovering"—the mastering of one's isometric tension is all that is necessary. It is, after a while, a very simple process.

But it is tiring. Hovering is intense, and I understand all too well now the life of a hummingbird. And that is the reason I have not been able to use the technique as a practical substitute for doing my explorations about the area—which I carry out quite satisfactorily I may say—on *shanks' mare*. Indeed, walking is still the fastest and most efficient way for me to move around. Perhaps in time that might change. But at the moment my new-found aerial ability is little more than a novelty. In fact I can rise and remain aloft for not much longer than half an hour at varying heights two or three times a day.

Only a handful of imitation, *soi-disant* citizens have seen me perform, and I imagine they did not know what they were witnessing and no doubt perceived me as a large bird. I have learned, as all people eventually discover, that most of our species see what they wish to see and that absolute reality is convertible into all sorts of convenient views.

Once I hovered above and by two men hunting ducks in a blind on the south end of Beaver Dam Lake. They waved. One of the men was smoking a cigar and let it fall from his mouth. I suppose I am lucky they did not see me, in slow motion, as a flight of teal. I cannot say whether they ever said anything to anyone about the event. I could not have known, as I was in hiding at the time.

Now for the second "piece," which was not at all produced by Leland Shaw, unless, unbeknownst to anyone of my acquaintance, he was ambidextrous and wrote it with "the other" hand; so far, I have not been able to verify that as a possibility. Still, the notion persists because I have come to understand, in these parts, that the improbable can so easily be the usual. In any case, here it is, and if by chance you have read Junior Ray's first book I think you will find the following rather satisfying, if not somewhat overdue. It calls itself . . .

THE HARRIER'S EYE

The world is of one perplexing consciousness. It is only mankind that is cut off, separated, from that single eye and the one voice of all there is. He, *Human Being*, is the observed. We, the raptors, are the observers.

Thus, it is not merely I but my kind that will tell the story. I am the harrier, the marsh hawk. For centuries I have seen it all and indeed all that was unseen as well through the agency of my fellow creatures wild, the hunters and the hunted, both winged and terrestrial. Indeed, Nature sees and listens whether by day or at night. In Nature there is everything, everything that ever was, and in Nature all is known and understood and, in a sense, preserved, not forever but until the sun expands and swallows the earth. It is only men who are ignorant of the world around them and who believe that what they do and say, where they move, and what they think go unrecognized, unnoticed, and unaccounted for, in this case here, on the alluvial flatness of Mississippi's Yazoo Delta.

I am the harrier, the low patroller, but my brothers and sisters keep me informed. Indeed you have the eye of grandfather Horus, the falcon, on your dollar, It was he who knew it all. He was the Sun God of the Sahara and the Nile. But falcons are nothing compared to me. Eagles are buffoons.

Unlike other so-called raptors, harriers are more in contact with the earth because, as you know, we fly low; yet, of course, the operative word is that we do "fly." So, low or not, we are also always above it all. Flying is quite different from slithering around in the grass as a mud-snake might do on a warm day in February. Rock breaks scissors. Harriers eat snakes.

Oh! Cut out my eye! And you will have the history of the Pleistocene in minute detail, the Quaternary in three-D, and, of course, in blazing color, regardless of what you may have heard from those ridiculous experts.

These are those who, silly-headed in the extreme, believe that I and the red-tails, the merlin, and the sharp-shins—*buteos, falconidae, and accipiters*—spend our lives in search of rodents and that we fixate solely upon the urine trails of voles, in the grass. Let me add, that of the categories, above, I, too, there included in a general sense, am apart and, yes, though perhaps more accipitrine, still, I am an *isolato* when it comes to hawks. My face is more like the mugshot of an owl.

But how then do the manuscripts of birds of prey come to be? There are ways. Remind yourself of ancient times when there were practitioners of the occult who had their "familiars," their "animal" creatures who linked mankind to the larger world of birds and beasts, and connected men also with the realm of the absolute, the world of spirits, and to all of time and space.

And how can it be so difficult to believe that a bird could produce a manuscript when the unbelievable seems to find no obstacle in the daily lives of ordinary people. The average Presbyterian has no trouble at all accepting as true the stories of miracles, or of a god who impregnates an earthly maiden in order to have a child whom he can murder to make himself happier about having created people in the first place. So why should the words of a bird present even the tiniest problem for sensible folk?

Here now is an untold story. This is what I, the marsh hawk, say to you. Listen to me. These are the words of the harrier:

In the spring of 1942 a German submarine surfaced off the coast of Louisiana and entered a short way into the mouth of the Mississippi River.

Three years later, on March 15th, 1945, at four o'clock in the afternoon, the U-Boat *Baron Fensucher*, a Type-IX, with a range of 11,000 nautical miles, rose to periscope depth just at the southern edge of the brown waters of the Mississippi River, a short distance from the river's mouth in the dark gray-green slosh of the Gulf of Mexico.

At 5:30, just an hour after that, the submarine entered the Mississippi and proceeded electrically, at barely six knots, to ascend the stream. Once darkness had fallen, the 251-foot craft switched to diesel and snorkeled past Pilot Town, then on by Liberty and at first light the next morning the *unterseeboot* lay by the east bank three miles downstream below the ferry run, between New Orleans and Algiers.

From there it slid past the sleeping Coast Guardsmen and moved—not quite submerged—past the lights of New Orleans and onward up the river, hiding by day in the chutes among the willows and the vines—continuing its journey at night, slowly, against the current, and onward upstream toward their destination until, finally, about forty-seven miles as the crow flies (ha ha) south of Memphis, with fuel to spare, the Gothic crewmen carefully concealed their boat of war in the virgin forest of the flooded batture land of Mississippi's Yazoo Basin and made their way by foot southeast to Hamlin then straight south along the train track on into Lula, where they found lodging at the small, barely conscious, railroad hotel, the *Margaret Valiant*.

Their mission had been to rescue Oberleutnant August Sommer who had been captured in France and sent to a prisoner of war camp in Como, Mississippi, located to the east, up in the Hills. The camp accommodated three hundred and fifty German and Italian POWs who were put there primarily to work in the cotton fields. The reasons behind the mission were not at all clear to the U-Boat's captain and crew. Although, as one might imagine, that was of utterly no concern.

The submariners did not know about Delta Planters or about Southerners white or black. And they did not question the authenticity of the costumes their superiors had given them for disguises.

Dressed in what they believed to be the fashion of American "farmers," they—referring to themselves in English as "Old Mac-Donalds"—hiked the muddy springtime roads eastward from the River, across the sucking mud of the Delta to the clay-rich Loess Hills, and, still eastward and mostly at night, into Como. Each submariner was outfitted with an enormous straw hat, a red bandana, bib overalls, rubber knee boots, and a corncob pipe.

"Who are they?!" was the rhetorical question asked by a tiny few, both black and white, too burdened with work to give the question any more thought. And there were no constables. That was that.

Walking by night and sleeping during the day in the plentiful woods, the Teutons reached Como, a not-so-easy fifty miles from where the boat lay hidden, in a little less than a week. They found the camp and discovered that Oberleutnant August Sommer was not in it. The young officer had in fact married a local girl and was living happily with her in a lovely old house not far from the Estes place just west of town on the road to Crenshaw. The *oberleutnant* had married not just a "local" girl, but one who was the daughter of a well-to-do Planter. So the foreign officer himself was now working for his father-in-law, growing cotton and raising Herefords. Astonishingly, the gates to the "prison" were not locked, and the "prisoners" walked in and out and back and forth to Como quite as they pleased. Moreover, the American guards had taught the Germans and Italians how to play softball and stud poker.

There was homebrewed beer and a movie projector, and the local residents supplied the foreigners with a steady stream of indigenous delicacies which ranged from wild game to pies and cakes made with government sugar. In addition, there was for the helpless captives no end of church groups and curious maidens. Life in the Fatherland had rarely been so good. And those that took up English said things like "y'all," "Yay'ess," and "Thang-kew." There was patriotism and there was "Christian Duty," and it was the flexible elasticity of "Christian

Duty" which, there, in the Deep American South, prevailed.

More than anything else, the sub rosa submariners were exhausted. The thought of the overland trek back to the boat and the voyage downstream to the Gulf of Mexico and then of motoring back across the Atlantic to a war-torn life, just before the end of the War in Europe, had no appeal . . . commercial or otherwise. The result of these feelings was that a sizable component of the U-boat's crew decided to take up the business of living scattered about in parts of the Loess Hills and in portions of the Mississippi Delta, and all of them rapidly assimilated and throve in their new environment. The rest, the ones who were determined to return to their families in Germany, made their way to Mexico and thence back to Europe. Of those who stayed, most were bachelors, but I cannot say all. Mates had been readily available. The seamen's Southern wives believed either a fabrication about their husbands' origins and their accents or simply remained tight-lipped and sank no ships for a lifetime. (One, however, who left her undercover spouse went about "revealing" everything and got nowhere. She was quickly deemed insane and became a pariah in her own land.)

Through the ensuing years, the children born to these unions graduated from Mhoon County Consolidated High School, the white one, and from the segregated systems in other Delta counties: those of Coahoma, Quitman, and Tunica; while the offspring of others graduated from the public schools in the Hill counties of Tate and Panola.

The clandestine submariners' children accepted without the slightest question that these men, their fathers, had "come down from up north," or had been sent to Mississippi as a DP, or even, in two or three versions, for example, "had been a POW at one of the several prisoner-of-war camps in the area—over in Como, down at the airfield in Clarksdale, farther on at Pace, also in Indianola, and near Belzoni—and they had liked it here so much they had asked to stay." And because they were not funny looking and indeed appeared quite handsome and exceedingly Caucasian, the government had simply responded: "Why, yes, of course, please do!" All of that was plausible and easy to believe. For example, First Watch Officer *Oberleutnant Zur See* Friedrich Jaeger quickly became Fred Hunter, whose life was rich and full as a successful father, involved citizen of Tate County, and respected breeder of Polled Herefords in the Hills, just up from the Delta, between Arkabutla and Bucksnort. A search at the courthouse in Senatobia revealed no records of his past. He had merely appeared . . . then began to live. No one gave it a thought. There were three who did not settle into the steamy agrarian life of that area and who, wifeless, found their way to New Orleans where they opened a "club" on the shore of Lake Pontchartrain, and they named their nightspot "Nothing But the Wurst." It became famous.

It is well to remember that outside the limits of the "larger" small towns—of which there were only a few—the rural areas in those days did not universally enjoy the comfort and communication provided by electricity nor the convenience and sanitation of running water and indoor plumbing. Moreover there were not many whites in those gridless remote reaches—nor even many in the towns themselves when one considers the fact that, ethnically, Caucasoids made up, in some cases, less than ten percent of the population of the Delta counties, and although more plentiful in the Hills those non-affluent, less-fortunate whites at either elevation who inhabited the fields and forests of the countryside would not have been curious. Paying attention to others was a luxury in which they had neither familiarity nor the slightest interest. Of course the better-off whites were not like that. As for the Delta blacks and likewise those blacks living in the upland fields of the Loess Hills there on the edge of the Delta, they, perhaps thinking the German sailors were merely poor-white sharecroppers who had migrated thither from the older, red-clay counties on the western side of the state, apparently felt little concern. It is not difficult to presume that the deprivation that still defined the peonage of blacks in that time and place was, itself, further smothered by the supernatural heat and humidity of the region and thus drove away all desires save those buried in the limbic system, negating any scope of inquiry and all existential probabilities beyond the present indicative.

The above is just as I found it and has not been altered by me or others. *Vostrum Servitor in Perplexitas Aeternum.* —ogbii

P.P.S.: Since my first arrival here so many, many years ago to locate the notebooks—ledgers—of Leland Shaw, a great deal more of his work has been discovered. As you know, there were a number of trunks and packing crates in his mother's house on both floors and in the attic. Indeed, while Shaw was hiding in the silo during the coldest months of 1958 and 1959, he was apparently transferring some of his work from town to his lofty hideaway. It goes without saying that the reason for that is strangely unclear because he would never have been able, piecemeal and by hand, to have moved the entirety of his ledgers from St. Leo to the silo. Further research will be required for a complete understanding of his situation at that time.

Ancillary to the necessity of my continued research into the life and work of Leland Shaw, I wish the reader to know that I am currently and aggressively seeking grants and other funds with which to establish a library, in honor of my uncle, that will be the first of its kind: The Brainsong National Library of Mysterious and Unfinished Manuscripts. It is my intention and my deepest wish that it be housed and maintained in Mhoon County, Mississippi, within the corporate limits of the town of St. Leo.

WELL, THERE YOU HAVE it, or part of it, I guess. With the exception of Mad Owens's one-legged polly parrot, my old buddy Gene LaFoote, I don't know how much stock you can put in what some gotdam bird says. Plus, I don't yet know what Brainy actually thinks about them papers he found on his doorstep. But, for right now, fukkum. I got sumpm good for you to eat.

Junior Ray's Famous Ice-Gloosh

If you want the most de-fukkin-licious thing you could ever think of to put in your mouth, you have to fix yourself some Ice-Gloosh. It's real simple:

First: Go to the store and get some fat-free and maybe also sugar-free vanilla ice cream or frozen yogurt.

Second: Take it back to the house.

Third: Open it up.

Fourth: Pick out a big-ass coffee cup.

Fifth: Spoon in as much of the ice cream or frozen yogurt as you can get in the cup.

Sixth: Jab down in it with a stainless steel spoon.

Seventh: This is how you make the actual *Gloosh*! Pour cold, strong-ass coffee down into the jab-holes, and jab some more so that the coffee gets on into the ice-cream or the frozen yogurt. This is the *Gloosh*-makin process—jabbin and pourin. Don't over-do it. Don't under-do it neither.

Eighth: Take it with you to the T.V., and turn on *Seinfeld* or *The Office*.

Ninth: Eat it up. Wolf down the Ice-Gloosh like the Fantastic Mr. Fox woulda did. And don't stop till it's all gone. Or, sumbich, you don't have a hair on your ass.

CHAPTER NINETEEN

*Shaw Mighta Hovered—The Endless-Ass Slough of Time—I'm
Not the Only One Who Wanted to Shoot Somebody for No
Reason and Say It Was for the Public Good—Miss Shoot-from-
the-Fukkin-Hip Attica—The Believinest Place I Ever Saw—
Deep-Ass Thoughts—Why Country Singers Are So Lonesome—
Life Is Sumpm No Sumbich Can Survive—Whacker's Solo
Sexual Bar—Pride and Prejustice—Recipe No. 19: Bob's
Sammidge & the Joe Boone Asparagus Sammidge*

I f all of what Brainy wrote is true in the fukkin chapter before
this'n, or even just part of it, then that does help to explain
some of what happened back in the winter of '58 and '59
when me and Voyd was chasin around after Leland Shaw, hope'n
to get to shoot his ass—which is probly dead by now, or damm
near, wherever the fuk Miss Helena and Lawyer Montgomery
and Boneface and Atlanta Birmingham-gotdam-Jackson sent his
ass, which is supposed to have been Chicago to live with them
muthafukkin black-ass Mohammedans so Mr. X, the head of them
roscoe-tote'n sumbiches, could get the title to Miss Helena's piece
of land. Which he did, but didn never do nothin with it, though
there was, not too long ago, a little talk about some outfit wantn
to drill a' oil well on it.

The *inter-restin* part of that is I happen to know that Miss Helena
kept the mineral rights, which now might in fact belong to Mad. I
can't be a hunnud percent sure of that. Quite frankly, I don't think
there is ever gon be no gasoline, nor no WD-forty crap neither,

comin out of Mhoon County—but maybe there will farther down the road in C'homa County.[81]

Don't go nowhere. IR-refukkin-gardless of what Shaw said about hisself bein able to hover and all, I do not think the whole story has all been told. Some muthafukkas might get the idea that that's it, that that's the reason Shaw's footprints would disappear and nobody couldn never figure out why. Well, fukkum. That aint all there is to it. And it wuddn *necessarily* no gotdam hoverin that caused it.

Oh, hell yeah, he mighta hovered! Hoverin, however, aint the problem nor the solution. I don't doubt one teeny-ass bit that the sumbich could hover. I wouldn doubt nothin that had to do with him, no matter how crazy it might sound. But unlike religion, the answer when it comes to Shaw aint that fukkin simple. Aint nothin ever just *that* simple, and I know it and you do too, cause if a sumbich could just th'ow a thing in a sack and say, "Here it is, that's it!"—then life itsef would be an easier duck to pluck.

Personally, I think Shaw's footprints disappeared because of somethin havin to do with the fact that they *always* disappeared on, or right by, the old trace that served as a road for the cocksukkin buffa-fukkin-lo and then the gotdam Inyans and later on, afterwards, for every other swingin dik that stumbled into this stump hole we like to call the Delta.

I believe more than anything else it's the Endless-Ass Slough of Time that has the most to do with the disappearin of Shaw's footprints. That's what I think. The imprint here and there of the old trace and the vanishin of that crazy coksukka's footprints has got to be connected somehow or another down in there inside the darkness of Big Cap'm Time's eternal muckmire! Here's the deal: The track of that old trail is still in the gotdam past. I mean, me bein a' historian and everything, I've got a certain second sight

---

81   Coahoma > Choctaw koi (panther) + homa (red). —ml

about stuff when it comes to the past. I think the sumbich *disappeared back into time*, because, as I told you in the last book, the past don't never go away. It can't. And don't roll your fukkin eyes and screw up your face like that! Gotdammit.

Now, with the regard to that other thing about *the harriest eye,* which Brainy showed you that gave all the skinny on the submarine, you know and I know SOME of that's got to be the gospel-ass truth, because Voyd and me found the sumbich rustin-out over cross the levee not long after New Year's in 1959. And Brainy's uncle, the real Mr. Brainsong, and Miss Florence, too, down at the Mhoon County Courthouse can verify it. Well, they could if they was alive, and I am certain they would.

Be that all as it fukkin may, it wuddn the principal thing I wanted to tell you.

Turns out, bygod, I'm not the only one—except of course for them sumbiches up in *Worsh'nun*—who wanted to shoot somebody for no real reason and say it was for the public good. Plus, I wouldna never believed it woulda ever cropped up again anywhere near me . . . but, really, I just guess, when you come right down to it and from all I can see from the TV and everything else, wantin to shoot each other is a major part of human nature. If it's not, then humans sure are busy doin a helluva lot of *unnatural acts.* Anyway, fuk *them* peas.

ALL I GOT TO say is that now knowin about it helps to make some sense out of that submarine. Plus, aint none of it hard for me to believe and wouldn be for nobody else down here neither. Because in the Delta and I suppose in the whole rest of the Deep South in general, if you can name it, some sumbich will believe it. I mean, if a' individual can swallow all that hoohaw about them old robe-wrapped, sandal-flappin ass'oles back in Bible days, then a sumbich can put his faith in anything, include'n High John the Conqueror

Root and Lucky Oil. ChrEYEst, I believe this is the believinest place I ever saw.

Anyway, I feel I ought to point out that if Brainy hada actually got hissef kilt by Miss Shoot-from-the-Fukkin-Hip Attica and/or any of the rest of them so-called *Aunty Belles*, it woulda been for not a soybean-suckin thing more than what you're gon to see next, in PART-fukkin- TWO! And that's comin up in just a few minutes, dependin on how fast your ass can read.

Right now I want to mention one or two other things I've had on my mind that I feel I ought to tell you in case you hadn put much thought on em. You know how it is when you're just sitn around thinkin a bunch of deep-ass thoughts—like why all the old country singers was always singin about how fukkin lonesome they was. I figured that one out. It come to me in a flash—those coksukkas was lonesome cause they lived so far out in the gotdam sticks couldn nobody ever come to see em OR might not never have even wanted to on account of there wuddn no plumbin, no lectric lights, and no phone . . . plus, the fukkin roads wuddn worth a shit, neither. I'm tellin you, if you set down and think about things, you'll come up with the answer. And I'm livin to tell the tale.

Dyin, basically, is just sumpm every sumbich has got to do. Even if you're a gotdam Planter or Banker, it's THE appointment you cannot get your fukkin secretary to postpone.[82] Plus, it's the last place you'll ever just have to be. Put another way, life is just sumpm can't no sumbich survive. Still, that aint no reason not to live it. Them preachers could be right, but I don't think so, so I say fuk all that. Maybe this aint all there is to it, and maybe it is, but life, right now, is a roosted chicken, and death aint nothin but a backward-ass breech birth—into the same kind of nothin'ness we come out of in the first fukkin place, which wuddn anything but

---

82   Junior Ray heard that at a black funeral in Teoc, Mississippi. —ml

a blank swirl of the same kind of odds like the kind they give you up at the Lucky Pair-O-Dice where, as you know, I work part-time in law enforcement.

Anyway, you done beat the odds just by getn here in the first place, so if a muthafukka has any sense a'tall, he'll cash in his chips and spend his money, and not give it all back to the gotdam house on a bet that probably wouldn be no fun if he won. That's why I intend to do what I want to do every gotdam day as much as I dadgum can. Them preachers really aint nothin but dealers.

Also, the other day I saw a white sumbich, who obviously don't never notice nothin, wearin a T-shirt that said: "I Am a Proud Black Woman." And I thought, you ass'ole, you ought to have on a T-shirt that says you are a "Proud Dum-ass Pekkawood." But I didn have the heart to brighten up his day.

Anyway, that's just some of the issues that was on my mind.

I DO MISS GOIN up to Meffis and bein a regular at the Magic Pussy. I still go to Meffis like ever'body else for things you can't get in St. Leo, like all that tasty stuff that's already cooked in one nem fancy-ass grocery stores out east of Perkins—man, it looks so fukkin good that I like to just go in and watch it for a while and then go back home with a sack full of yellow cherries, big-ass scallops, and a tame duck that come off a lectric rod jammed up its butt. Oh, and a loaf or three of that banana-nut bread, which is way better'n what some of the Baptist Ladies put out at EX-mas. I can't explain it, but the whole experience is like goin on a trip to a fukkin food museum, and in a how-good-it-makes-you-feel sense, it's not all that unlike bein back at the ol' MP Cabaret & Club. But I don't want to get too philosophical on your ass.

Once in a while I stop in and speak to Tally Shannon at his new bar he's got up there on Brookhaven Circle. You'd think it was a dignified place cause it's in East Meffis, and I guess it is, but it's

called WHACKER'S . . . because that's what the boys he grew up
with in St. Leo named him. You know, *Tally . . . Tallywhacker . . .*
on account of he jerked off all the time. They did, too, only Tally
seemed to prefer it to getn a' actual date and goin out with a real
girl—or hell, a goat, for that matter. He used to say he was "independent" and he would talk about an old-timey Yankee sumbich
who wrote somethin about "Self Reliance." Anyway, Tally does like
to take matters into his own hands. That's just the way he is. And,
no matter what you might want to think, you got to respect it.

So when he opened up his bar, he called it a "solo-sexual pub."
The regular, *normal-ass* folks had their places, the girl queers
had theirs, and naturally the men queers had a raft of em as
well. But there wuddn no place for the sumbiches who liked to
maintain their personal privacy, if you know what I mean. And
Tally seemed to be doin real successful—for one thing because it
looked like the law just did not know how to handle his kind of
establishment. I mean, what were they gon do, arrest a sumbich
for scratchin his own balls?

However, for fifty dollars Talley will rent a muthafukka a
doll—and I'm not talkin about one nem scary blow-up things
like Mad and me had stuck up in the sand in front of his shelter
there when I went down to see him on Horn Island. Unh-unh,
Tally had the kind that's truly-ass life-like and comes shipped in
a crate from California, where all that kind of high-quality shit is
apparently made. Son! This thing is somethin else! So Tally rakes
in fifty dollars for the rented dummy sex playgirl and also racks
up on the extra drinks which the customer is obliged to buy for
it—her—whatever—which means that every time a sumbich who's
set'n in there with one nem good-lookin dolls orders a drink, he
has to pay for two. Tally mighta been a *masturbater*, but he was
a fukkin mover and a shaker when it come to makin a profit in
business. Plus, condoms is required.

Inside, there's little intimate booths "for one," a sign on the wall that reads, "No breaking on the dance floor," another sign up over the bourbon and gin and such up behind the bartender that says, "If you're by yourself, you're not alone," and yet a further sign over the door of the place—a big one—that's got, "Tally Whacker's Solo-Sexual Pub for Independent Adults. Come in and pick *yourself* up."

But that aint all. Tally is a fukkin Democrat, so he also provides *male* sex dolls for his women customers, and, once again, condoms are mandatory. Plus, Tally does not charge the women who rent the male sex dolls for two drinks like he does the men, because, as he rightly-ass said to me: "For heavensakes, Junior Ray, they're *ladies!*" Overall, Tally was brought up right and is somewhat old-fashioned in his beliefs, the way a sumbich ought to be. Take for instance what he done the time he caught some muthafukka givin a blowjob to one of the male dolls. Tally th'owed the sumbich out on the street—the customer, not the doll, cause it hadn done nothin wrong—and Tally told that artificial coksukka never to bring his sorry ass back there ever again, on account of it wuddn that kind of a place. Old Tally told him he wuddn gon stand for it, that it was fukkin unsanitary and also against the gotdam Bible, and Tally made it pretty gotdam clear he wuddn gon put up with nothin like that. Nossuh.

I do admire Tally for maintainin his ways, but I'm thinkin he might oughta give the Bible another look.

Anyway, he is a helluva bartender. Plus, the sumbich loved Mexico, and he loved that t'keela shit they drink down there with the fukkin worm in the bottle. I can handle the gotdam worm but I truly don't care for the t'keela. Anyway, he could th'ow nothin more than t'keela and Co-fukkin-Cola in a short glass of crushed ice with a slice of lemon floatin on top—he called it a t'keela mockin'bird—and people talked about that for-gotdam-ever, though I never could figure out why unless it had sumpm to do with the fact that Miss'ssippi's state bird is the gotdam mockin'bird. But I didn ast, I just listened . . . and laughed, too. Fuk.

Some of that reminded me of the old Dew Drop Inn a long time ago in Meffis, up off Crump, on Florida Street. It aint there no more, but, when it was, the lady who owned the place had a sign on her wall that said "No Dancing Allowed."

Didn nobody pay no 'tention to the sign, and they'd dance whenever they felt like it. The owner would come out on the floor, and holler: "No dancin!" And the customers doin the dancin would say: "We aint dancin, we're just walkin." Then the owner-*ess* would turn around and go on about what she was doin, and that was the end of it. As you remember, I addressed that kind of a thing when I was tellin you about Merigold and how sumpm down here's got to be dam-near other worldly before anybody'd think it's unusual.

You know, even after it was clear that Merigold had murdered her mama—"just a little bit"—even after that, people still wanted to make a connection between what Merigold done and them other three killins. But there wuddn none. Merigold choppin up her mother at that time was just a coincidence. The sumbiches that thought there was a connection between that one and the rest didn know doodly about nothin, like me and Voyd and Secundus, and I guess Ezell, too, did. And God knows at the time our investigation was goin on, we sho wuddn gon tell nobody nothin about it.

On the other hand, cause she wanted to protect her rep'atation, Miss Attica had encouraged the stew out of all that speculatin. She'da give her grandmama's antique china slopjar for Merigold to have been charged with all four fukkin killins, and not a one of them folks to who she was pumpin the convenient-ass notion that Merigold done it all would ever have ever in this wide-ass world guessed why. But when you are a diktective, you see how people live their lives thinkin one thing when all the time it's sumpm else that's really the truth. Sumpm else entirely. I have to say it is a little bit disturbin, but, as a diktective, you've just got to learn to live with that bullshit and keep your thoughts, and especially what you might know, teetotally to yoursef. Everybody can't do it. You pretty much have to be a law enforcement professional, such as I am. Plus, it is somewhat easier to do if you know that if you was to open your fukkin mouth, Secundus Shipp and Judge "Rusty" Justiss Jr. would make you wish you hadn. And I don't even want to think about that.

Fortunately but sadly both Secundus and Judge "Rusty" Jr. is now dead and buried out at what I call No-Wood Cemetery. Secundus caught one of these godawful cancers people in the Delta gets from bein too fukkin close to all our chemicalized soil, and Judge "Rusty," well, he dropped dead with apple-plexy. Word was that when they found him he looked like he'd just that second had a big idea. Miss Attica and ol' Euster, too, has been gone a while as well, even though none of all this that went on was really that far back. It wuddn far back a-tall. But after a sumbich gets to a certain age, gotdammit, people die around you like poppin corn, and you almost can't keep up with it.

That Worthless Nigga Ezell is still around, though, just like Voyd and me. But can't nobody get him to do nothin. Fukkim. Well, hell, whenever I see him, I do like to talk to him. Gotdammit. I just wish the sumbich was really more different from me than he is, and then maybe I could get some things in my mind straightened out. When you get older it's hard to be real sure about stuff.

Niggas! I've tried awful hard to figure it out, but so far I aint come up with nothin. What is it, I ast mysef, that makes them sumbiches so fukkin different? Yet no matter how hard I try to think it out, I don't never get nowhere. Nowhere a-tall.

For instance I can't name nothin they do that we don't do. They knock up all their girlfriends, and we knock up ours. They shoot craps and kill each other, and that's what we do. Hell, when I was young we played baseball. Them muthafukkas played baseball too. I can't think of one single thing they did or that they do that we didn do and don't, except maybe two, and those are that they seem to be better at singin and, as I recall, they didn fuk as many barnyard animals as we used to. ChrEYEst. This is one reason I decided not to become no philosopher after I retired from sheriff work. Thinkin can fuk a sumbich up real quick. And I am that sumbich.

ANYWAY, NOW LITTLE QUIT Tait is the judge! As I have informed your ass, that lil sumbich is the smartest, wildest scownbooga that I ever knew! And when he went to the law school over at the University, Son, hold on to your fukkin girlfriend! Little Quit used to bring his law professorESS home to his mama and daddy's house, down in Clarksdale—well, right outside of it—which became his when they passed away, and they was passed away at that time, and he and his lady law teacher would drive up to St. Leo, which wuddn no distance at all, to see two of Little Quit's cousins, one a goodlookin girl and the other a hell-raisin' boy, and the four of em—plus whoever else might want to come along—would get drunk and jump in Quit's papa's big old yellow Cadillac convertible that had the gotdam fins on the back of it, and then they'd ride around all over Mhoon County at night, havin theirsevs a helluva time and drinkin it up like a T-shirt in a barrel of burnt oil, with the top down, nekkid.

Which is why I was not necessarily surprised when I hauled Voyd outa that gotdam coffin[83] where he was setn with them two professoresses in that coksukkin fraternity house. And when one of them professoresses told me she was a professoress in the law school, Little Quit was what come to mind absolutely immediate-a-muthfukkinly.

---

83   See chapter eight. —ml

Then and there I knew that's why there's so many lawyers.

IT'S TRUE I AM full of pride and prejustice. At least that's what Mr. Brainsong always said about me way back yonder when I first got hired on as a deputy. Yet I don't see what that's got to do with the price of pork skins in Indianola. Mainly I just think it's important to keep the record straight in order to nip a lotta unnecessary yip-yap in the butt.

In the first place, I never have thought there was a whole lot wrong with me, like it is with some-nem other sumbiches down here. And I don't spend a lot of time thinkin about sef-improvement. I've always known what I like, and I always done it, and so I can't see what there is to improve, except the size of my shot-group. On the other hand I can shoot a .45 automatic better'n most—I can put two targets up, side by side, stick an ax-blade between em, aim at that, split the round and hit both bullseyes at the same time. I only saw one other sumbich that could do that, and he was a Nigga. And I have to admit, as good a shot as that muthafukka was, I didn have no prejustice toward him a-tall.

Where you come from, guns may not be a big thing. But they are where I come from and always have been. Everybody has em. I 'member one time back in the so-called Civil Rights Movement, we caught some-kinda lillo Jew boy from up in Ohio with a big-ass load of single-shot twelve-gauges up in the trunk of his car. I didn know what to make of it. After a while he told Sheriff Holston he was bringin guns to give to the Niggas. Sheriff Holston just made him take em out of the car, and we stacked em up over in a corner of the office. Then Sheriff Holston told him to go on back up to Ohio, and I guess he did, but on the way out to his vehicle I felt like I had to say somethin to him, and I told him the Niggas already had guns. He looked at me kinda funny, and I looked back at him, and then he dropped his eyes, stared down at the ground, and said, "Damm."

He didn say it like he was mad or nothin but more like he was disappointed, and when he was paused before pulling out of the little gravel patch we used as a parkin space there on the side of the court house, I told him I was sorry he had done come such a long-ass way and that he probly didn have to worry about the Niggas because I had a feelin that, one way or another, they was gon be all right, which, it's always seemed to me, they usually are.

And I have to say, too, they are awfully handy when you need em, except for that worthless sumbich Ezell. Course, that mutha-fukka is most likely smarter than the whole state of Mississippi, which, I know, aint sayin all that much, but . . . !

A Double-Barrel Junior Ray Discovery—The Two-Gun Approach to Fine Sammidge Dine'n: One Mouth, Two Delicious Fukkin Sammidges

Discovery No. 1: *Bob's Sammidge*

My friend Bob Canzoneri is a good old Miss'ssippi Boy—and a fukkin EYE-talian as well.[84] Anyhow, the followin is a delicious-ass sammidge which him and his wife and me and my girlfriend, Dyna Flo McKeever, ate more or less on the edge of a ditch one day. Here, now, are the ten steps to good eatn:

1. Get some-nem English muffins.
2. Buy some ham already sliced.
3. Pick up a jar of roasted red peppers.
4. Don't forget the yellow hoop cheese.
5. Split the English muffin, and put Durkee's dressing on one half.

---

84   Bob is actually of Sicilian descent. I know him and his wife, Candy, and their two dogs. They forsook paradise and moved to Ohio. —ml

6. Slather on whatever you want on the other half, or let it alone.

7. I recommend some of that soybean mynaise.

8. Lay the dadgum ham over the Durkees; flop the roasted red pepper on top of it.

9. And place the hoop cheese over both.

10. After you have done all that, eat it up, and make anuddn.

Discovery No. 2: The Joe Boone Asparagus Sammidge

As far as I know aint nobody ever thought of this except Joe Boone. And I am convinced that is because, way-ass back, he might be kin to Daniel Boone, and that would explain how Joe Boone become the outstandin sammidge pioneer he obviously is.

This is how you make the Joe Boone Asparagus Sammidge:

1. Go to the grocery store and get you the tenderest, most fresh-ass aparaguses you can find.

2. Buy a loaf of real French bread, not that packaged-up soft crust crap. And if you do not have no home-made mynaise, reach for some of that well-thought-of store-bought kind, or get hold of a jar of real good soybean mynaise, and you might also consider usin a little of the Durkee's you was gon use on Discovery No. 1.

3. Go home.

4. Cut off any untender, woody parts of the aparaguses. You do not want none of that, in case there is some.

5. Have your plate ready, and know what you're gon drink, so you won't have to fool with getn them things together after you make your sammidges.

6. Also slice up a Vidalia onion extra thin.

7. You may want to put some cheese on your asparagus sammidge. I recommend a little French goat cheese, maybe some very ripe-ass brie or absolutely a chunk of runny-ass

camembert—and, yes, Muthafukka, I do know what all that is, gotdammit. The fact is that if you are gon use any cheese at all, pretty much anything you might think would be tasty probly will be. Just don't over-do it.

8. Do NOT add no coksukkin tomato! Your one green veg'able is enough!

9. Now, you can steam your asparaguses. You can boil em. And you can grill em. Personally I like mine sawtayed in olive oil, garlic power and black pepper. Don't over-cook em. And don't under-cook em. Use your fukkin head.

10. When your asparaguses is done the way you want em, leave em in the skillet.

11. Put your mynaise on both slices or only on one slice of your real French bread. If you sawtay your asparaguses, I'd say just let the olive oil that's on em be all you need on the piece of real French bread you lay em on, and put mynaise only on the piece of French bread you th'ow down on top of the one that has your asparaguses on it. Still, you might want to spread mynaise on both pieces of your real French bread.

12. Anyway, like I told you, arrange your asparaguses on one of the halves of bread. This is when you decide if you want to add on some of the thin-sliced Vidalias and a chunk of your cheese. As I said, do not over-do this part. You want the full asparagusal flavor to be the star of the *chomp*. Moderation is my motto. Ha. Ha. That was a joke, Muthafukka.

13. Slap on the top, and there you are.

14. Then take your Joe Boone Asparagus Sandwich and put it on your plate beside your Bob's Sandwich, get yoursef a drink, and go to the TV. You won't have no need for nothin else in your life for a good long while.

15. And that's the truth.

CHAPTER TWENTY

Voyd and Religion Don't Mix—Jesus Was in the New
Testicle—If Sunflower and Me was the Only Two
Sumbiches Left on Earth, There Wouldn Be No New
People—Miss Hospitality—Mugged in Meffis—Lied and
Got Out of It—The Mugger Apologized—It's the Gotdam
Planters' Fault—Dahkies—Cap'm Please!—Whickies—I've
Told It the Way I Seen It—Recipe No. 20: Go-To-Hell Cow
College Casserole!

Voyd and religion don't mix. Take the Bible for instance. That dumb little fukka don't even know there's two separate Testicles—the Old and the New. ChrEYEst, even *I* know *that*.

Voyd tried to tell me Jesus was in the Bible right from the very beginnin, and I told him, "No, he aint," and that Jesus don't even begin to come up till over half the whole big-ass book later, when you get to the New Testicle.

You can't get a read on Voyd. That little sumbich is incomprefukkin-hensible. I mean, even after all the time I have known him and been around him, even I just *can not* understand what makes that little head of his work.

For example, he is and always has been in love with Sunflower, and that is sayin a lot because it's hard enough just to like Sunflower, much less to reach up your ass and haul out any sho-nuff affection for her. But he does, and I guess in that regard you could say he's definitely one-up on Mad who, in spite of all his philosophy, fell way short of bein able to *love* Money Scatters as he had intended to and for a few months even managed to think he did.

So I say you have to hand it to Voyd for bein in love these many desperate-ass years with Sunflower who, no doubt, is the worst fukkin female on this earth. I'mo level with you, if, way back, there hadn been nobody else in the whole coksukkin Garden of Eden but me and Sunflower, I swear to you on a stack of preachers' daughters, there wouldna been no new people.

Anyway, feature this: Voyd has all of a sudden decided to use lovey-dovey terms, you know, of en-fukkin-dearment, whenever he talks to *Miss Miss'sippi Delta of 1957*—Miss Hops Your Tally-ty!—and his idea of an endearin term is *Booga Pie.* So, now, anytime he is around the afore-fukkin-said Love-of-Your-Life-from-Hell, it's *Booga Pie* this and *Booga Pie* that and Okey-dokey, *Booga Pie . . .* be there in a minute, *Booga Pie . . .* see you later, *Booga Pie . . . Booga Pie,* can I bring your sorry ass anything? . . . . And I'm thinkin, "Oh Lord! What's it gon be next: *"Gimme some booga?"*

You may be different, but I almost can't stand it. I've got a real strong stomach, but I near bout th'ow up when I think about a gotdam *pie . . .* made outa, you know . . . *boogas.* Watch out! You better move yo' ass. I think I'mo vomit.

Yet I know human beings is complicated, and I didn used to think that, but there are a lot of things, I guess, I didn used to think; only this sure defeats me. Anyway, you can't talk to Voyd. The sumbich is convinced he knows it all. And that probably comes from bustin too many bubbles in the bathtub with his nose.

ANYWAY, JUST WHEN YOU believe you've got it knocked, sumpm else falls outa the ceilin. I got, whatchewcallit, *mugged* the other night in Meffis at a basketball game—which I don't give a big bouncin fuk for, but I went with Voyd because he likes that shit and, I don't know why, I told him I'd go with him. It was at one nem east Meffis high schools that used to be white and now is mostly black. Well, you know, it wuddn long before I flat couldn stand no more, mainly just had to have me some air, so I stepped out into the parkin lot. It was a nice night, with a moon, and them little wispy-ass clouds racin cross the sky. And I said to mysef, "Don't go off far from the door," but of course I said fukkit and did, and it was nice. For a while.

After a few minutes I noticed three or four black teenagers bobbin and bumpin around a car on the far side of the lot, and the long and short of it is that I could tell they was upset, and then two more come out of the gym and was runnin over there, and in a second or so a girl was pointn over to me, and I heard her say, "He saw it." What it was *was* one of em's car had been broke into and they thought I was a security guard that had seen the whole thing take place and hadn done nothin about it. I could hear all that.

Then two of them boys come walkin at a angle by me goin back to the gym and they was cussin and callin me a muthafukka, so I said, "I don't work here." And one of em looked at me and said, "I'mo blow your gotdam head off, you white-ass muthafukka," and he and his friend come lope-walkin over toward me, and one of em, the one who done the talkin, had his hand jammed way down in his jacket pocket, and he come up to me and, right in my old ugly face he commenced to holler, "Gimme yo wallet, muthafukka, gimme yo money now, I'a blow you gotdam head off, gimme yo money, gimme yo money now!" His friend was standin by my left leg. He didn say nothin. Both of em was light-skinned. You know, the way they are these days.

Fuk a snake! I knowed I was not about to ast the sumbich to produce his pistol, even if he really did happen to have one. And, two, I figured I was a goner and that they was just gon shoot my mean old ass and nobody would never know why, or, I might add, give a shit. So, I lied. Mostly it was true when I was sayin I didn work there, but the rest was made up. I said: "My wife teaches here." And that britches-draggin lillo sumbich never took a breath. He just kept on blastin out with: "Gimme yo money, muthafukka, gimme yo money NOW, I'mo blow yo gotdam head off, gimme yo money!"

And I kept on lookin straight at him and sayin: "My wife teaches here." I said it about eighteen fukkin times with no visible result. Then, I remembered what Mad told me about write'n. He said that when you said somethin or when you wrote somethin to always *put a picture with it*, sumpm somebody could see in their mind!—that way, *see*, what you was saying would not be just a fukkin generality that wouldn get nobody's attention. So I hollered out: "My wife teaches mathematics here!" I wanted to add, "You little shitbird," but I didn. And that was probly for the best. Cause even a little shitbird can kill you if he really does have a gun.

Anyway, *blap*, the coksukka stopped. He turnt hissef around and walked into the gym. His real light-skinned buddy, who was on my left flank, looked up at me and said, "Uh, what kinda math does she teach?" I thought for a split-second and said, "Aw, you know, *algebra*." And him and me walked on into the gym behind the little turdsniffer that claimed he had a gun, and probly did. I was a lucky sumbich.

But that aint all. When me and the *bandido's* light-skinned buddy walked into the gym, the bandido—Mr. Low Pants—who was gonna blow my head off was leanin over talkin to the ladies on the ticket table. I walked up beside him and told the ticket ladies: "Apparently this young man's car was broke into, and he and his friends thought I seen it, but I didn." Then I stepped around to the side of the table. I was between it and a fukkin wall, just tryin to get my ass pulled together.

The I'mo-Blow-Yo-Gotdam-Head-Off boy was then talkin up a storm on his cell phone, cause you know every sumbich on this gotdam earth has one. But quick as a wink and slap-ass outa the unknown blue, he turns to me. He sticks out his right hand and says, "I apologize. I was just so upset. I apologize."

I stuck out my hand, too. I shook his and said, "Don't think nothin of it. I've been there." I do not know what made me say that. It was the only thing I could think of at the time. Later, not too much later, I did mention the whole episode to the principal. He went out into the parkin lot, but I never did know what happened after that.

Anyway, the next day, back in the Delta, I stayed home in my pajamas—which have pictures of food all over em. I aint been able to get no more like em. Didn start wearin none till I got to be about fifty-eight.

But here's the thing about every fukkin bit of that. It's the Planters' fault. Them ass'oles brought them black sumbiches over here. They worked their raggedy asses into the ground. And they not only *did not* educate the wild muthafukkas but even made it against the law to do so! Those cotton-pickin big rich seersucker pissguzzlers thought slavery was here to stay. Yeah, *they did!* Then, when it became obvious it wuddn, they made those po black bastuhds set at the back of the bus.

Oh, hell, everything was fine as far as them Planters was concerned as long as the Niggas was out there pickin cotton, eatn watermelon, singin about Jesus, and thinkin up nice things to do all the time for their white folks. And, worse, them Planters loved bein big daddy to all their "darkies." Givin em a quarter here and there and getn em outa jail and patn em on the head made them Planters feel like bein a Planter was a real fine thing to be, kind and generous, and long-sufferin, believin God Hissef knew how sweet they was to their black folks. All that was true too as long as *Rastus* and nem didn holler about wantn to vote and have a buncha fukkin civil-ass-rights.

Anyway, it wuddn them two black boys that held me up in that parkin lot, *it was the gotdam Planters that did it.* Them sumbiches caused it by long distance through the wiry, tangled-ass years of American history, and them two black teenagers wuddn nothin more than what these gotdam Planters made em into two hunnud years ago. And that's the fukkin truth.

The funny thing is them bigshot white muthafukkas gets all upset about what they say is black ir-refukkin-sponsibility. They say blacks don't never want to own up to nothin and always want everything to be somebody else's fault. That knocks me out!—because the very things these highclass white turdheads complain about is the very things they, *they-gotdam-sevs,* created . . . and THEY'RE the ones who refuse to take the coksukkin responsibility!

You'd think these big-shot land-ownin shit-heds woulda figured all that out by now, because they are smart as all get-out; but, I suppose it's more like they're smart about just about everything but what's in the mirror. Shoot, they want to have it that it was my kinda folks that fukked up the Niggas. That's bullshit! We was too poor and too beat down to fukkup anybody—oh, well, yeah, ChrEYEst, we done some terrible things to the po sumbiches, that's for sure, but we done them things with the full-ass approval of them bigshots—and you know who I am talkin about—the coksukkin Planters and *their kind*—who sat they big soft all-cotton asses on the fukkin screen po'ich while we done the chasin and the killin. Yeah, that was us, me and my kind. We done that, when the real truth is we shoulda been chasin and hangin them rich-ass bastuhds that owned all the land and owned all the po' ignunt work-whupped people on it as well, black AND white!

You just can't see things for what they are a lot of times when you're in the thick of em. I learned that when I was a historian. And that's why most of the time I do try *not* to say "Nigga," and, as much as I can, so as to be more polite when I want to talk about em, I use the word "Niggra." And, of course, Miss Peekyboo wouldn

even never let me say that! *She* always said "*Dahkies.*" I wuddn gon
go *that* far. Fukkum. Cap'm, please!

Anyway, I remember one time that Worthless-ass Nigga Ezell—
and I will have to give the no-count sumbich credit for this—he
said to me: "Junior Ray, y'all all calls us *Niggas* and 'pears to think
we don't mind, but how would y'all like it if we was to call y'all
"Whickies?[85] Y'all wouldn like it one bit."

"You got a point," I told him, and he did. I mean, Son!—If a
Nigga called me a *Whicky*, I'd wanta whop that muthafukka up-
side his head—or worse, step on his gotdam toe; that'd damm well
fix his ass. You know, hitn nem sumbiches in the head won't make
no impression on em one a-tall cause it's a signtific fact they has
a skull-bone three-inches thick, but now *ALL* emm muthafukkas
got a sore toe! Yeah! You stomp em on the foot, and that'll stop
em every gotdam time. That's a joke, ass'ole. But still I wouldn do
none of that if I was you.

On the other hand, even though I used to think down here
we knew how to *han'l em* and that we was experts at it, the truth
is I expect they're the ones doin most of the hanlin. And we're the
shit-heds. Fuk a mudpuppy. It's complicated.

The truth is I couldn do nothin to nobody now, since the
change and all. They can call us anything they damm well please,
and we can't do one fukkin thing about it. I mean in the old days
we coulda beat em, hanged em, and jumped up and down on
their ass, and even the Congress of the whole Uninety-Nine States
wouldna lifted a fukkin finger to keep us from doin it and, under
the right conditions, woulda sent the U.S. Army down here to
give us a hand.

But now! Oh, gotdam, now! Everything's changed, and even
though I do try my best NOT to go along with the new way that

---

85   Eutoria Kelly, ca.1949, Tunica, Mississippi. —ml

has come upon us, I know I can't act—and I can't *be*—exactly like I used to, gotdammit.

ANYWAY, WHEN IT COMES to what I know, I have told it all the way I seen it—plus some, I suppose, but that only helped the facts move along and made everything seem somewhat better than what it was. From here on out, though, I intend to advise McKinney and Mad and Brainy whenever—and *if* ever—they want to write a book of their own . . . or elect to talk one like I did. I expect my experience could come in pretty handy for em, or even for Robert Galbraith, if he was to ast me. Write'n a talkin book aint that hard, you know. All a sumbich basically has to do is just set back and begin to say what's on his mind, but the truth is most muthafukkas don't really have no idea what's on their minds till it falls out of their mouth.

Junior Ray's Super-Controversial "Go-to-Hell Cow College Casserole"

1. Get one nem casserole dishes. That makes the dish official.

2. You'll need a can of regular mushroom soup and whole lot of fat-free soda crackers, plus some already cooked fieldpeas or ladypeas and one cup of un-cooked Miss'ssippi brown rice—which will give your ass the amount of it cooked that you'll need. Don't buy that crap they put out over in Arkanfukkinsaw!

3. Round up a hunk of Miss'ssippi State's "Cannon Ball" Edam cheese, and grab a handful of fresh hollapainyohs and slice'm up.

4. Add the main ingredient: ground lamb, and a lot of it. You can, if you just have to, toss in a dab of mint jelly. But, personally, I'd wait on that. You might not want your casserole to taste sweet. On the other hand, I recommend you could th'ow in a third of a cup of medium sherry or *Eye Doctor*, and a buncha sliced, unsalted almonds.

5. After you cook your rice, mix everything together. And don't do it like a gotdam sissy. Stir it all around; pop in a dash of salt, and glop all of what you've got into the official casserole dish.

6. Put it in the oven and cook that sumbich for at least an hour at 350 degrees. Then take a look, so you won't burn up your mouthwaterin masterpiece.

7. If the muthafukka looks done, don't dik around: put it on the table.

8. Eat it with a big EYE-talian salad. Or even with just a big EYE-talian, which, you know, if you ride around the Miss'ssippi Delta, ought not to be too fukkin hard to find.

CHAPTER TWENTY-ONE

How Did Miss Attica Do It?—The "Interlocking Southern Elite"—Tooter Tait Saw Miss Attica and Three Other Women— Miss Nona May Drew, Miss Decima Boyle, and Miss MortaSue Gunnison?—They Wore Mosquito Nets—Miss Attica Had a .410 Pump—Miss Attica Turns Pale on the Phone—Tisiphone— Brainy Tells Us about a Figment of the Ancient Imagination— The Hippopotamuses Swim Down the Tallahatchie—They Might Make it Back to Africa—Recipe No. 22: Junior Ray's SurPrize- Winnin Poached Delta Farm-Raised Spicy Kimchee Catfish Sandwich

I know you are wonderin up a pissfit how Miss Attica could have done them killins, how she knowed to go to Shelby where she stabbed Farley, how she got into the woods and shot Tombo, and how in the name of Peanut the Holy-ass Doughnut Maker she come up to Froggy Waters and gigged him in the th'oat with his own gig! Course, she confessed to doin it all right there in the room with Judge "Rusty." But, here's the deal: She never said *how* she done it. And neither Judge Rusty nor Secundus pressed her to do so. Which I thought was kinda peculiar.

I wouldn lie to you. Sumpm's been botherin me a lot—especially me bein a law-enforcement professional and also now as a private diktective. Here's what I've thought: First, when Tombo was shot out on the edge of the Cut-Off, under the Visitor's Tree, in the Evans' Woods, then when Farley was found stabbed-dead in his car and, later, when Froggy was discovered sem-EYE face-down in

Beaver Dam Brake with his own frog-gig stuck in his mouth—all the way through to the back of his head—there had to be a connection. *No gotdam place* on this present day earth coulda had all that and there not be a fukkin connection. Voyd and Secundus and Crazy Baines thought so, too. So did Ezell, but that was later; for the most part he didn't really give a crap till we made him part of the investigate'n task force.

On the other hand, really, there was a number of other folks who all said they thought there had to be a "common denominator," and that's why a lot of em had thought Miz Potts's death was in there as well, which, as I told you a while ago, it was not and that it was just a coincidence. However, because the nature of the crime was so gotdam gruesome, with the hedge clippers and all, it looked like it fit right in with the killin of those three men. But, see, the folks that thought all that did not know, like Voyd and me and Secundus and Brainy and *Chumly* and Crazy Baines—and that Worthless Nigga Ezell! . . . about the threater letters!

Then there's the second thing. Lemme jump ahead. I always believed somehow or another Miss Attica murdered them old boys. And of course as you now know, she up and confessed to doin it, right there setn in Judge "Rusty's" office, in front of Secundus and, technically, me and Voyd who was listenin at the door. However, as I told you way back, even though we bullseyed her ass with the letters and even though she confessed, we couldn never figure out *how* she done it. That's the strangest part of all. Miss Attica was setn there flat out declarin she and she alone done the whole thing!—that she committed all three of the killins and that she mistook each one of them po sumbiches for young Mr. Brainsong II, and that she felt real bad about havin made the same mistake three fukkin times hand runnin. Yet, in all of that confessin, she did not offer no explanations whatsofukkinever as to how she knew to go to where each of the killins took place or how she got them sumbiches to roll over dead.

And that's why, number three, I am certain as a muthafukka she had to have some help. I mean, who told her Froggy Waters had invited Brainy to go frog giggin with him? How in God's name did she get Froggy's gig away from him and then stab his ass in the mouth, all the time of course, lookin straight at him and knowin he was Froggy Waters and not young Mr. Brainsong? That's another reason I am convinced there was some more of them Aunty Belles involved and, further, that they well coulda been from outa town so that, even though they mighta known Froggy's cousins, they might notta knowed Froggy personally and wouldna knowed what he looked like and thus could easily have mistook his ass for Brainy. But even if that was true, it still don't explain how Miss Attica, or some other powerful female of her type, got the gig outa Froggy's hands and into hers—again whoever's—and then into the back of Froggy's head by way of his lips.

See what I mean? Froggy's killer coulda been some *Planter* woman from Ittabena or Hushpuckena.[86] It wouldna mattered in a lotta ways because they are all part of what a smart sumbich once called the fukkin "Interlocking Southern Elite."

ChrEYEst. All of em—all them gotdam Planters and their coksukkin *types!*—and bygod all these blacks down here that made em what they are!—they're all the same thing, one way or another, and every fukkin one of em, both black and white, is kin to each other either on purpose or accidentally! That's what I think anyway. Fukkum.

Now, I have to say this real quick. Owin to the nature of the killins, the way they was done and all, I have discounted en-dam-tirely the possibility that a man was involved. None of what happened has anything about it that would indicate male participation.

---

86   Pronounced Hush-Puck-Nee. —ml]

Aint no man gon stab another sumbich with a gotdam little silver letter opener. And a man wouldn gig another man in the mouth— although Brainy says otherwise and talked about some kinda of knockdown-drag-ass-out involvin two coksukkas named *Thestor* and *Patroklos*. But you can see by their names them sumbiches was Yankees. There's no tellin what they'd do. It's true that here among the white folks and the blacks, we got plenty of EYE-talians and Grecians and Jews and Lebafukkinese and Chinamens all over the gotdam Delta, but, Jeezus ChrEYEst!—*they* are one of us, and not no gotdam foreigner.

Now with Farley, Miss Attica was, as you know, on the scene. The big question is how did she know "Chumly," Brainy's *friend*, was gone off on a trip to see his mama and nem in wherever it is he come from and that Brainy had gotten invited to come down to Shelby and spend the night at Farley's so they and some other of their you-know-what buddies could go down to Greenville and suck up a big steak and hot-tamale supper at Doe's Eat Place.

Frankly, as a diktecktive and as a law-enforcement professional, I have learned you don't have to understand somethin to know pretty much all about it.

I HAVE BEEN WAITIN to tell you about this next thing. A pretty good while after all of what I've been talkin about was over, actually, some years later, Tooter Tait, who is a cousin of little Quitman Tait, told me this. Tooter, like his cousin, was maybe one of the busiest sumbiches you'd ever want to meet. Anyway, among a slew of other pies and various wild-ass financial cobblers he had his fingers and toes AND his gotdam hands and feet into, Tooter *owned and run* a fishin camp out on the Cut-Off, which is now called Tunica Lake, even though all of it aint actually in Tunica County. But people calls it Tunica Lake so as not to confuse foks by callin it Mhoon Lake—which of course *is* here in Mhoon County. And natchaly that always gets further-ass confused with Moon Lake down in Coahoma County. So you can see, when it come to where you mighta told your wife you was gon be when you and some of your yo-bob buddies was goin fishin—if in fact you was goin fishin and not just tellin her that—it could sometimes turn into a completely fukked-up mess. And not a mess of fish, neither.

But here's what I want to tell you. Tooter told it to me one late afternoon in the early fall, when I was just fukkin around out at the Cut-Off, havin a beer in Tooter's baitshop with Pappy Saniston, who was setn there take'n his watch apart, and when I ast him how come he was doin it, he said, "I b'lieve I've figured out how to stop time."

"Good luck," I told his ass.

Anyhow—and, see, this was officially after me and Voyd had stopped bein diktectives—Tooter said, "Funny thing . . . on the day they found Tombo shot by the edge of the lake, down in the Evanses' woods . . . funny thing . . . ."

And I said, "Funny thing *what?*"

"Funny thing," he said, "before daylight and before even the first turkey hunters had showed up to put a boat into the lake to go wherever they was gonna hunt—Miss Attica and three other women pulled in here in a big black Ford FieldMaster Super SUV, towing a trailer with a new-looking electric catamaran on it. It was like the kind the Abbay boy sells up in Meffis. And the lady driving the vehicle whirled that big ol SUV and the trailer around like a pro and backed it right down the ramp."

"Who was the other three women?" I ast him.

"Well," he said, "all of em were wearing mosquito nets over their faces. Miss Attica had her net thrown back over her hat, so I knew who *she* was—of course you and I both know you couldn't disguise Miss Attica if you were to toss the Meffis Pyramid over her."

"I don't think it would fit," I said.

"But, the other three ladies . . . I believe . . . and I wouldn't bet the new baby on it . . . were *Nona* May Drew, from down at Jonestown; *Decima* Boyle, from Indianola; and Miss *Morta*Sue Gunnison, who lives with Stovall Jones out there from Friars Point on her family's land in that old house that belonged to her grandmother.

"If I'm right, it was Decima Boyle who was drivin the SUV. I went to Ole Miss with her! She was a Tri-Delt. She was nice, too, and I tried to go out with her, but she wouldn give me the gum off her loafers and wound up pinned to that sumbich Sheppard Landing, from down there around Rising Sun . . . his plantation's called *Ponolalawa*. He didn't marry her, though. And she lived up in Washington, D.C., for a long time working for the Bureau of Standards—you know—checking on weights and measures—and all that. Far as I know she never did get married and is now retired and came back to the Delta to live in her aunt's old home. It's right there slap in the middle of Indianola. Come to think of it, the only one of those four that ever walked down the aisle was Miss Attica!—I mean, if you can call living with Euster Draynum being married. But, like I said, Junior Ray, I couldn't see their faces."

My skin bubbled up. Old Tooter was on a roll. And I said to myself, "I'll be a mutha-fukka!" What he was tellin me explained everything about what happened to Tombo! It was good enough for me. And it also let me know Miss Attica *did have help* in killin at least *one* of those po' unsuspectin fukheds.

Sometimes I think almost all of life is like lookin out through a haze of bouncin heat waves. Everything is there; you just can't see it.

"I could be wrong," Tooter said, "but, even though none of em spoke a whole lot, I am pretty sure that's who they were, well . . . *pretty* sure."

"I be dog," I said.

Tooter went on to say that all four of them old gals was decked out in their huntn clothes, briar britches and all. He said he swore they coulda all been stannin in the window at T. B. Ronson's sportn goods store, up there in Meffis, out near Chickasaw Gardens. Plus, that's probably where they got all their stuff, unless it was from that new place you can order from I been hearin about, *HORviss* or sumpm.

Anyway, Tooter said each of them women, include'n Miss Attica, was dressed for turkey season, 'cept the onliest one carryin a gun was Miss Attica. Tooter said she had her little Ithaca with her. Yassa!

Tooter wuddn finished. "I helped em put that big pretty electric boat in the water," he said. "They got into it, and again it was Decima who was sitting in the driver's seat. She was the only one who wasn't standing up. Miss Attica and Miss MortaSue were on their feet in the front, bolt upright and ramrod straight, and Miss Attica had her shotgun at parade rest. Nona May was standing up too, but more relaxed, directly behind Miss MortaSue and right beside Decima, who, as I said was sitting at the wheel.

"There was a lot of fog that morning, a lot of fog, you know how that can be, and it was a little on the chilly side, somewhat too chilly, I thought, for turkey season. But before they left the ramp, I asked them where they were going and what they were doing—I told you they just had one gun among em."

"So, what did they say they was gon be doin," I ast him.

"*Bird watching,*" Tooter said. "They told me they were going *bird watching* down below old Fire Foot Landing."

"Aint no gotdam birds down there," I said. "Not worth *watchin* nohow."

"Well," Tooter said, "They slipped right on out into the lake and disappeared just as quiet as if that boat didn't have a motor at all. Those new ones are really something! When they left I went on back inside the bait shop."

"How long was they gone?" I ast him.

"It wasn't that long at all," he said. "In fact it hadn't even gotten light yet. I was outside when they came back because in the meantime three hunters had showed up. One was from Senatobia. I think he has something to do with the college over there, and the other two were from Southaven. They fish down here a lot, and one of em wants to buy a house in the camp. That morning, though, the three of them were going over to the upper end of the lake to hunt back in the woods out on Bordeaux[87] Point. It was right after they had put in and gone on I thought I could hear those women talking and that electric motor purring toward the ramp. I was right, and, in just a minute, there they were."

"What then?" I said.

"Well," Tooter said, "when the boat touched the bank, they all had their mosquito nets down over their faces. I looked at Miss Attica, who, like I said, it would take more than a hat and a mosquito net to hide, and she was sitting in the front with her little shotgun—they were all sitting down when they came back—and I said, 'Did yawl get a turkey?' Miss Attica didn't say a word, but Miss MortaSue did—I could tell it was her, too, because Miss MortaSue is hard to miss; she's the tallest—she said, 'I believe you could say we got ourselves a gobbler.' Then they all kind of laughed. More of a chuckle actually, or maybe a . . . snicker. I tell you, Junior Ray, I really couldn't figure out what they were laughing at. I just thought probably I had missed something or was slow on the uptake. And I didn't ask them anything about bird watching."

"What happened after that?" I ast him.

"Nothing. Nothing at all. They got out of the boat, and I helped them haul that big, pretty, quiet thing back onto the trailer. Once the boat was strapped down, Miss MortaSue, Decima, and Nona May—if I'm right in thinking that's who they were—and Miss Attica, all of em, got in that big old black Ford FieldMaster."

---

87 Pronounced: bird-o. —ml

"And . . . ?"

"They hopped in that thing, shut the doors and drove away," said Tooter. "Didn't even say goodbye, just booked it on back toward the levee."

You could say that didn clear up all that much. Yet just knowin about that foggy mornin was plenty, and I felt like what I had heard more or less organized the past a whole lot better than it had been. Things have a tendency to come out, and I imagine if a sumbich could live long enough, he'd just about know everything there was to know in the whole gotdam world.

It's also funny that back when all that stuff was goin on I never did talk to Tooter. I did talk with that sumbich that worked out there, and he does appear to have some sense, but I never did talk to Tooter. On the other hand, maybe things just have to come around when they come around. I don't know. Anyway, I am glad I got to hear all that from Tooter. And I *am* sorry I can't tell Secundus so he could tell Judge "Rusty." I doubt either of em woulda wanted to do anythin, but I am certain they would want to know, if, of course, they was still alive.

Another inter-restin thing about it is that all three of them women and two more besides went off on long-ass trips right after Judge "Rusty" had his talk with Miss Attica. Now I guess I know more or less why. You can't do much in the Delta and expect people not to know your business, cause they *will* know it, and bygod sometimes know it before *you* know it. Course it did take some time to put the bee on Miss Attica, but not *that* long, and we sure as hell done it. *Now*, though, I am certain I have seen a little bit of what's below the tip of the chocolate *sundy*. And it aint all that sweet.

And I remember, too, some time later, when Ezell come up to me in the new park they got "uptown" and said: "Hey, Junior Ray."

"Hey, Ezell," I said.

"I was in Miss Attica's house last week, and th' phome rang."

"The phone rang?" I said.

"Uhn-hunh, th' phome rang, and Miss Attica, she picked it up, and I could hear from where I was stannin somebody say: 'Attica? . . . .' It sounded like a woman to me, when she say, 'Attica.' Th' voice come outa Miss Attica's phome loud enough that I could make out it was a woman, and that's what I wanted to tell you 'bout."

"'Bout what?"

"Miss Attica turnt the color of a bowl of day-old grits: And she say, 'Oh my God!'—like she was scared to death—and she say, 'Oh my God!' one mo time. Then she state th' woman's name; Miss Attica say, 'TiSIFuhnee?' After she done that, it went on like this: 'TiSIFuhnee! . . . It was a mistake . . . I know I did wrong . . . But it was a mistake! . . . I didn't mean to . . . Yes, I know you're furious . . . But TiSIFuhnee . . . TiSIFuhnee . . .' Junior Ray, I felt like somebody done step cross my grave!"

Didn none of that make my shirt fly up, but it had obviously made a big-ass impression on Ezell mainly on account of how Miss Attica had jumped and how scared she had appeared to be when she heard that woman's voice on the phone. Anyway, Ezell said Miss Attica stood there with the telephone to the side of her head, just lookin straight-ass out to Arkansas with her eyes big as two jumbo fried eggs, and that that was it. He didn hear the other person say nothin more, and all Miss Attica said before she put the phone down was, "TiSIFuhnee! Oh my God . . ."

I told Voyd about it, and neither of us could figure out who that TiSIFuhnee woman coulda been, but that maybe she was from Greenwood. Anyway when we told Brainy, his eyes got big as fried eggs, too—with the gotdam country ham th'owed in!—and he said the same thing Miss Attica had said to the woman that called her on the phone: "TiSIFuhnee!"

Then Brainy put his professor-hat on and explained to us that the onliest TiSIFuhnee he knew about was a woman that was not a real person at all but was, as he put it, "merely a figment of the ancient imagination" and that the spellin of her name was "Tisiphone." He said she was "purely mythological." Anyhow, the point is this female figment went all around and up and down the "ancient imagination" getn even for murders, which I believe was mostly mythological as well. Anyway, Brainy said what Miss Attica heard was, in his words: "That which could have been none other than The Voice of Revenge," which further, he told us, was what the *Tisiphone* woman's name means in Greek. And triple-which of course don't mean nothin to me. Nor to Voyd neither. If it aint American, fukkit.

He also mentioned that this *Tisiphone* woman had snakes for hair, and I said to him that I bet she didn get invited out a lot. But Brainy informed us that she didn have to have a' invitation because she went wherever she pleased, and none of the mythological people could do a thing about it. By then, I could tell he was tired of fukkin with us, so we let him alone. And he went off to go work on his *memwars*.

I WENT DOWN TO Marks on some roads don't many sumbiches know about and met up with Voyd near the wreck; and soon as I got there Voyd jumped, after a fashion, into my vehicle and him and me drove into town and over to Riverside Drive along the west bank of the Coldwater River to see if we could get a look at them hippopotamuses.[88] We seen a whole bunch of folks crowded onto the Walnut Street Bridge, so Voyd and me stopped for a while and stood among em. But there weren't no *potowopusses* in sight. So we whizzed on over to Highway 3, went south to Lambert, took a left on 322 and zoomed east to the bridge on that road between

---

88   Classically, *hippopotami*. —ogbii

Lambert and Crowder where the Coldwater comes into the Tallahatchie, to see if we could catch sight of them big old things. But we didn see em there neither.

I know you might think it was a real strange thing why that particular eighteen-wheeler was on State Highway 6, haulin a couple of hippopotamuses. But, if you have ever been in law enforcement, like me, then you know what might look strange aint strange a-tall once you understand how that driver was thinkin. That's where bein a professional comes in.

I talked to the po muthafukka there at the Coldwater bridge on Highway 6. Hell, he was just stannin there with his gotdam hands in his pockets. Anyway, he told me he was headed for the Meffis Zoo and was makin a beeline for it up Interstate 55, but, when he got to Batesville, over there in the Hills, he hooked a big-ass left because he said he had a girlfriend in Belen. That's a little town setn out there between Marks and Jonestown, in the middle of about as much of nowhere as a sumbich can get and still be anywhere, especially with two hippopotamuses on board. But he never made it. ChrEYEst, Belen aint even on Highway Number 6! It's off the road altogether and up to the north of it, 'longside Cassidy Bye-oh.[89]

So there it is. The driver fukked up. He gets on a road he aint supposed to be on; plus, he's some kinda independent operator who aint hooked up to the GPS, so he knows won't nobody know what he's up to. Things woulda probly worked out just fine if he hadna blowed a tire on that ji-mongus-ass curve just as you're comin up to the east side of the Coldwater bridge, which is only a few yards to the east of the Yellow Dog tracks, which is just a small string of fish, rilly, from the four-way where Highway 6 crosses Highway 3, right there at Marks.

One thing had led to another. The tire blew, the trailer swang

89   Bayou. —ml

around and pulled the whole rig down the embankment on the north side of the highway; the trailer busted open, th'owed the cages with the two *hipposausages* in em out into the grass, where, natchaly, the cages come apart. The hippos just stood around the scene for a few minutes and one of em took a big bite of weeds at the bottom of the embankment. He—or she—chewed on it for a minute and then let it fall out of his or her mouth back onto the ground. Neither one of em, somebody said, 'peared to be partic'ly upset about bein in a wreck. Anyway, I guess they musta smelled water, cause both of em trotted on over to the Coldwater, got in it, and headed south. That's the way I heard it.

Even though wuddn nobody hurt, include'n the driver, it was a bad-lookin wreck. The trailer and the cab was layin on their sides; plus, the cab was crossways on the road, and it was all tore up. And traffic was backed up to Locke Station on the east side of the bridge. But it wuddn long before the road was closed on the other side, damm near all the way over to Clarksdale, and them two wild-ass *willopuswallopuses* had done disappeared downstream. I'da hated to a' been that driver. Anyhow, bad as it was, still it aint like the Meffis Zoo duddn have enough of them big old *woposostrus* sumbiches as it is, at least cordn to what somebody is supposed to of said.

But when couldn nobody see the animals no more from the highway, everybody had stampeded on into Marks and over to the Walnut Street Bridge where Voyd and me had went soon as we got there, hadn saw nothin in the river, and proceeded to haul-ass all over the fukkin place from Marks to Lambert and beyond; then once again we was at the Walnut Street Bridge, and in a few minutes after we was back, a woman hollered: "Yon they come!" And bygod I seen em! There they was. Just a'floatn and a'driftin along, not payin no 'tention to *none* of us.

Before that, though, word had done spread. People over at Belen was worried the hippos would turn off into Cassidy Bye-oh and come their way. But, as it was, them *potomizers* stayed smack in the middle of the Coldwater and hadn even give the time of day to Cassidy Bye-oh. It wouldn surprise me a bit if, in some way, those creatures mighta knew where they was goin.

I do have to say one thing about Belen. It would not have been a half-bad place for them two *wompuses* to set up housekeepin. Belen is rilly kind of pretty, hugged in on two sides as it is by the bye-oh, and I suspect overall it's not too much unlike Africa or Hippopotamia or wherever the fuk they're from. I don't know. I was just thinkin.

Anyhow, just a little bit ago I was setn around the house, and I got a text message from Voyd who says his grandson, Coahoma,[90] just now told him them *fukkapotamuses* is definitely in the Tallahatchie and is on their way to Greenwood! The thing is, if they had got loose earlier, before the Oil Leak, they coulda kept on swimmin all the way back to Africa, and it wouldna been all that hard to do, startn right there in the Coldwater River at Marks, Miss'ssippi.

Since they was already strokin down the Tallahatchie, if they make it past Greenwood, they'll be in the Yazoo, unless they fuk up and turn off into the Yalobusha. Anyway, see, once they'da got into the Yazoo, all they woulda had to do was keep on cruisin right along till they come to just a hair north of Vicksburg at the place where the Yazoo burps into the Miss'ssippi River, and that's where those two big *humptidumpuses* coulda took a sharp left and gone all the way down the Mississippi to New Orleens—and then, of course, right on out into the GuffafukkinMexico . . . which, now, though, I hear the Greedhogs have finally about fukked up for good, so if you swim in it, it'll kill you. And that goes for them two animals just like it would for me and you. The muthafukkas. The Greedhogs, I mean.

---

90 Pronounced: k'homa. —ml

However, I hope the bigshots habm ruint the GuffaMexico forever and that maybe some genius will hop up and fix it all back pretty much the way it was, because Mad's real near it down there in Luzianna, as I have told you, down in the white space on the bottom of the map, right by all that mess I was referrin to. Plus, you know, him failin at love and then force'n hissef to break up with Money Scatters was *hard enough* for him. So, after all of *that*, I'd hate to see him just have to pick up, ka-whammo, and move from where he's livin and happy with Enliss Roux and the tri-racial isolates, and all.

This may or may not be the last time I ever say this, but I cannot emphasize to your ass ENOUGH that when I might say "Big Shots," I mean PLANTERS. Nowadays a Planter don't have to plant nothin to be one of em. They're everywhere and all over the fukkin place, not necessarily by any means just in the cotton-pickin Miss'ssippi Delta. Look, sumbich, I am talkin about a class thing. It aint even partic'ly a money thing, because you can be a gotdam Planter and not have a icebox in the kitchen to piss on. It's like they all have the same head and think alike. They see things in the world alike. Shit they move alike, dress alike, walk alike, laugh alike, LOOK ALIKE, and they are born alike and gotdam die alike. Plus, the muthafukkas run everything there is on this earth—they can be plantn cotton and soybeans and rice—or collecting gotdam USDA welfare for *not* plantin—or those ass'oles can be makin cars, drillin oil, sellin stocks, and just generally suckin up the world with anything else they can get their teeth into. They can be huntn doves in Sunflower County and deer at Rena Lara, or they can be shootn the shit and gaze'n outa one nem high-up penthouses up in New Yawk City. More-dadgum-over, you cannot get the better of em. Those diklikkas will win every time. For-fukkin-get-it. If you aint one of *them*, you're a po'ass pekkawood or a Nigga. And that's a fact—in a philosophical—or I s'pose I ought to say a *THINKa-*

sophical and also a *DO-a-sophical*—way, if you get my drift. I aint
tryin to be signtific. I'm just tryin to provide the final clarification
of sumpm that is highly important, because it is highly important
to me that you understand it and don't have no confusion about
it. It's technical. But I am confident you got the picture. Anyway,
it's like I have told you before: "Planters is as Planters does." And
that's the whole pole and the hole of it. Them sumbiches aint human, and they think it's the other way around. Gotdam! Don't get
my ass started!

Course, there are exceptions, but I don't want to get off into that.

Anyhow, if the hippos finally do get out into the GuffaMexico,
I don't reg'n they'll have all that far to swim in order to paddle
their big ol' hippabutts back to Africa, if, of course, they really
want to hold their nose and do it. These rivers is *sumpm*! They can
take your ass anywhere. I think. Only not now if you're swimmin.
Like I indicated, from what I hear, bobbin around nowadays in
the GuffaMexico can give yo ass a disease. So my heart does go out
to them two hippos.

On the other hand, even if them big fat *jumbosostuses* do NOT
or can NOT make it back to Africa, and if they just decide to lay
around in the Tallahatchie and maybe never ever get no further
down in the Delta than, say, Silver City—or Panther Swamp!—they
might not know the difference . . . even with the changes and all.

Anyway, I have got to go see them sumbiches again!—provide'n
Voyd and me and of course all the game wardens and wild-life
signtists in the *Mississippi Gay Men's Fish Commission* can manage
to locate em. Our rivers can be somewhat bushy. I'll try to keep
you posted.

THE GOTDAM JUNIOR-FUKKIN-CHAMBER OF Commerce put up a
sign the other day that said: Visit Historic Downtown St. Leo. I
bout had to fart "Jesus Loves the LittleFukkinChirren" on that one.

A while back they did all kinds of crap to dress up the *down-town* part of the town, which aint hardly got a' up or a' down to it, and make it look like it come out of a gotdam magazine somewhere. You know what I'm talkin bout—false fronts and such. So what they really done was what old Miss Charlie Hayes said about Beale Street in Meffis, before she died of course. She told me one day, "Junior Ray, those Memphis people are really something, aren't they?"

"Yes, ma'am," I said, "I spec they thinks they are." I knew she had just cocked the hammer back.

"I saw," she said, "in the Sunday *Commercial Appeal,* an article showing the 'restoration of Beale Street,' which is supposed to entertain tourists."

"Yes'm," I said, cause I hadn really been keepin up with none of that, but I liked Miss Charlie and didn want her to think I wuddn right up there with what she was talkin about. And that's when she pulled the trigger: she said, "Looks like they've restored something that never existed." Miss Charlie had to a'been about a hunnud and seven by then. But that wuddn nothin unusual. Plus, she said she thought it "rather odd" that tourists would want to come to Meffis. To tell the truth, I do too, unless maybe a while back they mighta wanted to take the whole family out for a lapdance at the Magic Pussy Cabaret & Club.

Anyway, lookin at *hiss-fukkin-stahric downtown* St. Leo, I see what she meant.

THAT'S ABOUT IT, SUMBICH. So I'll just leave you with this: I was thinkin about Leland Shaw, like I sometimes do, and it come to me that although it may not be for the same reason or happen in the same peculiar way, one day my footprints will disappear, too. Time and the rain will wash em away, off this earth forever, and none of what I ever said or did—or ever was or didn never be—nothin, not a bit of it will matter or even be remembered. And, knowin that, I can't help but feel as though I probably never was here in the first place. But I guess that's okay with me.

Junior Ray's SurPrize-Winnin Poached Delta Farm-Raised Spicy Kimchee Catfish Sammidge

Step #1: When I say "poached," I do not mean for you to go sneak-ass over into Nolan Howitzer's aquaculturized Catfish Ponds. No, Suh! Buy you some gotdam catfish fee-lays at the Piggly Wiggly. Make sure the catfish is *farm-raised* in the Miss'ssippi Delta, and Lord God be certain it don't come outa some gotdam river.

Step #2: Confirm that you've got your kimchee. Personally I like mine extra hot. You shouldn't have no trouble findin a Korean to get some from.

Step #3: Look to see that you have a jar of soybean mynaise. I like NaSoya. On the other hand, if you can make home-made mynaise, that would be the livin end and taste a whole lot better'n I could ever tell you. It's up to you. Maybe your mama has some in her icebox or can show you how to whip it up.

Step #4: Go in the kitchen, get out a skillet, fill it with water, and put it on the stove. Note: If you want to, you can sawtay your catfish. I would recommend you do it in olive oil and dose up both sides of your fee-lays with "lemon pepper."

Step #5: Season the water with crushed red pepper and salt; then, bring it to a boil.

Step #6: Flap in a couple of the catfish fee-lays. Poach their ass. Turn the fee-lays over a couple of times. You want your catfish to be real done. Freshwater sushi'll give you tapeworm.

Treat a catfish like you would a chicken or a pig. Cook the crap out of it. Gently.

Step #7: Have you a plate ready with your one-hunnud percent whole-ass wheat bread standin-by on it. Lay out four slices, because you're gon fix two sammidges.

Step #8: Put your soybean mynaise on all four slices.

Step #9: Dip out some kimchee and put it on two of the slic-es—not too much, just enough. Don't build a gotdam "mound."

Step #10: If you're convinced your catfish fee-lays is done, lift em out, and flopm down on top of the kimchee. Slap the other two slices of your one-hunnud percent whole-wheat bread on top of that so as to make it all be a fukkin sammidge.

Step #11: Grab you a glass of ice water, and take your plate with the sammidges on into wherever you have the big flat-screen, cut on sumpm you love to look at, and eat the stew outa your delicious Junior Ray's SurPrize-Winnin Poached Delta Farm-Raised Spicy Kimchee Catfish Sammidges!

THE END OF PART ONE

Now, SUMBICH, YOU ARE gonna see "Part Two" which is what caused all the fuss. The thing is, none of what's in "Part Two" woulda dis-turbed Miss Attica and them Aunty Belles one bit if Leland Shaw hadna been certifiably zanga-danga in the head. That was what they couldn stan, him bein shell-shocked and runnin off and hide'n in a gotdam silo fifty-five years ago, and after that, on up towards the present *pasticiple*, them Aunty Belles got to fearin everybody in the whole world would know he was one of them. It was embarrassin. Course them Planters was divided. There were those who wanted to protect Shaw and save him, which they did. Then years later there was Miss Attica's bunch that just wanted to hit delete on the fact that he was ever even on this earth in the first place. So that's why her and the Aunty Belles went after Brainy who was gon publish a selected portion of the whole cluster of Shaw's googoo nutsness. Craziness is the one thing all these crazy fukheds down here cannot han'l. They think your craziness or my craziness can do somethin to them, can touch em in some kinda way so that other people here and in other parts of the world might think there was sumpm wrong with some of these gotdam uppy-uppies. Which it is.

Yet I guess Miss Attica and me has more in common than I thought. She wanted to kill Brainy to keep him from publicizin Shaw's write'n. And in that ball-frostin winter of 1958 and '59, I wanted to shoot Shaw and have it viewed as a public service with me savin the Delta from a rovin, ravin maniac. See, back in that long-ass-ago moment, I was overfukkinjoyed the sumbich was insane cause that's what I thought was gon give me the excuse to shoot him. But, crap. You can't count on nothin. It didn work out for me or Miss Attica. I never got to shoot the muthafukka, and she couldn even kill the right sumbich three times in a row.

Anyhow, if Shaw hada been more normal—maybe only a high-class queer or sumpm—there wouldna been no death threats and nobody woulda got murdered by mistake in a' attempt to keep Shaw's "Notes" from hitn the street and harmin the image of got-dam Southern fukkin manhood. On the other hand Brainy said the problem them women had with Shaw might notta had anything to do with him bein mentally defective. He said it might be that Shaw's write'n was just too "reflective."

I don't have no idea what that means. But I'll think on it while you make up your own mind about what Shaw has to say.

·

PART TWO

Excerpts from the Notebooks of Leland Shaw

*Consciousness is the quicksilver of existence . . .
and fear was the core of the forbidden fruit. None
of this was pointed out by the talking snake.*

— LELAND SHAW

Leland Shaw was a shell-shocked veteran of World War II who never believed he had returned home to the Mississippi Delta after the war, and he always thought he was being pursued by a patrol of German soldiers. So he jumped through the picture window of the rest wing at the County Hospital and ran off and hid in the top of an old silo that, for no reason anyone could imagine, was filled with long-forgotten cotton seeds. Because of that, he was able to survive the winter of 1958–59. I have read these excerpts from his alleged notebooks, and, personally, I don't think he was crazy at all.

— MCKINNEY LAKE

The ramblings of a madman cannot be construed as inaccurate. Indeed, within them there is a precision not found among the sane, and that is because the subjectivity of the madman is far more comprehensive than the paltry, limited sort of understanding available to the rest of us.

— OWEN G. BRAINSONG II

When he come back from the war in '45, that crazy sumbich never b'lieved he was home. Then he run off. And after that, Miss Helena, Sheriff Holston, Lawyer Montgomery, and all them Planters and n'em sent him away with a buncha Niggas. I never did get to shoot him, and, later, I give these notebooks of his to young Mr. Brainsong II. And that's it in a rabbit's ass.

— JUNIOR RAY LOVEBLOOD

Selected Selections Among the Notes of Leland Shaw

Taken Directly from the Original Ledger Entries
Written in Shaw's Own Hand
Circa 1945 until the Winter of 1958–59
& Edited by Owen G. Brainsong II

Hic et Nunc Incipit

FROM LEDGER NO. 3:

When we are dust what will it matter? Do the smallnesses, the transgressions, the indiscretions, crimes, misdemeanors, and sins still actively exist in some way beneath the farmer's foot? Yes. And they always will—if one believes deeply in the Periodic Table. But all those things I have just mentioned, though they are not found among the Congregation of Elements, may qualify as dust. Especially words: They are what makes the energy matter.

Are they murmuring in the wind, sparkling in the sunlight, coating someone's coffee table, becoming mud on rainy days? The question is whether there can be good if the bad is cancelled. How can there be hope if there are no molecules of error? Can we smell the past? I maintain that I can hear the passage of time. It is the Doppler effect. In short, *what will be* in Mississippi comes to us on the western breeze and *what has been* is now in Alabama.

I know exactly what happens when my pursuers disappear. I disappear. I vanish in the road. The path cannot be separated from its beginning, cannot be erased by cotton or beans. Its ruts are the imprints of the past and, like those grooves in hardened wax, contain the music so that all who step upon them may dance a hidden rumba.

I am nothing; therefore I am. I take great comfort in that fact, or at least I try to. Nothingness can be as cumbersome as somethingness. And just as puzzling.

I must remember always, though of course impermanently—for memory is fragile—to keep in mind and to understand that, even with every beat of my heart and as long as I am conscious, I am nothing. Nothing at all. Not a philosophic thing*ansich,* only an illusion of matter in a strange arrangement. Yet one day I shall *disperse,* among the mysteries of a larger something which is infinitely and most likely an enormous nothingness.

Still, one's trespasses never go away. Indeed, the wrongs for which a person is responsible cannot be erased by any messiah, real or mythical. They will not be cancelled by the death of the injured nor by the dual deaths of both the injured and the injurer, because, unfortunately, those wrongs, unlike the wronged and wronger, except in terms of sheer matter and energy, are not finite. They will exist forever in the light that holds their place in time. And wherever that light reaches throughout this universe or another, there those regrettable moments shall shine again . . . and sadly be repeated.

AHA! THE HIGH WATER is God. The problem has always been that I could easily believe in the possibility—indeed, even the probability—of high water, but I could not believe in the existence of God.

Just as an ancient Plato might say: Now let us suppose there is a God . . . On the other hand, in my perfect-pitch rendition of the *idioma* Thomas Jefferson would have spoken, I could phrase it, with unerring verisimilitude: "Okay, so what? The existence of such an Entity does not imply any caring, communicative relationship with that Entity. My snuff box, please."

The high water should, at least so I *believe*, be useful to me in reaching my objective, but, even so, like the God of the Deists I do not presume to assume the high water has the slightest interest in me. Yet I have to observe that I have an interest in it, which is unavoidably essential. What therefore is God? Is God the capitalized "It"? If so I am exactly where I was and in fact all things are what they were, or were proceeding toward, before I made the discovery.

> *Ecco lo nooye ethno clumb—the secret tongue*
> *of marsh hawks. I am learning it*
> *daily as they pass above the grass along the ditch*
> *and, low, back and forth over the fallow fields.*
> *Ethno clumb. That is what the harrier whispers*
> *just before he grabs the rabbit. Ethno clumb.*
> *An exact translation is impossible,*
> *but the general meaning is fishbowl clear.*
> *I know it is for the rabbits,*
> *who always hear the whisper but who never,*
> *never, see the shadow which*
> *catches and consumes them.*
> *The harrier is smart in that respect.*
> *He understands the disadvantage*
> *of producing a shadow faster than himself.*

Like others we have known and loved, life for the marsh hawk is a constant battle against the natural tendency of shadows to announce us.

And, because of this, unlike the rest of us, except for pilots, mariners, bathing beauties, and a number of physicists, the harrier has become an authority on the positions of the sun.

> *But, still, they speak, converse in flight,*
> *in raptorial whispers with each other,*
> *acres and acres apart.*

Yes, sir, the speech of marsh hawks is a remarkable phenomenon. For instance, here at the top of the silo, occasionally a small, gray male will bank in toward me at peephole level, maybe actually a little below, and look up at me where I lie and say quite distinctly, *"Uish ta no lu"* ("Hunting is a mere formality"). And then he banks away to go about his predatory business.

> *It is a simple statement—nothing flowery,*
> *but lean like himself and not attached to the ground.*
> *Further, it is what I shall say*
> *once I have learned to jump and not come down.*
> *He is after rabbits; I am after starlight.*

It is well for all of us to note that if indeed the Creator *spoke* all things into Being; then, logically, according to the law of origins, all *things* can speak.

THERE SHOULD STILL BE a golden eagle that lives on and hunts The River's left bank. And there are whirlpools, too. Mammals come to the water's edge to look out across the speeding stream, come out to look at it the same as men.

And if that great rush of moisture is in fact the Mississippi, it will be my salvation unless, of course, Allah finds another way.

LATELY I HAVE TAKEN to jumping upward[91] a lot. I feel, if I could jump at just the right moment in just the right way, I could remain in the air, hovering, so to speak, by creating—as I mentioned earlier—under my skin the right amount of isometric tension. In that way I believe I could maintain the necessary lift and, in effect, fly. Hovering, however, I am convinced, is the way to begin.

My objective is to leave the planet
in order to find, there among the stars,
that light in which my home
is most surely contained.
The past is in the light.

It is like looking for a flea in a fur coat. But persistence is the key, and knowing my capacity for tenacity, I am confident I shall win out.

And if home is in fact among those glittering fourth-dimensional fires of distant space, I have made the bold assumption that my home is therefore in the past. That would be true because, like a star, the Delta is part of the past in general. The problem is that I am not in that past. Frankly I do not know when I am. But being lost in a difficult dream does not come as news to me. Assumptions often make fools of the assumer. Yet when a person lacks sufficient information and when courage is the last resort, assumption is the only option. No guts, no glory. One might as well be bold about it. Thus, I can remain where I am—and when I am—or I can step forth and act on my bold assumption. That is what I prefer. I cannot sit still. It's like waiting for the telephone to ring.

---

91 Editor's note: Beginning here the scholarly reader is politely asked to compare the following with Part One, Chapter 19, pages 000 - 000. Apparently, for many years, even while on active duty during World War II, Shaw had believed he might be able to defy gravity and lift himself, through some act of sheer will—and muscular control—upward into the air. I hesitate to use the word "levitate," because what Shaw wanted was far more than that would imply. —ogbii

English of course is a Germanic tongue with African improvements. At least that is how it seemed to me to be before I left my home and went to war. And now I must protect my verbs, my articles, and my prepositions from the talons of the marsh hawk, against whom or which I bear no ill will, but I am aware of how certain parts of my native speech could well be regarded as delicious by predators.

The lightness of our rhotacism
is soothing to the brain,
and indeed the slow andante of our sentences
matches the low allegro of our thoughts
and of our ambitions
But there is a smooth fire in our verbs,
a soothing quite, fine and rather light—
not the molto con fuoco and staccato
one braces to receive from the Midwest
and elsewhere above,
just the sotto voce pianissimo
in flagrante of my native bog.

Truly, my dialect is undiagrammable. I say that mythopœically but not with conviction. In the Delta conviction is not necessary. Truth is in the moment. And, finally, I understand it is the moment I am trying to locate, not the space. *The place is in the moment.*

There are special obstacles one must confront when dealing with time that is within the spaces. It is like being in the woods. There I am in the forest. I stand in a space upon the ground beside a tree, but it is the *space* beneath the tree that I wish to stand in, yet it is *that space*—the one beneath the tree that seems impossible for me to reach and to occupy—*which represents "time,"* and it is the time, *the time I am looking for*, within the spaces that I cannot put my finger—much less my foot—upon.

But that's it. Home, it turns out, is not a place. It's a time.

Now I am beginning to understand the meaning of the sign over the gate at Camp Shelby:[92] "Abandon all hope, ye who enter here." I paid it no attention then in passing, and it is only in retrospect that I now am able to read it.

Eyko peregrino omoz eesha noktis = I wander about each/every night. You may notice a Latinate element.

I am inventing my own language out of necessity as a precaution in the event that I need to leave messages for myself once in a while, and would not want the enemy to know my business if they should find them.

Eyko futuro-stat bankibus ke ma privadingding stabili sancturarius = I will be sure that my secrets will remain safe.

My familiarity with various tongues is adequate, to one degree or another, and I confess I've never been attracted, until now, to the idea of some further version of Esperanto or to Volapuk. But for the *momentito*, my fair knowledge of Italic, and Germanic—Slavic, Austro-Asiatic, Semitic, Muscogean, and other linguistic—roots, both dead and alive, allows me in these peculiar circumstances to protect my interests. If necessary, I shall invent another alphabet perhaps by simply turning the letters in our current system sideways. There is really no sense in making things complicated. On the other hand, I might find it pleasurable to contrive a syllabary. Indeed, if it were not so unwieldy, I should even like to use glyphs—original, of course, and not so "thick" as those of the Maya nor so rudimentary as the feathers and snakes of the Egyptians. And though insanely unwieldy, an ideographic system like that of the Chinese would not be entirely out of the question, but, please, no abjads. I've got to have my vowels.

---

92 Army post established near Hattiesburg, Mississippi, in 1917, important in WWI and WWII, now perhaps the largest state-owned military site in the U.S. —ml

Yi zo eyko cambul[93] *graffa vi zit tota daga* = And I can write like this all day.

A digression: How can you, the doctor said to me, pretend that you are at home and still not believe it? And I said to him: Why should I *not* pretend? If I did not pretend, I would have nothing at all to do. The doctor was of course one of *them*. He would not let me look at him, and I knew it was because he was not wearing his rubber skin. I don't know how *they* stand it in the summer.

> *Quan l' grigi brbruh whoosh*
> *Aprochi cruksx l' nooda grunda*
> *Nit wumba ports a wowgli*
> *Straf beh digi-ketz o heli brit*
> *Ke muta vzha l' soggasogga glump*
> *Andu a zappa whutwhut,*
> *Na ya bit*
> *Ta kinikini wowgelblap*
> *O brbrglazha plunda.*

Translated:

> *When the gray cold wind*
> *Comes across the bare ground*
> *It sometimes brings a shining*
> *Strafe in rays of sunly light*
> *That changes all the static mud*
> *Into a bright illusion,*
> *And I see*

---

93   A reverse rebus: Campbell's Soup comes in a "can," thus "cambul," from "Campbell," is a verb: *to be able* or *can*. —ogbii

That moving flash
Of frozen silver.

The above is of course a fairly literal translation, which I always prefer over one that is bastardized, contrived and fabricated; yet, even so, the rendering above carries over the meaning as well as the rhymes. As anyone knows, foreign rhymes were never meant to survive translation, although mine seem to have done so; they appear to have made the transition in spite of my fears that they would not and in fact actually overcame my outright efforts to prevent them from being *transported* safely into English. And all that is doubly upsetting because, hitherto, I have always regarded *rhymes* as one of the absolutes Plato forgot to mention, and Aristotle did not in this way address.

Nevertheless, having had considerable training in the liberal arts at home and elsewhere, which includes a dalliance or several both formally and informally with, as I have already mentioned, foreign languages as well as dialects, creoles, patois, pidgins, argots, slangs, and various jargons, I am served well by it all now that I find it necessary to create an unknown idiom with its own grammar and vocabulary.

Further, in terms of what I should be doing while seeking simultaneously to escape, I have long had it in mind to compile an *encyclopedia* that will include many of the phenomena of the region, the one I am from and, shall we say, am trying very hard to get back to. The work will take a long time.

From Shaw's Encyclopedia Volume One[94]

Ailothelemus shawus localis: The slender ailothelemus falls into no existing taxonomy. It is a creature, about the size of a crow, that spends almost all of its waking hours trying to fly, but, having no wings, is

---

94 Shaw's encylopedia is a separate work and deserves its own treatment at a later time, but a few entries are included in these "Selections" to give the reader the flavor of the material. —ogbii

unable to do so. It is often sighted but seldom identified. The quality that has enabled it to survive over the evolutionary aeons is in fact its greatest: namely, that this peculiar animal has no sense of the impossible. Thus, and I believe Mr. Darwin may have said it first, *irony* is the secret of success even if that success is not the success one seeks.

FROM SHAW'S ENCYCLOPEDIA VOLUME TWO

Belizius gramnocovertus covertus: An odd grass that grows among other grasses and appears to be those grasses it grows among. A keen eye is required to identify Belizius, which, apparently has made its way northward from British Honduras in shiploads of uninspected bananas.

FROM SHAW'S ENCYCLOPEDIA VOLUME FOUR

Cleliobranthumus sterlingencheribus duckmossiae: The loveliest of dragon flies, a species invisible by day but brilliantly—and indeed mysteriously—lit by night in a polychrome luminescence barely understood by science. Sightings of *Cleliobranthumus* are accepted without question by poets and with awe by theologians, yet rejected by fundamentalists on the grounds that there is no scriptural basis for its existence. *Cleliobranthumus* spends its invisible hours skimming the surface of the dark, swamp waters, feeding upon the freshest and tenderest of aquatic mosses. This hitherto undetected behavior was discovered by a bream fisherman in Beaverdam Brake, some five miles north of Itilawa[95] Slough, a few miles south of St. Leo.

FROM SHAW'S ENCYCLOPEDIA VOLUME FOURTEEN

Nanodeltus chickasawensis rodentii: A tiny rodent no larger than a field pea, who makes its home in the cozy dens of field mice and voles. *Nanodeltus*—or, informally, *Nandy*—is, one might say, a mouse's mouse, and though there are countless millions of them in any given

---

95   Many trees/Choctaw/Chickasaw. —ogbii]

area of countryside, within temperate zones and as well as the tropics, they have remained heretofore undiscovered. In the interest of modesty I did not name this remarkable creature after myself. Indeed, there is a credible possibility *Nandy* was first observed in 1943, on Iwo Jima, by Seabrook Silver, a contemporary of mine, who lives a short distance below Diana Landing, near the long-defunct town of Peyton. Clarification of Seabrook's sighting has not proved possible, for after a brief encounter with him, which occurred two or three days after he had arrived in this place, Seabrook—like me—could readily see it was *not* his home. Seabrook will not speak. We all have to deal with the enemy as best we can, in our own way.

FROM SHAW'S ENCYCLOPEDIA VOLUME TWENTY-EIGHT

Zzyxwelelia floramorassus eremitae beaverdamibus: A flowering aquatic plant related to roses, which always occurs as an isolato and in what appears to be the center, if such can accurately be determined, of large slough systems. Its colorful yellow, scarlet, and lavender bloom lasts for three unlikely months—from the last part of November into the middle of February! *Zzyxwelelia* has been sighted and verified only three times since it was first discovered near Tutwiler in 1925. The a second so-called discovery of the flower was made in 1949. The individual who came upon it, a sensitive duck hunter by the name of Furlough Tracker, cut the bloom from its fleshy stem and carefully carried it home later that day. The specimen was dried by members of the West Tallahatchie Garden Club and has been preserved quite successfully in a glass case on a table beside the baptismal font at the back of the nave in Saint Maude's Episcopal Church at Tippo.

THAT'S IT, OF COURSE. I have trouble controlling not so much the passage of time as its placement, and I have allowed myself to misplace a good bit of mine, either through a negligence born of the essential ignorance of the fiction that I could have maintained a great deal of control over the invisible and seemingly indisputable dominance of time's uncatch-able thingness or, indeed, that I have misplaced large quantities through no fault on my part whatsoever, a notion I absolutely reject because the fact is I am responsible.

> *Yet I could not*
> *in all the world*
> *find the footprints*
> *of the Self,*
> *footprints to prove*
> *there had been a time*
> *in such a place,*
> *both time and place connected*
> *by the passing of moments,*
> *by poets and the stretch of memory.*
> *If only there were wires*
> *to hold the time to the place*
> *and water there as well,*
> *high enough*
> *to lap the edges of the stars;*
> *then, oh then,*
> *could moments and their meanings*
> *be preserved*
> *Or shall I simply find myself*
> *down on all fours*
> *like some bewilderable beast, howling unreflective*
> *beneath the magnificence of uninteresting light?*

I AM SO LOST. I am lost beyond all finding; I am lost in the vanity of a search. I am Lost. *All* is lost, even place and time themselves, confounded in this mythical entangled swamp of escape and evasion where, if I am not careful, false will be true, bad will be good, and rainwater will be mist. There is a great deal to sort out; fortunately walking about seems to help. I love the winter. The bugs are sleeping. Trees, too, and the grass and even the ground, all are taking a large nap, and I am somewhere in the cold clear beauty of a kingdom's dream, and I imagine I could simply kiss it, kiss it all and wake it up.

I'd be frightened to find I had such power, and, really, I like it quiet when the fields are empty and bare. I like the air and the light and the country quiet, while farmers spend their harvest, go on trips perhaps, and buy their wives the joys of Memphis. I like it quiet but not so quiet as the tenant houses. They are empty, sitting now waiting for agriculture to bury them in a tomb of weeds and vines and then to sit disguised for a time, season after season through the green bouncing heat of the humming summers then again on the cold, picked-out ground of winter, with their lifeless eyes surprised and their mouths open to the wind, the pulse in them gone forever.

I get the impression it is not coming back and that I should follow the Negroes. I see no reason I should not. And I will—if I can be sure they are not imposters inside a rubber skin. I will—if I can be certain they know the right direction. I am sure that where they are I must go, and where they are I shall—or at least *may*—find myself at home again. The Negroes hold the key to the door of my house.

The problem is that the Negroes I see have *not* left and *are not* leaving. I am afraid I am going to learn that the difficulty is one of logic.

> *Lest I miss*
> *The rising of the waters,*
> *I must walk about at night*
> *To find*
> *The depth that floats me home*
> *Upon the starry light,*
> *Where, zooming like the river*
> *When the flood is on,*

I'll sail the great connector:
Those waters of the dawn.

What a troubadour I would have been! To have summed up the universe in only nine lines is not bad even for a knight on the town—or, more accurately, out on the county roads.

But should I not have begun with "Lest I miss / the rising o' the waters"? I can't decide. It all boils down to a matter of idiom, and I have tried, successfully, I think, to use the idiom of these latter-day Dark Ages which we in the Delta hold so dear.

But now about those waters . . . There are several to consider, with the exception of the oceans and the inland seas, and those streams I have in mind are the four rivers of Eden—Pison, Gihon, Hiddekel, and the Euphrates—and the Five Rivers of the Underworld—Lethe, Styx, Acheron, Cocytus, and Phlegethon. I am certain Mark Twain was able to float down every one of them.

The question arises, because of my need to find the high water or at least to find the stream that leads to all waters, whether any of those ancient channels are somehow involved in the possibility of my return, indeed, if perhaps the nearby Coldwater, the Tallahatchie, the Yalobusha, and the Yazoo could constitute a re-constitution of those timeless waterways I just mentioned?

I admit the lines are not clean—after all there are tributaries and that makes *replicas* of anything more complex.

The answer to things, regardless of whether those things are of time and its spaces or whether they are in a category of things apart from that, things of, shall I say, time*less* spaces and of a movement separate from the speed of light, a movement, say, like that of water. I am thinking deeply now about the speed of water and of water's capacity to go anywhere and to be anywhere—providing of course that there IS water to *have a being*, and I am aware that that is not everywhere the case; yet, water *could go to* and *could be in* a single or a multiplicity of real or supposed anywheres—and nothing could stop it.

Just because water is slower than light does not mean that it will not define the limits of space just as light in some way does. Besides which, I shall write a note here to myself that I met him. I met Dr. Einstein in 1936 when I was eighteen and had gone—just after I graduated from Cadwallader Academy—to New York in that early summer and over to see cousin Willis who was taking summer courses at Princeton.

I knew who he was when I saw him in the hallway. I said, "Good morning." He stopped and smiled at me as though I had said something very funny, and then he asked me if I could "define that." I looked down at my feet, as I usually did in those days, in an attempt to define "Good morning," and when I raised my head, he was disappearing around a corner, on, I suppose, an infinite curve with no outside edges.

Nevertheless I certainly saw him, and Willis verified it. He affirmed as only a relative might that I had in fact stood more or less face-to-face with Albert Einstein and that he, cousin Willis, himself, had come upon him several times under the same moving circumstances, at the same velocity. This is a marginal note:

> *I can feel time as it passes.*
> *It makes a scratchy sound on the silo's outer surface.*
> *I believe there is a crumbling, and somewhere*
> *Things are falling down, although*
> *When I look out or when I go out,*
> *I do not detect a great deal of change*
> *In the essential line and form of the tower.*

Yet, I recognize that there may be difficulties. For instance, I cannot tell the difference between what the rain has done and what time, in its abrasive—I should say *erasive*—way, has altered.

The temptation to say "*marred*" is huge, but in the context of "time," *mar* does not apply. And "change" is far too lightweight a term.

With regard to what in fact must be the *substance* of time, that is to say, the sort of matter it must surely be, I was never certain whether I should become a philosopher of the Process or of the Manifold. Both hypotheses are useful, and I intend to try them both; I really have to if I am ever to escape the insanity of this place in which I find myself captive.

If time is a "manifold," then, well, *Voila!* I am virtually already home, and I only have to understand how to recognize it in, so to speak, a crowded room. If, on the other hand of the clock, time is a "process," then I simply have to figure out whether I am going backwards or forwards. In either case—time as manifold or as process—I am confident I shall succeed, providing I don't panic.

Once a person learns the alternative route, the back roads, as it were, he may for a while enjoy a certain detachment from the restrictions of ordinary reality and, indeed, may even negate the famous "ineluctable modality of the visible."[96] I say one may discover the *ineluctable modality of the detour.*

It is from observing the Germans that I have come to understand that obedience is not always a virtue. With them it is a vice. And it has gotten them into a lot of trouble. Even so, it is likely that they are, in some ways, much smarter than we Celts. We may be cleverer, but they are smarter and can tolerate detail, which most of us cannot abide. I descend from men and women of broad strokes. Germans are composed, for all their seeming robustness, of fine lines and dots.

I pretend to believe I am home. But I know a charade when I perform one, and I know how clever those Germans can be. They can control the weather. The ruse does seem an awful expense unless I know something useful, which is possible but, I think, not very probable. However, they haven't yet asked me anything, so, I suppose, I won't know what sort of answers are possible until that happens. I must say I am puzzled at the lengths to which they have gone and the pains they have taken to *duplicate*

---

96   James Joyce, *Ulysses.* —ml

the Mississippi Delta; yet, anyone who is a native can tell, can see, can detect instantly that this is all a mere set, a contrivance on a grand scale.

This place is not my home! Nay, no home of mine!

Let me give an example: Memphis is too close, and there is no myth. *Memphis* should be more distant, not greatly perhaps, but *more* nevertheless. It's too close—I can see it shining in the sky at night. And there is not enough mist in between—and not enough dust when it is dry and not enough mud when the weather is wet. Moreover, the mirages are absent. As I remember, my home was a mirage. The upper Delta, at least, was a mirage. And I haven't seen those wonderful nonexistent lakes at all since I was brought to this place.

I always saw the mirage when I came home from Memphis—true, I have not been to Memphis for a long, long time. But, still, I ought to know if the mirage were here or not, and it is definitely nowhere to be found in this cleverly staged and crafted charade.

Indeed, if there were no subtlety, there would have been no Delta to begin with. After all, mountains could be anywhere, but not in the Delta.

Myth is reality. It is created by the past, the factory of all things.

And the past is the only certainty there is. The past is fact. The future is pure speculation, and the present does not exist. Personally, I have no time for it. "Present" is a mere function word for a non-moment. And I certainly have no time to devote to non-anything, particularly moments, which I must keep up with and manage well, because I have reason to believe time is the key to escape and the location of my home.

Any fool who reads Einstein knows time is just another piece of physical real estate—which means it can be mapped, and if place can be mapped, it can be found. Science was not my best subject, but I seem to understand it now more than I ever did before . . . before whatever or whenever or wherever it is that I am now. Everything else, though, is a bit on the murky side.

But let me make one thing very clear: the myth is alive.
It's simply that it lives someplace else.
I am not at home.
Neither is the myth.
But all that is a matter of time and space and, or course,
high water.

Further, it is not fair of me to say that the inhabitants here are Germans. Frankly, I do not know who they are or what they are, owing to their habit of wearing rubber skin. There are Germans present here, from time to time, and I have seen the soldiers, the patrol coming day after day, but I have always managed to elude them. That is the second principle of "escape and evasion."

Unfortunately, I have most definitely not escaped. Liberty is a destination and, therefore, mainly a question of direction. That is why the high water is so important. The direction of its flow would be the direction I should follow. The truth is I would have little choice, and that would be a relief.

I remember the soft cool of early summer
when evening came with the call of the dove.
Shadows grew out of the growing green,
and the familiar took on the look
of places I felt I had only seen in dreams—
or in memories that were not my own.
Those moments were thrilling,
as though I were somewhere else
but not quite,

more or less on the edge
of somewhere else,
an else that could be, had been,

or ought to be,

and there was a strangeness
about the colors in the dying day and
in the light that held them.
But all of it, and all that the senses saw,
were contained in the song of the dove, which,
inarticulate, even then, I knew
was the sound of cessation,
of setting suns, of passings, and
of a time that had never been.

Now, today's gray
fits with the humid chill like an old coat
on an old man.
And I,
like a dying soul, deflating,
swim here and there
in the colorless air

so that the desperate motion
itself
seems the way to ensure
that I, the rememberer,
stay alive and do not fade away,
or vanish suddenly,
into the cloudy light of these short days,
days and light
whose source—
assumed and huge, perhaps
just fire and force—
remains the unknown tick

before the tock of time
or hides more simply in the light
among whose bright particles
the future is always present.

What do I expect to find when I locate my home? I expect to see that everything I remembered about it was true and that my aunts were right about where the wind went and right about what the dove said when it sang in the late afternoon.

I have recently observed that, of the Seven Deadly Sins, I was never guilty of Avarice or Greed, though I cannot see a lot of difference between the two. Moreover it is only in retrospect that I now discover my rather shining capability in the other five. This is partly the reason I have considered a quest for the Grail as an alternative to my search for my home, and in some way, I can see that the objectives could be synonymous.

FROM LEDGER NO. 5

Old Mojo Jack! . . . how surprised I was to find out that afternoon from Mama's baby brother, Uncle John T., that the name of the ancient Negro out there in the woods was merely a title. Uncle John T. pointed out that there had been a Mojo Jack—or a Mojack—in that unlogged forest since perhaps before the days of the Civil War. The name Mojack pops up all through the county's history, and the present wearer of the mantle was an old preacher who had grown up on the Abbay place but had always lived his solitary life, fishing and hunting, and for a dollar or two obliging the other blacks with their requests for hexes and for cures.

As it was with many other things in our part of the deep American South, people simply accepted Mojack's existence and, indeed, treasured it. The mysterious part was not that he was somehow immortal but that there was from generation to generation always another individual to step into his rolled-down, often dry and dusty hip boots. Uncle John T. said that for a long time he had worried that the old man would fall out with a heat stroke in the summers because he lived in those hip boots; but, over time, Mojack did just fine and took his place—or places—in Mhoon County's haunted past and present.

I have seen him watching, seen him smile. We nod. We wave. But even so I cannot be certain, under the circumstances, that it is really he and not an actor.

> *But, of course, I am Señor Coca-Cola.*
> *Came I not here by fiat*
> *from the father of all fools*
> *lost in the magnificence of the mystery?*
> *I deem it a fool's goal.*

But lost is not *at a loss*, for I am certain that I shall find myself once again in my home, and so it is because I have no doubt about that, strangely enough, I never seem to despair—and, quite frankly, that is puzzling, for I am a desperate character. But hope in the face of impossible odds is not unusual. The odds are always, even under more definable, more locatable, more geographically known conditions, impossible. It is simply that I know I will go home before the lights go out.

I *am* Señor Coca-Cola because *then* I did not drink alcohol, and all the women in the bar there in Havana called me Señor Coca-Cola. I was eighteen. The summer of '36. I spent a week with my uncle Bob-Lowe in his apartment in New Orleans and through him got a job on a freighter bound for Cuba. It was a short voyage but a long leap into perspectives not obtainable otherwise.

Portions of Havana were very much like the French Quarter . . . and very much *not* like it, too. Afterward I returned home to St. Leo, in the north part of the Delta, spent about a week and departed to begin my freshman year at Sewanee—far from the *Prado* and the *Paseo de Colon*.

(*Se m'ya contaó que nobio mio se m'ya casaó*—that is what the *Chinita says* in "La Paloma." Or, words to that effect.)

I began to understand what "the Devil and all his works" might mean; those words rang in my ears from the moment I heard them at my baptism, which came late, at age ten, I think—I was asked to "renounce the Devil and all his works" which I did then and there but knowing I wasn't sure what those particular works were and that I longed to find out. I only wanted to do the right thing, hoping that, simultaneously, there might also be a way to do the wrong thing. I wanted to *know* how, in God's name, could I renounce something I had never "nounced."

But who could say it was the Devil that I found there in Havana? He and his works were more likely to have danced right under my nose in the French Quarter, though my eyes hadn't yet been opened wide enough to see him, or them. But, in Havana, how could it have been the *Devil and all his works* that I saw and fell so in love with? Surely, I thought, if these are the Devil's works, I do hope there are more of them.

And why hadn't the Devil seen fit to establish some of his wonderful works back in St. Leo? I began to feel that what my kind had considered sin may have been sin but it was not particularly interesting. A little embezzlement here, a bit of adultery there. God! How pedestrian could it be! I could easily have renounced most of that. But the women of the Music Box Bar *Cloob*, ah, I was unable to renounce a single one. Nor did they renounce me. It was the first time I understood fertility as something other than a field of mud. Havana was the Temple of Ishtar, and I believed. I worshipped. The only thing I felt like renouncing was the burden of virtue.

And I did so in complete sobriety. The end of that came a little later . . . at Sewanee. There the Devil had a hell of a time finding a space, and, there, one drank to dull the pain of his absence.[97] *Chaca chaca maraca.* And ever since those Mount Athos days, I have not been very spiritual. I

---

97   Sewanee has become co-ed, and the Devil has now been officially enrolled. Thank God. —ogbii

must admit, now, that goodness and mercy, except on several occasions when I knew I needed both of them, put me to sleep.

The majesty always seemed to be outside the church instead of inside. Existence did not need a vestment. Even so, there was no end to majesty on the Mountain at the University of the South.

But majesty was not enough. I wanted humanity. I was, after all, a mammal. And that's at the heart of it . . . of *it*. I am a mammal first and a man last. Like any of those mythological beasts whose combined corpus is composed of man and animal, the most accurate representations are those with the heads of beasts, most especially those with heads of mammals—the Minotaur, for instance. His feet and arms are controlled by a bestial head, unlike the cranially more capable centaur who symbolizes rational control over the lower mammalian self. I can honestly say I've hardly ever enjoyed the feeling that I was rationally in control of anything, particularly my own body, not that there is much distinction, if any, between mind and body. It's all the same rubbery housing for the same synaptic circuitry. And I'm not even a doctor.

I am Señor Coca-Cola.

FOR ONE THING, I never remember traveling to this place. I went to sleep in a foxhole, and I woke up here. So, something has been left out. Certainly, the missing piece is important: yet, I am not as concerned with it as I am with the fact that where I am now is not the place I am told it is. What I see is a chocolate *eclair* without the custard.

And Memphis is getting closer and closer. I have seen its light in the night sky, just a little way out of town above what is purported to be Highway 61. The light was red. However, I was eighteen when the highway, this so-called 61, was finally finished and paved between St. Leo and Memphis. That was 1937. Before that time the road to Memphis was different, and the city was far, far away. There was gravel but the old road was narrow, and it curved a lot and zigged and zagged, then when it hit the bluffs above Walls there was a hairpin curve, right on the face of the bluff where the road turned west, to the left, and crawled along the bluff to the lake at Lake View, though the view of the lake was brief and not at all spectacular. After that the road wound about quite a bit, coming into Weaver Road at Tully's gin, where, again, one turned left. From that point on it ran to the railroad yards, then right and east and, after a short distance, into downtown Memphis by way of Florida Street. Those were the days, by heaven—those were the days when a trip to Memphis was a trip to Memphis—by automobile, anyway. The whole thing was much shorter by train, and there were more than eleven trains a day through St. Leo. Four of them were for passengers.

But the brevity of the train ride compared to the longer journey on the road did not bring Memphis closer. The train ran as the crow flew. It was a machine which one had nothing to do with in terms of control. It was a capsule. A mechanical drug. The brevity did not count. Memphis was still far away. Just as a building can be very, very tall, but when one is in an inside elevator, one does not perceive the trip up the height—as *one* would if *one* climbed it on the outside of the building! That's my point.

What I have not figured out is why another country would go to such lengths to fool *me*. What is it I know that can be of value to it or them? What is my responsibility in this matter?

> *I did not write the Treaty of Versailles;*
> *I did not cause the Depression;*
> *I did not invade Poland; and, as a side issue,*
> *neither do I speak Japanese—Nor, earlier, did I*
> *sink the Lusitania*
> *or shoot the Archduke.*

What then, I am forced to ask myself, is the reason for this massive, and no doubt expensive, project the enemy has undertaken to try to make me believe I am home at last, when I know full well that is not true. I am not one to be tricked by *seeming* reality.

It will take more than continents or hemispheres to keep me from the high water. And I have seen hints of it in the flooded fields and in the gulls overhead. But that water is shallow and only a hint—beautiful, to be sure, but only a hint of what it could be if, indeed, the high water really came, as it did in '27 and in '37. I believe it was in '27 that Cousin Ivan went to Greenville and saw the steamboat in the sky. He left, he said, quickly and came back to the north part of the Delta. Later, however, he was killed by a locomotive as he crossed the tracks downtown. He did not see the train because he always carried a black umbrella as a parasol, so he did not see the train, and he did not hear it either, because as usual, he was quite drunk. He is now buried on the high ground, so that his coffin will not float up. Too bad the high ground is not also a temple mound. I do not think the Indians would greatly mind. After all, they, more than anyone else, understood the rules of high water.

If now the high water were to come, I could get upon it, and it would provide the connections I need to find my way home, for indeed, the high water would be here and also where I want to go. Heavens! High water would connect me with almost any place in the world, I imagine. And all I ask is the connection. That is the issue—the connection. I am, more than anything else, disconnected.

That is where these Teutons, or whoever they are, have the advantage. They are never not connected. I do not know what they do when I am asleep, but I would say, they hold organizational meetings to make sure the ruse continues smoothly. Then, too, they have to get out of their rubber skin for a while. I know that's what they do because it is logical.

They are very clever at impersonating Negroes. I'll have to hand them that, though Lord knows how they learned to do it—because no one can truly impersonate a Negro. The reason is that only Negroes know about being themselves, and any attempt on the part of anyone other than, say, another Negro to impersonate himself, will, ordinarily, immediately fail, as it did with Al Jolson. Negroes do not look like Al Jolson, and they do not behave like Al Jolson. Most especially, they do not sing like Al Jolson. Only people who have never seen Negroes believe Al Jolson even remotely resembles one.

These Teutons did not study under Jolson. They have obviously been drilled by a master dissembler so that it is extremely difficult to penetrate their disguise. However, there again if one really knows what to look for, the cover is blown. In addition, if one can find the back of the neck and the elbows, he can easily detect the presence of their rubber skin. Someday I shall write a handbook on the detection of these things if tricks like the present one prove to be a worldwide phenomenon. But I can't know about that unless I can escape and go home.

It is useless, at the moment, to run. The sun cannot be relied upon as a reference. In fact, I often call the place of its rising *false east*. For all I know, what appears to be first light may be a false dawn. I am just going by what the birds do. Surely they would be able to tell, unless, somehow, they are imported.

But let me digress. I have become attracted to one of the poseurs—a *poseuse*, to be more accurate. I realize I am enamored with her rubber skin, but it is of such high quality, I can't really complain. Not that I have touched her; that is out of the question. Moreover, rubber skin is not always an indicator of true gender, though I have reason to think that the designers made female skin for females and male skin for males. Still, one cannot be too careful.

Certainly, if there should be any real beauty there, it is deeper than skin. The truth is, rubber or not, I do long for the feel of skin, other than my own of course. I am not much enamored with my own flesh, although occasionally I've slept on my arm, causing it to become numb, and when I rolled over, it fell on me and startled me because I could feel it, but it could not feel me. It was as if I had been touched by another person. It is very difficult to do this on purpose, and I have not managed it. I would prefer a third party.

> *If only love, itself,*
> *could be as stretchable as rubber skin.*
> *But love is not elastic and not, of itself, enduring.*
> *It is only the lovers who must, or who can, endure,*
> *and they only until they are dust*
> *and their love less than that.*

Love is an absolute concept with a relative occurrence. But desire, which sounds a lot like dessert, is deep. Lust, or liquid dust, is just a Teutonic name for French desire. And longing is what I have the most of, and it is focused on nothing in particular, which can be very painful because it is a state much like this directionless world in which the sun is of no use as a marker. The thing is, when a person loves, he can see the thing he loves. He knows what it is. And when he lusts, he can see the thing he lusts after even though he may not know it very well. But *I* long and cannot see what it is I long for.

Even so, the longing is what propels me; it is my energy; it is meaning in itself, an unseen goalpost, and I move to its attraction in the same fashion deer and geese and squirrels move to the hand of nature. In that case, perhaps home is prehistory. Maybe it lies backwards in the evolutionary thrust. Wherever it is, that is where I am going. I have no list of other things to do.

I am *Pithecanthropus erectus* in a necktie. Thomas Wolfe is wrong. Moreover, he died the year after my Cuban adventure. You can't go home again if you don't want to, but I do, and I will. I say so because getting there is primarily a matter of *will*. I can see that. And will transcends ordinary boundaries, providing the high water is present.

It is the *not seeing* of the land that lends the mystery to the high water. It is the suddenness of a sea where there was no sea that gives it its power. And the water brings the gulls. And they are connected to the river which is connected to the real sea.

> *Oh,*
> *but there are fish then in the cotton fields.*
> *Carp.*
> *The dry land and the water meet,*
> *and for all I know, at that point*
> *the whole earth is united by the combination.*
> *It is the open door of ultimate desire.*

And, home, abstract, unseen and indefinite, remains the most potentially tangible necessity in my life. I should say it is my life. It is I and I is it. I am the myth made flesh. Here, I realize I said the myth was someplace else. So it is. I am someplace else. That's the problem.

The myth and love are synonymous. I could just as easily tell my beloved "I myth you" as I might say "I love you." Believe me, it is the same thing. In both cases the object of the feeling is largely imagined.

It is important to understand that the myth of my homeland is not its sweetness, not its peacefulness, its beauty, or any of that nonsense. It does not possess much of those elements.

> *The myth is in the darkness of its sloughs,*
> *the violence of its history,*
> *the heat of its summers.*
> *It's in the smell of its moon.*

FROM LEDGER NO. 8

There are no antebellum Greek temples in my homeland. There are antebellum structures here and there, but they are dogtrots. There may be an antebellum Greek temple, but, if there is, it is an anomaly. Those houses were in the hills, and the owners of those things, my ancestors, left their families and rode horseback, on a regular basis at specific intervals, from the hills into the Delta to tend to their land, talk with their overseers, and make sure their slaves were cared for. Big houses are not part of the myth, unless you count the Choctaw chief Greenwood LeFlore's *Malmaison*, but it is no longer standing.

Oh, but the bird-like qualities of captives cannot be denied. I can all but take flight in the most literal sense, and I do think that, if I could generate the right amount of isometric tension beneath my skin, throughout my muscles, and into the marrow of my bones, I could rise from the ground and stay aloft. Alas, so far I have not been able to do it. Yet, I am as certain of its possibility as I am of the passage of time— and, as we know, the high water is time in liquid form. It is space made displaceable to accommodate the heaviness of desperate need, to buoy it up and float it to its fulfillment. There is no other way that I can see. And I believe I can see alternatives the way a falcon sees mice. Let me assure you, if I cannot yet corporeally fly, I do soar about on the wings of incredible perspective when it comes to the local area, whatever that is and wherever it might, cartographically, actually be. Personally I think it is in Europe. The Low Countries, no doubt.

I believe the Atlantic would be no obstacle if I could reach it. Then, I could make my way northward to Norway. From there I'd turn left and proceed to Spitzbergen, Iceland, Greenland, Labrador, and VOILA!—the mouth of the St. Lawrence. I would make it all the way up the St. Lawrence, cross Lake Ontario as far as Niagara, accomplish a brief portage, get into Erie, slide through Lake St. Claire, zoom up Huron and dive down into Lake Michigan, so to speak, to enter the Illinois River at Chicago. Once I find the channel, gravity, itself, will be my engine all the way to the Mississippi at the big bend just above St. Louis, where the current will take me swiftly on toward Cairo, then Memphis, and in scarcely a day, finally, to the Mississippi Delta at Mhoon's Landing, west of town.

Life is thunder, and its meaning can be found in the names of bugs.

I should know. I have listened to them night after night and heard them singing like tenors and mad sopranos, even in the snow, tiny, too, but not small—in a larger sense. Yet it was the words I listened to the most, and words there were, our words, my words, words that could have come from anywhere or from the rhythm of the earth's core. In any case, I heard the words. Who would have thought it? Bugs speaking an articulate tongue, though Lord knows how they did it, as few of them have lips. Nevertheless, the words were words . . .

Which is why I think the *Scripture* should more accurately read, "In the beginning was the bug." Indeed, they are creatures of light and of string quartets, and from them there is much I have learned. First, they never tire. *Like the Cubans, they do not sleep,* unless, of course, they are of those buggish varieties that cocoon themselves for a decade or so and then emerge, choralic and voracious. Second, they do not fret over trifles; their activity is never paralyzed by guilt or by social considerations of the sort that hamper humans. Their aims are never thwarted, except occasionally by birds and pesticides. Third, they do not speculate about outcomes. They simply go about their bugly duties and persist and in the end they always accomplish what their watch-like mechanisms have been set in motion to do.

I intend to emulate them. I shall learn to do on two legs what they do with six—or more. Of course, I am at a disadvantage. I have warm blood and a memory. I know from my surveillance of them that they possess no memory in the sense that we might recognize it. But, then, it is understandable. They always do the same thing, and so, for them, memory serves no real purpose. Moreover, they eat their dead. We have tried to abandon that habit, but I do not foresee any change in their mores any time in the near future. And, yet, they are so advanced in other ways. The absence of lips has not held them back.

Next to high water, it is entomology that will show me the way home. I shall learn not to sleep and to know that persistence is the answer to all things: to success, to truth, and to the hardening of the senses.

Dionysos versus Apollo—that was the way old Eliot Gordon Quintard put it and let it be known that though he admired Apollo, he favored Dionysos. He drank his bourbon out of julep cups, loved long conversations into the night, called all girls "daughter," knew everybody in the South, was kin to most, and fought bitterly in the angry battle, the slaughter between the absolutists and the relativists, there on that strange and wonderful mountain.

He would never say, absolutely, whether he was a relativist or an absolutist but only that he thought his position was always absolutely relative to any given moment—because, he maintained, even the absolute is relative if one considers the possibility of other universes. And so it went, much to my delight.

One day, teachers like E G. will be found only in the fossil record, and there will be many who will doubt they ever existed. That will be because those unbelievers will have known nothing in their lives except the ordinary, the very pinnacle and epitome of which they believe is excellence.

To them a mule is a racehorse and a car is an investment. They are the same as some of those in large ephemeral cities who, not understanding the similarity between depth and elevation, do not know the difference between a basement and a penthouse and never know wonders when they appear.

Nothing can exist that they cannot conceive of, and they cannot conceive of very much; that explains their existence, anyway, in a nutshell.

ON THOSE COLD, CLEAR nights when I travel, if I do not look down at my feet or ahead or over to the side, but keep my gaze mostly upward, the illusion that I am walking through the starry heavens is transcendent in the extreme. The magnitude of the sensation is astronomical. It is a dimension of self in that the whole thing is going on only in the self, the self, namely me.

And that is at once both encouraging and disturbing, because the thought occurs that if I am able to construct such a cosmic exercise while I am merely walking alone along a country gravel road, then perhaps I am capable of having fabricated this place and, indeed, my own alienation. And what if when I find the high water, it takes me *from* instead of *to*?

"Don't holler before you're hit," as Uncle Sticks used to say. Yet I have a tendency not to worry about Heaven but, rather, to stew about infinity.

This has nothing to do with tides, nothing at all, but it has everything to do with one's ability to stay grounded—not that I haven't indicated my destination may be some distant speck of light. But, until that should become clearer even to me, I shall simply have to pursue both high water and the heavens, and hope diligence will supply the truth.

> *There are days gone skyward in the smoke of burning leaves,*
> *as though youth was but a dream or perhaps a hope now*
> *in the heart of an aging man.*
> *The performance of time is like a footprint on the senses,*
> *and it is they, not the soul, which put the match*
> *to those leaves of longing.*

Now I burn from time to time—the question is from *what* time to which—with deep nostalgia not for youth but for its weather, because if time is in the light, then so is the weather that filled its moments. And weather is mostly an overall sound and smell and touch among a multitude of other pieces of sensory business. But, of course, the atmosphere is not the food. Ask Alonzo.[98]

I said above "an aging man." I believe I meant myself, though my servitude is merely academic. That is because I have forgotten my age. The numbers are gone. However, I notice I am wearing glasses and do not remember having them when I went off to war. Things happen when I sleep.

---

98   Alonzo Locke was the famous and highly respected black maitre d' at Memphis's Peabody Hotel. —ogbii

Note: The silo is a perfect place to be if the high water should somehow find *me*. The silo would indeed be perfect—temporarily, because I dread to think what life in here would be like after the water soaked into the seeds on the bottom. The subsequent rot and fermentation might be intolerable to the senses, even in Silesia. But then again, I'd be gone—far away from tipsy fish. And the subsequent spontaneous combustion.

Note: Like Nero, I have tried scampering about on all fours. It occurred to me I might try it because it seemed possible, for a moment, that it might be a lost art and useful as well. However, art or n'art, as a mode of travel, I cannot recommend it. And unlike Nero, I would not bite my guests.

I AM CONVINCED, NOW, that it is the Goths who have created this enormous attempt at deception—an environment complete, I might add, right down to the last tack with mules and marsh hawks and, of course, the elaborate rubber-skin disguises. Where they got those I cannot imagine. As everybody said of Aunt Georgia in her coffin, it's so life-like.

I've never known how they get through the summer. It would have been hard enough to walk around naked in July, but to be inside that rubber stuff must be—well, I can only imagine they have invented some way to make themselves comfortable, a lack of interrogatives perhaps, a numbness that comes when there is an absence of fascination, which occurs once there are no *doubts*.

Yes, a genius obviously has invented a thing, a way, that keeps the wearer of the rubber skin cool. That is the only answer. Like "God." Whenever one is ignorant of the reason for something, I've noticed they will usually use "God" as the answer. God is very handy for those who wish to know nothing. Plus "God" saves time by preventing further discussion.

Let me also remind you that "God is love," and that, if you fail to believe it, He will burn you in Hell forever—as a demonstration of his divine sense of justice and concern for your welfare. And all of that, as they say, is in the Bible, which was written by a number of primitive and exceedingly superstitious people but which, nonetheless, is regarded as the vessel of all truth, again, by the same group of blockheads who always use God as the reason for everything, not because they know He is but because they are afraid He will be angry if they use their minds to try to determine if there are other causes.

They do not love God. They fear him and hate him and simultaneously believe that somehow He does not know the truth of how they really feel about Him.

Fortunately there are none of these people here, and I know there are not because no amount of, or quality of, rubber skin could ever disguise them. I cannot believe anything that exists would stretch to such absurd lengths.

I am having a very hard time. Mostly it is mental and not physical, although what's the difference? I am quite comfortable on top of all these cotton seeds, and the view is excellent. But I am having a hard time somewhere in my intangibles, much as one would in a dream in which he could not find an exit from an endless building, or in a dream in which he could not find a necessary something; the whole experience is very, very similar to one's attempt to escape from a large wave by running uphill in loose sand. The doom is inevitable even if it is not permanent.

That is the interesting thing about doom. It is often not permanent, though that does not mean it is not painful. But pain is not usually permanent either, although I am told and can understand that some kinds of pain never abate. That kind of pain dies with the man and, like the man, does not go anywhere else. Pain cannot travel on its own. It can, however, be transported.

I do not have pain, neither physical nor emotional. I have frustration. I have deep longing. Indeed, the absence of pain disturbs me a little because its absence does not imply pleasure, just a stillness, except for my anxiety about the German patrol, which is always, always out there, always coming, always searching, apparently for me—which I find odd because they already have me. Surely they know I have not left the premises. But undoubtedly they know that I am determined to do so and that I certainly shall, once I find the high water.

Just how high? At first I thought of it as the connector to all things on this planet, but now I am beginning to see it as having greater dimension, and I feel that it is also the connector to more distant regions, cosmic continents, and photonic archipelagoes in the night sky. My theory has something to do with the horizon and its connective nature, binding the whole book of sky and earth, at least visually, into one great field of habitation. Yes. It was the horizon that altered my view—well, expanded it, so to speak.

I cannot continue to search for truth. As I see it, truth must come to me, and I think it can because I believe it is everywhere and that it is like the air, so that it is pointless to thrash about searching for truth when one is bathed in it all the time.

However, the difficulty in discovering truth may be analogous to one's not being able to isolate hydrogen, look at it here in the air, and exclaim, "So this is hydrogen!" Of course, one is looking at hydrogen all the time, looking at it right smack in the molecule, and I am not really sure that it is, in a technical sense, invisible. I say it's visible. A person just has to know how to recognize, as James Joyce said, "The ineluctable modality of the visible." And I for one intend to be able to do that. And I have to if I am ever to get home again.

So . . . that is settled. I cannot continue the search for truth, because, in all truth, I realize that is not what I have been searching for in my program of escape and evasion, or vice versa. It occurred to me the other day that the effort to find my home again and the search for truth might be the same thing, and then I thought, "No. Home has nothing whatsoever to do with truth." Even I know that. And that is why I know I am not insane. Anyone who thinks his homeland has anything to do with truth is nuts.

The quest becomes the search not for reality but for a more comfortable illusion, which, if I were good with my hands and handy with tools, I might actually construct, on my own, from scratch. I would use parts of this present place, but I won't. I don't know where it has been: and the past of anything is of great importance unless one lives in California or in one of those other places where no one is from anywhere, not kin to anyone, and nobody cares. In a situation like that, myth does not stand a chance.

Everything is fashion. And fashion is everything, and by fashion I do mean everything—clothes, houses, attitudes, and aspirations—or the lack thereof. I have read about this in books, seen moving pictures, and heard tales from travelers. We did not have technicolor in the Mhoon County of my youth.

Now I am a bit worried. Regardless of what I have said about the connected nature of sky and earth at the horizon, never have those two territories seemed as separate as they do of late. I almost believe there is a growing gap at the plane of contact. And I am very concerned about what is, or is not, in the gap. After all, if what is there or not there is neither sky nor earth, there is no name for it, and I believe that could be a problem, because I have always relied on the notion that there is a name for everything, However, I do not think there is a name for this tear in the fabric of creation. Things may be coming loose. Perhaps I should not place so much importance on connections, but if I do that, then *that would put me in the tear*—which, now that the question has been raised, may be where I am this very moment, may be, in fact where I have been all these years, since my capture, and may be why I have not been able to find the high water and the way home. Also, somehow, this very silo and these very fields may indeed be that spot of separation on some other person's horizon. After all, a horizon depends on perspective and point of view. And I may be always on the horizon itself, looking back toward the place where one is looking at the horizon, if you see what I mean. My God! How is it possible to be so visible and yet so lost?!

FROM LEDGER NO. 13

Perspective on how the world is unified does not come from philosophical gardens. No, it is found in the simple observation of the nature of drainage and the realization that it is high water which has brought people and, of course, nations together—remember, flood stories are so abundant in ancient times.

The question is whether there was one flood or many local ones; not that it matters, because all water is connected, one way or another in any of its real or imagined states, unlike dry land. I do not include sloughs, bayous, and the floors of oceans in the category of dry land, although I can see a danger zone here owing to the fact that even so-called dry land may contain a certain amount of moisture. Here now is an even greater perspective: except for perhaps, and I guardedly now say perhaps, the Atacama and the Sahara, the Rub' al Khali, the Namib, and other notable dry-dry parts of the world, water remains the connector in a physical sense but not necessarily in a navigable sense, and it is navigability that may be the key.

Why do I think I am lost in Silesia? Logic. Where else but in Silesia would this silo be? Where but in Silesia would a silo be filled not with silage but with cotton seeds?

I may not know my geography perfectly, but I know about the law of anomaly, and my situation here, warm and comfortable beneath the roof of this agrarian round tower, conforms precisely to the ancient equation embedded in the anomalic theorem.

Location is as much a question of philosophy as it is of navigation or of geographic reference. Every Greek and Jew understands that. Indeed, without philosophy, they know there is every chance they might not now be anywhere at all. That is why I believe so strongly in a good liberal arts education. From a practical point of view, it may not constitute the can opener, but it is most certainly the can. First the can, then the opener, I always say.

If I ever succeed in reaching my home again, I will owe it all to liberal arts, its *trivium* and *quadrivium*, and the insight that marvellous foundation has provided.

I bleed on the sherds of ancient pots. Well, my feet would bleed if I were walking barefoot, which I am not, owing to the fact that it is, I believe, presently the middle of someone's winter; and, further, my feet would bleed if the sherds were sharp, which they are not, and, in fact, are very much, at first glance, like the rest of the mud. Besides, they are not ancient, for I am certain they are simply part of the complete decor put here by my captors—who must have known I would not overlook a single detail. As a re-creation of the Delta, it is impressive—even in much of its inaccuracy.

In any case they have included the potsherds in the fields, and for that I am, in a sense, grateful. Perhaps my own civilization is now as lost as that of those who left the pieces of their pots for people like me to pick up and ponder.

(Speaking figuratively is always a risky business. Yet the wind and the thermals are so powerful that I never keep my craft on the ground. It is a *soar* subject, but one I adore.)

Pots, however, and/or their remnants are significant in that they, first of all, are or were vessels and, as such, are containers of the past. Time is the water in the fragments, and time is still there even though the whole pot is not, proving forever that the package is not the gift—except, of course, from a cheerful giver.

I am numb with age in my, I think, forty-first year. Let me say quickly that though I may not be certain about place and time in the ordinary sense, *i.e.*, location and moment, I am constantly in touch with time in the extraordinary sense, which is not only the same as place and moment but also the same as the entities that occupy any such particular place and moment, and which, this time in the extraordinary sense, I have come to believe is both linear as well as dimensional and can be seen, quite clearly, in the light.

By the light, I am referring to almost any light which travels from any point into anyone's eye, and that includes the light that may travel away from someone, too.

Moreover it is in the light that age is seen and understood. That is why I move fast when I go abroad by night. I know about speed and how it slows time. Velocity does not give time to an individual. It puts the person ahead of time, in a way, by retarding time. And that is why I walk very, very fast. Doing so slows time and also keeps me warm.

Velocity equals warmth. Shaw's law. QED. No matter how cold it is, I seem to stay sufficiently warm and comfortable moving about at night, along the roads, through the fields, and close to the woods, by simply increasing my speed—but I enjoy the mastery of it, this walking fast, because now I regard it as an art form. Fortunately I am only forty-one, which by some standard somewhere, some place, I am sure, is counted as extreme youth.

I can easily see why men wish to be explorers and discoverers. I have discovered a great deal since my escape, and the secret to effective discovery is reflection. I have had the good fortune to be able to reflect on just about everything. And, in doing so, I feel I have joined the ranks of Columbus, Magellan, Newton, Bienville, Iberville, DeSoto, Churchward, Admiral Byrd, Herodotus, Alfred T. Mahan, and Ibn Battuta.

But, of time once more, let me add that, in fact, time is matter, like gauze, and not only *in* light but very akin to light except that, unlike light, there can be no absence of time; although one might also say that there can really be no absence of light because light, too, exists in its own absence in the form of presupposition. That is to say, if there is darkness, there must be the possibility of light. Concept, itself, is just a thing, like any*thing* else.

There is no scenic beauty to the Delta. None. Yet, it is beautiful. There is no grandeur, no "purple mountains' majesty" or sea foam and all that. There is mud and slough, flatness and bayou; there is bush and field and ditch, then dust, flies, mosquitoes, and summers so oppressive Hell might seem Alaska.

But that is where I belong and where I aim to go. That is home, and it is all I want—not this facsimile, this environmental charade born of some warped madness of the Hun. God (gawd)! How many others are trapped here, longing for reality.

Pardon me. I must be careful. The word HOME does not imply reality. I should say one's "preferred reality" complete with a marvelous mirage.

> *I have to go where*
> *life moves like a small stone*
> *dropped in a jar of oil, and thought*
> *proceeds at the same rate—with the notable*
> *exception of wit.*
> *There's the anomaly.*
> *Wit leaps.*
> *It pounces like a cat on a quail.*
> *Wit is*
> *the spear of light in the brightness*
> *of the summer's heat. But thought,*
> *just plain old thought in general,*
> *is but the buzz of a fly*
> *on a long afternoon.*

Still, I miss it, the tenseness of that daily sleep. I miss myself. Indeed, I may have literally *missed myself* somewhere along the line. I took the wrong turn, probably genetically, and I may have been my Uncle "Sticks" without the benefit of all the fun—or all the trouble . . . his driving around the county at night with the top down in a red convertible, that snazzy 1938 Ford Deluxe Club Coupe, naked and drunk, singing hymns, with Claudia, the sociologist from Columbia, who, as my mother said, "was ahead of her time and learned a lot more 'ology than she had planned on." And this was before I went to war.

Home was like that. Nobody in the nation knew where it was, much less what it was, but a person could always go anywhere and find someone who'd either been there or had been with someone from there. It never failed—which may be why the Germans have tried to copy it. They are also very serious and do not seem to love nonsense in the same fashion that we have chosen to adore it. Well, we must adore it, because we cannot separate ourselves from it.

"Sticks" had his valleys and shadows, his rainy days and muck-mires. And that is where wit came in. His wit, his own and anybody else's, was his only hope. The Delta was cleared by wit, sustained by wit, and endured by wit. The North had seriousness and humor. We had wit—and also murder, two things that seem to go hand in hand, mostly after the fact.

> *Wit and death, funerals on high ground*
> *so the coffins won't jump out,*
> *and wit was life—which is one reason*
> *people drank so much good whiskey.*
> *They believed they were consuming more wit,*
> *unlike those in the Hills who had no time for either.*

I mean, of course, the Hills far to the east of Como. Remember, the Hills near the Delta are "good" hills and are, in fact, the home of many of the early Delta dwellers. Nevertheless, there are the darker hills beyond, those far to the east, and down, that are alien. There's murder there, too, but no wit.

> *Steamboats in the sky and admirals*
> *sailing over cotton fields and up Deer Creek—*
> *the very idea of it! What a pity*
> *they were having a war.*
> *It would have been so much better if*

all that shooting had not been a hazard
to so much fun.

But, there again, as Uncle "Sticks" said in his unpublished book: "I love bodies of water I cannot see across, unless they're over my bean field."

My mother was a Ferry. She married a Shaw, but both my parents descend from Miss Anquilla and old "Snake" Frontstreet. *It seems we must marry our cousins if we are to marry at all,* which means, I suppose, that one becomes a cousin to oneself.

I believe I am related at least three times to me. It's hard to feel lonely in the Delta. I am a teeming stew of all I am.

Also, we think we're better than others in the rest of Mississippi—and in parts of Alabama, too—and, with the exception of our friends in Helena, we definitely hold ourselves above our neighbors in Arkansas. However, we are humbled by lower Louisiana. We worship New Orleans. We kiss its decay.

Yet, that is all part of the myth,
and the myth is the point.
I do not ask more of life than there is to be had,
but I do ask for all of that and not necessarily
that things be what they seem, only
that things seem what we'd have them be,
if you know what I mean.

And so I remember summer, the season of drama and violence, which is paradoxical because summer in the Delta is inimical to activity of any kind, much less dramatic activity, but the heat and the humidity bring it out, especially in the alley on the western edge of town, behind the stores.

There,
summer is a season of straight razors,

and fall
the time of scars.

Winter and spring bring the high water. But spring is filled with murderous storms which come out of Arkansas, across the river. I am sure the people in Arkansas feel that those storms come from Oklahoma and/or Texas. I have never seen such a blackness anywhere else. The wind turns the air green, and all the trees bend to the east. The rain is blinding. And one hopes the tornado passes overhead and does not touch us; one prays and wonders why God would particularly care to spare us and hopes, again, that all His reasons for not doing so, though perhaps justified, will not matter and that He will not be as smiteful and as bloodthirsty as He ordinarily appears when one hears of His activity once a week on Sunday. I have often thought His violence might be an indication that we are but in the summer of creation.

I should turn to Him—or HerM—in my search for home, but I have not done so. It occurred to me that a prayer or two might be worth a try, but I have not gotten around to it. So far I am not convinced He is on my side—or that He is near enough to hear and that if He is near enough whether He would care or not. The prevailing thought was that He is constantly concerned about each hair on our bodies, that He saw every sparrow, and that He cared only that we believed in Him—not so much what we did, but mostly that we believed.

And that is what threw me . . . and worried me more than anything else. How could the creator of the universe be so petty and human, so fallible and befoibled? I couldn't buy it. I thought more of Him than that. Popularity would be the last thing on His infinite mind.

Having escaped, for the time being, and now, lying out here in the top of this wonderful silo, walking about at night, I have approached the eternal in a different manner. The truth is I am not so certain about the word *eternal*, but for lack of a better, I will use it from time to time.

I do spell His pronoun with a capital "H." This stems from the maddening habit of Southern boys to say "Suh" to anyone who is the least bit older than they are. Northerners are driven crazy by this device. I know. I have driven several of them crazy. But it's ingrained. And it's a dodge. Apart from its being a form of respect, it serves, for the younger, as a shield between the younger man and the older one, although the older one is not aware of this. So, in a way, "Suh" is a sort of stiff-arm as one runs toward the vague and often ambiguous goalposts of life.

"*Suh*" is for Southern boys what fluttering is for Southern girls: a means of control. As long as you say "Suh," you're home free. It's the same as "Cap'm please," if one is black and on the Mhoon Country Penal Farm. "Cap'm please kin I have a drink of water?" And when the white deputy with the gun says, "Sam, go get that saw," Sam, in his striped suit, responds energetically, "Cap'm please!" and trots off to get the saw. Of course, Sam's situation is a bit different. For him there is a tangible hazard with real consequences in not saying "Cap'm please"—in some cases possibly a cat-o-nine-tails, and in fact one hung quietly on the wall in the warden's office at Parchman. And that was not the county; that was the state. Colorful as it might have seemed, I don't know that "Cap'm please" is the best part of the Delta, but it is a part of it nonetheless.

> *It might not have been the sweetest sound*
> *in the Southern symphony, but it was still a member*
> *of the orchestra,*
> *and I don't think it is good for things, plus or minus,*
> *to be forgotten, or erased, or tidied up,*
> *not even one's own egregious behavior.*

A piece of the price of admission to this extravaganza is that one must live with one's actions, real or merely contemplated. The trick is knowing which is which.

> *Memory is imperfect, so that now I have a tendency*

to wonder whether I did something
or merely thought about it,
whether something was
or was not and only put there
in the past,
not by my forgetfulness
but by desire.

FROM LEDGER NO. 21

The whole thing, really, is desire. Buddha sought to rid himself of it; I have *sought* to wrap myself inside it, to tumble away in its infinite cosmos, and to see the lights of creation everywhere as I sail into its starry sea, so that, finally, the only desire is desire itself.

In the beginning was desire.
In the interim there is longing.
And, in the end there is neither.

Personally, I do not think the soul hops up out of the body, equipped with invisible eyes and ears to see and to hear the living—or the dead. Phooey. I have not lived for that; I have lived for living itself and for the running, the hiding, the living again, and the search overall, but particularly for the place I belong—which, though I may never find it, will ultimately be wherever it was I was at any time I was. The goal is always in the runner. The posts are just an illusion.

Let me add that I do not see lust as a beast with fangs. I love lust. And though during my captivity I have not had an opportunity to enjoy much of it, I fully intend to lust a great deal when I am home again. Frankly, that is one reason I am so anxious to get there. Life without lust would be like spaghetti without the sauce. That is why lust is popular, even with those who condemn it.

Further, He invented it.

Therefore, lust, though pesky when unfulfilled, is divine—as, one might also include, is the rest of existence, in some fashion; though I admit it is difficult to permit oneself to say that pestilence, disease, war, and natural disasters fit that description.

Nor is imprisonment easily folded into the category of the divine. Yet, all of those opposites of celestial light are indeed part of the divine something-or-other, just as darkness is part of light. It is *not*-light, just as tails is *not*-heads.

The big "H."

But now to the question of where I am or *not*-am now. It is my firm belief that I am among an alien people who seek to hold me with them for reasons I cannot discern. Further, they have constructed an environment the sole purpose of which is to make me think I have returned from the war to my homeland. Of course, I saw through that the first day. Even if I had not been clever enough to catch on to the farce, I would have known I was not home simply by the presence of the *ever*-present German patrol. There were certainly no German troops at home when I left. I was led to believe we had won the war, so WHY would there be a squad of German infantry always nearby at the ready?

Smart as I am, I cannot figure it out.

Unless . . . these Teutons think there is something I can tell them about the Delta, that there is something about where I come from that they feel is essential and should be incorporated into their own way of life. The question then is what that would be. Gravel?

Or, perhaps I am to be exchanged for one of theirs. The question now is why I would be of value. Moreover, their having fabricated this amazing facsimile of the Mississippi Delta should show them there is utterly nothing of Germanic interest. After all, the *time* is not the same.

Delta time is flexible. Germanic time is rigid. The only thing rigid in the Delta is flexibility itself. And the need for fast cars.

Fast cars for flat roads, so flat, in fact that the engineers had to put curves in them to keep them from running off the earth itself in a line tangent. Who does not know *that*? There is such a curve just south of Saint Leo, one north, and also one above Clarksdale. I, personally, am not so certain, in my case, that those curves were a good idea, for if they were not there, I might more easily leave this place, high water or no high water. I could simply stay on the pavement and, voila!, there I'd be, out in space.

Too bad there is always an *if* or an *and* or a *but* every time something could have been just the thing one needed; but that's circumstance, and circumstance is the same thing as divine will, which is why I never say something is "God's will." I usually say, "It's circumstance." And, unlike God's will, circumstance can be proven and also understood. I have mentioned this to clergymen, but they did not appear to agree, preferring instead not to understand—a *circumstance* in itself which possibly enables them to remain clergymen.

But how now a Merlin would play so well to my Percival, not that Percival and Merlin had all that much to do with each other, but I cannot bring myself to liken myself to Arthur, and certainly not to Galahad or to Lancelot. It was Percival who, when I was a boy, struck me the most with his imperfect self. It was Percival who, unlike Galahad, did not actually get to see the Grail. He was too imperfect; in short, he was human, and the others were fictions. In fact, I'll bet Percival hated being a knight—except of course when the girls were watching, and I'll also bet he hated jousting or fighting of any sort, and that he was constantly saying, inside, "Oh, no! Not that again," when he knew he was going to get the stuffing whacked out of him by some tin-wrapped ape who thought blood, pain, and broken bones were a way of life, and liked it. That sort was the same kind who liked football practice. They did not all die out in the Dark Ages.

But that is because the Dark Ages never died out. The war is an example of that. The houses are built, and then they are destroyed. The children are reared, and then they, too, are destroyed. The field is ploughed and planted, and then even the field is erased by steel and fire.

I believe Percival would have felt the same way, and, like me, he would have done his duty, as I feel I have, and am, in a manner of speaking, still doing. I am not running away, exactly. Indeed, when I arrive home, I shall explain the whole thing and tell them to send me back to the front, if necessary; and I hope it won't, by that time, be.

The whole thing is just too strange. Even I may include myself in that indictment of strangeness, because I have known for years that those around me were wearing rubber skin; yet I did nothing about it. I made no move to get free. What was I thinking!

It is just such lapses of moral action that make me more and more like Percival. In my case, I should have been racing to escape. Yet even now I am hiding and not running. However, in spirit, and, I think, also in actuality, when you take my enormous nocturnal hikes into consideration, I am as ardent a questor as Percival was. But though I am imperfect as he was, unlike him I shall find the Grail and throw it in a plastic sack.

Why should the prizes of life be reserved for angels? I think they are not! Imperfection can be aggressive. And, remember, Galahad was a fiction. The Grail was, too. But fiction as an objective is perfectly acceptable, which is why mine is the Mississippi Delta in general and Mhoon County in particular.

I am extremely fortunate, even in my present circumstances, to have the leisure to think things out. And, frankly, if I had known about this silo, I might well have moved here sooner.

The only problem is that I can tell that when the weather warms up, someone is going to come into the field around me, to till it. Also, when the weather becomes too warm, I won't be able to stay here. The silo will turn into an oven.

So I've got to get busy. If I am going to escape, I'd better start escaping. I cannot just hide under my captors' noses indefinitely. That would mean finding spring and summer quarters, which present more of a problem because keeping cool will be more difficult than keeping warm.

And, then, of course, there are the bugs.
And, even in the winter, I can hear them,
deep down in the ground . . . where the Devil is.

Yes, well, I have looked into the sky.
I have sought the high water, and I have certainly
been patient in waiting for it to appear.
But I have not opened the third package
of possibility: the earth, or, more accurately,
I have not combed the banks
of the massive subterranean rivers,
nor have I explored the canyons, dark plains,
and shadowy meadows of the lower world
that lies between every fugitive and the Abyss.

I have capitalized Abyss not only out of respect but largely out of terror. Indeed, if Bosch's third panel is frightening, I do not think even mathematics could describe the horror of the Abyss.

But, perhaps, "Abyss" is a bit dramatic. I really only meant "down in the ground," a mile or so beneath the topsoil, but I got carried away and fell to believing that I knew more than I actually did, not making the important distinction between imagination and truth, not that I think there is all that much difference separating the two well-ploughed fields of *is*-ing.

Thomas Wolfe mentioned "a stone, a leaf, a door," and Swedenborg thought like that, too, that there could be a hidden entrance nearby, always nearby, but unnoticed, a vestibule of eternity. The task was to find it, and I have to say I am not enthusiastic about going under the surface of anything, much less the earth itself. I don't like the idea very much at all. I don't like depth or height—except in the case of this silo, which is pretty high for me and also for the false Delta that surrounds, but this is as far up as I go, in actuality but not in, of course, intent. I am aware that my limits are cosmic and unbounded. It's just the terrestrial and the practical of the here and now that makes me phobic.

Nevertheless, in my relentless chasing after home, I shall crack the crust and descend to the mantle. I shall discover a local Mohorovičić Discontinuity, which may mean I shall have to cross the Mississippi and go to Helena, Arkansas, to investigate Crowley's Ridge, or, as we say in Mississippi, "It's not our fault." But I must consider swimming the river, I suppose, because it simply does not seem likely that I will find an entrance to the underworld here in the false Delta, this Delta *manque* designed by enemy geopoliticians. And geopolitics was especially loved by the Germans, as we all know—*because naming it was next to conquering it.*

So what'll it be? Home or the Grail? I have suspected the validity of a subterranean route for some time. And now I know the real meaning of the phrase, "going underground." Those before me who have known have successfully guarded its true meaning by having the term "underground" presented to the philologic public as though it were a mere metaphor.

Bah! Metaphor my foot. The deceit is so clear. And I must say that if I had not been in my current predicament, I would never have discovered the prodigious lie concerning things thought to be "underground." In fact, only because I was pushed by necessity to try to find every way possible to get back home—or to find the Grail—I eventually, or inevitably, undid a chthonic denial.

> *However, I am slightly concerned*
> *that no one is there "down there,"*
> *Anymore than there is in much of Wyoming.*

And where I aim to go
is like Wyoming without the sky.

When you think about it, it is silly to imagine that there is not a land in every direction: up, down, that way, this way. The journeys to these territories may be different in character and in scenery, but the destinations are assured.

As far as going into the innards of the earth is concerned, there are holes all over the place. So it's just as I said: if there's a direction, there's a place, though, and I repeat: *"The journeys to these territories may be different in character and in scenery, but the destinations are assured."*

Only an idiot would believe otherwise, and that would be because that person had trouble with logical thought and to boot was ignorant of modern scientific advancement. The earth is as hollow as regret.

But, are there women there? I have so seldom asked myself that question; yet it is a matter that is always on my mind, not that I have had time to pursue it. I have not had time even for time, though it, somehow, has had me in its control in an extraordinary way. I have dealt with time as if it were alive and could be contacted, which it cannot.

But are there women down below?
If there are rivers, there are women
because they are rivers,
though some are rivers of air,
and others are rivers of darkness and the earth.

Likewise there are women of the moment
and women of the continuum.
I do not know for certain which of those
are the most attractive,
and even if I seem to lean toward those of darkness,
whether they are of the moment or

are of the continuum,
I can still lose my ability to think clearly
when it comes to a girl of the air,
like Kimbrough—though alabaster,
alabaster is not enough.

She was lighter than air
and more beautiful than sky
on the elbows of the day.
But I am afraid it will always be academic,
like an event that one prepares for which never occurs—
like approaching but never reaching
the speed of light.
Yes, she was lighter
than a cloud at morning.

But her lightness is not hot enough. There is no heat. The sight of her should be seen in no uncertain terms of thermal units. The touch should be hot. The fingers, the hand, the cheek, the hair, should be hot. Their smell should be hot, and their heat should collide at incredible velocity with my own so that all of life is consumed in the meeting—and consumed again and again each time my eyes touch the line and form of her face. I long to be consumed in such a way. To heck with home, even if that were available . . . If it were, why would I or any man yearn for geography or for place when the entire, unmapped magnificence of the universe could explode in his heart? Why should I stretch so to hold a cloud, when I can have hot flesh?—well, philosophically, in theory anyway, in theory. Hot flesh is not plentiful in my situation except in dreams, and, I can assure anyone, philosophy is not and, in my opinion, never was a consolation to Boethius or anybody else. That's just a lot of hooey, if you ask me.

Thus, if I go down into the earth,
I shall look for darkness and heat;
then, if I find it, and like it,
I shall attempt to bring it up with me again,
forsaking all rivers and all mythology,
to the surface where I shall try to combine it
with light and sky, with distance, with time, and
with the brightness of high water across the fields.
and, after day has gone
and the view of infinity is at last above me,
I shall find that darkness and that light
in the fires of night, and I
shall be neither here nor there nor at
any particular spot on earth or in air,
but I will be love itself, caught in the arms of existence,
holding in my arms the woman,
that eternal girl, both of air and of darkness,
the one of the moment and of the continuum;
and her touch, her smell, her skin,
her eyes, her lips, and the shape of her words
as they come from her mouth into mine,
everything, every molecule of her, and all that I
want her to be,
will be hot—very, very hot.

If I could have that, I would never give home a second thought. But I am a practical man, and I try to remain in touch with reality. That is why I chose to run. Boogety boogety.

Hot, very, very hot—I suppose that is why Dante put the Devil in ice. He knew Hell would be an eternal coldness, a biting one if you will, and that Heaven would indeed be something akin to the hot, hot skin of a girl. Besides, ice cubes have no smell.

It is in these moments that I do not know if I am running to, or fro; and, being the organized individual that I am, I do not function well in confusion. I like to know what's what. And that's that.

But, a change of direction may be called for now that I have tried up and out and over. I shall go down. The logic is elegant, as they say, though questions arise concerning how to get "down there."

FROM LEDGER No. 34

I have made an observation that whenever human beings seek to go "home," they seem to be caught between two opposite directions: up and down. Either they look awestruck to skyward, or they sigh and look comforted toward the ground beneath them. Perhaps I am the one chosen to settle this matter. Although, I could not say who might have chosen me or why or what difference it would actually make in the life of man. I have, of course, also observed that not knowing has never stood in the way of believing. I won't fall into that trap. I will pursue this matter intellectually and physically. And that's going to be a problem because the way "down," though obvious in directional terms, is complicated in practical terms. I can't just start digging. In a few feet, we'd be back to the issue of water again. I must find a passage.

But where? Maybe behind the Baptist church. The church is on high ground, safe from high water; at least the ground is high for such a low place as the Delta, even a false Delta. And there is a door back there, as I remember, which was always closed, and no one knew what it led to or why there would be door there in the first place, plumbing and heating notwithstanding. Vines grew over the door. And if one leaned against it and put an ear to it, sounds could be heard as though from a depth and a great distance. Someone said it was merely the sound of the train way down the tracks, and we had eleven a day rumbling through town so I felt that explanation was plausible. But now that I am older and more desperate, I am inclined to ascribe more possibility to the door and its cover of creepers. Certainly no Baptist was ever known to go near it and, as far as I knew, I was the only half-Presbyterian/half-Episcopalian to do so.

I remember thinking of the door as we crossed the Rhine. I wanted to go home then, but that was when I believed home was geographical. Now I know that the way home may involve an infinite journey and that there may be serious wrong turns that could require light years of correctional activity—not that I can walk that fast.

Let me clarify something. There was not much in the way of depth in the Delta, so "down there" never occurred to most people. Mostly, "in the earth" meant just under the topsoil, which, granted, was extremely deep for topsoil, but no one ever really thought about depth in any significant way, as I am doing now.

So that door may have been the entryway to "down there." It may still be that, and I must investigate. The church is sitting right where it was when I was in my early teens. Well, there had been an older one that burned, but, when the present one was built, they put that door in the back, down a step or two . . . and never opened it. Who, I ask myself, was the builder? Who was the carpenter? The contractor? Was he one of those tough, sinewy men from over in the Hills? Did he, in a moment of resentment, hook us up to the underworld? And, if that were the case, had he been there?

You see, people do a lot of things they never talk about. So, it would not shock me to learn that a number of my fellows have been below the earth for one reason or another, other than for mining purposes.

The sounds we heard were not made by trains. They were the sounds of something inhabitable, something reachable, and not altogether unpleasant. As I say, just because the earth is dark and, I presume, deep, does not mean that it contains an evil. That was a misconception promoted by early Christians. *Why would be prince of evil live inside the thing from which we grow turnip greens, corn, and field peas? It wouldn't make sense.*

And I pride myself on being a sensible person. That is why I think it is possible that if the door leads to "down there," "down there" will

not be an evil but rather a level of profundity we all needed but didn't
know where to look for it.

> *The sounds were undoubtedly made*
> *by the moan of subterranean winds*
> *blowing over the rush of those great underground rivers*
> *that separate the shadowy plains,*
> *and, just like a miner, I will,*
> *within that deep environment,*
> *find the jewel of existence*
> *and once more discover myself safe at home . . . if, of course,*
> *all this turns out to be the correct direction.*
> *Right now, however, I'm about worn out*
> *with stars.*
> *And I am sick to death of waiting*
> *for high water.*
> *So, in the interest of therapeutic change,*
> *I intend*
> *to descend.*

Unless there is an alternative, and there may be. I have noticed for
some time the presence of two or three false Negroes who only stand
and watch. They know that I am here. The two white men do not, and
the black ones have not told them.

> *But first: I shall go down to fields*
> *of dark cotton, mud of blacker soil,*
> *through a portal inconspicuous,*
> *but a door nonetheless*
> *that has called for ages*
> *to ears that have not wished to hear*
> *the dark music of*

unthinkable alternatives.
Indeed, except after treasure,
men do not go downward in pursuit
of fleeting paradise.
Men do not think that they long
For darkness, or that they sigh
for depth when touch and light
seem so much to be the ingredients
of beauty and the objects
of soul and groin.

I can see that my focus has shifted. This is disturbing because I had thought, like the universe, I was proceeding in an orderly fashion toward something higher than my groin.

My assumption was wrong. The universe is not proceeding in an orderly fashion. It is proceeding toward dissipation, and that is where I am headed if I don't get back on track.

This metaphysical approach to the remedy of my circumstances is beginning to break down. God help me.

I must be nuts . . . thinking of finding the entrance to the belly of the earth through a door in the back of the Baptist church. Great Scot! How flawed can a premise be?! The Baptist church!? What Baptist church? The one that is here now or the one I remember? If this is not my home, then that Baptist church is not the building I remember; *ergo,* the door in back of it is not the door I remember, which means it is simply not the possible passageway—not to Hell—but to the Land of Lost Deltania. If nothing here above is what it is supposed to be, then how could I have thought that any of it had any validity.

In short, if I don't know where I am, I'd best understand that nothing around me is as it seems—although that does not necessarily mean that what there is or what I see is worthless. After all, even if the inhabitants are wearing rubber skin, I presume they are all still quite human, mistaken humans but humans nonetheless, which doesn't put me any nearer to my original objective than before I leaped through the picture window at the hospital. I have thought for a long time that being human is not that impressive. If you ask me, people make more out of humanity than it is worth, which is surprising considering the frightening things we have done and more that we are surely capable of if left to develop the full horror of our potential.

I'm just going to have to run.

From Ledger No. 55

Was it all true? It seems that when people come into the world at any particular time and place, they, for the most part, accept that time and place as the norm and as the way the world should be. I call it the is-ness of the moment.

In any case this unrelenting question of truth has got me wondering whether I am on the right track and whether my objective, namely my home, ever really existed. But, here, I am not going to indulge in the *Cogito ergo est,* "I think, therefore it is." That would be insane and putting the Descartes before the horse. *Cogito ergo sum* was bad enough.

Proving the existence of anything is too much to deal with under the present circumstances—with which I am perfectly satisfied and do not for a single second entertain thoughts of giving up and leaving the sanity of fresh air and the safety of this silo for a life of resignation among creatures who run around in rubber skin. Give me the open road any day. "There's a long, long trail awinding into the land of my dreams." Possibly it is the "trail of the lonesome pine," though I should much prefer a lonesome cypress.

What was it Longfellow wrote?—

"Tell me not, in mournful numbers,
Life is but an empty dream!—
For the soul is dead that slumbers,

And things are not what they seem."

I am sorry I cannot phone him up. What would I say, "Number please"? We would have a lot to talk about as it appears he, himself, may once have been lost. I do have to disagree with him on one point, though: I do not think sleeping kills or ever injures the soul, providing, of course, that there is one. Plato was convinced there were souls, but, there again, how did he arrive at that conclusion?—certainly not by astronomy or by archaeology.

Nor would I say that life is an empty dream; a dream perhaps, but not an empty one. But as to the business of things not being what they seem to be, Longfellow and I see that like a Cyclops.

With regard to the "mournful numbers," I am not talented in mathematics. Thank God for that; and though I do believe that mathematics is the ultimate language and the only one that can adequately and accurately deal with the world's reality, I still, even so, would not want to look about me and see any of those numbers, particularly the *mournful* ones, especially if there are fractions involved, or decimals.

HIGHWAY 61 WAS A pure delight—no more winding through the gravel and the dust to go to the dances. Highway 61! A ribbon of line-tangent from White Oak Bayou to the Oil Mill at Clarksdale, Clarksdale and the Odd Club Dance, where, even in winter, young men sweated through their tuxedos, and the faces of the girls were blushed and hot, on fire with the music of black musicians and the constant, infinite queue of would-be beaux in love and rut who broke in for only a moment's touch. Om my Oh Maya, quoth the sage.

Highway 61 was a line into the lair of distant fish. It split the morning and the afternoon and ran, I think, from Labrador to Buenos Aires. It was the high water of highways. It did not wind. It did not hesitate as some roads have been known to do. It sliced. It collected. It remembered the paths that were lost. And I must cross it when I leave this silo and

walk to my great-great grandfather's landing—Shaw's Landing—which
is more than all right but north of O.K.[99] And the site of our landing is
south of Mhoon's Landing where the river bends and widens to more
than a mile. There are sturgeons in its murk.

> *Oh!—and Oh again—for a single osculum sanctum!*
> *Just one, tiny philema hagion. I*
> *shall have to do it myself and be careful*
> *not to kiss my elbow and thus*
> *turn into a girl.*
> *Smack-ola. This acta reverentialis:*
> *The kiss o' peas.*

The real issue is why cathedrals do not harbor wildlife, but more
interesting than that is the quality of music I hear when I am walking
about the countryside, mostly on the clearest and coldest of days. That
is at least some compensation for my being trapped in what I believe is
Silesia—or, certainly, possibly Saxony.

However, though I may function in that gorgeous sunlight as a
seemingly celestial being, I am not that at all but am only filled with
a *joi de vivre* peculiar to fugitives. *Let us now pray for the whole state of
Crass church. Armed men.*

So much good fortune was wasted on me. Yet, forsooth, my life is
a piazza of teeming remorse, a souk of dark regret, and would contain
even more hyperbole had I lived longer when I was younger. But I have
remained close to that earlier and more juvenile moment, and still in
my blackest hour I have always been able to hear, even if only barely,
that old Yahoo of birth above the booming of the guns, and the crying
of the wounded.

My mother was a Presbyterian but not much of one and even in

---

99   An old landing in another county, no longer on the Mississippi River. —ml

her most irrational moments never believed in virgin births, rising from the dead, or heavens and hells. Oddly, though, she thought it might be desirable for me to study theology at Sewanee and become an Episcopal minister. My father, on the other hand, was an Episcopalian and felt I should study law or go into the Foreign Service. Hah! Well, I have certainly done that! And now can't get out of it.

In some respects the Second World War was a fortunate occurrence in my case because, if nothing else, I was saved from law and the diplomatic corps. The truth is, all I ever really wanted to do was look at naked women—wherever I could find them: *National Geographic*, the Art Museum in Memphis, the Metropolitan in Manhattan, and at the Art Institute in the City of Broad Shoulders. To that end I feel it was tragic that I was revolted by pornography owing to the ease with which I could have obtained it.

I simply could not abide Popeye's relationship with Olive Oyl. And those postcards! My lord. They were enough to turn one toward horticulture. No. Give me the work of the great masters of the brush; let me sit quietly in the presence of marble where, in some igneous way, I would be happy.

I doubt if Dad could have understood my obsession, or if he did, I am sure he would have had to reject that understanding because of his own upbringing. On the other hand I didn't understand it a bit; I merely accepted it.

And in the midst of hormonal weather, I always, always, knew I wanted to be in love, to be in love and to be loved back, and with marble that was . . . hard.

Religion, in general, among my uncles and aunts was not much of an issue, as it was with some of my cousins in other quarters of the family. My uncles John T. and Bob-Lowe were about as far away from theology as it possible to be and still be in the American South, but, save for a slicing remark here and there about the Baptists, they kept their opinions to themselves.

My aunt Booley, on the other hand, had been brought up like my mother as a Presbyterian, but in the course of time completely discarded Calvinism in favor of Rosicrucianism, Swedenborg, and Madame Blavatsky. And then suddenly one day out of nowhere, she decided to convert to Roman Catholicism and did so. Even at that, by no stretch of the imagination could one have ever said she was religious. Nor would she have.

Aunt Helena had no use for catechisms or for Jesus, whom she regarded mainly as a gentleman who was kind, gracious, brave, and true, the sort of person one should be and has to like, and always does. Finally, to all my mother's siblings the Devil shared a seat on the sofa with *Rawhide and Bloody Bones*. The idea that one would or could burn in Hell for eternity just because one did not "believe" properly was incomprehensible and likely too primitive to consider.

FROM LEDGER NO. 89

Of course I know that choice *is* one of the pillars of freedom. But freedom, in itself, is not what I am after. I want only to go home. That's the long and the short of it. If I could get there, I might think about freedom later.

But I must go now where all is swamp. Wonderful swamp! Snake Brake, Beaver Dam, Phillips Bayou, Hollywood Brake, Cassidy Bayou,

> *The Tallahatchie Scatters,*
> *and Dead Nigga Slough . . . Swamp . . .*
> *All was swamp before my time, but the remnants*
> *of that great bog beckon audibly, visibly,*
> *in the eyes and ears of my flesh and bone—*
> *where all is swamp!*
> *Oh,*
> *There are slow reptiles in the memory,*
> *amphibians of the soul,*

water turkeys of the imagination,
long-necked avian divers, swift and serpentine
below the surface of some cypress enclave
in the beauty of a bog.
Dampness is a perfume, magnetic and aphrodisiac,
locational and welcoming.
Decay is the fruit eaten by the nostrils,
ingested by the brain and translated into the dance
of life by the flowers of the libido.

We had it in the Delta; it is soaked into the city of New Orleans, where mixed with a little salt and a bit on the brackish side, the full madness of delight rises up, screams out, and wears an orange dress at noon. With us in this lowland, this alluvial mud, sperm is never very far away, and always somewhere nearby breasts are heaving in a river of sweat.

Thank God! *Gratia* [Lat.] to the Great "H." Yeewoo, Yoway, Yahwee, Yeewoh, Yahweh, Jehovah. The sacred, unpronounceable but not unmisspellable name of God.

The magnificence of the mystery
Is the highest of worldwide waters,
Whose whitecaps expand the planet
And, to some degree,
Cool the sun, finally
To be consumed lukewarm,
Like sugar, a gumdrop
In the mouth of munching Kronos,
Whose esophagus
Is the gurgling home of time,
The obverse of desire,
The blind man's thread

That binds "forever" to the mind
And splendor to the fire.

From stars to marsh hawks
It is all the same, except for
Perspective and the magnitude
Of the light.

I am here; I am there. Motion
Is merely a form of matter and therefore
An illusion. The leaver stays;
The stayer speeds away, or
Day is night and night is day, or
Each is neither
Nor.

I know that I should love my enemies, but, with the exception of soldiers in the German patrol, I don't know who they are. People who dress in rubber skin obviously do not wish to be recognized, although it is logical that they are Germans too, and I have really simply assumed that they were. However, in all fairness to the principles of science, I am allowing for the possibility that they might be something other than the Teutons.

Further, I have checked, thoroughly, to determine if any of my own skin is rubber, and none of it is. I am I from head to toe. Remember, the verb "to be" never takes a direct object. And I intend to remain in the nominative zone.

Speaking of zones, I am not interested so much in the scenery of my native one. I am only interested in the way it penetrates my neurons, and penetrate it does. In fact, all my life I never really saw where I lived; I felt I lived where I lived and recognized it by the way my flesh came alive whenever I rode through it, hypnotized by its lowness, entranced in the smell of it. There were other smells by the time I arrived here, smells I did not know and were told that they were the smells of potions used to kill the boll weevil. There were biplanes—yellow Stearmans—and black men covered with white powder. Everyone was happy except, of course, the boll weevil, who, if he were larger, might make an interesting pet. For a bug, he seems to have a rather dog-like aura.

In any case, the evenings began to smell
like the white powder,
and that was the tell-tale sign
that something was wrong.

It would suit me if I could find my unit, but I think there is less chance of that than of finding my way home. Tonight I must visit the store. An odd thing, that. The chest on the porch of the store is always filled with almost everything I need, and always—always—has plenty of those wonderful PayDay candy bars![100] The sign says, "Casequarter's Grocery." I believe it is owned by one of *them* disguised as a Negro. At night, and even during the day I see several of *them*, clumsily made up to look like Negroes. I see them watching me. The whites do not appear cognizant of my presence, but those who attempt to look like Africans observe me all the time; yet, they never make a move as though they intend to recapture me. I don't understand the situation at all, but I have learned to accept it in the hope that it means rebellion is brewing within the camp of the enemy. Twice now that I know of, the black ones have not told the two whites who show up every once in a while where I am. And they know.[101]

They appear to look down on the two whites. I can tell, because the black ones always laugh a great deal after the white ones leave. Some-

100 See *Junior Ray*, 38. —ogbii
101 Ibid., 117. —ogbii

thing tells me the black observers want me to escape. Yet, they show no signs of impatience.[102]

The fact is, one is always observed, and the observer does not necessarily have to be other than the one observed, who, if he is halfway intelligent is observing himself automatically. One's awareness of oneself is one's observation of oneself. A cow cannot do it. It cannot observe a human, and it cannot observe itself, any more than it can observe the heavens and know that it is a cow observing the heavens. Cow reflection is minimal. It eats and defecates and remains unaware that it is even a cow. And although a cow is a mammal just as I am, a dog is different. Oh, yes. I like to make a distinction even if it barely exists. A dog is a "fellow" mammal. That's because his brain is large enough in proportion to his body to allow him to appear to reflect just enough to understand affection, and then he will go and roll in dung. Much like folks we know.

I do not fault them, and the dung is not literal; it is figurative dung. Nonetheless, if they do it with any frequency, they become hard to be around. It becomes difficult to pat them and to allow them to lick us in the face. Still, I do not fault them but merely wish they would change their ways, which but for the grace of the big "H" might be my ways.

But not until I get home. I cannot turn my attention to ordinary life while I am in an extraordinary situation.

I am no sluggard. I do not sit and wait for high water. I go in search of it. That is how I discovered the U-boat.[103] It sits in the bed of the old river, across the levee, somewhere south of Flower Lake. I spent the night beside it, because I could tell no one was home and that no one had been aboard for a long, long time.

As long as I keep tabs on the patrol, I am not afraid. I can always stay one or two jumps ahead of them. And they did not follow me into the woods. Apparently it is one of the oddities of escape and evasion

---

102 Ibid., 117.
103 See Chapter 18, or for the full saga, *Junior Ray*, 95, and *The Yazoo Blues*, 29, et al. —ogbii

that the soldiers do not seem to like the forest and rarely if ever come in to look for me.

Still, I am not about to abandon my tower. In my view—and in the view I have of the land around me at large—the top of the silo is the best apartment any fugitive could wish for.

But what I want to know is where the crew of the U-boat went. The possibilities are numerous. And one is that they are still here, though for some reason I do not think any of them are members of the squad that clumps about after me. And I would like to know why the submariners came this far up the Mississippi. Surely it was not to shell Friars Point. Or to disrupt ferry traffic between Lula and Helena. Still, war is absurd, and one of their strategists may have believed putting a scare in turkey hunters could somehow give Germany an advantage. I don't have the answer.

But I'll say this. *The U-boat had to have come up the river during high water.* There we have it. Long ago, to be sure. But there it is. With high water anything is possible. And the presence of the submarine near Hawk Lake, which is south of Flower Lake, proves it.

This is the kind of knowledge Prometheus brought us in the torch. Very strange that the gods never want man to know anything, much in the same way Jehovah did not want Adam and Eve to eat the fruit of the tree of enlightenment and exactly in the same way those Mexican loggers in 1940 did not want the Indians in Durango to learn how to drive trucks. Bolivar Deeson and I drove down there, by the hardest in his grandmother's car, the summer of our twenty-second year, after graduation. We fell in for a time with the loggers, the Indians, and a missionary who was translating the Book of Luke into Southern Tepehuan.

> *It is not that when one eats the fruit or*
> *catches the fire or drives the truck that all is known.*
> *On the contrary,*
> *it is at those moments in which one realizes*

that not enough is known and that more can be known,
and that is the difference between a man
and an obedient serf.

Oh, of course, the gods prefer the serf! Mortal serfdom makes it easier for those Olympian jellybeans to be gods. "Don't think," say the deities. "Yassuh," says the man. "Shuffle your feet once a week on Sunday," say the gods. "Thank you, Jesus," says the man.

But, here is the answer: Naturally, the presence of a German submarine anywhere in this vicinity does not surprise me in the least. True, deduction when it comes to enemy submarines stuck in the woods across the levee would be a difficult matter if it weren't for the salient fact that I am wandering about in enemy territory, so that answers that.

The more likely question would be why wouldn't there be one stuck over there? If a person like myself is behind the lines among the enemy, he should not be shocked to discover one of their boats . . . Unlike the *Northern gunboat* Jimmy Mack and Lewis Andrews found in Moon Lake.[104]

It was probably the driest summer we'd ever had, and the lake was way down. Even in the middle you could stand. And it was over on the island, the northeast side, that Jimmy saw something sticking up out of the mud, he called Lewis over, and they discovered it was a cannon.

Then, of course, there were the professors from Ole Miss and Mississippi State and even the University of Alabama who came there that summer and dug up the gunboat, which they called a tin-clad. They even found its name on a brass plate. It was the *Patroklos*. And they said it had been part of the Yazoo Pass expedition, a thing that everyone had always talked about but, really, no one understood all that well, as indeed the Yankees themselves had not.

After a while the cannons were gone, and so were the professors,

---

104 See *The Yazoo Blues.* —ogbii

and no one knew any more about the Yazoo Pass Expedition afterwards than they had before. As for Jimmy and Lewis, they were quite upset, because they felt that at least one of the cannons should have been theirs. And most people, as I recall, thought so, too and, later, had nothing whatsoever good to say about the professors, especially the one from the University of Alabama, who, as far as they were concerned, was the next thing to a Yankee.

That may not have been all bad. My father used to remind me that his mother was a Northerner and that his grandfather on that side of the family had fought for the Union and had been captured by the South and put into Libby Prison in Richmond, Virginia, where he ate black beans and rats.

I have thought a good deal about that particular great-grandfather lately. I feel I have come to know him better than my Southern ones. There he, too, was but *not was* in his country. I do not know if he ran off as I have, but I am certain that he dealt with his captivity in some ways similar to my own methods. *There is, I believe, a brotherhood of captives.*

I am more than a little afraid that the U.S. Corps of Army Engineers is working in concert with my captors. Observe: the levee is enormous and more than 200 miles long. When this new levee was built after the flood of 1927, it was the highest earthen dam in the world, though now it may not be—indeed, I believe, in terms of height only, Sardis and all the rest of those reservoiral projects have taken the title away from the levee along the Mississippi and all the semi-mysterious, batture wilderness between it and the channel.

All I am saying is that these obstacles make it more difficult for the high water to get anywhere close to the silo. It is not impossible, perhaps not even improbable, but difficult nonetheless.

> *If only I had thought to construct my special shoes.*
> *Indeed, if snow shoes are appropriate for deep snow,*
> *golf shoes suitable for walking over a castrated field,*

and tennis shoes for tennis,
why then should there not, I thought,
be shoes designed for high water—
other than hip boots of course.
I do not want walk in the water;
I want to walk on it.

There again we have it. If one is perfect, things are different—
Galahad got to see the grail, possibly to touch it, caress it even; and
Jesus hiked out over the Sea of Galilee as though it were a parking
lot in Memphis.

Understanding then my personal imperfection, I knew I would
have to have special shoes. After all, I may be a great-great grandson of
Colonel Duncan Sherard Benoit, but I am not the Son of God, not in
the sense of immediate family anyway.

The colonel may not have been God, but I was led to believe that
whatever the colonel might say *let there be*, it generally was. And I am
sure he could have invented such footwear if he had seen a need for it
in his time.

There is no way now for me to construct my shoes. I've all I can
handle and no material suitable for the project, nor do I have any
tools. Besides, there would have to be testing and redesigning and all
the stages of development that go into a quality product. But, oh, if I
had had more foresight! The "foolish virgins" used all their oil and had
none to burn in their lamps so the bridegroom could find the way to
their doors, and I wasted my time and did not invent my shoes so that
I could walk across the waters of the flood.

Unlike Noah, there are those of us whom God does not warn, and,
I must admit, that unlike Noah, there are those of us—as there were
then—who wouldn't have listened if He had, and I know that I am
one of that batch: "He was just hard-headed and wouldn't listen" is
what my mother always said about me and about most people besides

herself. At least I am in good company, or just a lot of it, depending on one's perspective.

FROM LEDGER NO. 144

I don't know why I endured my captivity as long as I did. I kept thinking that possibly I might be wrong, that I was simply too critical, but inevitably I came back to the conclusion that all was false and everyone was merely an actor in rubber skin, including Lawyer Montgomery and Aunt Helena—how the enemy managed to almost duplicate them I do not know, but it almost worked for quite some time, until I realized . . . I think it was about the time I saw the German patrol hiding in the aisle at the Liberty Cash grocery on Main Street that I really began to understand I was going to have to make a run for it. And then, after I was put into the hospital, I worked out how I was going to do it, although I was a bit surprised when I jumped through the picture window. Fortunately I was wearing my father's woolen robe.

I was on my way home from the lumberyard and stopped in the Liberty Cash. The day was lovely, crisp, just into fall, and I went inside. Everything appeared normal until I went toward the back of the store, and I saw them. They were pressed together, one behind the other, like dark sardines in the shadow of the last aisle on the left. I looked to see if the butcher, Mr. Rolinstowe, had seen them, but he seemed unaware of their presence, which I thought was rather odd. The Liberty Cash is a very small grocery, and there are only three aisles, rather short, running lengthwise from the check-out counter at the front of the store to the meat counter at the back.

The soldiers stood as still as a can of peas, their eyes fixed straight in front, as though they did not see me, which I knew was balderdash. Their entire reason for existence is to pursue me. Surely they understand that. However, you know how those Germans are, obedient; they never ask questions, so maybe they don't realize that clomping about, hunting me, is their sole purpose in life, if indeed this is life (it could be a dream, but I certainly, at this point, would not know the difference even if there were one).

But, goodness, enough about me! There were other matters of greater importance. For example, under all the sweetness, the laughter, and the warmth, there was, I think, the malice—malice and death, and loss, and deep, oh deep, deep sadness because of it, and yet malice was the fuel that ran the household, that, underneath it all, defined the family and determined the shape of every life within it.

But it was the malice of only one, perhaps. And that was Aunt Booley, small, so lady-like, and in the early years, rather charming, at first, but vicious in her hatred of her siblings. Why, Aunt Booley couldn't put her foot flat on the floor because she had worn high-heels all her life. And she thought, when she was married to John Hamilton, that it was her monthly dose of Epsom salts that prevented pregnancy, when the truth was she had an infantile uterus and couldn't have had children anyway. (Celeste told me that before I got on the ship to go to England. Celeste had grown up in St. Leo and was older than I and had gone at the age of twenty-two to live in New York City, and, when the war broke out, she had become an Army Nurse. It was that latter fact that caused Aunt Booley to confide certain things to her. Celeste was a nurse, and so one could reveal things to her that would not be interesting or even understandable to someone with no medical training.)

Mother said John Hamilton would have left Aunt Booley, but he up and died young after only four years of marriage—crashing head-on into another car on a one-lane bridge near Tchula and dying, later, drunk and singing hymns with his two best friends in a hotel room in Yazoo City, of a ruptured spleen.

But it is the malice that is sadder than the sadness and more devastating than the loss—not of John Hamilton but of my cousin William and of the possibility, ever, for happiness to be anything but forced. Yet forced is better than not at all. And after a while I believe it resembled the real thing. William—"Billy"—was blown into statistical history before I was born, during the "Last War" at Chateau-Thierry in '17 . . . at seventeen.

That loss is the strangest and the most powerful, though as a child I saw almost none of it and only heard the laughter and saw the shape of place and belonging, mostly on the side porch of Grandmother's house . . . which really, it turned out, somehow through scheme and euchre was owned and controlled by Aunt Booley, who I thought simply read palms and fluttered about in a way that she believed was charming.

That is just my point: things can be entirely other than they appear, no matter how close one may be to them, no matter how well one thinks he knows them, and that is why Buddha was the way he was, and he lived nowhere near Mhoon County. Still, he shot from the hip and leaped to the wrong conclusion when he became hipped on that business about ridding himself of desire (qv). That was bad business because, ultimately, desire is life itself no matter how the philosophers wish to gussie it up with higher *thisses* and spiritual *thats*. My God! If I should rid myself of desire, I would merely be pod of flesh on a heap of seeds! In short, I would have no business being anywhere at all. And that is the very essence of death. The life of statues.

High water and passivity do not go hand in hand. Only the aggressive, the fast, and the fierce will ever find it, if I read my scripture right. Indeed, the timid, the phlegmatic shall never find the high water—I think that is in Noah, one through something, or is it from the Book of Ham?

Or the Book of Bone?

Imagine that scripture (personally, I just don't think holy writ is very hard to write), for example:

> *Go ye into the land and rid all men of desire, for I the anthropo-*
> *morphic god of the preachers do command ye. Yea, exorcize the*
> *thighs; bind the pelvis so that it shaketh not and lay not thy hand*
> *upon thy navel, lest ye pierce the wall of thine abdominal cavity.*
> *Go forth and do this as I the Lord of Cytoplasm hath charged thee.*

And, lo, they did bring the transgressors unto the back porch and there they bade them alter their wicked ways and cease to violate the ethics of their bodies, but the words of the righteous fell upon deaf ears, and the goodness was left undone. So were the righteous infected by life and caused to laugh without reason.
[from the Book of Bone 1:1–2]

I shall see that a copy of the *Book of Bone* is placed in every tourist court in Memphis, including the Ditty Wah Ditty on Bellevue.

Or better yet I shall pair it with the *Book of Saurians*:

. . . Beaked and ornithic came the bipedal terror and lept upon his slower kin, which, having but three short horns, could not save itself from the raking talons and razored jaws of the wingless death. Thus, cowlike, the creature surrendered to the greater terror of that Jurassic moment.
[from the Book of Saurians 7:11]

Indeed, when one realizes the possibility for hoax, one comprehends the folly of faith—faith, which has always seemed more like a shackle than a comfort.

Further, golden angelic tablets are to be found everywhere if one knows where to look, beneath ferns, for instance, on the eastern edge of the Delta and in abandoned barns, especially those that once held mules. Angels have rather particular if not fairly regular places they prefer to leave samples of angelic texts for mortals to find and to translate. I just skip all that and write mine from scratch. My words sound about the same as those of God, except when the words of God are written as equations, and that throws me, but for the most part the regular "words" are easy to mimic once I catch the rhythm. After that, the wisdom just falls right into place.

Winter, 1944
Somewhere in Silesia

Dear Mother,

Sorry your dirt has gone so cold and dry, but then it is now a cold dry time of year—one, I might add, that I prefer. But your fertility was never in question—even though we all knew a lot of it was just big talk and that the dirt held by those Yankees in Illinois and Iowa is blacker and richer than this silken swamp of yours, except for the light sandy kind of soil that grows the cotton, bale on bale, for us to blow our noses in.

I mention your agronomy because it was that that made the way everything else in the Delta became, which was what made people feel about the place the way they did, even though nothing about it, apart from the dirt, was real. It just seemed to be. Consequently our Delta acquired a reputation as such, and the image was passed along for at least three generations until it began to acquire a sort of palpable mass, in the same sense that up would be down if people called it so, over a long enough period of time.

That is why men like me have a hard time with the plain-spoken, bare-bones factuality of other regions that are less invented. It's not enough. Just an egg without toast, or grits. Worse, we always carry our place-ness with us and try to find a way to fit it into another environment, which is impossible, and which always defines such men as "characters." Of course, that is what we are. If one lives in fiction, one is most certainly a character. How could it be otherwise?

Well, that's all right as long as one does not also become disagreeable. Trying to fit the unfittable into a space it won't fit into apparently makes some of us bitter. That has never been one of my peculiarities. I may long for my native illusion, but I am not bitter about not being able to enjoy it *in situ,* so to speak.

Indeed, I can be as genuinely American as *Ozzie and Harriet,* or

Just Plain Bill, or *Portia Faces Life*. "Duz do*es* everything," and I am extremely flexible, as my captors likely agree.

But there comes a time when one must decide upon a life of acceptance or a life of gratification. I have chosen the latter. And I have crossed the Rubicon. "*Alea iacta est*." Caesar the day.

But wait. The gratification does not necessarily imply that I mean to be ecstatically happy when I am where I say I long to be. Oh no. I will be gratified simply knowing that I am there. And once that is established, I may in fact wish to leave it, but, first, I have to BE there. That's it; I cannot go forward until I return home. First I have to go back. One cannot go to war and not come home, one way or another, although I know that there are special circumstances that prevent an actual return, but in most of those cases the person never knew the difference. I am not one of those: I am alive.

> *I intend to go where the weather always changes,*
> *where nothing is familiar except the lowness of the land,*
> *and where the forest grows suddenly around me*
> *but where there is quite a distinct path*
> *which can disappear,*
> *along with the weather and the trees,*
> *just as quickly as it appeared in the first place.*
> *I do not understand the mechanics of the phenomenon.*
> *But, being flexible—and agreeable, I accept it.*

And I am always on a well-worn path, a road, if you will, though only made so by the track of many feet over many, many years. Often there are the wheel ruts of wagons but not always, just as, also, often there is a cleared field, but not always. Sometimes there are blacks in the fields, but more frequently there are Indians, with stone hoes. I see them, hear them, and am among them, and, if I want to, I can touch them.

The path runs more or less east and west, from the hills to the Mississippi and vice versa, although, certainly there are other tracks that run generally north and south, but they are not as wide as the east-west/west-east ones—or one, I cannot be sure.

And then, just as suddenly, I am back in a field near the silo, and the forest is gone, as it is now except for a fair expanse over the levee and a remnant or so on the dry side. Still there are patches here and there that have not yet heard the ring of the ax. But I know they will, if what I see here is representative of a trend. Clearing. This must be how Kansas was formed.

But why these Nords would want to erase their forests is beyond me. Here they don't quite duplicate the Delta, and they go about destroying even what I would consider a pretty fair replica of some of it.

It is, however, these abrupt changes in the immediate environment that, (1) apparently are not controlled by my captors, and (2) appear to have the stamp of New World antiquity. So, then, if in fact those changes are not really in the environment per se but in time, it stands to reason that I might be able to use those jumps[105] as a means of going home. The trouble is I don't know how to control the jumps. There are no dials. I cannot, say, set the jump for 1941, the year before I went into the army. If I could, I would still have to go through all that again. So, frankly, maybe it is a good thing that I cannot program the change, because I am unable to decide which point in time I should jump to. Anything technical always gives me a fit.

Therefore, for the *time* being, I will simply enjoy the phenomenon and the fact that when the patrol is out there or when there are others in pursuit, as from *time* to *time* there have been, all other people vanish except of course the ones I find along the path, those I just mentioned who cannot see me, and, not being visible in the place I've jumped to, I presume I vanish too in the place I jump from. All this is sheer speculation.

And as long as I get back to the silo, I am not overly concerned. All

---

105 cf. *Junior Ray,* 128–29. —ogbii

I do know is that this peculiar stuff has something to do with a path.

> *I think the law*
> *of this kind of gravity*
> *Is that*
> *A path never goes away*
> *And that it always goes in two directions,*
> *Forward and backward*
> *And that paths, by nature,*
> *Are worn not only into space*
> *But into time as well.*

Perhaps it is what Professor Wigfall at Sewanee would have called "the dao" (Please, read: *Tao*). Whenever he was asked by a student: "What, sir, should I do?" Professor Wigfall would lower his eyes to the way in front of him and say, "Find 'the dao,' young man; find 'the dao.'"

None of us knew what that meant, until one day at the library Bowman Byars found a reference to Taoism and "the Tao," pronounced, it said, "dao." And it meant, "the way" or "the path."

Since then I have constantly looked for the "tao/dao." I know what Wigfall was trying to say, and I know how important it is to every person, though only a few comprehend that importance.

And now I have found it, or, shall I say, sometimes I seem to stumble upon it.

Occasionally I have thought that perhaps I am home and that it has simply changed, though to what specific degree, at first, I could not say. But I did admit, slightly, of the two possibilities: I was home; I was not home . . . and somehow I preferred to believe the latter were true—which may mean that it is I who have constructed this false Delta, that it is I who am my captor, and that it is from the same I am trying to escape. All of which is almost too bizarre; yet, being a high-forceps delivery as I am, I can see how I could have done it.

It is always preferable to feel that one does not have a hand in the trouble one causes, always preferable to assign the origin and the engine of it to Teutons—who by God I have seen! They are here!

I cannot deny the reality of the rubber skin. Winter, summer, spring, and fall, these creatures wear it. The question is how long can all this keep up, whether it is my doing or theirs. And I don't know that it makes that much difference who is responsible. The main consideration is how I feel about the situation. And, even if I, myself, have built this preposterous scenario, that doesn't mean I have to live in it.

Nor does it mean that it is real. After all, the capacity one has for delusion is enormous. It is enormous enough for me to have created the rubber skin. But, even though I know that, it would still be extremely hard for me to accept. And I would still have to escape and to try to find the point at which all this was begun, or when I began it, and how I am to think of it.

On the other hand, unreality is just the other side of the coin. Flip it, and one has either reality of unreality—except in the rare, rare event that the coin falls and lands standing on its side, and I think that might be what I am dealing with. The coin can land in a crack; it can fall and bounce against the side of a shoe. Any number of things can happen that can cause a quarter or a nickel or, less frequently, a fifty-cent piece to land on its edge and remain standing. Anyone who has had difficulty making decisions and has tossed a lot of coins knows this.

So I have the third possibility that the whole situation is neither the doing of me nor of someone else but that I am somehow caught on the edge of what is true and what is not true.

Your loving son,

Leland

FROM LEDGER NO. 233

People tend to like the fictions that suit them. I am no different in that respect from others. But I can't tell fiction from fact, and that's the rub.

However, simply knowing that, or at least believing that, does not relieve the awful frustration of not having a clear idea of what I need to do.

That is why, through an act mostly of sheer will, I continue to believe that I am a fugitive from captivity in a foreign land and, therefore, must do all I can to get back across the lines, wherever they happen to be, and ultimately to my home, the *Delta*—even though there is a lot about my native region that leaves even more to be desired, as I remember. Regardless of what Thomas Wolfe may have thought, I *can* go home again and shall. Wolfe had forgotten his Hardy.

But, about the "a lot to be desired": For example, the year that I decided not to play football—two years *before* I was sent off to Cadwallader Mountain Military Academy, which was founded of course by Leonidas Polk, the "fighting bishop"—was, though brief, all in all a bad experience. I was ostracized by my peers and by the older townsmen, particularly those down at the barbershops, who, at one of those establishments, when I was very small, threatened to cut off my penis. As I say, there were two barbershops. There was that one, and there was the other one where the men played dominoes in the back room and talked about the crops and expressed no interest in my or anybody else's penis; so naturally that was where I went for my haircuts, as soon as I had anything to say about it.

As for football, I hadn't realized it was such a big issue, though it did not take long for me to understand that I had done something unspeakable and that it might even imply that I was homosexual—a loathsome queer!—(I was terrified I might be thought to be a girl, thus to this very day I stolidly maintain that the world does not need any more Southern fairies, although, next to cotton and fiction, homosexuals are the South's most successful product, but it was the war—it was most assuredly the war—that made me realize that more of almost anything would be better than more war, and, also, the truth be told, I could not manage to convince myself that homosexuals had ever been the cause of very much damage, not near as much in my view as the lethal messes non-homosexuals appeared to have caused; on the other hand, for all I know President Roosevelt, Mr. Churchill, General DeGaulle, and even Joseph Stalin could all be homosexuals)—then, to fuel my fear, I received not one but two bouquets of roses, anonymously from the coach and, thoughtfully, also from the team.

Exactly like my situation, now, with my presumed captors, I could not understand why it made so much difference to anyone whether I went out for football or not, since I was not a very good player, and never enjoyed any of it except when the girls were watching. Then my running form became godlike, slow but godlike, and I seemed to receive boundless energy and a desire to excel. But, as soon as the girls were gone, gone also was my love for the sport.

Before high school, though, when we played "football" in the side yard of my grandmother's house, where I was constantly embarrassed at being plucked away by Miss Sandra, from whom I took tap-dancing lessons, I did love football, no pads and all. What happened later when I went out for the team in high school, I cannot say. There was an important change, and I can only speculate that it had to do with the sudden imposition of the *official* stamp, the overwhelming fact that the game was no longer an idea of a group of boys but an activity of the school district, run by large, burly men, who seemed not to mind the weather or the time and had us beating the tar out of each other in order to teach us the love of the game. I observed that some did love it. It was their cup of tea, and I found that totally baffling.

Somewhere, somehow, I had slipped behind, and though I did not realize it, I was not where I should have been in what I might have imagined was my development as a warrior. Maybe, when I really think about it, I can understand the shock my friends must have felt when I announced I was not going out for football. They were, I suppose, afraid that might happen to them, too, and if it did, that they, themselves, and perhaps the whole little town, would discover they—*they* who turned their backs on football—were girls. That was in the '30s.

I can see how great was the matter of masculinity. I remember deliberately speaking in what I hoped was a basso profundo, so that I would sound manly. Indeed, I learned later from a noted musician that women respond positively to low notes.

And yes, yes, as I maintain,
A thing, I think, that may not change:
I respond to dark women,
Women who have the darkness of a forest,
A large darkness of some genetic depth
Unplumbed by white men in hats.
It is the darkness of origins.
And that is where I aim to go, back to the beginning,
Not of the Delta but of everything.
I don't like waiting for the last dance,
And I am not happy with intermission.
I want the downbeat, and that is why I like dark women;
The explosion is buried in their metabolism—
Oh, I suppose one might say that is also true
With fair-skinned girls, and I admit
From a technical standpoint,
That is laudably democratic.

But I am not being technical. I am being cosmically perceptive, and I have devoted my life to the perfection of that capability. Hovering, I have not yet mastered, but cosmic perception through dark women, yes, I have.[106]

---

106 The date of this entry is uncertain, as is the case with much of Shaw's work. However, as the reader knows, what is certain is that Shaw does tell us, that eventually, he was able to "hover." —ogbii

Without cosmic perception, one is very limited. So much goes by unnoticed or appreciated. It is like standing in line, waiting. But, when one feels the "Fiat lux" and the nudging tongue of God urging into *Being* the fire of all time and matter, then a person has cosmic perception. And you can get it in a glance, fully clothed . . . from dark women.

> *There is a darkness in the light that comes from them.*
> *And the darkness contains a fire, a smolder,*
> *That draws the heart and the hand to the source of it*
> *Somewhere beneath their skin,*
> *Where the olives grow.*

There is another question. Who waits for me? When I do finally return, will there be anyone who remembers that I was gone? This is important. Suppose no one waits for me. What if no one cares whether I am there or not? What then should I think about that? Will home still be home? That is to say, what was it that made the place my home? I have not considered these points before.

Of course, not knowing who is there or how they may feel about my absence is not what I must base my own feelings on, because I could be wrong. After all, I may be cosmically perceptive, but I cannot know what is unknowable. Unlike the Swiss, I have no concept of time's passage in an hourly sense. I lost that in the war. There, a wristwatch was only useful if one had a wrist.

I always said that absence was the core of my charm. I said it because I really believed people would rather miss me than be with me. There again, this attitude may be a product of my having been a high-forceps delivery, which has made me feel intrusive all my life. Some things I have stolen like hot pies cooling on the window sill, because I merely assumed they would never—or could never—be mine and that I would live and die without knowing the taste of any it. This habit has caused me to act impulsively and has brought me great regret, all before my twenty-fifth year. Since that time, I've not been in a position to do things that I might have regretted in a moral sense. There has not been much opportunity for impulse in this no-*land's* land where all my energies and thoughts have been directed toward eventual escape. Even my leaping through the picture window was not an act of impulse. At least I didn't regard it as such.

It is possible that reading corrupted my life. After the first book, I no longer had a clear view of the difference between myself and the characters—and I believe I identified with them all. It was they, not the writer, who were alive. It was they, not the writer, I wanted to be.

If I had it to do all over, I would not read. No. I would maintain contact only with the immediate and in that way stay in touch with reality. You will understand my attitude if you first understand that, for me, all writing was scripture—every novel was a work of holy writ, a world of possibility for me. It never occurred to me that a person had to sit alone in a room and invent most of what I was reading, or that, even if they did not invent it, they still had to sit alone in a room to get it down on paper. My God, the very idea of that is hideous!

So here I am: alone in an infinite room, a room whose walls have no shape but which keep me in and everyone else out. Now do not imagine that I am going to say, "Oh, I made this room." I certainly did not. Nor am I sure who did, but that it exists and that the condition I just described exists is true.

And, yes, even after my arrival, I wanted to marry the fictional women, especially the brunettes. I wanted to win them in a knife fight, in Louisiana, on Frank Yerby's *Benton's Row*. At about the same time, I did not want to be the Corsican Napoleone Buonaparte, but I did fall in love with Selinko's Desiree in *Desiree*; although much earlier, I was quite smitten with Planetty, the Silver Princess in one of the Oz books—not a brunette but, even more attractive, from another planet. It was the illustration more than anything else that caught my attention.

Romantic relationships with real women were made difficult. The kissing and embracing—and the dancing—were not a problem, but the being with them on a non-embracing, non-dancing, non-kissing basis was somehow flat and unattractive, like watching baseball, or sitting in a waiting room. I could observe that somehow married couples rarely appeared to be embracing, kissing, or dancing, and I knew that a lifetime of conversation was going to be hard for me to get used to.

My reaction to ordinary life was not the fault of the women I met. It was the result of my having read. Indeed, should I ever organize an ideal society, no one shall read. There will be books, of course, but they will be books one ought to read or books that one should have read, but not books that anyone will actually read; and in that way, I believe I may come closer to creating a utopian environment than any of my predecessors.

Vee feely tahnken geebt ess? Nik sheeza! I could call that out to the patrol when they get too close, but I am not certain if my German phrases from my army handbook would be acceptable. After all, this affair is not quite war, yet not quite peace, so the rules do not apply and, in fact, may not even be there to be broken. Clearly I can see what Aunt Booley was talking about when she discussed the possibility of someone's child dying and going to Limbo, which was a Catholic subdivision for people who were nowhere. Aunt Booley was a Catholic convert—after John Hamilton's untimely death—and a Rosicrucian, so that when one of the two organized systems of credulity fell short of imaginary power, the other filled in.

Theologically, I know now that the relationship between God and man is like that between man and turtle. For example, when a man sees a turtle in the road, the man knows there is every chance in the world that the turtle will be crushed by the tires of an automobile, even on roads that are fairly remote. So the man detours from his appointed or self-appointed path, picks up the turtle and carries him—or her—to the turtle's apparent intended side of the road and deposits same into the grasses of the ditch . . . from which the turtle turns and proceeds again to the road where it will sit until a car kills it. Man is the turtle. And God is the man. The road is, of course, the way to Ludlow Fair and an unnecessary destiny. But man-as-turtle does not know that.

But there we are: big frogs get gigged; tadpoles get eaten. In the end it's all more or less a never-ending ending.

FROM LEDGER NO. 377

Perhaps the dead giveaway was not merely the subtlety of the change that I perceived when I was told I had returned, but more the rate, the rapidity, of change that I have seen since I have been here. We Alluvians did not change with such alacrity. Enthusiasm for progress is Germanic. That is what tipped me off as much as anything, and then when I discovered the elaborate disguises, I knew I was not at home. It was a trick.

And this thing goes on. My captors die and are born, and I remain a man without a clear idea of where I am, yet patriotic to the end. I will not surrender, and I will not give up. Escape and evasion is the only alternative if I am to live an honorable life.

There is freedom only in opposition, though I know that my captors would simply counter with the proposition that what I am opposed to is what I want, that what I flee is what I seek. The thought that they may be right is upsetting. And the business of being right is certainly an issue, because I really only wish to do what is right, and if I am mistaken, and I discover, somehow, that I am, I shall have to change, too, and admit that I was wrong—and I would not hesitate to do it if I could become convinced that I was home, but every time I have tried to feel that way, something has intervened, some little something has always presented itself so that I was always forced to say, "No. Watch out. They do not pronounce the 'shibboleth' quite in the proper manner. You are among Philistines." I cannot be at home if I do not feel at home, particularly if home does not appear to be home, especially because, in this case, there are simply too many white people.

I have found that as upsetting as anything else. Worse, I have lately heard country music, which means—if this were my home—that whites had brought it in and that it could infect the Negroes.

But there's no danger of that happening here. What appear to be Negroes are merely individuals elaborately concealed in rubber skin, the same as my parents and all my friends.

The truth is, from an artistic point of view, I would be the first to give them awards for their performances. Their grasp of character and of the general subject is remarkable, for foreigners.

For God's sake, where is the Atlantic! If I could reach the coast I might be able to spot a landmark.

But this may mean that I cannot continue to come back day after day and night after night to this refuge, comfortable though it is. And warm. I can only fault myself for lack of daring, and for waiting for high water to come *to me*.

It is very much like hunting. Some things you chase; other things you wait for. In either case a hunter may be successful, but he has to understand his game to know which method to adopt. And I am afraid I do not understand enough about the nature and the origin of high water.

This may mean ignorance is my captor
and delusion has propelled my rebellion.

I cannot bear the thought of it. Why should I be deluded any more than anyone else? Why should I not know the truth as much as the next person? True, I am exceptional, but Dear Sweet Jesus, not that exceptional! There is such a thing as being TOO wrong.

Mainly, I have deluded myself by believing that I am escaping and evading. Escaping what? Evading what? I am still here. I have not left in years, and the only difference is that now I am sleeping in a silo full of, of all things, cotton seeds, which never should have been in a silo in the first place. But I am thankful they were, and isn't that just life in a shotgun shell?

Further, I have come to like it here. I don't want to leave. From the top of the silo, I feel I am almost really home. What I see is so real to me, and so pleasant to look at in all its lack of scenic grandeur that it lulls me into what can only be described as a happiness.

I do not feel captured anymore. I feel free, and the idea of waiting on the high water to get me to the ocean is only a dodge, and I know it. Somehow, I have already sailed as far as I want to go. And I am weeping now, because I don't understand what has happened to me.

I suppose that if I did not have a place I wanted to escape from, there would be no place I'd want to escape to, so that escaping has become my reality, and my reality has become a dream, or a memory that has begun to shift or that has become false, much like the beautiful French girl Uncle Sticks used to talk about, though at the time when he told it, she had grown to be old, too, like Uncle Sticks, and would no longer have even resembled the person he remembered. He always vowed he was going to take trip and look her up. But the closest he ever got back to France was the Peabody Roof and a lobster thermidor.

Or, as he said the French said, "Ooowee, Baby!" And he loved to dance to a song called, "Roll 'Em Pete." It was boogie-woogie.

> *But, wait.*
> *Hold fast.*
> *Stuff stuff in your ears.*
> *Lash yourself to a bourbon and water;*
> *Do not answer the Sirens' song.*

The fact that I may hold a foolish consistency does not mean that that consistency is a "hobgoblin" or the property of a "little mind."[107] What if I am right? After all, there is something really wrong if I am constantly pursued by a squad of German infantry. And I am. But,

---

107 Ralph Waldo Emerson. —ogbii

of course, I have become used to them and, in fact, have come to the conclusion that even when they almost have me, they don't really want me, because they have just kept on marching, like rabbit hunters who have not seen the hare they've nearly stepped on. Well, even rabbits can be too scared to run.

I have tried to see the other side. I have not been small about it. But I reject the notion that I have come to love my situation. When all is said and done, one cannot love what is false. No, that is not true. Christianity and a long list of other creeds may be prime examples how easy it is to love what is not there. So, then, my position is in line with the acceptable. Is my fixation on returning to my home any more peculiar than that of a monk's longing for Heaven?

> *The major difference is that he believes*
> *he must die in order to reach it,*
> *and I have no intention of dying before I reach*
> *the true Mhoon County and the true Mississippi Delta,*
> *even though, as I have said,*
> *those things may not exist*
> *except in the fictions*
> *of imperfect memory.*

Furthermore, I realize that it is unreasonable for me to think that I know ALL about the Delta. I only know what I came into contact with and what my elders passed along, which, in at least one case, could have been syphilis.

However, if one allows for the expansion of knowledge through the intuition as well as through love for fiction, one comes to comprehend that he knows a vast amount he hadn't known he knew.

That is one of the more charming qualities of the human brain. And Southerners seem to have been blessed with a set of extra genes in that regard.

But that summer
in a dry, dry year,
how deep did the cracks in the buckshot go?

That year the rain came in isolated showers that could be watched
as they selectively washed this field or that one, never touching the rest
of the cropland.

Where did the water go?
Deep, deep down, I suspect,
Way down deep, where it sloshes about in the mind,
as a hope, perhaps, beneath the earth
even in unseen whitecaps
and storms of a seismic bent.

Was it there and then that large carp
were sucked down, too,
deep into the dried and splitting dirt?
I think so. Where else would logic put them?
They were down there,
and I could feel them schooling
far beneath my feet, schooling,
cool and happy in the dark.

It is all just a matter of level.
And on the upper air, the plane of my existence,
the world caught fire, and smoke was everywhere,
particularly in my eyes.
There were blazes all around the town, fire,
dancing in the night,
and men and boys rode the roads believing
that they could contain its beauty.

Yet somehow the dust beat them to it; the dust rose up and the dust fell down and choked the fire, along with the men and boys, but the dust saved the day, and saved the homes of countless mice who, otherwise, might have been driven to their deaths in the sugarditch.

> *. . . as dust will do, before, later, it becomes mud,*
> *the mud, perhaps, that is the source of life*
> *here and elsewhere, now and long ago.*
> *Earth, like water and fire, has its states,*
> *and dust is its gas, mud the liquid,*
> *and those dry, hard, cracked-apart fields*
> *of being are its solid mask*
> *. . . that hides the face of fish below.*

So, if water is the connector to everything in the present, I say the alligators at Ossichuca[108]—and all alligators in general—hereabouts, providing hereabouts is indeed hereabouts—I say the alligators are the dragons of time, the direct, unmistakable, lookalike link to the days of the dinosaurs, and they are right here nearby, if my captors have chosen to include a Ossichuca in their program, and I am sure they have.

The Ossichuca alligators are particularly significant owing to the fact that they are so far north and at the highest latitude of their inland reproductive range, on a line between Rudyard and Rich. But, then, even as far up as Mhoon County is, these great saurians have been sighted, lost perhaps, but here nevertheless and almost always found in association with high water, even with low high water, not necessarily *the* high water. Therefore I know they are here, and I feel I can communicate with them on the basis of their antiquity, which I am sure they, themselves, are aware of, and appreciate.

My only real regret in this matter is that they are not crocodiles

---

108 Crudely translates from Choctaw/Chickasaw as "eagle house." —ogbii

whose teeth are ever so much more impressive, and whose mouths open from the top instead of the bottom, a difference the reason for which I do not yet understand.

And I have looked carefully for these reptilian
embodiments of the aeons.
Yet, neither along Beaver Dam nor over the levee north
or south of Austin, except on special occasions,
can I find scale nor tail of them.

But that is only true of the present, here, in Mhoon County. I must prepare to camp out. That means I must become a better judge of the weather so that I do not get caught in a blizzard without a means of shelter. And this could be a problem, even though my woolen robe keeps me warm when it is wet.

The issue is time and place, and I feel I can tie the two strands together, somehow, by running them through the alligator, metaphysically of course. For within each alligator there ravens at least three hundred million years of time and of space through which that moment-and-place has traveled. I could put those ages to good use if I could find the right harness to fit them, and I believe I can.

But it won't be a snap, no pun intended. Harnessing the creature is one thing, but harnessing the fireballs of millennia—from which he is constructed—is entirely another, and I will need special equipment for the job.

It is a good thing that I am no stranger
to the intangible
and that I know the hypothetical
like the back of an unrequited lust.
This is no time to deny the ridiculous.
All things ridiculous at one moment or another

become the commonplace furniture of the future.

Therefore time and place via the *saurian alternative* will cause the rising of the water that will carry me, or at least allow me to navigate, backwards to a point where I can understand all this by which I am now held captive. There is more than one way to skin a dimension. I remember the scripture: "In my house are many vestibules." And I must find the right transom to go over.

It may be the mirage, which has grown since I have been here. The mirage could be the door. If memory serves me, and it usually does, there was throughout the year a mirage or two on or beside highway 61, and perhaps one of the more spectacular appeared just east of the highway, near Robinsonville. It is a convincing image of water that is not there but that is somewhere . . . else. And I feel, therefore, that in that image there must also be the images of all that is contained in the thing itself, wherever that thing-itself-of-which-there-is-only-an-image may be, and that would possibly mean alligators.

Alligators should be in the mirage, and just because one does not see them in the apparition does not mean they are not there. Indeed, one does not see them in places where they are in fact numerous, but they are most certainly there, lolling about in those little sloughs such as, say, the tupelo slash and among the willow runs and scattered cypress, near Teoc.

Image is substantial. Everything one sees is seen because it has an image, so I don't downplay the importance of what is seen, which is why I place image on the same level with substance, except, of course, in the professions, where substance is everything and image not much of anything.

But for metaphysical purposes image and *thing* are equals. A person does not have to be a Rosicrucian to understand this.

Without light everything is shadow. And I am not sure which is the more aggressive. The world I live in is pinched in the middle, and that is why there seems to be such a variety in the contents that furnish the "efficiency" of existence.

What was it? "In my father's house there are many studio apartments?" I have beaten the odds on that one. The silo is a wonderful find. It's not great for entertaining, but I never did much of that anyway. I never found entertaining very entertaining. Moreover, I do not truly recall when I did any of it in the first place. Possibly I have memory now of a non-event. If this is so, then it is disturbing because I cannot, as man of honor, incorporate more fiction into my life than I can handle. The question is how much I can handle, have I handled, am I going to handle? The truth is nobody cares but me. People have their own lives to create and cannot be getting emotionally involved with someone else's plot or lack of same.

I want to mention something about the war, but I can't. What could I say?

> *It was loud.*
> *I was wet.*
> *I was cold.*
> *I never saw the enemy until I got home.*
> *And no one ever told me what happened*
> *to President Roosevelt.*

I kept asking, and my friends only talked louder to each other, so I learned to sit quietly at the table. I couldn't eat there. Always I would eat before I ate so that I wouldn't have to eat when everybody ate. I didn't want to be encumbered, and I wanted to be constantly ready to leave at the first sign of danger. Later I understood that my voice had no sound, and then I realized why no one had ever answered my question. There was the possibility that no one saw me.

Now, of course, I have proven that to be true on one occasion or another during my present program of escape and evasion . . . *on those times in the fields when everything around me suddenly changes and my pursuers are no longer visible.* When that happens, I know that they can no longer see me, though others can, others who happen to populate that other weather.

Oh, my god (with a little "g" because I don't know his name)! And because I feel it may be best to go back to the pantheon. There some lofty Olympian, or perhaps a mere Memphian, has the picture of my destiny already sketched out in his celestial notebook. Ohmmmm, eye god.

The difficulty of my life is only two-fold—how to live and where? The former seems to be going quite nicely, but the latter has become a *raison d'etre*, though not an unpleasant one.

Often, the condition of being lost feels very satisfying—though "lost" may not be accurate because I know perfectly well where I am, and I know exactly where I want to go. And, as high water is the Great Connector, I know that by finding it I can find my home. Simple.

I realize I am pursued mostly by two—the taller skinnier fellow and his smaller stockier companion. The other day they fired upon my tower with a water-cooled machine gun. It was only after the third burst that I knew they had no idea I was here, and they seemed to aim well below my hideaway located just beneath the roof. It was late in the afternoon, and right before dark, and, while they were changing the belt, I slipped down the chute and ran into the little woods across the ditch just to the south, about one hundred yards.

My enemy were arguing and did not see me, although, for a moment, the tall one, I think, thought he did. Nevertheless, they were not prepared to find me. *One must be ready for discovery if one is to be a discoverer.* The predator must be ready for the prey. And those two were not.

I cannot say the same for the German patrol. I believe it is always ready, and that is one reason I am so careful and, to be truthful, so frightened of them. They never stop. But the difference between them and their persistence and the kind with which the Greeks were familiar is that the Germans do not think the stone will roll back down the hill.

That is the most significant indicator that, nationally, they are crazy and should be constantly dreaded. A fact is a fact. I know what I am talking about.

A while ago I mentioned something about my friends. I should have qualified that remark by saying that they were either my friends or the enemy, on duty, in rubber skin. But, often, I get tired of uncovering the truth, and, rubber skin or no rubber skin, I just let them be who they think they are and who I want them to be. I feel that is, at this point, the most sensible path to follow, even though all that now is not anything I really have to think about too much. I have flown the coop, skipped town, twenty-three skiddooed, jumped ship, left the premises, and tootle-looed—as they say. I have left *everywhere*, in fact. And there are no new friends when a man is on the run. That is a price one must pay, I suppose. After all, a fugitive cannot maintain a close relationship to the posse. There is no home for the hunted.

Oh. But I have also been the hunter. My, how that cane-cutter ran! His long body stretching and contracting, desperate for sanctuary, and how different in size he was from his smaller cotton-patch cousins. I always meant to investigate the difference.

I carried a gun. I wore boots. Hunting gave one a rugged, manly feeling about oneself, as though rabbits were ferocious beasts, as though the hunter were bringing home a necessary food, a quarry dangling dead from his belt, or bulging darkly inside the game pocket in the back of his canvas hunting coat.

> *Oh. I subdued the earth.*
> *I came home.*
> *The cane-brake rabbit did not.*
> *Oh.*

From Ledger No. 610

What I really ought to do is take French leave and make my way to Memphis and call up Kimbrough. I do not know how long it has been since I have seen her, and I am still not in love with her, though I wouldn't mind kissing for a bit. If she can do without the love business, I think things will work out splendidly. Otherwise, I don't believe kissing would be in the best interest of either of us. But, LORD, I would love to KISS. Yes! . . . Kiss . . . kiss . . . kissie . . . kiss-kiss . . . okeydoke . . . tongue poke.

Kissing is a kind of food, a dish without nutrients but a dish that one cannot help thinking one needs from time to time. And I suspect even monks and nuns find that this is true, though they aren't going to discuss the matter much with a freelance eremite like myself.

Oh, but kissing . . . the touch of lips and tongues,
the desire to swoon, to swim downward
into unconsciousness
deep in the sea of another person.

And Kimbrough's sea smells good and is, I think, sufficiently deep, even if indeed it is not by any means dark enough. And that is really not to say that a blonde cannot have the necessary darkness. Blondes can contain it. Oh, yes. Although, I admit, the darkness is more readily apparent in a dark woman,

and, when I find it, when I feel it, when I touch it,
it is like the closing of the soul's eye,
the drifting off of immediate life,
and the possibility of living elsewhere
still buried and submerged forever
in the skin and hair and breathing
and the darkness of the girl.

Oh, of course—most certainly!—
I remember who she was, the girl,
and that she and her darkness
would never have made her debut in Memphis
but might only have lived
on the edges of a plantation economy, or
gone back to Arkansas and the half-Caddos
that spawned her.
But in the darkness of the Palace Theater,
beneath the branches of the mimosas at the courthouse,
in the car after the basketball game, before the war came,
that was where I learned to love the difference
in what she was and who I was;
yet, as now, I could not then see
how I was to get from who I was to where she was,
even though, I must say—let me be perfectly clear!—
that I was not exceptionally clear on who I might have been.

At present, of course, I seem to know
precisely who I am but
not at all where I am.
And the girl was the place
where I first began to know
that I was lost.

(That's right, Miss Minnie, a person can be a place; even though only
in metaphor can a place be a person. The ends of that teeter-totter are
not equal.)

But, sometimes, it seems I scarcely know
the difference between love and meteorology
or between dream and location.

And I can see that Aristotle would be confounded
by my juxtapositions.

However, I am sure he would have seen the connections with blinding clarity once he had time to really think about it, being Greek and all and, therefore, as bound by myth as I am. Clarity is the product of the will. Aunt Booley knew that, as did, I believe, most of the other women in the family, except perhaps for Aunt Helena.

Their lives were much like mine in that they felt they belonged somewhere else, or, more accurately, some *time* else, but, not knowing how to get there and not being enlightened about the properties of high water, as I am, they did not move but remained in their silos until the end, although for Aunt Helena the end has not come unless she has died since I made my escape, and, there again, I cannot be sure if she is she and not the enemy disguised inside an elderly rubber skin.

I am pleased with the fact that,
Before the war and during the tornado
That came out of, of course,
Arkansas across the river,
Uncle Dick's ashes were picked up by the storm and
Sucked into the clouds.
He was the only member of the family to be cremated,
That we know of, and certainly the only member
To have ascended into the heavens.

He ordered that he be cremated because
He believed, and for good reason, that Aunt Mamie
Was going to have him pickled,
Like a pig's foot
Or a piece of fruit without appeal.
An elegant man, he always wanted

To be sure he looked his best or,
After death,
Looked not at all.

But he understood something, too, about youth and time and light and movement, and for all I know I have inside me whatever he and I must have inherited from some of our kin, and that is a sense that death, though it does not imply Heaven in the Presbyterian sense, does not, either, imply an end and that what lasts may be some kind of turbulence of passion translated into an indelibility that cannot be erased, a permanent dent in the fabric of the cosmos, so to speak, a hint, a mere impression, a shadow, a never-ending I-have-been.

God knows, the past is my future. Even *I* am beginning to see that, and even though I know it is probably true, I cannot do anything about it, because I am lost.

One minute the noise, the next minute I found myself on the platform being "welcomed." I did not have time enough to fill in the blanks. There was no progression from there to here but only a there and then a here without anything in the middle. It drives me crazy.

IF I WERE A madwoman I would sing. But if I were a madwoman they would have had me in the jail, where, in my experience in St. Leo, there was always a madwoman of some type, and she was always singing—or screaming, and there is a thin line between the two utterances.

In fact, I remember that there was one who did not want to leave the jail and another whom they could not keep IN the jail; they never knew how the latter managed to get out, though when she did, she never went very far, only to the town pump. And there, directly in front of the courthouse and exactly between two law offices, she would sit and sing until Sheriff Holston, or someone else, came and took her back to her cell. Her name was Louisa. She was not a Negro. She was the adopted daughter of Miss Clara Powen, who was an old maid because, I heard, she was much too intelligent to believe marriage was a suitable way to spend her life. As for Louisa:

It was not so much
that Louisa was adopted
but that she could not adapt
and kept falling out of the cradle of myth.

And that may be, apart from a desperate search for truth, because it was suspected her real parents had been Northerners. This was not implausible because, every summer, as far back as anyone could recall, Miss Clara had driven all the way from St. Leo in her Model A to Nova Scotia where, unlike the rest of the town, she had connections who were near enough to Quebec so that they knew how to speak French, which in Miss Clara's view was extremely important.

Therefore, as everyone said, there had been plenty of opportunity to run into Northerners of all sorts, who might have wanted their baby daughter to be raised by an old maid in the Mississippi Delta. It just stood to reason.

Wherever Louisa came from, Miss Clara brought her up, educated her, and loved her no less than if the girl had been her natural daughter. But that could be another story, and another and significantly longer vacation.

But love was not enough to protect Louisa
From the waywardness of her own brain, and, so,
She became a madwoman.

One would think all it would have taken would have been a simple conversation for someone, more in possession of himself, to say, "Look here, Louisa, you've got it all wrong. Let me show you the right way to see the world around you."

Of course I know it must be more complicated than that, but I have never seen any reason most crazy people would not respond positively to that approach. Certainly I would, if I were insane.

Yet, I have also noticed,
The truly sane never seem to take the obvious route.
And, like Columbus,
They always think they're in India.
They do not trust simplicity.
I have observed this.
Perhaps it is, for one thing,
They do not hear the voice of God
Giving them directions,
As do madwomen, and men,
Who think they are Napoleon.

And that is why truth is so odd. Plato said, I think, or he might have said, or I don't know why he shouldn't have said, that, on one level, any opinion is as good as another—because it is an opinion. I will not get into weights and measures here. That would make this matter unnecessarily complicated. Nevertheless, if Plato is right, then the crazy man's opinion that he is Napoleon is therefore just as valid as Napoleon's opinion that Napoleon is Napoleon.

Alors et aussi zut, Monsieur Descartes: I failed, therefore I am! I have failed so far to find my home, and I have failed in my quest for the Grail. It would be a comfort if I could regard those twin lacks in character as merely temporary. I hope very much that they are. Still, that is laughable. Those concerns are small compared to the more permanent if not in fact perhaps *infinite* lapses that, in me, abound.

I have failed, failed the hearts of my parents, failed as a soldier, and as a man of honor; I have failed in countless good intentions, contravened my own morality, and scarred my own image and, possibly, also some fine thought of me which others might have wished to hold. My sadness is massive and my regret is without measure. In the end, the only thing I can think to say for myself is simply that I have always wanted to be better than I am.

THE END OF PART TWO

AMF[109]

W ell, there you have it, Shaw's googah. Women like it, but I don't. Course they like the recipes I put in the book, too, and I do like those. Shootchyeah! Anyway, women read Shaw's write'n and say, "Oh, he's so sensitive!" That sumbich aint sensitive. He's just hairball nuts. That's all. Hell, I'm just as sensitive as that fukhed is. ChrEYEst.

Plus, while you was readn Shaw's hootydoo, I got the latest update on the hippos! They made it to Greenwood. Some sumbich deliverin the *Wall Street Journal* seen em early this mornin, eatn grass, up on the bank straight across the Yazoo River from what the Greenwoodians calls Cotton Row, right there in downtown Greenwood. I be *double* dog.

Anyway, right now, it looks like the people down there want to keep em and want em to be fulfilled and feel at home, so a buncha civic-minded buttholes are tryin to ever so quietly sneak a fence around em. The G-woodians have fell in love with them big old things, and I'd say that was pretty lucky for the hippos. Even if you wuddn a gotdam hippopotamus, you could do worse than have the whole fukkin town of Greenwood in love with your ass, dependin, I guess, on what you had to do for it.

---

109 Here Mr. Loveblood wanted to use the term *BackisPiece*. He believes that if there can be a "frontispiece," then there can be a "backispiece." The definition of "frontispiece" was of no concern to him. McKinney Lake and I should have agreed with him, given what he came up with next. "AMF" is a colloquial shorthand used among Mr. Loveblood's cohort for, as he puts it, "Adios, Muthafukka." —ogbii

Of course, there's already some questions about how to keep the hippos happy in the winter, so some sumbich said; and *now*, a whole lot of folks are hope'n there IS global warmin, cause, see, they don't want nothin to happen to the potamuses. Natchaly, all the preachers and the uppy-uppy women is involved.

Course, I got to thinkin: another time with another set of circumstances—and you know this as well as I do—them hippo-lovin coksukkas woulda been out there tryin to carve them old *woopatus-wompuses* up for sausage. Folks *are* funny, aint they?

And that's it, Sumbich. AMF . . . *Addy-os* . . . *Muh-THEH-ro . . . Fuh-KEH-ro.*

Oh, wait. I been thinking a lot about *this*. I have finally decided that I firmly-ass believe that them *TchEYE Omeegases*—the Ex-horseshoes!—and nem *Try-Dultresses*—the Three Arrowheads!- -did not have nothin to do *whatsomever* with Miss Attica Rummage nor with the Aunty Belles. And that's all I have to say about that.

Course . . . wouldn nothin surprise me.

ACKNOWLEDGMENTS

J ohn Pritchard sends enormous love and appreciation with all his heart and soul to his beautiful partner, Leigh Davidson Fraser, who, though exceedingly smart and sane, laughs at what he writes and keeps him grounded, if not always upon the actual earth, at least in Memphis. S.W.A.K.!

For support—literal, figurative, or even just semEYE-moral--Junior Ray loves always, never forgets, and hereby acknowledgizes: Lynn & John Adams; Anne & Lawrence Anthony; Ahab Music; Anne & Lawrence Anthony; Ben Beard; Cubert & Lacie Bell and the Mississippi Choctaws; Neil Block; the Boll & Bloom Cafe; Joe Boone; Bordeaux [Birdo] Point; Adam Borod; Nan Borod; Howard & Ann Brown; Jim Bullard; Candy & Bob Canzoneri; Jim Costello, Ty Gorman, and the Irish Travellers; Ellis W. Darby; Mick Davenport; Carol DeForest; *Delta Magazine*; John W. Dulaney Jr.; Anne & Joe Fisher; Michael Flanagan; Peter & Mary Lee Formanek; Fort Knox; Frank Hardy; Coleman Harwell; Richard, Will & William Houston; Michael T. Kaufman, Rebecca & all the Kaufmans; Diane Keeney; Jane Lettes; Will Long; Suzanne La Rosa, Randall Williams, Brian Seidman, Sam Robards, Deric Sallas, Lisa Emerson, Noelle Matteson, & everyone at the NewSouth Shoe Factory; Newt Lovvorn; Linda & Layng Martine; Max Pearsall & Marcella Williamson; Dan McGown; Cheryl & Corey Mesler; Mhoon's Landing; Shelley Mickle; Colin & Carl Middleton; Ken Neill; the *New York Times* 1960 & 1963–65; Cherie & Sterling Owen; John Tait Owens;

Uncle Percy; the Palace Theater; Betsy & Phillip Prioleau; Alston Purvis; Betty & Bill Ruleman; Joel Sanders; Tom Sanders; Robert & Anne Sayle; Bard Selden & Wendlandt Hasselle; Chad Selden; Tait Selden; BlackJack; David Shands; David Tankersley; Brooks & Dick Taylor; Tommy & Tom Tucker; Joe Vecchione; the White Horse Tavern on Hudson and West 11th; Ed & Calvert Williams; John M. Willcox; David Womack (Dr. Wu); and all the wonderful friends near and far, and kin, close or distant, of John Pritchard and his beloved son, John Hayes Pritchard III—the man to whom this book is dedicated.